In...

Ahmed grabbed his ri[...]
in the fading light. Be[...]
He brought his weapon to bear, one finger hovering on the trigger as his ears strained.

On the ragged face of a shallow ridge of sedimentary rock, the soft glow of an unattended phosphorous lamp illuminated a large sheet of plastic. Ahmed reached down and whipped it aside, and a superstitious awe crept like insects across his skin.

Within the rocks was carved a tomb of immense antiquity, now partially exposed, and inside were bones. There was no question as to the age of the sediment in which they lay, the levels of strata as ancient as the hills where time had formed them.

The remains bore testimony to an enormously powerful creature, over eight feet long. The bones were huge, and tissue anchoring points suggested immense musculature. Broad hands were clasped neatly across a vast chest, long legs crossed at the ankle.

"Get the cameras rolling—*Indiana Jones* meets *Alien*."
— *New York Times* bestselling author R.L. Stine

"Scarily realistic science, earth-shattering intrigue, and hyperdrive action . . . a major new talent in the thriller world."
—Scott Mariani, bestselling author of *The Hope Vendetta*

DEAN CRAWFORD

COVENANT

POCKET BOOKS
NEW YORK LONDON TORONTO SYDNEY NEW DELHI

Pocket Books
A Division of Simon & Schuster, Inc.
1230 Avenue of the Americas
New York, NY 10020

This book is a work of fiction. Names, characters, places, and incidents either are products of the author's imagination or are used fictitiously. Any resemblance to actual events or locales or persons, living or dead, is entirely coincidental.

First Pocket Books paperback edition December 2012

POCKET and colophon are registered trademarks of Simon & Schuster, Inc.

For information about special discounts for bulk purchases, please contact Simon & Schuster Special Sales at 1-866-506-1949 or business@simonandschuster.com.

The Simon & Schuster Speakers Bureau can bring authors to your live event. For more information or to book an event, contact the Simon & Schuster Speakers Bureau at 1-866-248-3049 or visit our website at www.simonspeakers.com.

Manufactured in the United States of America

10 9 8 7 6 5 4 3 2 1

ISBN 978-1-4516-7255-8
ISBN 978-1-4516-2854-8 (ebook)

For Emma

And Azazel taught men to make swords and knives and shields, and breastplates, and made known to them the metals of the earth and the art of working them . . .
Bind Azazel hand and foot, and cast him into the darkness; and make an opening in the desert . . . and cast him therein. And place upon him rough and jagged rocks, and cover him with darkness, and let him abide there for ever, and cover his face that he may not see the light . . .

—The Book of Enoch

HAR BEN YA'IR
NEGEV DESERT, ISRAEL
AUGUST 22

She's out here somewhere."

Ahmed Khan had to shout above the hot wind tugging at his thick black hair as he wrestled an open-topped jeep across a desiccated landscape of thorn scrub and dusty riverbeds. Desert sand whipped past the windshield, stinging his eyes as it had those of his Bedouin forefathers for a thousand generations. To the west, the sun descended into a sea of molten metal.

"Can you find her before dark?"

Dr. Damon Sheviz sat in the passenger seat, a diminutive man with a feeble ponytail of white hair that twitched in the wind behind the collar of his tweed jacket. An associate of the Hebrew University in Jerusalem, the elderly academic was clearly unhappy in the merciless firmament of the Negev. Ahmed saw him glance nervously over his shoulder at a rifle in the rear of the jeep, there to guard against foxes, rogue ibex, and anything else unfriendly they might encounter.

Ahmed did not reply, yanking the wheel of the jeep to one side as they climbed a steep escarpment peppered with thorn scrub. The engine growled as the wheels clawed ever upward through drifting sands until the jeep breached the top. Ahmed eased the vehicle to a stop and switched off the engine. A silence as deep as eternity descended around them as the Bedouin vaulted from his seat and walked to the other side of the ridge.

The Jordan Rift Valley sliced across the wilderness ahead, an ancient seismic scar slashed by the tributaries of long-extinct rivers that snaked their way into the endless deserts. Ahmed sighed and squatted down. He lifted a fistful of dust from the earth and let it fall in the hot breeze as he looked at a pair of parallel tire tracks descending into the valley below.

"Well?" Sheviz demanded, moving to stand alongside him.

"I can, but time is not on our side and she has a head start." He glanced at the sun as it bled into the trembling horizon. "This is a restricted area. We should not be here at all."

"I have no desire to travel the desert at night, Mr. Khan."

Ahmed slowly rose to his full height. "Then go, and peace be upon you. *Ma'assalama.*" He strode back to the jeep and leaped into the driver's seat. Crunching the Rover into gear, he suppressed a smile as Sheviz skittered with the speed of a frightened hare and clambered in alongside him.

The drive down into the shadows of the valley took another half an hour, Ahmed cautiously guiding the jeep into the shadow of a deep wadi before killing the engine once more. In the distance the shore of the Dead Sea glistened, overlooked in silent vigil by the fortress of Masada. Ahead, Ahmed could see a white vehicle loosely concealed by a thicket of thorn scrub.

"That's one of our jeeps," Sheviz whispered.

Ahmed grabbed his rifle as he climbed out of his seat, cocking the weapon and creeping forward in the fading light, the land around him already laced with long blue shadows and the sky above darkening swiftly. Behind him followed Sheviz, treading only where he trod and moving only when he moved.

The Bedouin edged forward and caught sight of a small fire flickering in a clearing ahead. Beads of sweat trickled into his eyes. He brought his weapon to bear, one finger hovering on the trigger as his ears strained, but he heard no voices or footfalls as he lowered himself onto one knee at the edge of the thicket.

The clearing was thirty feet across, ending in the ragged face of a shallow ridge of sedimentary rock that stretched away to his left. Scattered across the clearing were various devices including a portable satellite dish, vacuum hoses, and a laptop computer.

Sheviz pointed ahead. "She's here, that's the university's equipment she—"

The Bedouin clamped his hand across the academic's mouth and glared at him. Sheviz obediently shuffled back out of sight.

Ahmed crept into the camp and saw a discarded mug near the computer. He dipped a finger inside it, and a trace of residual dampness told him what he wanted to know. He moved down the rocky edifice toward where a soft glow illuminated the sedimentary rock.

An unattended phosphorous lamp sat beside a large sheet of plastic concealing something in the sediment. Ahmed reached down and whipped the plastic sheet aside. He stared at that which lay before him, and then felt a superstitious awe creep like insects across his skin.

Sheviz appeared next to him. "Oh my God."

Within the rocks was carved a tomb of immense antiquity, partially exposed by tools wielded in someone's patient grasp, and in the tomb were bones. There was no question as to the age of the sediment in which they lay, the levels of strata as ancient as the hills where time had forged them.

The remains bore testimony to an enormously powerful creature, the internment a cavity over eight feet long. The bones were huge, bearing the depressions of tissue anchoring points that suggested immense musculature. Broad hands were clasped neatly across a vast chest, long legs crossed at the ankle. The body was flat and level, perfectly supported within the sediment in which it had been interred.

"Purposefully buried," Sheviz said in wonder, kneeling before the excavation.

"How old is it, *sadiqi*?" Ahmed asked the professor.

"Not less than seven thousand years. It's quite possibly—"

The sound of boots crunched on the parched earth behind Ahmed and he whirled, swinging his rifle up to aim at the figure striding purposefully into the clearing. In the glow of the camp lights a tall blond woman dressed in khaki shorts, T-shirt, and bush hat came to an abrupt halt.

"What the hell do you think you're doing?"

Sheviz stood and pulled his jacket neatly into place as Ahmed lowered the rifle.

"I might ask you the same question, Lucy."

Dr. Lucy Morgan placed her balled fists on her hips. "Overtime. Who are you?"

"Dr. Damon Sheviz. The university has demanded the return of this equipment," he announced, "and your return to Jerusalem immediately."

"This equipment is on loan to my survey team."

"Indeed it is," Sheviz said as he took a pace toward her. "And that survey was completed two days ago in Be'er Sheva. I was on the verge of reporting you missing to the authorities and the equipment stolen."

Lucy shrugged. "They don't need any of this right now, anyway."

"And what are you doing with it, Dr. Morgan? You realize that this is theft, do you not? The university does not condone the use of its resources for personal projects."

"Perhaps they would if they knew anything about this," Lucy snapped, and then glanced at the remains nearby.

Ahmed watched Sheviz falter, following her gaze. The fastidious little man straightened his tie absent-mindedly and cleared his throat.

"How long ago did you find it?"

"Three days ago. I've been back whenever I've had a chance."

Sheviz's voice edged a tense octave higher. "Have you classified it?"

Lucy gestured across the camp to her laptop. Sheviz leaped across to the device with the speed of a man half his age. The computer hummed into life, the blue screen lighting his features.

Ahmed, bemused, moved to stand behind him.

"Good God," Sheviz uttered, reading from the screen. "Remains located south of Zin, Israel. Previous carbon-fourteen dating suggests specimen died approximately seven thousand years ago, confirmed by obsidian hydration-rim dating of accompanying detritus within strata."

Lucy joined them as Sheviz went on with increasing excitement.

"Subject cranium fully intact. Postcranial structure present with mild erosive damage concurrent with recent exposure."

Ahmed looked at the bones, confused now by the unfamiliar terminology and the doctor's excitement. "What's so special about it?"

A ghost of a smile touched Lucy's lips. "It's not human."

2

Ahmed Khan struggled to understand what Lucy Morgan had said.

"The remains are completely unmineralized," Sheviz gasped before Ahmed could speak. "They are not comparable to any known variant of *Homo sapiens*. Awaiting analysis from Field Museum, Chicago."

Ahmed shot a questioning glance at Lucy. "How can it not be human?"

"Look at the chest structure, the cranium, the fused sternum."

Ahmed looked again at the remains and a tingling sensation rippled through his nerves. The skull cap was elongated as though stretched to double the height of a human cranium, the eye sockets were cavernous and shaped like giant teardrops, and the vast plain of the chest was a sheet of fused bone, only the base of the ribs visible, protruding from the spinal column still buried in the rocks.

"Cranial capacity, three thousand cubic centimeters," Sheviz whispered, shaking his head. "A bigger brain than ours."

Homo sapiens—modern man—had been believed for millennia to be the only intelligent species of life in the universe. Now, Lucy's discovery had extinguished that fallacy as brutally and instantly as man's first fires had banished the darkness and the beasts of the night. Here were the remains of an unknown species, immensely powerful in stature and yet seven thousand years old. Bigger. Stronger. *Smarter.*

"In the name of Allah, what is it then?" Ahmed asked.

"We don't know yet," Lucy said. "We need the measurements I've made to be examined and I need this specimen out of the ground and back in Jerusalem. Whatever it is, it didn't evolve on this planet."

The Bedouin glanced at the blackened void above, now shimmering with legions of stars.

"We should leave the camp. It's dangerous to be out here at night."

"I've never seen anything like this," Sheviz whispered reverentially, ignoring him. "This is going to change everything, rewrite the history books. We're never going to look at ourselves the same way again."

"We're never going to look at anything again if we're arrested by Israel," Ahmed pointed out patiently. "We should return to Be'er Sheva and maybe come back tomorrow."

"No way," Lucy snapped. "We need to complete the excavation. Do you understand what this is? It shouldn't be here."

"Neither should we. You're digging in a restricted military area."

"This is more important than Israel's damned restrictions."

Ahmed struggled for words.

"Those remains have been here for seven thousand years; they're not going to get up and run off any time soon."

"This could be the most important scientific discovery of all time," Lucy said.

"Perhaps, *sadiqati,* but I don't want to be the next set of bones you dig up out here. Your camp lights are visible for miles. How long do you think it will be before Israeli soldiers notice them, or maybe even insurgents from across the Sinai?"

Before Ahmed could stop her, Lucy reached out and slid his rifle from his shoulder.

"Fine, we'll see you back in Be'er Sheva in two days if you're worried about guerrillas or a prison cell."

Ahmed hadn't expected such a thinly veiled challenge to both his authority as a guide and his courage as a man. He straightened his posture a little.

"As you say, I would not make a big deal out of nothing."

Lucy tilted her head in acknowledgment. "Neither would we."

Ahmed sighed heavily, shaking his head.

"I'll radio the university from the jeep and tell them that you are safe." He gestured to the rifle. "Six rounds. I'll come back with supplies in the morning. *Ma'assalama.*"

Ahmed turned and strode away into the darkness, pursued by Lucy's mysterious words. *It's not human.* A profound thought crossed Ahmed's mind. We are not alone in the universe. It occurred to him that the remains could be worth a fortune. He was attempting to calculate how much when a scream shattered the silence of the night behind him.

Ahmed whirled. "Lucy?"

The air burst out of Ahmed's lungs as the weight of a man slammed into him and he fell hard to the unforgiving earth. He rolled onto his back and lashed out with one foot toward the silhouette of a man against the star-light above, slamming him hard in the groin. The man gagged and staggered backward as Ahmed scrambled to his feet.

The Bedouin lunged toward his attacker, but before he could reach him something heavy cracked across the back of his head and plunged him into a deep and silent blackness.

3

COOK COUNTY JAIL
CHICAGO, ILLINOIS
AUGUST 24

The pain woke him.

He lay motionless as a throbbing began to grind around the interior of his skull. His eyes ached as though needles were being driven into his retina, bolts of nausea churning through his stomach to the labored rhythm of his heart.

Open your damned eyes.

A white wall, defaced by the remedial scrawlings of occupants gouged into the brickwork over countless decades. The creeping odors of stale food, sweat, and unflushed latrines caressed his senses as they reluctantly reconnected themselves, revealing forgotten aches and injuries. He breathed a long and weary sigh and tried to free-fall back into the dreamy oblivion of sleep.

"Warner. Ethan!"

He rolled over on the hard bench to see a holding cell where about thirty men dressed in orange Department of Correction coveralls, most of them angry young gang hoods, watched him suspiciously. Something heavy clanged against the cell's steel black gates loudly enough to send spasms of agony shooting through his brain.

"Yeah?" he uttered in a dry rasp.

The young bloods remained silent, but the portly face of a white-shirted prison officer sneered in at him from beyond the gates.

"Get off your ass and over here."

Keys rattled as the door opened and Ethan Warner struggled to his feet. The floor heaved beneath him as fresh waves of pain scraped across his eyeballs, and he steadied himself with one hand against the wall before shuffling to the gates.

"But you haven't served breakfast yet," he said as he yawned.

The guard reached out and grabbed Ethan's arm in one chunky hand.

"You're a born comedian, Warner."

The guard offered him no mercy, prodding him out of the cell and down a corridor lined with more identical cells holding hundreds of felons. Muffled voices called out a mixture of greetings, insults, and threats. Having spent overnight in holding, Ethan knew that he would now be processed and given his own Department of Correction clothing: standard procedure, along with the strip search and the questions.

The guard guided him to the front desk, where a young cop with tightly bobbed blond hair looked up at him with a disapproving gaze.

"Warner, Ethan. Public disorder. Again," the guard said from behind him.

Ethan offered her what he hoped was his best smile. "Morning, Lizzie, how you doin'?"

Lizzie rolled her eyes, placing a piece of paper on the

desk before her and grabbing a sealed plastic bag filled with loose change, a watch, and a packet of Lucky Strikes.

"Your belongings, Mr. Warner. Sign here."

Ethan looked down, seeing an unfamiliar form before him.

"Signature bond?" he asked, looking up at Lizzie.

"Anonymous," Lizzie said without interest. "Somebody obviously cares what happens to you, even if you don't."

Ethan reached down and scrawled something approximating his signature on the slip of paper. Lizzie handed him the plastic bag. As Ethan took it from her she gripped his wrist, catching his gaze.

"Get a grip on yourself, for God's sake."

The guard gave him a shove in the direction of another set of heavy-looking doors, and moments later Ethan was propelled through them and out into the cool morning air. After passing through two sets of security gates a bustling street greeted him, vehicles thundering past and cloaking him in clouds of exhaust fumes as the jail gates slammed shut behind him.

Ethan turned and trudged wearily down the street, ignoring the traffic and the hordes of people passing him by. He walked by a shop window and saw his reflection staring back at him, a cut beneath his left eye. He vaguely recalled arguing with someone in the street the previous night after drinking perhaps a little too much: a running volley of shouts, threats, and then blows as he'd punched someone, only to find himself flat on his back moments later.

Then the flashing lights and sirens, more shouting.

Then the booking and the jail.

Just another day. Nothing matters.

Ethan continued on his unsteady way, grabbing the "L" elevated train and following the Red Line south until he reached 47th at Fuller Park, getting off and walking toward a soaring housing project. Cars parked bumper to bumper lined the sidewalk of West 42nd Place, the project that had been his home for the past six months. An old man sitting outside with a cane greeted him with a broken-toothed smile as he walked inside.

As he reached his apartment door he saw a broad bouquet of carnations propped against the wall, the petals battered and wilting with age. Ethan sent them ritually once a year, every year, and they were ritually returned unopened within a few days. He sighed and grabbed the drooping bouquet. The damned things were an expense he could ill afford, and he wondered again why he sent them at all.

If you've got nothing, then nothing matters.

Ethan closed his eyes, his fists clenching as a wave of despair rose up from somewhere deep within him. He inhaled and struggled against an unyielding tide of hopelessness, scrambled above it, and stamped it back down into some deep place where it could no longer bother him. *Nothing to worry about. Nothing matters.* He stood in silence as the panic receded, breathing alone in the center of his universe, and for a brief instant he was asleep on his feet.

And then he heard the sound coming from within his apartment. Ethan's eyes flicked open, his senses suddenly hyper-alert. Footsteps, crossing softly across his living room. Heavy enough to be male. Left to right. Right to left. Ethan glanced down at the door lock and saw a few tiny bright scratches against the dull steel of the barrel.

His heart skipped a beat and a hot flush tingled uncomfortably across his skin.

Without conscious thought Ethan set the flowers down in the corridor and slipped his key from his pocket, taking a deep breath before sliding it into the lock, turning it, and then hurling himself through the doorway.

4

Ethan lunged at the form of a man standing in the center of the apartment, catching a brief glimpse of a dark-blue suit and gray hair as he swung a fist toward the man's face.

A knife-edged hand shot into Ethan's view with practiced fluidity to swat his punch aside into empty air, and he felt a hard palm thump into his shoulder and propel him across the apartment. Ethan staggered off balance as the man stepped neatly aside from his charge.

"You're getting sloppy, Ethan."

The old man lowered his guard and jabbed a thumb over his shoulder at the apartment door. "And your security isn't up to much. Lucky I was here, in case somebody broke in."

"You could have just called, Doug," Ethan muttered, regaining his balance and ignoring the old man's wry smile.

"Where's the fun in that?"

Ethan retraced his steps and grabbed the bouquet from the corridor outside before closing the door.

Doug Jarvis glanced curiously at the decaying flowers in Ethan's hand.

"The bail?" Ethan asked before the old man could

say anything, and was rewarded with a curt nod as Jarvis glanced around at the apartment.

A small couch, a coffee table, and a television that Ethan hadn't turned on in a month occupied the uncluttered room. The coffee table was stacked with library books.

"How have you been, son?" Jarvis asked.

Ethan had met Doug Jarvis when the old man had been captain of a 9th Marine Corps platoon. Ethan had himself served with pride as a second lieutenant in the United States Marines after finishing college, leading a provisional rifle platoon with the 15th Marine Expeditionary Unit during Operation Enduring Freedom before taking up employment as a war correspondent. Despite the advice he'd been given not to resign his commission, Ethan had been driven by a desire to document the horror of war and to expose the injustices he had witnessed, to be more than just a foot soldier. He had been embedded with Jarvis's unit in Fallujah during Operation Iraqi Freedom, and had obtained footage of the war that had helped secure his career as a correspondent. They had gone their separate ways after that, maintaining only occasional contact since. The last he'd heard, Jarvis was working for the Department of Defense or something.

"I'm getting by."

"Sure you are."

Ethan decided not to respond and gestured to the couch, acutely aware of his meager surroundings. Jarvis removed his jacket and sat down as Ethan discreetly tossed the bouquet out of sight into the kitchen.

"So, what brings you here, Doug?"

"There are some people from the Defense Intelligence Agency who want to talk to you."

The DIA, that was it. "Why would they want to talk to me?"

"Because I recommended you. I need you to come with me."

Ethan felt another wave of anxiety flood his nervous system. "What the hell's going on?"

"How long have we known each other, Ethan?"

"Twenty years, give or take."

"Two decades," Jarvis agreed, and then hesitated, rubbing his temples. "Son, I know what you went through in Palestine, but so does the department, and it's why they want to talk to you. They're confident that you're the man for the job, enough to have fronted your bail on my say-so."

"I'm not in the business anymore, not after what happened in Gaza."

"I know," Jarvis admitted. "But this time it's different."

"Surprise me."

"Two days ago, an American scientist went missing in the field and we need to locate her."

Ethan knew all too well that thousands of people around the world went missing every year, vanishing from the face of the Earth and leaving their families unable to grieve or abandon the hope to which they clung so desperately. The suffering of those they left behind, people like him, could not be measured simply in terms of grief, of regret, or even of guilt. It was the corrosive anxiety of not knowing, the terrible pangs of helplessness searing and scalding through the veins.

"Where was she when she went missing?" he asked.

"The Negev Desert, Israel, near the border with Jordan."

"So call the Red Cross, inform Interpol, and hopefully she'll turn up."

Jarvis smiled tightly.

"It's not quite that simple. Israel is in the middle of peace negotiations with the Palestinian authorities, and for once the various factions that make up Palestine's resistance have all observed a strict cease-fire. If we raise the alarm with Interpol or have the Red Cross scouring the Gaza Strip, and either Palestinian insurgents or Israeli right-wingers are accused of abduction, both sides could walk away from the table before the signing ceremony on August twenty-sixth."

"So what do they want from me?"

"They want you to go in there, discreetly, and find out where she is."

Ethan had seen it coming, but hearing it still felt as though someone had clubbed him around the head. On the rare occasions when Ethan could be honest with himself he accepted that his life was dull, shitty, and almost entirely devoid of hope. But if there was anything that the last two years had taught him, it was that he didn't need the endless traveling and the artillery-shelled hotels, the vacant stares of traumatized children and the undiluted misery that war inflicted upon the innocent masses groveling for mercy beneath its wrath. The memories were a swollen abscess of pain festering deep within his chest that was slowly being drained by the passing of time. A daily diet of cigarettes, nihilism, and little else had taken its toll, but hell, he was getting somewhere, wasn't he?

"I can't help you, Doug."

"Can't help," Jarvis echoed. "You working?"

"No." Ethan didn't meet his gaze.

"I wouldn't be asking if this wasn't important, Ethan."

"Israel has excellent security forces."

"Israel has put a cap on this," Jarvis explained patiently, "to avoid upsetting the peace process. There's a total media ban in force too."

"There's nothing that I can do out there that they can't."

"Except look. You're good at this, Ethan; you always were. You found those people in Bogotá, didn't you, and Somalia? You've got history in Gaza, friends who can help." As Ethan continued to stare out of the window in silence, Jarvis changed his tone. "But if you'd rather just sit here and let yourself go to hell, then that's fine by me."

Ethan kept his tone neutral. "My life's good as it is."

"What life?"

A stab of pain pierced Ethan's chest. "The one that doesn't involve me risking my life or anyone else's. I don't want to go back out there."

"So what *do* you want, Ethan?"

Ethan opened his mouth to speak but found no words. His rage withered and he wondered why he had shown it in the first place. Two years with nobody to vent it on.

Jarvis jabbed a finger in his direction.

"You're sitting here with your thumb up your ass waiting for your life to begin again. I'm giving you some direction, something to move toward before you self-destruct. Christ, it took some effort for the agency to even consider hiring you."

"I can't," Ethan said repentantly. He sought desperately for something to say, and was disappointed with what finally came out. "I still don't sleep much."

"You think you'll sleep better if you just keep running away from what happened?" Ethan shot him a hurt look but Jarvis continued without mercy. "You're not that kind of man, Ethan, and you know it."

"So I should spend some time trying to avoid being shot in Gaza instead?"

"Sure, or you can sit here on your ass feeling sorry for yourself. Your call."

A laugh blurted unbidden from Ethan's mouth. Jarvis stood, his hands at his sides.

"There's nobody else I can think of who can help, Ethan. I wouldn't be coming here asking for this after what happened to you, unless I was out of options."

Ethan felt as though he was slamming a door in Doug's face.

"I'm the last person you should be asking." He looked up, suddenly curious. "What's your stake in this anyway?"

Jarvis's features creased as he spoke.

"The missing scientist, Lucy Morgan, is my grand-daughter."

5

You should have said something sooner."

Ethan reveled in the breeze funneling in through the open window of the Ford Taurus as Jarvis drove them out onto South Lake Shore Drive, heading north toward the city skyline and the Willis Tower.

"The Defense Agency's being discreet about what is really a civilian matter. They wouldn't front your bail until I'd had you checked out."

Ethan doubted the agency had been impressed by what they'd heard. He sighed and shrugged inwardly. *Nothing matters so don't get involved.* Since he'd lost everything it had been easy to just ignore the world around him. What was the point in worrying? What was the point in anything? *If you've got nothing, you've got nothing.* Why would he want to fly halfway around the globe searching for some damned fool scientist?

Ethan looked at his reflection in the car's side-view mirror. Narrow irises floated in discs of sun-flecked gray beneath a thick mop of light-brown hair. His skin seemed more heavily lined than his years deserved, creased by both time and neglect, and the cut on his cheek was forming a line of purple bruising. *You shouldn't be doing this. You're not ready. Go and see what*

*Doug's associates have to say, advise them as best you can,
then walk away. Just walk away.*

"You okay?" Jarvis asked.

"Where are we going?"

"The Chicago Field Museum of Natural History."

Ethan gave Jarvis a curious glance but said nothing,
looking back out of the window. The sparkling expanses
of Lake Michigan glistened in the hot sunlight, the
beaches and neatly maintained marinas making the
South Side look more appealing than it actually was.

It took more than twenty minutes to reach their
destination through the laborious traffic, the immense
porticoed edifice of the museum towering over them.
Jarvis avoided the main lot and turned instead through a
discreet side entrance and into a small parking lot, pulling up near a loading bay at the rear of the building.

Ethan followed as Jarvis got out and led him toward
an access door, beside which stood a tall woman. Ethan
surveyed her disheveled black hair and features creased
with exhaustion as they approached.

"Ethan, this is Rachel Morgan, my daughter."

Rachel Morgan's handshake was firm and dry, but
her smile was feeble and her green eyes haunted by
drifting shadows of pain that Ethan recognized all too
quickly.

"Thank you for coming, Mr. Warner," Rachel said,
hope twinkling like a newborn star in her eyes, before
withering as she observed his tired features and the
bruising on his cheek. "Please, this way."

Ethan followed Rachel down a narrow corridor that
wound endlessly through the depths of the museum.
Ethan whispered to Jarvis from the corner of his mouth,
"Why the hell are we going down here?"

The old man shook his head, refusing to be drawn.

Rachel reached a large door and beckoned them through. Ethan found himself walking into a cavernous hall closed off to the public. Shafts of sunlight from soaring windows sliced through a galaxy of dust motes drifting on the musty air. The walls were dominated by scaffolding draped with the hallmarks of ongoing renovation, workmen in hard hats laboring high on the precarious walkways. A huge mammoth fossil dominated the center of the hall, standing three times as high as a man and with tusks as thick as Ethan's waist. It stared solemnly down at him from the depths of prehistory as he passed by.

At a table near the center of the hall sat two men, dressed in identical gray suits and bearing identical serious expressions. They stood as Ethan approached the table, the taller of the two extending his hand.

"Andrew Woods, Defense Intelligence Agency. This is my colleague, Adrian Selby."

Ethan shook their hands as Rachel Morgan and Doug Jarvis stood unobtrusively to one side.

"My apologies for the circumstances of your arrival here, Mr. Warner," Woods said, "but we're in the midst of a crisis and attempting to keep a lid on things."

"Doug informed me of the situation," Ethan said.

Woods sat down and looked at a series of papers spread across the table.

"Ethan Warner, born 1978, Chicago, Illinois. You worked as a war correspondent."

Ethan was about to respond but before he could open his mouth, Selby spoke.

"And you're a man with a talent for finding people."

Ethan said nothing.

"Some fifteen individuals over a period of several years," Woods added. "Half a dozen from inside the Gaza

Strip, Lebanon, and Somalia, and many more prior to that in Mexico and Colombia."

Ethan glanced at Jarvis, who refused to catch his eye. He turned back to the two men. "What do you want?"

"Reassurance," Selby replied quickly, "that you can be trusted and that you can do what we require. We have . . . concerns. We understand what happened in Gaza and don't wish to dredge up any unnecessary regrets."

A dense pall of sadness swelled in Ethan's chest.

"Help us with what we need," Selby said, "and in return we can help you find closure."

"What the hell is that supposed to mean?"

Woods raised a pacifying hand as he spoke.

"Israel is a powerful and influential nation, but they are not without diplomatic vulnerabilities. We could provide sufficient leverage to help you find out what happened to your fiancée in Gaza."

Ethan experienced a transient blurring of his vision, his fingernails digging into his palms as he shouted, "You want to tell me why you haven't been doing that all along?"

"We're doing what we can," Woods said immediately. "We're as uncomfortable about this as you are, and felt that an incentive was required."

Selby stood and held a photograph out to Ethan. He reached for it, suddenly and inexplicably afraid. He looked down at the grainy image and felt something sharp sting the corners of his eyes as a gasp leaped unbidden from deep within his chest.

A woman held firmly in the hands of masked men, being transferred from a building into a battered-looking sedan on a dusty street. Distress etched into her features. A Kalashnikov wedged against her side. Hair in disarray, wrists bound. Joanna.

Tears that Ethan struggled to conceal burned like acid across his eyes, and his voice was a rasp as he spoke.

"When? Where?"

"January, near Jabaliya in the Gaza Strip," Woods replied. "Israel only released this image after considerable diplomatic pressure."

Ethan looked at the picture for a moment longer, a face he hadn't seen for three years, then cleared his eyes and throat. He glanced at Jarvis. The old man was watching him hopefully, as was Rachel.

"A paleontologist has gone missing in Israel," Ethan said as he pocketed the photograph.

Woods looked down at his paperwork.

"Dr. Lucy Morgan had been involved in an excavation for the Hebrew University near a place called Be'er Sheva in the Negev Desert, along with a team of scientists. The team completed its work and returned to Jerusalem but for reasons unknown Lucy remained in the field. Members of the university sounded the alarm after no contact with her for twenty-four hours."

Apparently sensing Ethan's change of heart, Jarvis picked up the story.

"Lucy has always complied with standard safety procedures in the past."

"She found something," Ethan suggested with a clairvoyant flash.

"That's the last that was heard of her," Jarvis said. "We've no idea where she went or why."

"Any news on possible abductors?"

"Nothing," Selby answered. "Most insurgent groups out there consider foreign hostages a major coup. They should be screaming at the top of their lungs by now."

"Anything else?"

"Lucy's research program was involved in the study of . . ." Woods hesitated. "Mitochondrial deoxy . . . ribo . . . nucleic acid."

Rachel Morgan spoke for the first time. "Mitochondrial DNA. You know, the double helix?"

"There have been some major studies going on out in the Middle East and Africa," Woods continued, "looking for traces of our earliest ancestors."

"Why would someone abduct her for that?" Ethan asked.

Woods, Selby, and Jarvis all looked at Rachel.

"My daughter was involved in an off-the-record dig at an excavation site she herself discovered. I only received a single e-mail from her, sent here to the museum and copied to me before she vanished. She also sent the museum a bone fragment from her discovery that the DIA has acquired. During her excavations, Lucy found the remains of a species of humanoid buried in the Negev Desert."

"So?" Ethan asked.

"It was a species unknown to science."

The hall seemed oddly silent in the wake of Rachel's words. Ethan stared blankly at her for a moment before Jarvis spoke.

"Such remains are reputed to have immense financial value," he said. "We believe that Lucy may have been abducted by groups seeking to sell the fossil on the black market."

"There's a black market in bones?" Ethan asked. "But why would they take Lucy too? Surely they could just steal the remains?"

Woods shot Ethan a look.

"Not if they're politically motivated too. The profits

from the sale of such remains could fund weapons and explosives for insurgent groups, and a Western hostage could be used to derail the peace process."

"It sounds too complex," Ethan said thoughtfully. "They'd never be able to get the remains out of Israel."

"We haven't come to any firm conclusions yet," Woods cautioned. "Right now our priority is to locate Dr. Morgan and the remains that she discovered, and repatriate them both to the United States."

"Israel's position is sensitive," Jarvis added. "Our embassy in Tel Aviv is doing everything that it can but they don't want to push Israel too hard. You have friends, Ethan, contacts in Israel and Palestine, people on the ground. You can work without attracting attention."

Andrew Woods spoke solemnly.

"We can't conduct an official investigation without arousing suspicion in the Knesset and the media. You'll need to be discreet."

Ethan felt something cold creep through his veins.

"Israel doesn't know what Lucy Morgan found out there," he said quietly. "And why would you want these remains recovered too? Why not just focus on Lucy?"

Selby winced.

"We would prefer that this entire affair remain secret," he said stiffly, "if you take my meaning."

"Just how much support will I actually have?" Ethan asked.

Jarvis's reply was swift.

"The agency doesn't consider Lucy's disappearance a priority," he said bitterly. "You'll be able to call me for assistance from the Israeli Defense Force and maybe assets here in the States, but officially the department has no active investigation running there."

Ethan closed his eyes, running through his mind

everything that he had just heard. He opened them and found himself looking down at the photograph of Joanna. *If you've got nothing, you've everything to gain.*

"Can you get me into Gaza?" he asked.

"We will do everything we can to support you," Jarvis said. "Just call me once every day, so that we know you're okay, understood?"

Ethan hoped that his voice was not trembling as he spoke.

"Okay, tell me how you want me to do this."

6

POTOMAC GARDENS PROJECTS
G STREET ON 12TH, WASHINGTON DC

What do we got?"

Metropolitan Police Department detective Lucas Tyrell drove in a characteristically sedate fashion along a deserted G Street. Streetlights above drifted past against an overcast dawn sky that sealed in a sweltering blanket of late-summer heat. Beside him sat Detective Nicola Lopez, reading from a notebook.

"Search request from the DC Housing Authority on an abandoned town house opposite the projects. Neighboring residents have reported unpleasant odors."

Tyrell winced, his black skin creasing around his eyes as he turned onto 12th. He looked in the rearview mirror to see a pair of brown eyes watching him from the rear seat. Bailey, his four-year-old dachshund, tilted his head and flopped an ear to listen to his voice.

"Who's down there?" he asked Lopez as he cruised toward ugly apartment blocks weathered by years of neglect.

"Kaczynski and his guys are on-site, coroner's got jurisdiction. An FBI incident team's on its way under Axel Cain."

"Cain," Tyrell muttered, as though he had something unpleasant in his mouth.

"Can't have everything."

Tyrell watched from the corner of his eye as Lopez glanced over the paperwork, a strand of black hair dangling in front of her face. She was petite and slim, with butter-smooth skin, a third generation Latino from down on the gulf. Tyrell, on the other hand, was obese. Like two-hundred-eighty obese. Most all the detectives at the First District Station joked that if Tyrell ever caught a criminal red-handed, the perp had better hope that Lopez was the one to pin him down.

Nicola closed the file in her lap.

"It's probably just another crack den."

"Never reach a conclusion without first evaluating all of the evidence," Tyrell cautioned. "Most everybody does that and they usually get it wrong."

"This is it," Lopez said, gesturing ahead. "Twelve fifty-five G Southeast."

Four MPD cruisers were parked across the road, incident tapes cordoning off the last in a row of abandoned town houses. The cruisers' lights flashed like nightclub beacons in the pale dawn. A few dark-skinned faces appeared on balconies on the projects opposite, smoking and wiping sleep from their eyes but watching with interest.

"Let's go see what's up," Tyrell said, and turned to look at Bailey, who whined softly. "Now, you stay here and guard the wheels, 'kay, boy?"

Tyrell levered himself from the car, pausing to catch his breath before leading Lopez through the police cordon. A cheerful-looking officer by the name of Kaczynski walked toward them.

"Hope we didn't get you guys up too early," he said,

glancing at the thin sheen of sweat glistening on Tyrell's brow. "Warm enough for ya?"

Tyrell shook Kaczynski's hand and gestured to Nicola.

"Detective Lopez, Lieutenant Terry Kaczynski. Any news from the inside?"

"Nothing," Kaczynski admitted, smiling at Lopez in a manner that suggested the only thing he'd ever successfully flirted with was rejection. "We're just waiting for you to show us the way."

"What we're here for," Tyrell said without fanfare, wiping the sweat from his brow with a tissue.

"Best get on with it then," Kaczynski said with a shrug. "If there's anyone inside lookin' to give us trouble, they can't have missed this goddamn circus."

Kaczynski turned and cleared the way for them to the windowless front door of the town house. Tyrell glanced at the trees growing outside the row of abandoned buildings, gnarled branches concealing the clapboard houses and their mangled chain-link fences. Dense weeds thrived in long-abandoned gardens. Living opposite the Potomac Gardens projects with its drug trade and gang warfare had driven the occupants out long ago.

He could see that the front door of the house was blanketed with a kaleidoscope of sprayed tags and gang colors, the signature of misled youth on a citywide scale. Mara Salvatrucha 13 was the dominant gang in the District, an assortment of El Salvadoran gunrunners and drug dealers who had migrated across America over the past twenty years. Brutally violent, they complemented the local peppering of Crips, Bloods, Surenos, and La Razas fighting for turf as far out as Prince George's and Maryland.

The two detectives drew and checked their weapons one more time before Tyrell nodded to a tall, robustly built young officer. The officer hefted a black iron ram from where it had been leaning against the sidewalk.

"You guys take the upstairs," Tyrell murmured as Kaczynski took position outside of the door. "No heroics this mornin', 'kay?"

The young officer's face was taut as he lifted the ram. Tyrell aimed at the door, Lopez covering his shoulder and flank. He checked everything one last time and raised the barrel of his pistol once, twice, and then with a final jerking third movement.

The police officer lunged forward and slammed the ram into the door with all of his impressive physical strength. A dull crash echoed across the projects, the door splintering but holding firm. A chorus of whoops and obscenities drifted down from the balconies behind them. The officer swung again and the door smashed open, hanging from one twisted hinge.

Tyrell rushed forward into the darkened maw of the house.

"Police! Stay where you are!"

Tyrell's voice was muted by the narrow hallway ahead, lost in deep shadows. He crept forward into the darkness, Lopez close behind. An intense blanket of heat cloaked the inside of the house, sweat drenching his skin and trickling beneath his shirt.

"Police! Stay still, face down on the floor!"

The silence taunted him as he caught the sickly sweet aroma of putrefaction drifting on the air. The walls of the hall were bare but for a few tattered scraps of paper hanging entombed in gossamer webs, the carpet thin and caked in the filth of ages. Tyrell advanced toward a passage at the end of the hall that opened left and right.

He gestured to the left, and Lopez silently shifted position against the left wall as Tyrell moved to the right, crouching down as she remained upright. The drill was ingrained into their respective psyche with the same intensity as the will to breathe. Without words, their weapons whipped simultaneously into the open corridors, each covering the other.

"Clear," Tyrell whispered.

He covered Lopez as she moved left to the edge of a kitchen littered with spilled pans, tubs, and cutlery. The odor of congealing mold mingled with the musty, stale air. He watched as Lopez took a breath and then whirled into the kitchen, sweeping the boxlike room with her weapon.

"Clear."

Tyrell turned and moved back down the hall. Another open door ahead led into what he presumed was the living room, while one to the left led into a bedroom. The sickly stench of decay became stronger, and a dull humming sound sent a spasm of disgust rippling down his throat.

He turned, sweeping the bedroom with his pistol. A bare mattress lay upon the rusting springs of a double bed. Shredded curtains dangled limply from a small window, accompanied by the bodies of several dead rodents on the floor, tiny white teeth gaping from mortified bodies.

"Clear."

The smell was overpowering now, and Tyrell already knew that his weapon was unlikely to be discharged. Still, he kept it trained ahead of him as he moved to the edge of the doorway, Lopez covering his back.

With a final breath that felt as though it coated the back of his throat with something slimy, Tyrell lunged into the living room and stared into the half darkness.

The room was dominated by two sagging couches. Plates of half-eaten food littered a table amid a crumpled sea of crushed beer cans and empty packets of potato chips. A handful of cockroaches scampered over rotten morsels of food. The hum of blowflies filled the room, a chorus of life flourishing in the presence of death.

Three bodies sprawled naked across the couches. A handful of syringes lay discarded around them, while others dangled awkwardly from the blackened veins of bare arms or were wedged between lifeless toes. Crack pipes lay scattered on the thin carpet. Tyrell's voice was raspy with repulsion as he called out.

"Property clear, three dead."

He holstered his pistol before gingerly stepping across the grisly scene, donning latex gloves, and opening the curtains. The pale morning light filtered reluctantly into the room, illuminating the corpses and their attendant swarms of flies.

"Jesus," Lopez murmured, clearly struggling to prevent her breakfast from making a dramatic reappearance as she put on her own gloves.

"You'll get used to it," Tyrell said quietly, surveying the scene.

Kaczynski appeared in the doorway and winced. He was followed by a tall, portly man with mousy hair and a pockmarked face whose frame filled the doorway. He stood there, his jaw chomping loudly on a piece of gum until he saw the corpses and caught a whiff of their scent.

"Christ's sake," he muttered in disgust, covering his nose and mouth with one hand.

Tyrell ignored FBI special agent Axel Cain, who gathered himself together as he surveyed the scene.

"Crack den it is then," he said. "Coronor can take it from here."

Tyrell didn't reply, staring at the bodies. Lopez turned to Cain.

"We'll need forensics. Make sure nobody else comes in here until they've finished up."

"The District doesn't have a forensic department," Cain said with an oily smile. "They'll have to go to Quantico."

"That'll take months," Lopez pointed out.

Cain shrugged without interest as his lips began grinding around his gum again. "I don't suppose these dudes are in any rush."

"We'll handle it," Kaczynski said. "Lucas, you done here?"

Tyrell remained silent for a few moments, looking around the room before nodding vaguely. "Sure, Terry, just give me a few minutes."

Cain rolled his eyes. "It's a bust; let's get this place swept clean."

Tyrell took a few careful paces amid the detritus on the carpet, skirting the table in the center of the room. He crouched down beside one of the bodies, the corpse's dark skin graying with decay. Reaching out, he lifted the man's lips with a plastic spatula and peered into his mouth.

"Jesus," Cain choked, "I'm sure he flossed before he took his ticket out of life."

Tyrell moved to another of the corpses and then to the third, performing the same task with each before finally standing up.

"What's up?" Lopez asked. "You smell somethin'?"

Tyrell ignored Kaczynski's chuckle. "This wasn't a crack den."

"It sure as hell wasn't a frat party," Cain said.

Tyrell gestured to the bodies.

"One crackhead ODs himself, I can handle that. Three at once, simultaneously and naked? That's pushing it."

Tyrell saw Cain shake his head wearily.

"Isn't the first time. These losers probably tripped each other out all night before going off the edge in some kind of binge. We're wasting our time, let's go."

Cain left the doorway, covering his nose with his hand. Nobody followed.

"This guy's mid-thirties at least," Tyrell said, "not classic crack-addict age."

"Profiling shows addicts come in all shapes and sizes, and he could have gone out on crystal meth and not crack," Kaczynski countered, but his tone conceded the point.

Tyrell crouched down again beside one of the bodies, motioning for Lopez to join him.

"Tell me what you see, Lopez."

"No tattoos or major scars, no gang colors like the other two," she said. Tyrell nodded, and her tone became more thoughtful as she placed a gloved hand on the corpse. "No rigor mortis."

"Exactly," Tyrell agreed, "and decomposition has begun."

"Rigor mortis only lasts a few hours," Kaczynski said, moving closer, "which would mean they died yesterday evening latest. What else?"

Tyrell looked at Nicola, who shook her head. Tyrell gestured to the arms of the corpse.

"Puncture wounds and evidence of drug abuse on the arms, but look here." He pointed to the backs of the hands. "This one shows signs of intravenous medical procedures like saline drips."

Kaczynski squatted down alongside Lopez and looked at the marks.

"Homeless people often check into clinics with various ailments, get free medical aid and so on, even substituted drug programs."

Tyrell pointed to the undignified mouths gaping open in silent death throes.

"This guy has good teeth," he added. "The others don't. I'd bet he's had dental work done and we'll see it in the autopsy. Not the mark of the crack addict. And look at this"—Tyrell pointed to the man's index finger, where a pale band bisected the dark skin—"he could have been married long enough for the ring to have marked and—"

Tyrell stopped, holding the hand still as Kaczynski stared at him.

"What?"

Tyrell turned the hand over, examining the fingertips.

"They're darkened, see?" he asked, showing the tips to them both and shaking his head in confusion as he looked at the feet and saw the same discoloration. "It looks like frostbite."

"Frostbite?" Kaczynski echoed. "Are you kidding? It's been eighty degrees or more across the District for two weeks. Ain't nobody gettin' frostbite round here."

Tyrell frowned. "You got any ideas as to what the hell else it could be?"

"Decay of some kind?" Lopez hazarded. "Livor mortis?"

"It's in the toes too," Tyrell pointed out, "and the legs are elevated on the couch, which rules out livor mortis."

"Maybe circulatory distress during overdose?" Lopez said.

Kaczynski shrugged. "What are you suggesting? It's a setup? Drug-motivated homicide?"

"I'm not suggesting anything other than that we

should get forensics in and run a check for missing persons," Tyrell said.

Kaczynski exhaled noisily. "You think that they weren't alone?"

"You're damned right," Tyrell replied. "I want to hang on to this one, see what turns up. Can you get them down to the medical examiner's office in a hurry?"

"They're not going to push three crackheads up the list for you."

"They're not doing it for me, Terry." Tyrell smiled playfully and nudged Kaczynski.

Lopez stood up and looked at Tyrell as Kaczynski left the room. "What d'ya make of it?"

Tyrell shook his head slowly, still looking at the bodies.

"Don't know yet, but there are enough questions to make postmortems a priority. Let's keep this one to ourselves, okay? At least until we hear back from the examiner's office tomorrow morning."

7

AMERICAN EVANGELICAL ASSOCIATION
NEW COVENANT CHURCH, WASHINGTON DC

What is the meaning of life? Where did we come from? What happens to us when we die?"

Pastor Kelvin Patterson's words echoed as successive ranks of speakers amplified his voice around the church gardens, where two thousand pairs of eyes were fixed upon him. For a brief moment he caught himself waiting to hear the voice of the Almighty thunder down in reply and break the live current of anticipation flickering through the congregation. He was a small man dwarfed by the broad stage upon which he stood, yet although the ranks of speakers gave amplification to his voice it was his passion that truly powered it.

"What would life be if it had no meaning?" Patterson demanded of his flock. *"What would be the point of a universe without purpose? Nature never does anything without purpose, for to do so is a waste of resources."*

Television cameras focused on him from nearby, broadcasting his image onto massive television screens and to millions of Americans across the United States. He could see his own image, his big, round gray eyes glowing beneath his short gray hair and a light sweat glistening on his brow from the stage lights. The man of the moment. Pastor to the nation. Patterson momentarily recalled his unhappy childhood as he looked at himself on the huge screens, a lonely and ostracized youth where his bulbous eyes and earnest desire to be accepted by other children had earned him the hated moniker *Bug*. *If only they could see me now,* he thought, before realizing once again that they were probably watching him on television.

Across the rear of the gardens, a huge banner spread between two towering trees was emblazoned with flowing red text: GIVE BLOOD FOR JESUS!

Patterson glared at his congregation, his bulging eyes ablaze with the utter conviction of faith as he clenched his fist beside his head.

"The Darwinists, the atheists, and the secularists claim that the scientific method, pure logic, is the only way to find the answers to such questions. I say unto you now: if the universe is here and it is governed by the laws of nature, then it must have a purpose, and to have a purpose it must by that same pure logic have had a cause!"

A surging wave of cheers thundered down as though from the heavens to swamp him as he spoke.

"And all of you know that there is only one cause that fits every criteria, supports every fiber of our human instinct, and provides us with the answers we need, and that cause is God, and His word brought to us by our Lord Jesus Christ! This is not a movement for God, this is a movement because of God!"

The congregation roared their approval, applauding and swaying as Patterson gathered his breath and waved them down to silence. From the corner of his eye he saw a tall figure watching him from the wings of the stage. Patterson's voice trembled with emotion as he spoke.

"*Yet every day we see our Lord's mission corrupted by the secularists! They infect our country with their filth and despair, their disregard for the sanctity of human life, their disrespect for God. There can be no peace on Earth, there can be no Second Coming, and there can be no Rapture until the prophecy is fulfilled!*"

The pastor's face twisted upon itself in righteous indignation, teeth gritted and spittle flying in the bright glare of the stage lights.

"*Until the Holy Lands are returned to whom they rightly belong there will be no peace and there should be no peace! Peace before the glory of our Lord's coming is a heresy, and I for one shall not rest until God's will has come to pass!*"

A tsunami of approval surged up into the vault of the sky before crashing down around Patterson. The ranks of the faithful bolted to their feet and punched the air, faces shining with the fervor and the fury of the chosen. Cameras flashed, flags and banners waved, faces beamed with conviction.

Patterson turned to the figure lurking in the wings of the stage.

"*Thank God that we have in our government today the kind of men who would have made Moses himself proud. I'd like you all to give a warm welcome to a man with whom I'm sure you're all very familiar, United States senator Isaiah James Black!*"

A rush of surprise swept through the congregation as two thousand heads turned to look at the stage wings. Senator Black walked out into the brilliant sunlight, waving and smiling at the crowd, perfect white teeth and wavy salt-and-pepper hair. The pastor extended his hand to the senator. Black took it and leaned in close to be heard above the tumult of the crowd.

"No peace? What the hell are you talking about?"

Patterson kept a smile fixed as he vigorously shook the senator's hand.

"Keeping up appearances, Isaiah, as should you."

The senator managed to keep a smile slapped awkwardly on his face and turned to face the expectant flock of the American Evangelical Alliance, some two thousand souls from a total of thirty million faithful Americans.

Tread carefully, Isaiah, Patterson thought as he watched the senator speak.

"I can scarcely begin to say how proud I am to be a part of this initiative by the New Covenant Church to refill the empty transfusion reserves of this great city, our capital. There can surely be no greater, yet simpler, sacrifice than the offering of our blood for the hospitals that save American lives every day. It takes only a little time, only a little effort, but a really big heart, and that makes us special in our own way, knowing that this one act of selflessness could tomorrow save the life of our fellow Americans, perhaps even one of us here today."

The senator cultivated a smile for the crowd, who applauded him vigorously as he spoke through a carefully choreographed flash of brilliant white teeth for the cameras. *"I know without a doubt that I'll be seeing each and every one of you down at the donor stations, and if it's okay with all of you, I'd like to take a moment out of my campaign here to donate blood myself right now."*

A further burst of applause thundered across the gardens, followed by a chorus of "Amen, Amen," chanted as though God Himself were listening. The senator strode off the stage, waving as he went, followed by Patterson. As Black reached the shelter of the wings he turned to glare at the pastor.

"What the hell was that?"

The pastor smiled calmly.

"It was on a whim, Isaiah. You were here, the people were excited. You're a member of this congregation, after all, and so rarely do we get to hear the great and good of our leadership say a few words to the humble masses."

Erratic spasms twitched across Black's eyelid.

"I'm also a member of the Senate of the United States of America," he snapped, and then appeared to quell his rage. "We need to talk."

The pastor led him into the modern megachurch, a maze of carpeted corridors and offices far removed from the archaic European monuments of austerity hewn from ancient stone. A suitably imperious oak door bore Patterson's name on a polished brass plate. The pastor led Senator Black through, closing the door after them and noticing the senator's visible relief at a brief sanctuary from the endless cameras and questions of the press.

The office was vast, dominated by a heavy desk and broad bay windows that looked out across Memorial Park and the distant silvery strip of the Potomac. A fifteen-foot-high chrome crucifix dominated one wall, a small altar and candles arranged before it.

"So, Isaiah, what can I do for you? Your call sounded urgent."

Black turned from examining the glorious vista outside.

"Do you have any idea how long the Senate and the president have been working on a peace initiative for the Middle East?"

"As long as Israel has existed as a state," Patterson replied. "I'm not unaware of the efforts made to secure a deal with the Palestinians."

"This is the first time in over a decade we've had any

real chance of a deal and you're here preaching fire and brimstone. Peace in the Middle East a heresy? How the hell do you think that will look on tonight's news?"

Patterson sighed heavily.

"That is what we stand for, Isaiah, the kingdom of our Lord as the destination for the Second Coming. The administration must return the faith of its people toward God, put God back into the public sphere, and save this soulless, secular, decaying society of ours. You, my friend, will be the next man in the White House to support the cause."

Black stared at the ceiling as though searching for a safe escape. "It's not as simple as that."

"Why?" Patterson snapped. "Isaiah, on the day of the Rapture the Christian faithful of this world will ascend to Heaven while the remaining few billion people on Earth are cast unto everlasting fire. That will be deeply unpleasant but not one of them can say that we haven't tried to warn them. You've been a member of my congregation for forty or more years, you know this."

The senator rubbed his temples wearily.

"Being a member of a church is not the same thing as being a member of an administration. I can't be seen endorsing a man who favors war. If I go into the primaries on that ticket, I won't last five minutes."

Patterson's eyes transformed into tiny, probing points of ice that pierced Black's soul.

"I had no idea your faith was built on such weak foundations."

Senator Black raised his chin as he spoke.

"The American people will watch the news tonight and see me as a member of a church that preaches hate. Despite what you seem to think, not every American wants a theocracy."

"Are you sure? Fifty percent of all Americans believe the Bible to be the literal truth. They know that the Earth is less than ten thousand years old, that it was created by God, and that His judgment upon us is soon to be realized. All of the prophecies support it, Isaiah."

"Prophecies don't win elections," Black muttered, crossing the room and sitting on a brown leather chair. "The people are not going to support a president who is so openly associated with . . ." He struggled for a suitable word.

"Fundamentalists?" Patterson suggested with a mocking smile.

"Conservatives. We've been down that path before."

Patterson adopted a soothing tone, sitting on the edge of his desk.

"Don't be so dismissive of the Word, Isaiah. The Second Coming, the End Times, and the Rapture are all preceded by what we see in the world around us today. The revival of Israel as a nation, witnessed by the last generation before Christ in the parable of the fig tree—Matthew Twenty-four. A strong and united European state, or a United States of Europe similar to a revived Roman Empire—Daniel Two. The role of the European Union in the Middle East, the Antichrist, and the peace treaty—Revelation Thirteen. The mark of the beast, in commerce, so that none can buy or sell without the mark, which is the UPC bar-code system whose bars are encoded as three groups of six: the number of the beast—Revelation Thirteen."

Black shook his head. "I think that you place far too much faith in ancient texts."

The pastor smiled again. "Peter Three—the Apostle says that in the End Times even religious people would dismiss the idea of Christ's return."

Black looked the pastor straight in the eye.

"My allegiance is to this country and its Constitution. I cannot be seen to openly favor one faith above another."

Patterson kept his expression neutral.

"Yet this country is one nation under God, Isaiah. Look around us, at what is happening to our world. America is crumbling beneath the weight of crime, corruption, and societal decline caused by atheists and secularists. America is rotting from within and God is the only one who can save us."

"One nation under God indeed," Black echoed. "Yet our crumbling America is the most religious of all the world's democracies, which kind of lets the atheists off the hook."

A stab of indignation punctured Patterson's studied calm. "God is the light, not the darkness. Only a lack of faith can see His light deflected from a true path."

"I can't support your church any further if you continue with these inflammatory speeches," Black said firmly, standing.

Patterson regarded Black for a long moment, masking his fury at the senator's resilience. A man who had survived the political machine due to his popularity with ordinary folk, hockey moms, and liberals, Isaiah Black had always been a more pliable man in time of need. He decided to turn the screws up a notch.

"The voters may not forgive you lightly, Isaiah."

"What do you mean?"

"If you turn your back on us, then you turn your back on God and abandon any chance of redemption. I command the allegiance of thirty million faithful Americans, Isaiah. They do not vote for a president or a party, they vote for God, and if you abandon us, then I'll make damn sure that ten percent of this country's voters abandon *you*."

Senator Black's jaw dropped open. "You can't control voters like that."

The pastor shook his head slowly, a smile creasing his thin lips.

"Can you afford to take the risk? I would suggest that you ask yourself something, Isaiah. What matters more to you: misguided government policy or your place as the president of the United States of America?"

Senator Black ground his teeth.

"I have blood to give," he said, and turned for the door.

"We too are prepared to shed blood, to seal the covenant between man and God," Patterson said after him, "no matter what the consequences."

8

AUGUST 25

The woman stared at him from across the street, her hair in disarray, her wrists bound, guns wedged into her side as she was wrestled into a battered sedan by masked men. Ethan shouted at her, but his voice was muted. He ran toward her, but his legs refused to move, dragging like lead weights beneath him. He saw her scream in desperation, and he heard a strange whining noise assault his ears as the world shuddered beneath his feet.

Ethan's eyes blinked open, the turbulence shuddering through the aircraft jolting him awake.

He stared out of his window as the Boeing 737 turned steeply over the sparkling azure Mediterranean. The coast of Israel drifted past five thousand feet below beneath a scattering of cloud, and to the north he could see the metallic sprawl of Tel Aviv glinting through the early-morning haze. His eyes ached, and he realized that he had drifted into sleep, the first time since taking off some seven hours previously.

Beside him Rachel Morgan sat in catatonic silence, as she had done for the past four hours. Ethan had spent half of his life crammed into aircraft flying from one godforsaken war zone to another, and had hated the narcissistic chatter of journalists from a dozen countries sharing their unwanted opinions on whatever crisis they were heading to document. Rachel's silence had been initially a great relief. Now, he suspected that there was something more to it, emphasized by the empty seat between them.

"We're descending," he said in a vague attempt to provoke conversation.

"So it would seem."

He tried again.

"You ever been to the Middle East before?"

"Only when family members go missing."

"Is that some kind of joke?" Ethan snapped.

Rachel's eyes swiveled to peer sideways at him. "No, I'm sorry. I'm just not in the mood for talking right now."

"Is there some kind of problem here, with me?"

"Should there be?"

"You've barely spoken since we met, and if this trip is going to achieve anything at all, I need your help." Ethan leaned across the empty seat between them. "If we can't work together and start uncovering what happened to Lucy, you know what will happen?"

"What will happen?"

"Nothing at all."

Rachel stared ahead for a few moments before replying. "I'm not comfortable with the idea of running around a foreign country with someone I don't know anything about and who clearly has problems of his own."

"You think I want to be cooped up on an airliner bound for the Middle East?" Ethan challenged. "I was perfectly happy where I was."

"Is that so?" Rachel said. "You see, that's my point. Even Doug admitted to me that you're troubled, and whether that's because of whatever happened to you out here or not is irrelevant. If you're unable to help yourself, then what use are you to me or to Lucy?"

Ethan struggled to erect a harbor of dignity around his shame.

"Do you think Doug would have asked me here if he thought that?"

"By his own admission, there was nobody else he *could* ask."

Ethan gave up and stared out of the window. "Glad I could help."

For a long time Rachel sat staring into space, but eventually she glanced across at him.

"Look, I appreciate you being here."

"Thanks," Ethan said quietly. "As you've pointed out neither of us has much of a choice, so why don't we just get on with it?"

Rachel stared at him for a long moment with an unconvinced expression. "Fine."

"I need you to tell me everything you can about your daughter and what she was up to out here."

"Lucy was born in 1981, but her father Robert died when she was fourteen."

"I'm sorry to hear that."

"So were we," Rachel said, her voice softening. "He died before his time. I've questioned a thousand times what would make God take someone from us, but I've never found an answer."

"You're Catholic," Ethan guessed.

"I'm a theologian. You?"

Ethan held up his hands. "I'm on the fence, doesn't interest me much."

Rachel looked away, but he saw a ghost of a smile touch her lips. "You'd have liked Robert then. He was a humanist."

Ethan blinked.

"A humanist, a theologian, and a scientist? Family dinners must have literally been a riot."

Rachel smiled again and Ethan watched as her green eyes blossomed briefly with light, but the moment vanished as quickly as it had come and the smile melted away.

"How on earth did you and Robert meet?"

"He was a friend of a friend. We met at a barbeque, and he bet me ten bucks that I couldn't convert him from his humanism over a dinner date."

"Nice move," Ethan said.

"It was."

Rachel's features were no longer strained, and though she continued to stare straight ahead Ethan could see that her mind was wandering among the phantasms of the past. She barely noticed the mechanical grind of the aircraft's undercarriage coming down somewhere beneath them. Ethan glanced briefly out of the window at the fields and palm groves sweeping past beneath the Boeing's flexing wing tips.

"How did Lucy end up in Israel?"

"She had been doing field research in Kenya's Great Rift Valley near Nairobi, before moving to the Hebrew University under a new posting. She'd been awarded a grant for new research into early human evolution and was being mentored by someone called Hans Karowitz, a Belgian scientist, and a cosmologist called Hassim Khan."

Ethan made a mental note of the names.

"Okay, so why don't you tell me what was so important about what she found out there?"

"It was an unknown species of human," Rachel began, "that hasn't yet been classified by science and—"

"That the Defense Intelligence Agency for some rea-son wants to recover?" Ethan challenged. "I need to know everything, or this is all for nothing."

Rachel sighed.

"They asked me not to reveal it to you unless it was absolutely necessary."

"Is finding your daughter alive absolutely neces-sary?" Ethan asked.

Rachel closed her eyes and nodded before speaking softly.

"The remains that Lucy found were in a tomb esti-mated to have been about seven thousand years old," she said. "But the remains were not human."

"Not human?" Ethan echoed. "They said that the bones were humanoid."

"Yes, they were."

The aircraft around Ethan seemed to recede as he tried to grasp what Rachel was saying.

"So it was some kind of ape?"

"It was a species that did not originate or evolve on this planet," Rachel said.

Ethan dragged a hand down his face, trying to con-ceal his disbelief.

"An alien," he said finally. "That's why they're send-ing the DIA after Lucy, because they think she found E.T. camping in Israel and they want possession of the remains."

"It's the only reason they're willing to take an inter-est in this case at all," she said sadly. "If it weren't for what Lucy found, do you think the DIA would invest in a search for her? They wouldn't give a damn. This is about the remains, not Lucy."

Ethan leaned his head back against his seat and chuckled in disbelief.

"I'm being sent halfway across the world to dig up some bones for the DIA," he murmured, "that'll probably turn out to have belonged to a frickin' rhinoceros or something."

Rachel shot him a toxic look.

"My daughter is still missing out there, whatever you think about this, and she's smart enough to be able to tell a rhino from a human."

Ethan shook himself from his torpor of disbelief.

"Okay, indulge me. Why would she have found something like that out there?"

"There's a big problem in human history that nobody has been able to explain," Rachel said. "The ancestors of modern humans, people essentially identical to us in every way, had existed in a hunter-gatherer state for at least sixty thousand years. But suddenly, out of nowhere, mankind began building cities, forming agriculture, and producing advanced technologies. And that growth blossomed simultaneously in vastly separated geographical areas, from the Indus Valley to the Levant to the Americas."

Ethan leaned back in his seat.

"Surely that's just natural growth after the end of the Ice Ages?"

Rachel shook her head.

"There had been some developments, of course: simple dwellings, domestication of animals, and rudimentary agriculture. But then the people of the Indus Valley in today's Pakistan began the construction of major cities around five thousand years ago. At the same time the Sumerians began to build cities in Mesopotamia, between the Euphrates and Tigris Rivers. The point is that there is no record of gradual development or progression—the cities sprang up almost instantaneously.

Both civilizations supposedly independently invented the wheel and a script called cuneiform. The Indus Valley script, known as Dravidian, hasn't been fully deciphered even today."

"How big were these cities?" Ethan asked.

He was surprised by her answer, never having known that such ancient cities could harbor populations of up to forty thousand people. Nor had he known of the complexity of their technologies: that the Indus civilization had built domestic bathrooms, flushing toilets, and drains using burned and glazed bricks; or that it built public basins with two layers of bricks with gypsum mortar and sealed by a layer of bitumen, a remarkably astute method. The Mesopotamians had built docks and seaworthy vessels for trade, and had developed extensive irrigation comparable to modern agriculture.

"Okay," Ethan said, "but so did the Egyptians, right, and they came later?"

"The Egyptians rose at about the same time," Rachel said. "Egypt's first king, Menes, ruled some five thousand years ago in its capital Memphis, but the kingdom was ancient even then and had already developed its hieroglyphic script, again apparently out of nowhere."

Ethan frowned.

"And you don't think that this could have happened naturally?"

"It's possible," Rachel conceded, "but it should have taken longer than it did, and it seems that the ancients suddenly acquired knowledge sufficiently advanced to still be used today."

The Babylonians, Rachel explained, were descended from the Sumerians, and their mathematics was written using a sexagesimal numeral system: one which has as its base the number sixty. From this derived the modern-day usage of sixty seconds in a minute, sixty minutes in an hour, and three hundred and sixty degrees in a circle.

"Which remains after almost eight thousand years," Ethan said.

"Along with various customs and traditions," Rachel agreed, "which are continued today in recognizable forms."

"And Lucy thinks that another species," Ethan guessed, "perhaps an extraterrestrial species, gave them knowledge, which they then passed down through time ever after?"

"If it seemed crazy before, it doesn't now after what Lucy found," Rachel said. "I've spent some time researching all of this since Lucy first mentioned it months ago, long before she disappeared. There have been many books written in the past that have attributed all manner of activities to alien visitors from distant planets, from the founding of Atlantis to building the pyramids. All of it was rubbish, of course."

"So what's the difference here?" Ethan asked.

"Real historical events that match the supposed myths of a thousand religions," Rachel said. "We are familiar only with the religious histories that survive to this day, but they have existed in many differing forms for millennia. Oral tradition was the only way for ancient civilizations to record their past until scripts suddenly appeared simultaneously around the world: the Neolithic script, Indus script, Sumerian and Bronze Age phonetics all appeared around six thousand years ago. In all of their creation myths, these early civilizations almost identically describe gods who came down from the skies and passed to them great knowledge."

Ethan himself had read of the legends of the Sumerians, Egyptians, Amerindians, and Japanese, describing such visitors as traveling in fiery chariots, flaming drag-ons, or giant glowing birds that descended noisily from the sky.

A loud thump reverberated through the fuselage.

Ethan looked at the sun-baked runway flashing past outside. "So we don't know who hired Lucy to go digging in the Negev for alien remains, but whoever it was must have known what they were looking for."

"I doubt that she would have abandoned her original research on a whim."

Ethan unbuckled his seat belt and turned to face her.

"I need to know everything you know about this," he said. "When someone vanishes, the first forty-eight hours are the most critical and they've already passed. Knowledge is our only resource now because X never marks the spot."

Although Ethan could still see doubt shadowing her expression, Rachel unbuckled her seat belt and looked at him expectantly.

"What do you want to know?"

9

BEN GURION INTERNATIONAL AIRPORT
ISRAEL

That's crazy," Ethan said.

"Why?" Rachel challenged. "Just because it sounds ridiculous doesn't mean it's not correct or even likely."

The main terminal of Ben Gurion International was dominated by a circular glass-vaulted ceiling from which poured a cylindrical sheet of glittering water. The waterfall drained into a pool that reflected light across the domed roof in a shimmering kaleidoscope of color. Ethan had the impression that he was passing through a giant fish bowl as he walked with Rachel toward the airport meeting point.

"Yeah," Ethan conceded, "but UFOs in the Bible?"

"And in all other ancient creation works. Ezekiel speaks of such events in the Bible," Rachel said, and her expression became distant as she spoke. "'And I looked, and, behold, a whirlwind came out of the north, a great cloud, and a fire infolding itself, and a brightness was about it, and out of the midst thereof as the color of amber, out of the midst of the fire.'"

"Could have been a meteorite," Ethan suggested.

"'Also out of the midst thereof came the likeness of four living creatures,'" Rachel continued. "'And this was their appearance: they had the likeness of a man.'"

Ethan looked at her for a long moment.

"I'd have thought Lucy would need more to go on than that."

Rachel was about to reply when a thunderous voice boomed across the terminal.

"Ethan!"

Ethan saw Aaron Luckov the moment he entered the terminal, a bearded and barrel-chested man who swept through the crowds like a tornado through an olive grove. The man possessed shoulders like a harbor wall and a grip that felt as though Ethan's hand was being stood upon.

"Aaron, been a long time."

"Too long, Ethan!" The towering Israeli swung an arm around Ethan's shoulders, one hand clapping loudly against his back.

"Is everything ready?" Ethan whispered as he returned the embrace.

"It is prepared," Luckov replied equally quietly.

Aaron Luckov had served as an Israeli Air Force fighter pilot before starting up an air charter company with his wife. Ethan had known him for over a decade, and together they had shared both the best and the worst of times out in the ancient cities and deserts.

"Aaron, this is Rachel Morgan," Ethan introduced them.

"Ah," Aaron said, gently shaking Rachel's hand. "I have heard much about you. I am so sorry to hear of your loss."

Rachel flushed. "Hopefully, it's not a loss."

Aaron took Rachel's bag in one meaty fist.

"I hope so too. Come, I have a ride waiting for us outside and we'll need to hurry."

"Why?" Rachel asked in confusion.

"Because we're not alone," Ethan said, glancing across the terminal to where two suited men stood and observed them with fixed gazes. "How many?" he asked Aaron as they began to walk.

"Two inside, two outside," Aaron replied.

"Why are they watching us?" Rachel asked.

"They're not," Ethan said. "They're watching *me*."

Ethan felt his lungs spasm reflexively as Aaron led them out of the air-conditioned terminal into a merciless heat. A white convertible jeep was parked by the sidewalk, a petite and dark-haired woman sitting behind the wheel. Safiya Luckov was Aaron's wife, a Palestinian with dark olive eyes and a bright smile. She got out and helped them with their bags before driving them out of the terminal and east toward Jerusalem.

Ethan leaned back in the rear seat, finally able to stretch out after the long flight. "What's the situation in Jerusalem?"

Aaron's rolling basso profundo voice carried easily above the wind.

"Fragile, how else would it be?"

Ethan had spent several months living within the disputed territories. He had seen the shattered, scarred wreckage of the Gaza Strip, where the Palestinians lived in a near-permanent state of squalor and oppression. And he had friends in the West Bank who had lived under Israeli military occupation for more than forty years since the Israeli-Arab War. Likewise, he knew many Israelis who lived under the constant threat of terrorism, their lives dominated by the wailing sirens warning of unguided Qassam rockets being fired into their backyards from the Gaza Strip by "freedom fighters" of a dozen obscure sects sworn to Israel's destruction.

"This doesn't make our job any easier," Ethan said, glancing over his shoulder. Behind them, a pair of glossy black SUVs followed at a short distance. "Are those guys Mossad?"

"Just an NGO," Aaron said, glancing at the following vehicles in his side-view mirror with a wry smile. "You're not *that* important, Ethan."

"Surely if the authorities are following us, then we're being protected too?" Rachel said.

Ethan turned to her.

"The authorities don't like me here," he said simply.

"Why not?"

"This discovery that Lucy supposedly made," Ethan said, ignoring her question. "You really think it's real?"

"You're not buying into this, are you?" Rachel muttered. "Even the Defense Intelligence Agency is showing an interest, regardless of their motives."

"I doubt they're holding their breath," Ethan pointed out.

"No?" Rachel challenged. "NASA launched its *Voyager* space probes in the seventies with solid gold discs aboard, bearing greetings in fifty-five different languages. One of those was ancient Sumerian. Why else would they include a script that is several thousand years old and no longer used by humanity?"

Ethan shrugged.

"Not for me to say. Why would Lucy have been looking for alien remains out here?"

Rachel gestured to the parched land around them as she spoke above the wind.

"Israel is part of the Levant, the cradle of civilization."

Ethan glanced across the barren landscape baking beneath the equatorial sun.

"Doesn't look like much."

"Not now it doesn't," Rachel agreed, "but twelve thousand years ago the Levant was a very different place. Back then, this would have been a lush and fertile land, and the Sumerian legends describe the origins of their civilization here through unusual means."

"Like the Bible?" Ethan asked.

"Sumerian legends tell of a god named Oannes," Rachel explained. "Oannes rose out of the Persian Gulf in what is described as a diving suit, and is depicted as an amphibious being. Many legends state unequivocally that Oannes came from under the sea. Oannes is the culture bearer for the Sumerian civilization, who is said to have brought them the arts of writing, agriculture, and tool making."

From the front seat, Aaron Luckov peered at them curiously.

"Is this what you're going to tell the government when you meet them—legends?"

"What contact have you had so far with the Knesset?" Ethan asked.

"In this, I have excelled," Aaron stated proudly, not noticing Safiya rolling her eyes. "I have an appointment for you at the United States embassy this afternoon, and there will be a member of the Israeli Foreign Ministry present."

Rachel turned from looking out across the sun-scorched land and the twinkling blue Mediterranean beyond. "How did you manage that?" she asked.

"I spoke to a few contacts in the West Bank and Tel Aviv and they put me in touch with the Foreign Ministry. Your name was mentioned, and they understood immediately. There's a lot of sympathy for what's happened, and they understand your frustration at their reluctance to broadcast your daughter's disappearance because of the peace negotiations."

"Well done," Ethan said, clapping his friend on the shoulder.

Aaron smiled awkwardly. "There was a price to pay."

"What do they want?" Ethan asked.

"Security," Aaron said. "They're determined that you remain under armed guard throughout your stay here, to prevent any further kidnappings. We're to meet with your escort first, and I don't like any of them."

10

MEDICAL EXAMINER'S OFFICE
MASSACHUSETTS AVENUE SE,
WASHINGTON DC

Y ou know I hate this part."

Lucas Tyrell grinned at Lopez as he drove the car into the parking lot and killed the engine.

"You've gotta get used to it. Just don't get *too* used to it, or I'll have you sectioned." He turned to Bailey, who sat quietly in the rear seat. "Sit tight, buddy, shouldn't take too long." He tossed a handful of biscuits into the rear of the car and then clambered out, mopping his brow as he caught his breath.

Truth was, he felt the same about morgues as she did, and he had far more experience than she. Not for the first time he wondered what had kept her in the District.

Nicola Lopez had emigrated with her family to DC almost twenty years before as a gangly nine-year-old from Guanajuato, Mexico, a ramshackle town nestled in the Veeder Mountains. She had been raised a Catholic amid the cobbled streets and quaint markets far from the hustle and bustle of America's capital city. Dragged by a family searching for a better life away from the crippling silver mines of Las Ranas, they had found instead only a better quality of misery, where endemic poverty and poor sanitation had been replaced with housing projects, fast food, and type 2 diabetes. Her disillusioned parents had returned to Mexico five years previously, closely followed by her two brothers, one sister, and last remaining grandparent. She said that she hadn't seen any of them since, although they wrote and spoke on the phone often.

Nicola had stayed, apparently enthralled by the rush, glamour, and danger of America. It had been the drastic change of surroundings and endless junk television that had prompted her to join the MPD as soon as she was old enough, her imagination flying high on a diet of cop dramas depicting police department and FBI offices as marvels of high-technology fecundity: ranks of glossy black desks and glowing blue lights, giant screens with satellite links and connections direct to the White House. The reality, Tyrell knew, had been far more austere. Even so, it was a better life for her than stabbing needles into her arm in some frozen subway shelter or running with the Latino gangs out of Shaw and Columbia Heights.

The medical examiner's office was tasked with the investigation and certification of all deaths in the District of Columbia that occurred unexpectedly or as a result of violence. Positioned conveniently alongside the General Hospital, it was the first or, depending on how you looked at it, last stop for corpses in the city. A single ambulance sat with its rear doors open as a gurney was rushed with indecent haste from the building's interior. Tyrell and Lucas watched in amazement as paramedics fussed over what looked like a surgeon lying on the gurney, his face pale white beneath his oxygen mask and his eyes rolling up in their sockets.

"Don't patients normally get wheeled in, not out?" Lopez asked.

At the entrance, a beat cop barred their way. "Been an incident, sir, I can't let you past right now."

Tyrell and Lopez flashed their badges.

"What's happened?" Tyrell asked. "Was that a doctor being wheeled out?"

"Toxic-material breach," the cop said. "Something to do with three John Does brought here yesterday."

"Out of the Potomac projects?"

"Yeah." The cop nodded. "The hell's going on with them? They're supposed to be dead, but they've half killed one of the top surgeons in the hospital."

Tyrell and Lopez shot a glance at each other.

"The Does are our case," Tyrell said to the cop, "we need to get in there."

The cop nodded and opened the entrance doors for them.

Tyrell led the way through the corridors and down a flight of stairs toward the morgue. A series of polished steel doors partitioned the morgue from the autopsy rooms, where corpses afflicted with the gruesome lesions of crime, neglect, or both were dissected and their decaying remains examined for silent testimony to their demise.

A small dressing room provided the chance to don gloves and a filter mask before Tyrell and Lopez pushed through into the autopsy room proper.

Three of the four steel trolleys dominating the room were covered with pale-blue plastic sheets, the interiors of which were flecked with ugly spots of fluid that even after all these years still made Tyrell's stomach turn. He looked instead at a man dressed in a surgical gown approaching him. Tall, wiry, and with thin-rimmed spec-

tacles adorning an aquiline nose, he looked every bit at
home in a morgue.

"Detectives Tyrell and Lopez," Tyrell announced.

"Dr. John Fry," the surgeon said. "You guys pick up
the three crackheads here?"

"Yeah. What's the story?"

"You ever thought to check them over for toxicity?"

Tyrell shook his head. "We figured that was your
job."

"I've got one of my surgeons on his way to General
with cyanide poisoning after he cut into one of your John
Does."

Tyrell stopped in his tracks, Lopez alongside him.
"There was nothing at the scene to suggest poisoning.
Your man going to be okay?"

Fry regarded them briefly before turning to look over
the top of his spectacles at the three corpses.

"He'll be fine. Have you spoken to the district attorney yet?"

"Thought we'd wait and see what you had to say."

Fry nodded almost absentmindedly before waving
them to follow.

Tyrell watched as the surgeon lifted the sheets off
the three bodies. Each had been opened with a Y-shaped
incision across the chest, encrusted around the edges
with dried blood. The skull caps had been placed loosely
back atop their respective craniums, the brains still inside. Tyrell wondered briefly whether it made a difference
if they somehow got mixed up, but refrained from asking.

"You say these were found in a crack den, a group
overdose?" Fry asked.

Lopez took her cue when Tyrell remained silent.

"That's how it looked to have played out, but Tyrell
has reservations about it."

"How so?" Fry asked him.

Tyrell voiced his doubts over the crime scene as he had found it. Fry appeared lost in his thoughts for several seconds before speaking.

"Only two of these men died from overdoses of crack cocaine."

Tyrell noticed Lopez smile quietly beside him, but pretended not to. "What makes you say that?"

Fry gestured to the bodies.

"One of the victims shows none of the usual external signs of crack addiction. Crack is smoked through a hot pipe in order to obtain the maximum high between evaporation and inhalation. This gives habitual users *crack lip*—dry and blistered lips. This individual, we'll call him Alpha, shows no sign of this affliction."

"Sometimes addicts getting their hits off low-quality crack who then smoke something pure can inadvertently overdose," Lopez suggested.

"Possibly, but when large amounts of dopamine are released by crack consumption," Fry explained, "it also releases a large amount of adrenaline into the body, which increases heart rate and blood pressure, leading to long-term cardiovascular problems as a result of the release of methylecgonidine. Alpha shows no sign of such disorders, which precludes any kind of long-term addiction for him at least."

"Cocaine-related deaths are often a result of cardiac arrest or seizures followed by respiratory arrest," Tyrell pointed out. "So Alpha could've crashed from misadventure."

"Indeed, but then why the crack den?" Fry asked. "In addition, Alpha shows external signs of recent medical procedures. Placing patients on saline drips is a common practice in order to rehydrate them and replace lost vitamins. Either way, checking in for medical help doesn't fit the profile of someone contemplating suicide."

Fry moved across to a metal trolley, upon which lay a file. He picked it up as Tyrell cast his eyes across the bodies.

"What would you estimate his age as?" he asked the doctor.

"Not less than thirty. Dental work and mild erosive damage to enamel suggest an age closer to forty."

"Not like a homeless person to have access to good dental practice," Lopez said.

"That's not what bothers me the most," Fry said, propping his spectacles farther up the bridge of his nose. "Rigor mortis does not give a reliable indication of death; however, livor mortis can and it tells me that Alpha did not die where he was found. The accumulation of red blood cells in the lower extremities suggests that he was lying on his back when he died."

"So he was moved after death?" Lopez said.

Fry shrugged noncommitally.

"You're the detectives, I'll leave that to you. What I *can* tell you is that he suffered. His blood and lungs contain excessive levels of hydrogen sulphide, which is the compound that sent my colleague into hospital."

Dr. Fry moved across to the corpses, his eyes scanning them with intense curiosity as though he could speak to them with the power of thought alone.

"Alpha's body also shows signs of intense hypothermia."

"You mean the discoloration on the fingers and toes?" Lopez asked. "Frostbite?"

"Yes," Fry said. "Some of the tissues near the surface of the skin show signs of trauma consistent with sustained low body temperatures."

"Maybe he was refrigerated to alter the apparent time of death?" Lopez suggested.

"That might make some sense." Fry nodded. "Homicide victims are sometimes chilled by the killer in order to provide a plausible time alibi. What's unique is that hydrogen sulphide has been shown to induce a state of hypothermic suspended animation in some mammals."

Tyrell's mind began working overtime. "Suspended animation?"

"Hydrogen sulphide binds to cytochrome oxidase and thereby prevents oxygen from binding," Fry explained, "which results in a dramatic slowdown of metabolism. Most animals and humans naturally produce some hydrogen sulphide in their body, but not at the levels I've encountered here."

Lopez stared at Fry.

"Why would somebody want to slow down his metabolism?"

"Like I said, you're the detectives," Fry replied. "But this man cannot have ingested such high levels of hydrogen sulphide in a natural environment: it's a broad-spectrum poison, meaning that it can affect several different systems in the body. Its toxicity is comparable with that of hydrogen cyanide, forming a bond with iron in the mitochondrial cytochrome enzymes, thereby stopping cellular respiration."

"You got any other evidence of this?" Tyrell asked.

"Other than the victim's blood turning purple in color?" Fry asked. "The treatment for exposure can involve immediate inhalation of amyl nitrite or pure oxygen, injections of sodium nitrite or administration of bronchodilators. I found excess sodium nitrate in Alpha's blood pathology."

"So he was poisoned and then revived?" Tyrell

asked, struggling to connect the disparate pieces of information.

"Apparently so," Fry agreed, obviously enjoying the mystery. "In addition, at his lower extremeties we have evidence of the extraction of reproductive materials from the testes."

Tyrell felt a momentary spasm of disgust shiver through his own family jewels, and didn't bother moving round the gurney as the doctor continued.

"But what is most astounding about Alpha is that his blood contains a genetic signature that I have not been able to identify."

"Genetic signature?" Lopez said. "You mean blood group?"

"I mean *signature,*" Fry said to her over the top of his spectacles. "But as you've mentioned it, Alpha bears the rare O-negative blood group that is the mark of the universal donor. Only seven percent of human beings possess this blood group and its origin is completely unknown, the purest human blood on Earth."

"You mean that his blood has been altered in some way?" Tyrell asked.

Fry nodded. "Transfused. The blood now in Alpha's body is not his own, and I've been unable to determine its origin. I'll need to run more tests."

"Dr. Fry," Tyrell said, "what's your assessment of what happened to him?"

Fry exhaled a lengthy breath.

"I've never seen anything like it before. He must have undergone an ordeal that required suspended animation," Fry answered, his enthusiasm for the mystery apparently tempered as he considered what the victim had endured. "My guess is that his metabolism was slowed in order to hinder the immuno response to whatever process he was enduring. I'll have to run more tests, but I'd say Alpha died from acute hemolytic reaction to a blood transfusion that replaced the original AB blood I found traces of in his kidneys with the rarer O-negative blood. Alpha was originally a universal recipient, someone who could receive blood from any other group, but this transfusion still killed him because his T-lymphocyte cells mounted an attack on the foreign blood entering his body, causing hemorrhage and liver failure."

Tyrell shook his head slowly.

"I need something that I can follow here."

Fry turned to a smaller table beside him, retrieving from it a long, slim metal object that he held in his hand.

"You'll be needing this then," he said. "It's a titanium implant belonging to Alpha."

Tyrell smiled. "Serial number?"

"All in order," Fry said, handing him the rod. "It's from the right femur, probably a result of an automobile accident. Maybe whoever caused his death wasn't as thorough as they thought."

"What about the other two?" Lopez asked.

"I'll send blood specimens to the state crime laboratory," Fry said. "I can use radio or enzyme immunoassay here, but only gas chromatography or mass spectrometry will give us a clear answer as to what happened to these poor souls and be admissible in court. My guess is that they're genuine overdose victims, although still homicides, and that Alpha was made to look like one of them."

"Keep me informed," Tyrell said, turning from the gurneys, "and let me know of any developments, no matter how insignificant."

Tyrell led the way out of the laboratories and into

the fresh air outside. He heard Lopez breathe an audible sigh of relief as they left the labs, but managed to keep his own quiet enough for her not to hear.

"How do you want to play it?" she asked as they reached the car.

"Carefully," Tyrell murmured. "Our victim Alpha's had his blood transfused after being cryogenically frozen and had God knows what extracted from his body, for reasons I can't possibly fathom. If I can't work out why, I doubt the district attorney's going to see this as anything other than a freak overdose."

Tyrell leaned on the roof for a moment, looking thoughtfully back at the office building as he retrieved his handkerchief and mopped his brow once again. He noticed with a sigh that Bailey was watching him from a rear seat covered by a sea of biscuit crumbs.

"Get in touch with the International Commission on Missing Persons. I want details of all individuals reported in the last four weeks who match the bodies we've got in that morgue. Whoever they were, it's my bet that someone's missing them. As for this," he said, tapping the titanium rod, "get in touch with the hospital administration and find out who it belonged to."

Lopez nodded and opened her door.

"Captain Powell won't want us chasing this down, Tyrell. He'll have it tagged as another bunch of po' crackheads wiped out on misadventure once he gets the FBI report from yesterday morning."

"Indeed he will," Tyrell agreed, "but we won't. We keep this to ourselves, for as long as we can."

11

UNITED STATES EMBASSY
HAYARKON STREET, TEL AVIV

Greetings and welcome to Israel."

A smartly dressed envoy led Ethan and Rachel through the large, modern building of concrete pillars and smoked glass situated in the heart of the city. Supported by a consular section in the nearby Migdalor Building, the embassy was home to Ambassador Jeb Cutler, a buoyant Arkansan with a long history of diplomatic wrangling who welcomed them into the conference room as though it were his own living room.

"Ms. Morgan, welcome to Tel Aviv."

Cutler was middle-aged, his features creased by the years of worry that marked the career politician, but his brown eyes danced with genuine delight.

"Thank you for seeing us, Ambassador," Rachel said.

"It's Jeb," he insisted. "I'm glad that you're here, although I wish it were under better circumstances."

Cutler turned and gestured to a wiry little man in a neatly pressed suit who stood behind a table dominating the room. Ethan looked on as Rachel was introduced to

Shiloh Rok, a representative from Israel's Foreign Ministry.

"Welcome, Miss Morgan," Rok murmured, then glanced over Rachel's shoulder at Ethan. "I believed that you were traveling alone."

"This is Ethan Warner," Rachel said. "He has come to help me here in Israel."

Cutler's handshake was firm and dry, but Ethan saw an undercurrent of unease rippling like a cloud shadow behind Rok's eyes as he watched them. The Israeli reminded him of a bird of prey, hawkish and alert.

"Come," Cutler said, "let me pour you a drink. Iced tea? Cola? We've much to discuss."

Rachel wasted no time, speaking as soon as Cutler had handed her a glistening glass of Coke and ice as they sat down around the table.

"Has there been any word at all from Lucy?"

"Alas, no," the ambassador admitted as he handed Ethan a glass and sat down. "We have contacts across the government and security services working on this but so far there hasn't been a lead."

Rachel's face fell, and Ethan realized that she had placed too much hope in this meeting with the ambassador. Cutler caught the look on her face and leaned forward in his chair.

"Don't worry. We'll find your daughter no matter how difficult it might be. I apologize for Israel's inability to act more decisively at this time."

"The Knesset dare not take the chance of broadcasting your daughter's disappearance for fear of upsetting the delicate balance achieved with the Palestinians in the current peace negotiations," Rok said. "I know how much this must distress you."

"Media attention could increase our chances of finding Lucy," Ethan pointed out, "either through word of mouth, the bait of a ransom, or even terrorist abductors seeking media sympathy by releasing Lucy."

Rok shook his head. "That is not a chance that I would like to take with my family, Mr. Warner."

"And if Lucy's abductors are trying to influence the peace process?" Ethan challenged. "If you ignore them, and the process goes ahead, they'll have no further use for her."

"Again," Rok said, "an assumption, not an analysis, Mr. Warner."

"We don't have the time for indecision or analysis," Rachel snapped. "Right now we don't even know if Lucy's still alive."

"She is alive," Cutler said. "This was an organized abduction. In Israel there is always a motive, always a statement to be made."

Ethan saw Rachel take a breath, controlling herself.

"I understand that it's quite unusual for there to be no word from abductors regarding a Western captive," she said.

"It's downright unlikely," Ethan chipped in. "Abductions achieve nothing if there's no political or financial gain."

Cutler took a thoughtful sip of his drink before replying.

"It's a problem, all right, but insurgent groups have no illusions as to the ability of Israel's intelligence services and special forces to liberate Lucy if she is found. They may be laying low."

"I agree that Israel's security forces are capable," Ethan said, "but Israel is a large country and much of it remains sparsely populated. There are thousands of square kilometers of terrain and Lucy could be concealed anywhere out there in the deserts."

"We do not have the manpower to search for her there," Rok said.

"What about the excavation site Lucy was working on? That could harbor some clues. Could we visit it?" Ethan suggested.

Cutler was about to answer, but a gruff reply came from behind them.

"That will not be possible."

Ethan turned in his seat to see a man with severely cropped brown hair, dressed in khaki combat fatigues and a dark-blue beret. Rok stood as the soldier strode into the room and stopped at the opposite end of the table.

"This is Spencer Malik, head of security at Munitions for Advanced Combat Environments—MACE. He is responsible for security in the area where Lucy disappeared."

Malik nodded curtly but remained silent. Ethan glanced at Malik's stubbled jaw and defensively folded arms. He looked more like a mercenary than a trained soldier.

"Why can't we go to Lucy's dig site?" Ethan asked.

Malik met Ethan's gaze, the rest of his body remaining as still as though carved from rock.

"The Israeli Air Force is conducting low-level flight training operations from Ramon Air Base in the Negev Desert. Dr. Morgan's excavation site is within the training area near Masada, and off-limits to civilians."

"I thought that the area around Masada was used as a tourist destination?"

Malik nodded. "The Masada complex lies outside of the practice range, which is concentrated in the canyons to the west, but sometimes the aircraft have to fly overhead at low level."

"Lucy found something before she disappeared," Ethan pressed. "It could be relevant to the reason why she was abducted."

Malik shook his head.

"Not until the exercise is over in three weeks' time."

"The area could have been pulverized by Israeli bombs by then," Ethan pointed out.

"Such is the price," Malik replied, "of living and working in a country oppressed by terrorism. We cannot delay our work over one missing foreigner who knew damned well that she shouldn't have been there."

"What about Gaza?" Ethan insisted. "I have friends there. If you can arrange visas, then we could travel into the Strip and ask around for—"

"That also will not be possible," Malik cut in with an insincere smile. "Gaza is too dangerous and it would not be politically prudent for us to request a search within the territory."

Ethan turned to look at Rok, who shook his head.

"We can't allow you access to the Gazan territories without risking further abductions or political repercussions from their leadership. I'm sorry we can't help you further."

Ethan felt a lance of anger pierce his guts.

"You're not helping, you're hindering. Lucy's been missing for over forty-eight hours and we're running out of time for political niceties. If you're right and her abductors are trying to affect the peace process, then Lucy only has twenty-four hours to live. Are you willing to act or not?"

The air in the room suddenly felt thick and heavy. Rok set his glass down and stood up, peering at Rachel over the bridge of his nose.

"We will continue to try to resolve this tragedy, but

I must ask that for security's sake you do not inform the media of your daughter's disappearance."

Rachel appealed quickly to Ambassador Cutler as Shiloh Rok turned and left the room.

"If anything is heard, you will let me know as soon as possible?"

"Of course," Cutler promised.

Ethan watched as two young men in smart suits with cropped hair and a military bearing appeared in the doorway and Spencer Malik gestured to them.

"Agents Cooper and Flint here will act as your escort. Obey them at all times. They are here to protect you."

With that, Malik turned and left the room.

"Brilliant work," Rachel snapped at Ethan.

"We're wasting our time," Ethan said, gesturing to where Rok had been sitting. "He was never going to help us."

"How the hell do you know?"

"Been here before."

"And you think that they're conspiring to ensure that I never find my daughter?"

Ambassador Cutler spoke quietly. "They're not conspiring. I suspect that they genuinely fear any further abductions from within their borders, or the media uncovering the story and upsetting the peace process with baseless conjecture or accusations."

Rachel turned to Ethan with a venomous look in her eyes. "So, what's your next genius move?"

Ethan ignored her sarcasm and thought for a moment.

"We talk to people who knew what Lucy was doing out in the desert, starting with Hans Karowitz. The Negev isn't entirely devoid of life and Spencer Malik said that Lucy's dig site was near Masada. If we're lucky, Karowitz may know something that Shiloh Rok doesn't."

Spencer Malik walked outside the embassy and lit a cigarette, watching as a stocky Arab man emerged from a car nearby and approached. The index finger of his left hand was missing, an injury Malik had once been told he'd suffered in the Balkans at the hands of Chechen rebels years before. Now he wore black leather gloves to conceal the disfigurement.

"I have work for you, Rafael," Malik said as he walked down the steps.

"Something else that you can't handle?" Rafael murmured in a soft voice touched with an Arabic lilt.

"Find out what you can about an Ethan Warner," Malik said, ignoring the jibe. "The name seems familiar to me. Get this guy's life history as soon as possible and let me know what you find."

"It shall be done," Rafael said, glancing at the building behind them. "But why would you be concerned with an American? Byron Stone will consider it a waste of resources and . . ."

Malik looked down at the Arab as they reached a large black SUV parked nearby, puffing his chest out as he spoke. "Byron Stone pays you to do what *I* damn well tell you to do. I just saw Ethan Warner insult the Foreign Ministry's representative. If he's willing to do that, then he's likely to cause more trouble. Get on it."

12

HEBREW UNIVERSITY OF JERUSALEM
GIVAT RAM CAMPUS

The Hebrew University of Jerusalem lay outside the Old City near the district of Rechavia, perched atop Mount Scopus. Ethan guided Rachel around the immense campus using a hastily scribbled set of directions, their MACE escort following, and after retracing his steps more than once finally located the Berman Building.

The Natural History Collections and Institute of Archaeology was enveloped in a hushed atmosphere as Ethan led Rachel through a maze of corridors, Cooper and Flint following in ominously silent formation until they reached a door bearing a plaque with the name *Doctor Hans Karowitz* etched into the surface. The door was half-open, the room apparently empty.

"He was Lucy's mentor, according to her e-mails," Rachel said, peering into the room.

Ethan knocked gently on the door, but there was no response. He walked inside, Rachel and their agents following behind.

The office was like a miniature lecture hall, complete with a lectern. Chairs were stacked neatly to one side beneath broad windows overlooking a sculptured garden. The room was silent, dust motes winking in the musty air as they floated between two rows of large display cases that dominated the rear of the office.

Ethan walked past the cases, each as tall as he was. Within each was the skeleton of a human or, more precisely, an ancient species of hominin. Ethan looked in fascination at each of them as he passed by, each specimen progressively taller and more recognizably human than its predecessor.

As he rounded the far end of the first row of cabinets, he found himself looking at the back of an old man who was staring into one of the second-row displays against the wall. From Ethan's perspective, the old man's reflection was ghoulishly superimposed over the ancient remains of a Neanderthal within the case.

"Dr. Karowitz?"

The old man seemed startled at the sound of Ethan's voice. Ethan extended a hand and introduced Rachel. At his realization of who Rachel was, Karowitz's eyes saddened.

"I am so sorry to hear of what has happened," he said.

"Do you know where my daughter is?" Rachel asked.

"No, but there is no shortage of likely candidates for her kidnapping, creationist groups being the most likely to—"

Before he could finish, Agent Cooper barged in. "That is an unsubstantiated comment with no basis in reality. Keep your opinions to yourself."

"Shut up and let him speak," Ethan snapped.

Cooper's jaw twisted around a shit-eating grin as he rested one hand on a Sig 9mm pistol at his waist.

"Accept my judgment or you'll be on the next plane back home, Warner, understood?"

Rachel looked at Karowitz. "Please, just tell us what you can."

Hans Karowitz sighed, glancing warily at the MACE agents as he spoke.

"Creationists believe that the universe was created in seven days," he said softly. "Yet the Torah, the Old Testament as recorded by the Hebrews, makes no such claim. It refers only to seven 'periods of time,' or *yom,* which meant aeon in ancient Hebrew. The error appeared as a result of translation between Hebrew, Greek, and Latin. Therefore, the supposed creationist age of the Earth as less than ten thousand years is baseless."

"What difference does it make?" Ethan asked.

Karowitz smiled faintly.

"Almost every major faith on our planet has a creation myth, in which their devotees believe without question regardless of evidence to the contrary. But it may be that such myths found their origin not in fantasy but in a sort of distorted historical record."

Ethan glanced at Rachel before replying.

"I thought that science would oppose such a concept. You think that religious myths have a genuine historical origin too?"

"Possibly," Karowitz qualified. "How much do you know about human evolution?"

Ethan, caught off balance, shrugged. "We evolved from apes, right?"

Karowitz spread his arms to encompass the room around them. "Look around, you're surrounded by examples of evolution. These are the fragments of a human story that began eight million years ago in Africa's Great Rift Valley and continues to this day."

"To this day?" Ethan asked. "I thought that we were the last of our kind, the best of our species?"

"Evolution does not have a goal, it's driven by unguided natural selection," Karowitz said. "It is constantly in motion and simply represents change over time. It is driven in biological species by random genetic mutations and environmental influences that govern how species adapt to their environments, and thus how efficiently they can reproduce and pass their characteristics on to their offspring."

"I never understood how one species can suddenly change into another," Rachel said.

The Belgian shook his head and whistled through his teeth.

"They don't. Creationist groups have long spread such rumors in an attempt to deceive uncritical minds into believing that humans are special, the product of a god. For decades they have deliberately spread disinformation, misquoted scientists and invented conspiracies, or claimed that evolution is only a theory, despite knowing that the word in science doesn't mean the same as in daily life. You don't hear them criticize Einstein's *theory* of general relativity, another well-proven foundation of science that underpins everything from space flight to nuclear power and GPS systems."

Karowitz gestured to the cases beside them, filled with ancient human skeletons.

"Part of the problem is that we're not familiar with geological and evolutionary timescales. Humans live for perhaps a century, but life has evolved over billions of years, and only those who have a religious motive continue to deny what stares them in the face."

"So you think that they're afraid that what Lucy found might cost them their influence, these creationist groups?" Ethan hazarded.

"Exactly," Karowitz said. "You said that we evolved from the apes, but that's another creationist myth. We evolved *alongside* the apes and continue to do so. Our evolutionary paths diverged from a common ancestor some eight million years ago, eventually diversifying into some twenty different homonin species. But by the last million years or so, there were only four species of man left walking the Earth: *Homo heidelbergensis*, from whom *Homo erectus* and *Homo neanderthalensis* evolved, and our direct ancestors, *Homo sapiens*, who dwelled in Africa. As a result of natural selection, only we, *Homo sapiens*, remain to this day."

"And our ancestors were what Lucy was originally looking for?" Ethan asked.

Karowitz nodded.

"Under my mentorship, Lucy made some incredible finds out in the southern Negev over a very short period of time. But she also began undertaking work for a private group, and somewhere out there she found something entirely different."

"Something that was not one of our ancestral species," Ethan said.

"No," Karowitz said, "what Lucy found was—"

"Unknown," Cooper interrupted sharply again.

"We have e-mails from Lucy," Rachel said to Cooper, "detailing the remains and their appearance and—"

"And I get e-mails every day telling me I've won the Nigerian lottery," Cooper rumbled. "But I haven't started showering in frigging champagne."

Ethan ignored Cooper, barging in front of him to speak to Karowitz. "What makes you so sure the remains were not human?"

"The physiology Lucy described was remarkably different," Karowitz said. "The specimen's bone structure was far more robust than a human and the chest plate was fused, therefore its lungs would have differed from ours. Its bones were latticed, something known to have been common in some dinosaurs to save weight, and it also bore an extended cranial cavity that may have served a communicative purpose by infrasound, again a known adaption in some species on Earth."

Ethan nodded. "And you think that this species might have been responsible for interfering with human evolution?"

"Not our evolution," Karowitz cautioned, "but our developmental history." He looked at Rachel and began quoting. "'And Azadel brought the men knowledge, and taught them of the metals and the fields and the things of the earth, and made them strong . . .'"

Rachel's eyes glazed over as she instinctively took up the recital.

"'. . . and God struck down the angel Azadel, and buried him amongst the earth, and covered him with sharp rocks and covered his eyes with earth so that they may not see.'" She looked at Karowitz. "The Book of Enoch."

"Among many other books," Karowitz said, pacing up and down as he spoke. "The supposed contacts between ancient man and their various gods share remarkable details that some people believe may record the presence of beings on this Earth of technological superiority so great that they would have appeared to early man to literally be gods."

"Arthur C. Clarke said as much in one of his books," Rachel said. "His *Third Law* states that any sufficiently advanced technology would be indistinguishable from magic."

Ethan frowned thoughtfully.

"But if life in the Levant at the time was good, why would man have needed help?"

"Man was surviving, but only just," Karowitz said. "The warming after the Last Glacial Maximum was interrupted by an event called the Younger Dryas, an extreme thousand-year chill that caused the Holocene Extinction Event, when all of the megafauna like mammoths became extinct. Mankind also almost died out, and those few who survived would have been greatly separated in small groups with poor genetic diversity."

"What caused the event?" Ethan asked.

"Nobody's sure," Karowitz replied, "but a charred sediment layer at many sites that includes nanodiamonds, iridium, charcoal, and magnetic spherules is consistent with a major cometary strike at that time. The airburst explosion of a carbonaceous chondrite comet could have caused the major extinction around twelve thousand years ago."

"Okay, so we survived, but things went down the can," Ethan said.

"To put it mildly. The point is that it's after this catastrophe, when human numbers and resources were severely depleted, that human civilization is born when it probably should have collapsed. We came out of the so-called Clovis culture of making flaked stone tools and entered the Copper Age. Suddenly, we're forming civilizations and technology. The earliest true civilizations known to history appeared around seven thousand years ago in Mesopotamia shortly after the Younger Dryas."

"So you think that any intervention occurred between those two dates," Rachel said.

"Perhaps because of the near extinction of mankind," Karowitz said. "If we were indeed being watched by advanced species of unknown origin, then our near extinction may have prompted assistance. To impart the knowledge to achieve this leap would have required only the most basic of assistance in developing script, language, and novel construction methods."

Ethan frowned again.

"This doesn't help us figure out who exactly abducted Lucy."

"But it could," Karowitz said. "Lucy may have been abducted by people for whom faith is more important than truth. Such people are willing to pay mercenaries to locate such remains."

Ethan tossed the idea around in his head, and somehow it seemed less desperate than radical jihadists abducting obscure scientists in a futile effort to change Western foreign policy. He glanced curiously at the remains in the cabinets around them.

"Mercenaries? Like fossil hunters? How much money would Lucy's discovery be worth?"

"If Lucy's discovery was the complete skeleton of an unidentified extraterrestrial species, then the value of the find would be astronomical."

Cooper opened his mouth to speak, but Rachel ignored him and looked at Ethan.

"You think that somebody abducted her in order to steal the remains that she found?"

"It's possible," Karowitz answered for Ethan. "Fossils of prehistoric creatures often sell for hundreds of thousands of dollars, and creationist organizations have access to vast amounts of money."

"If insurgents haven't abducted Lucy, then Israel's fear of media coverage is unfounded," Ethan said. "We could use that to get the word out."

"Israel's media ban stays in place," agent Flint said from beside them, speaking for the first time.

Ethan turned to face the two escorts.

"Anyone would think that you wanted her to stay kidnapped."

"Our purpose," Cooper said, smiling, "is to willingly put ourselves in harm's way to protect both of you."

"Please, you're making me feel all warm and fluffy inside," Ethan muttered.

Cooper didn't respond.

"If it's true," Rachel said to Karowitz, "then Lucy could be anywhere by now."

Ethan shook his head. "Not likely, they'd have to cross the Sinai into Egypt and they'd face the same problems there as here." He turned to Karowitz. "Where was Lucy's dig site?"

Karowitz balked as Cooper and Flint shook their heads at him in unison. "I don't know."

"Did the university send anyone to search for Lucy before raising the alarm?" Ethan asked instead.

"Yes, a local guide named Ahmed Khan, but I haven't seen him since."

Ethan made a mental note of the name and then came to a decision. He turned to Cooper.

"I need to use the can. You want to come hold my hand?"

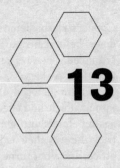

13

Ethan walked down a corridor with Cooper following silently, turning as soon as he found the toilet door and going inside. The white-tiled interior was mercifully devoid of students as he strolled to a cubicle and unzipped, glancing over at Cooper.

"Want to hold it for me, or is that below your pay grade?"

Cooper stood with his hands clasped before him at the entrance to the cubicle, saying nothing. Ethan shrugged, finishing his business and washing his hands before turning and following Cooper toward the exit. As expected, Cooper held the door open for Ethan to pass through.

"Too kind."

Ethan stepped through the open doorway onto his left foot, and then pivoted sideways and slammed backward into the half-open door, ramming Cooper against the tiled wall and pinning his arm against his chest. Ethan turned and jabbed the locked knuckles of his left hand up under Cooper's thorax. The guard's eyes bulged, swimming with panic as his throat momentarily collapsed under the blow and blocked his windpipe. Ethan yanked the door open, driving his left knee into

Cooper's plexus before hammering the point of an elbow down behind his ear as Cooper doubled over. Cooper crumpled sideways onto the tiles, his eyes rolling up into their sockets.

Ethan dragged the unconscious guard backward into a cubicle and checked that he was breathing clearly again before shutting the door behind him and hurrying back the way they had come. He walked into Karowitz's office, and Flint turned to look at him.

Ethan wasted no time. Even as Flint's jaw opened to ask where his colleague was, Ethan strode forward a pace and shot a fast left jab. Flint was quick, but not quite quick enough for the unexpected blow that caught him just above his left eye. As Flint's head flicked backward and sideways, Ethan swung a roundhouse right that smashed across his temple with a loud crack. Flint's legs quivered as he toppled across a desk and slumped onto the carpeted floor.

Rachel's eyes flew wide. "What the hell do you think you're doing?"

Ethan turned to Karowitz.

"Which one of the fossil hunters you mentioned is most likely to have known where Lucy was?"

Karowitz stared in shock at the fallen guard.

"Bill Griffiths," he stammered weakly. "He's staying in Beit Hakarem, not far from here. Hassim Khan in Gaza might know too, but I haven't heard from him in a week."

Ethan approached Karowitz and clicked his fingers in the Belgian's face to focus his attention.

"I need you to tell me the truth: what's the chance that what Lucy found was just some kind of deformed human skeleton?"

"Zero," Karowitz said confidently. "Lucy would have

easily identified any kind of forgery or deformation of natural remains."

Ethan turned, grabbed Rachel's hand, and yanked her out of the lecture hall.

"You're insane," she snapped, struggling against his grip.

"If you want to find Lucy, we need to lose these MACE goons," Ethan said, releasing her. "You can either stay here with them or come with me. Your call, but I'm leaving now."

Ethan set off without her, suppressing a smile as he heard her run in pursuit.

"I just know I'm going to regret this," Rachel muttered as they hurried out of the university compound.

14

THE REFLECTING POOL
NATIONAL MALL, WASHINGTON DC

Thank you for seeing me at such short notice, Byron."

A humid, overcast sky was reflected upon the glassy surface of the Potomac River in the same tones as the steel-gray-haired man with whom Kelvin Patterson shook hands. Byron Stone was a sepulchral, gaunt figure with frosty turquoise eyes who towered over the diminutive pastor.

The two men sat down on a bench overlooking the river.

"How is the boy?" Stone asked in a broad Texan accent.

"He is safe. For obvious reasons I could not bring him with me today."

The Texan nodded slowly, though Patterson could not tell whether it was a sign of regret or relief.

"He's safer at the institute," Stone replied before casting a serious gaze at the pastor, "and reliant upon your care, Kelvin."

"I never wanted him there. He is your responsibility."

"Some responsibilities are best shared. Agreed?"

Byron Stone was the son of the legendary Bradley Stone, a Texan oil prospector turned munitions salesman who had built himself a small empire from the profits of conflict. Munitions for Advanced Combat Environments, or MACE, had grown from a minor arms developer in the 1950s to a major defense contractor by the 1990s. Bradley Stone—a whiskey-drinking, cigar-smoking womanizer—had run himself into an early grave just two years after his long-suffering wife had expired into hers. Thus, Byron had inherited the business and reached out into the burgeoning private security industry, providing former military soldiers as security advisors for companies across America and Europe. The fact that MACE had been investigated on numerous occasions for alleged atrocities in both Iraq and Afghanistan had not stalled the company's growth, but costly investments in developing a series of remotely operated aircraft called Valkyrie that had failed to achieve production orders were crushing MACE beneath unbearable financial burdens. Once a giant, MACE was now struggling, a fact not lost on Patterson when he had acquired the controlling share of the company. He had known Byron for almost twenty years and had ministered to Bradley Stone for a decade before that, for what little good it had done. Now he guided MACE policy.

The pastor looked out across the river as he spoke. "The situation in the Senate has not proceeded quite as we expected it to."

"That is your responsibility," Stone drawled.

"Only for now," Patterson reminded him. "The current administration's search for a peaceful resolution to the Middle East problem continues to hinder both of our causes."

Stone shook his head slowly.

"Our causes, or yours? Your power comes from the tithes of your faithful flock, not from the puppets you orchestrate in the Senate."

"Senator Black's success is key to our own, and Israel's future may depend upon his ascension."

"Israel and Palestine are committed to each other's destruction. That's been the way of things for the last fifty years and it ain't gonna change overnight."

Patterson frowned.

"This is a conflict between what is right and wrong. A divided Jerusalem is a divided nation of God."

"Everything this administration has done is a disgrace," Stone agreed. "The emasculation of America by limp-dicked liberal hippies."

Patterson managed to ignore the profanity, speaking softly.

"Israel must ensure its survival in the Holy Lands."

"Israel can take care of itself. If the Arabs want to blow themselves to hell, then let 'em. We're just providing the hardware."

"And if the conflict should end?"

Byron Stone ignored the pastor for a moment, pausing to light a thick cigar that spiraled hot smoke into the already humid air around them. He dribbled a thick stream of aromatic fumes from between his lips to hang over the listless water.

"As long as Senator Black supports the export of arms and promotes a policy of zero tolerance toward terrorist-supported governments, we both win."

"How can I be sure that you will honor your part of the bargain?" Patterson asked. "I don't want your people dropping rocks if they get too hot."

Stone's eyelid twitched. "You sayin' I don't got the balls for this?"

"I'm asking if you have the *will*."

The Texan's features creased into a thin smile as he examined the glowing tip of his cigar.

"I would say that we have mutually assured destruction, wouldn't you?"

Patterson nodded. "And the experiments?"

Byron Stone worked his jaw silently for a moment before speaking.

"Rapid hypothermic surgical response to battlefield trauma is a useful addition to MACE's armory, but it's not essential and your goddamn experiments sure as hell aren't. I'm not willing to risk a federal investigation here in DC."

"Security for the experiments was part of the bargain when I bailed MACE out," Patterson reminded him. "Thirty million Americans follow my church. Think how many will follow it if these endeavors succeed."

"I think you put far too much faith in the power of your flock," Stone murmured, "and not enough thought into how you're using it."

"You have the photographs?" Patterson demanded, and grabbed the envelope Stone handed him with greedy hands, flicking through the images. "My God, look at it," he marveled. "Look at the chest plate, built to support wings, and the cranial cavity, a brain far larger than our own. A Nephilim, a fallen angel of God."

Stone drew on his cigar. "Whatever."

"Science supports it," Patterson said with quiet confidence. "We have already extracted the mitochondrial DNA from the other fragments we've acquired, and the full genome is not far behind. This will change the face of humanity forever."

"Strange," Stone murmured, "how your church denies science with one breath and yet embraces it with the next."

Patterson struggled to cope with Stone's ignorance. That any man could display such indifference to the divine staggered him.

"We're searching for creation, searching for the face of God. What greater purpose can there be than finding the cause of everything in our universe and communicating with it? How can we sit on the precipice of discovery and not act when we have the chance to prove the divinity of the Lord?"

A long silence ensued as the Texan inhaled deeply upon his cigar, expelling blue smoke in diaphanous whorls.

"Do you have faith, Pastor?" Stone asked finally, as he stared out over the Potomac.

"I have absolute faith," Patterson replied instantly. "God is always with me."

Stone smiled without warmth. "If that were truly so, you wouldn't need these experiments of yours, would you?"

Patterson kept his gaze fixed on Stone. "I seek only confirmation," he insisted, "for the sake of all manki—"

"You seek proof because you're not sure," the Texan interrupted. "People who claim absolute conviction without evidence are setting themselves up for a fall. Don't wish too hard," he said with a cold smile, "you don't know what you might find."

"Our influence is waning," Patterson lamented. "Americans do not worship with the passion of previous generations. There have been too many scandals, too much corruption, too many empty promises. The people are turning to personal faith and this is the only way to save them from the abyss, to prove that what we believe is true by cloning these remains and resurrecting an angel on Earth, a Nephilim."

"I'm in this for the money," Stone said as he stood, "not for heavenly glory or your supposed salvation."

"A pity," Patterson said, "that you place money above faith. It would be a shame to see MACE assets sold off to avoid bankruptcy."

Stone glared at Patterson for a long beat before flicking the smoldering butt of his cigar into the Potomac.

"MACE will continue to protect your grotty little experiments—for now—but if you push this too far, you'll end up exposing us all, and then you can go to hell for your protection."

Byron Stone turned his back and strode away down the path beside the river.

15

JERUSALEM

The golden dome of the Al-Aqsa Mosque shone like a second sun against the hard blue sky in the distance as Ethan hurried Rachel through the Old City. While Rachel was distracted by the sights and sounds around them, Ethan instead struggled to conceal conflicting emotions that rushed upon him in waves. Long forgotten images of these packed streets and the throng of life in a city where the three great monotheistic faiths met in a potpourri of holy worship and primal hate flushed through his mind.

Orthodox Jews in black coats and fox-fur hats weaved their way toward the Western Wall past Palestinian street hawkers touting their wares. Tiny shops wedged into recesses in alleys sold Jewish menorahs, olive-wood crucifixes, and ornamental plates depicting the Al-Aqsa Mosque. The air was filled with the hushed murmur of Hebrew and the musical ripple of Arabic echoing down endless alleys. Amid the human traffic darted dozens of cats, and the meat market scented the air with the odor of a bewildering array of foods. Incense wafted from churches and the potent aroma of roasting Arabic coffee drifted through the narrow walkways, competing with the pungent reek of rotting vegetables and all of it filling Ethan with a regret-stained nostalgia.

Forget it, Ethan. There was nothing here but misery then and there's nothing new here now. This is a city of suffering and always has been.

Ethan's perception started to change. Groups of different faiths walked together for safety under the watchful eyes of Israeli soldiers cradling assault rifles. Children skittered on bare feet through the alleys, their faces smudged with grime. Ethan heard the sounds of the city haunting his past; the warbling Muslim call to prayer drifting from minarets at dusk across the ancient rooftops, the bells of the Holy Sepulchre Church, and the mournful horn announcing the start of the Sabbath.

As he turned a corner, he looked up past the bobbing swathes of turbans and Hasidic Kipots and saw a brief flare of blond hair. Ethan froze, his eyes locked onto the shining hair as an image of Joanna blazed brightly in his mind. He changed direction, lurching through the crowd toward the woman drifting past stalls near an ancient stone wall.

"Ethan?" Rachel grabbed his arm, hauling him to a stop. "Where are we going?"

Ethan blinked, turning to look to where the woman was still standing beside the stall, her face turned toward him now, deeply tanned, middle-aged. A tourist, maybe a local or one of the countless European Jews who had returned to Israel after the diaspora.

Ethan shook himself and pointed down one of the myriad alleys toward a small square that buzzed gently with the conversation of tourists sitting outside cafés in the bright sunshine. A group of Israeli-Arabs smoked aromatic hookahs and bartered gifts from makeshift stalls, all under the watchful eye of heavily armed Israeli troops manning a checkpoint nearby.

Ethan negotiated his way between the tables outside one of the restaurants, moving toward a stocky man sitting with a newspaper and wearing a broad-rimmed hat. A glass half filled with ruby-colored drink glistened before him on the table.

"William Griffiths?"

Ethan stood in front of the man, who made a show of finishing reading his sentence before squinting up at him from beneath the shelter of his hat.

"You are?"

"Ethan Warner, and this is Rachel Morgan."

Bill Griffiths folded the newspaper he was holding and set it down on the table before lazily gesturing for them to join him. Ethan ordered drinks from a passing waitress, and regarded the man opposite him.

Griffiths looked every inch the outdoorsman, with a broad and thickly forested jaw, his shirt undone at the neck and the sleeves rolled up his chunky arms. His weather-beaten skin told of countless years spent toiling beneath the burning sun, as did what appeared to be a permanent squint. Dirt was encrusted under his fingernails, and his heavily creased shorts bore patches of recent dust and sand.

"What can I do for you, Mr. Warner?" he asked without apparent interest.

"I understand that you have something for sale?"

Griffiths squinted at Ethan behind the rim of his hat. "For sale?"

Ethan got down to business.

"I thought that it might be worthwhile me coming to you directly, rather than wandering around fossil markets looking for trinkets."

Griffiths regarded Ethan and Rachel for several long moments, as though trying to size them up.

"I don't deal. I work privately, and right now I'm on vacation."

Ethan nodded as he glanced around at the square.

"Nice spot. You always take vacations in war zones? I thought you'd be better off down in Eilat."

Griffiths let his gaze return to his newspaper.

"I like the architecture here. What do you want?"

"I want you to be honest with me," Ethan replied. "You're not on holiday, you've been working. You've got dirt under your nails, which suggests to me that you've only recently finished an excavation, probably worked through the night to complete it." Griffiths looked back up as Ethan went on. "I represent a collector, and I think that you've happened upon a specimen that he may be interested in."

Griffiths shook his head. "As I said, I work privately."

"Whatever you've been offered, he'll beat."

"I doubt that."

"So you *have* found something then."

Griffiths sighed as though tired of the game already. "Who are you representing?"

"That's not important," Ethan replied smoothly. "What is important is that they are willing to pay handsomely for the specimen."

Griffiths shook his head again.

"You know nothing of what we've found, you don't know where it is and you have no idea of its value, yet you're sitting here trying to cut a deal with me over it."

Ethan leaned back in his chair, taking a sip of his drink. "Alien fossils are hard to come by."

Griffiths's squint vanished completely and hard gray eyes bored into Ethan's.

"How did you—"

"We have people," Ethan cut across him, forestalling his question.

"Who's *we*?" Griffiths asked, glancing at Rachel.

Ethan gestured around the square.

"We'd like to see the remains before making a bid. If they live up to expectation, then I'm sure that you'll find our offer to be *extremely* generous."

Griffiths stared at Ethan for a long moment, apparently unable to weigh up whether he was being played or had just walked into the deal of a lifetime. Ethan pushed harder. "Come on, you know that you're sitting on a fortune. Why reserve it for one client when an auction would be far more lucrative. It's not like we're in Montana: you're not going to be arrested for theft as long as nobody knows about what you've found."

"My client is reliable and I am not greedy," Griffiths said.

"I'm sure," Ethan agreed, "but money is money and these remains are going to be in high demand if you open them up to the market."

"You want me to make you bid against others for it?" Griffiths muttered. "Why would you do that instead of pushing for a bargain here and now?"

"Because we would win. Price is not an object, Mr. Griffiths. It is the quality of the specimen that counts."

Griffiths's eyes narrowed.

"And if the remains are of sufficient quality and I was willing to sell?"

Ethan took a breath.

"Five million dollars, delivered in bonds or wire transfer. Anything you want."

Griffiths promptly got up from his seat.

"Not even close, Mr. Warner. My client has already paid a deposit greater than that."

Damn. "A deposit? So he has seen the remains, in person?"

"Not yet," Griffiths replied, shoving his newspaper under his arm. "But images were sent."

"May I see them? It will affect our offer."

"Client confidentiality," Griffiths muttered as he turned away. "And your offer was shit."

Ethan stood as Griffiths walked away, ignoring Rachel's dismayed expression.

"You're not a trained paleontologist," he said. The fossil hunter kept walking. "Which makes me wonder, how did you know where to look to find such a magnificent specimen? It's almost as if someone else had to find it for you."

Griffiths slowed, standing for a moment with his back to Ethan before turning and looking at him. "What do you mean?"

Ethan was no longer smiling, and spoke loudly enough for people at other tables to hear him. "Doesn't it make you wonder, who it was who found the remains and what happened to them?"

Griffiths looked about anxiously and then paced back toward the table, muttering under his breath.

"They were found by a security company conducting trials in the Negev using explosives. They turned something up and called us in to examine the remains."

"Wonder why they didn't call scientists instead, or the police?" Ethan mused out loud. "How would ordinary soldiers have known that they were looking at ancient bones that had such value? It could have been a murder scene for all they knew."

Griffiths's features creased with irritation. "I have no idea and it's none of your business. Stay out of it."

The dealer turned away, but Ethan carried on talking loudly.

"Pretty convenient too, those explosives perfectly excavating the remains without damaging them." Griffiths kept on walking, but Ethan managed to get one last sentence in before he was out of earshot. "Although if somebody else, a scientist, say, had found and excavated the specimen, I'd be wondering what on earth happened to them. Worried, even."

Rachel watched the fossil hunter vanish beyond the milling tourists, and turned to Ethan.

"Brilliant work so far, I don't know what I'd have done without you."

"He knows something," Ethan said.

"And he's told us nothing."

"Didn't need him to," Ethan said. "Just needed to plant a seed of doubt in his mind for now is all."

"So now what?"

Ethan finished his drink and stood up.

"Now we go and find Lucy's dig site."

16

FIRST DISTRICT STATION
M STREET SW, WASHINGTON DC

Lopez leaned back in her chair as she watched Tyrell heft his way laboriously toward her between ranks of desks and computer terminals.

The station covered everything from New York Avenue in the north of First District right down to Buzzard Point and the old navy yard on the Anacostia River, which meant that Lopez got to see America in all its guises. From the immaculate White House down to the decrepit projects of East Side along the border with Maryland, America's heart bared its soul. One hundred eighteen fatal homicides this year. Better than the last.

Tyrell's phone began ringing before he'd even had the chance to sit down. She watched him pick it up wearily.

"Tyrell." He paused, frowned, and sighed. "Be right there."

Lopez looked at him as he set the phone down. "Problem?"

"We've been summoned," he intoned deeply.

Lopez got up and followed him down a long corridor lined with partitioned offices. The Hall of the High and Mighty housed the district commander's office. They turned at a door marked *Powell,* Tyrell knocking briefly before striding in.

"You beckoned?" he asked as Lopez closed the door behind them.

Captain Louis Grant Powell was a robustly built African American with a thick mustache that seemed to be trying to make up for his receding hairline. Lopez had often wondered why Powell, a long-service officer who had somehow never made it past the rank and file to the true upper echelons of the MPD, had never been promoted, despite bearing a name that made him sound like a confederate general.

"Sit down, Detectives."

"Too kind."

If Powell was ever amused by Tyrell's laconic humor, Lopez never noticed it. It was a wonder he knew whom he was actually talking to, given that he had yet to look up from the file he was scrutinizing. The word in the locker room was that Powell was up for retirement and had invested in new real estate, down Tampa way. Lopez waited in silence with Tyrell, and was rewarded with a question as Powell looked up at her.

"The bust over on Potomac Gardens, what's the score?"

"Alleged crack overdose, three victims locked themselves inside an abandoned property just off the projects."

Powell closed his file and looked up at them both.

"Victims, alleged," he echoed thoughtfully. "You sent the bodies down to the medical examiner's office."

Tyrell answered, saving Lopez from incriminating herself.

"I didn't consider it likely that the victims were crack

addicts." Powell folded his hands under his chin expectantly, his jowls bulging as Tyrell went on. "I wanted the pathology before we wrote this one off."

Captain Powell nodded briefly.

"Axel Cain at the Bureau, the MPD on site, and even the DEA consider it to be a closed case. They've acknowledged the discrepancies but see little point in referring it to the district attorney. I agree with them."

"With all due respect, sir," Lopez said carefully, "this isn't a drug-related crime. Dr. Fry has confirmed that they didn't die from crack."

Powell smiled thinly at her, and looked at Tyrell.

"From what I've read, Surgeon Fry has been unable to determine the exact time of death, let alone the exact cause. Tyrell, this one's dead in the water and I haven't got the manpower or the time to allow either yourself or Lopez to run around the District on another wild-goose chase. The border with Maryland and Prince George's has enough crack 'n' meth addicts for the entire country. I'd lay down serious bucks that there's another dozen stiffs out there waiting to be stumbled upon. This isn't a priority case."

Lopez watched as Tyrell sucked in his cheeks.

"Last time I looked, death under suspicious circumstances warranted our attention."

"Not above greater needs," Powell cautioned. "This country is still under a level-three terrorist alert, and I need officers and men to maintain a vigil against God knows who planning God knows what. This can be left to beat cops. If something comes up that they can't handle, then I'll send it back your way."

Tyrell's face twisted into the kind of smile that looked to Lopez as though he were trying to bend an iron bar with his lips.

"Local PD will take one look at those bodies and be glad to have swept them off the streets. I doubt a coroner would even glance at the paperwork before signing it off."

"He probably didn't," Powell agreed.

"What?" Lopez and Tyrell asked in perfect unison.

"Recorded a verdict of misadventure."

"We've got a crime scene here and we're going to shut the door on it?"

"The door, Tyrell, is already shut," Powell insisted.

"What if this is just a small piece of a bigger picture?" Tyrell pushed. "Those people were moved there after they died. If you give me just—"

"Just what?" Powell asked. "A few hours, a few days, a few careers? We haven't got the resources for this right now. People die, Tyrell, sometimes for no other reason than their own damned stupidity. Let it go."

Lopez watched as Tyrell took a deep breath, and closed his eyes. Powell tossed the file into his out box with a flourish as Tyrell hauled himself out of the chair in disgust, walking across to the door and opening it. Lopez got up to follow him. The open corridor beckoned, but she could see that Tyrell couldn't help himself as he turned back to look over his shoulder at the captain.

"You remember 2000? Y'know, Y2K and all that?"

"My parents' golden anniversary," Powell replied without looking up.

"An FBI agent reported high numbers of people attempting to acquire pilot's licenses in local schools down in Florida. He reported back to the Barn in DC several times, documenting what they were doing and rating the activities as highly suspicious and worthy of extensive resources. He got turned down."

"Your point?" Powell muttered, finally looking at Tyrell.

"The people he was watching hijacked four American airliners a year later, and killed over three thousand American citizens."

Powell winced. "Tyrell, your three dead bodies aren't going to become a national incident no matter how much you might want them to be."

Tyrell shook his head. "I'm sure that's what they said back in 2000."

Before Powell could retort, Tyrell lumbered out of the office. Lopez made to follow him.

"One moment, Detective," Powell rumbled.

Tyrell glanced back at her, a glimmer of suspicion crossing his features, and then she closed the office door and sat back down opposite Powell.

"He's onto something," she insisted.

"Jesus, not you as well?"

"What's your problem with Tyrell? Why reject everything he says?"

"Because most of it's bullshit," Powell said sharply, and then visibly reined himself in. "You haven't worked with him all that long. Tyrell's desperate for the big bust and he's been looking for it for years."

"C'mon, he's just willing to look a little further than most all cops working homicide."

"He looks too goddamn far into everything," Powell shot back. "He's been up in front of a committee three times in the past four years for misappropriation of resources, chasing everything from Russian spy networks, JFK conspiracies, and the friggin' Illuminati. For all I know, he thinks the *Apollo* landings were faked. Commissioner Devereux's nearly suspended him twice."

Lopez's train of thought changed track. "You sayin' he's on an agenda or something?"

Powell ran a hand over his face as though rubbing the fatigue from his body.

"You ever been to the Big Apple?"

"Not yet."

"You ever do, make sure you visit Ground Zero and the memorial there."

Lopez's skin felt suddenly cold in the breeze from Powell's desk fan.

"The attacks?" she asked, and was rewarded with a quiet nod.

"Tyrell lost his wife and both of his daughters in the attacks and his brother to drugs two years later," Powell said. "He's been on the warpath ever since, no matter how carefully he thinks he disguises it."

"How'd they get caught up in it?" she asked, as gently as possible.

"Amelie Tyrell had family out in Boston," Powell explained. "She'd traveled to visit them while Tyrell was working in Maryland. She took their daughters with her, Ellen and Macy. Tyrell knew nothing of what had happened until he returned home; it was only supposed to be an overnight stay. They died on the return flight home."

"He doesn't talk about it," Lopez admitted, feeling strangely disappointed that Tyrell hadn't confided in her, and then guilty for having thought that he should.

"The investigations and commissions all found failings in the intelligence community to prevent the attacks, and that's what put a rocket up Tyrell's ass," Powell said. "He knows that the towers were dropped by suicidal lunatics from another country, but now he can't help but see neglect and conspiracies wherever he goes."

Lopez rubbed her temples. "Why you tellin' me this?"

"Keep an eye on him, okay? He's a good detective, but he needs a balance."

"I'm not his mother. If he decides to go after something, he's not going to turn around and ask for my permission."

"No, but he asks for your advice," Powell countered. "Make sure you give it to him, but if he goes off the range, then you make damned sure you come back here and tell me."

"You're asking me to spy on him," Lopez said. "He's my partner."

"I can't afford to lose either of you right now, especially not on another one of Tyrell's goddamn conspiracies. That clear?"

Lopez stood from the desk and turned to leave.

"That clear?" Powell repeated.

Lopez hesitated at the door and sighed. "Clear."

17

WADI AL-JOZ
WEST BANK, OCCUPIED PALESTINE

The darkness changed shape.

From a deep and featureless blackness came distant textures, touching her skin and caressing her hair. Slowly, the fragments of her awareness began reassembling themselves one by one as they tumbled from the abyss.

She opened her eyes, but could see nothing. Her limbs and back ached and she tried to move, but she was bound firm. Her throat was parched, and for one terrible moment the belief that she had been buried alive injected panic into her synapses. She fought to free herself, and a gasp erupted from between her cracked lips as she squirmed.

A noise came from the darkness somewhere to her right, and she fell silent and still. She turned her head, the stiffened muscles in her neck protesting at the movement. Beside her a thin muslin sheet hung from a tall rail, like a hospital shroud. She could see that she was lying on a bed, her limbs tied down with canvas straps as though she were an incarcerated psychotic patient.

She looked down at her body and saw an intravenous line in her right arm, and from the dull ache she guessed that it had been there for some time. Where was she? What was happening to her?

Another noise, like two pieces of metal being tapped together, then a voice whispering softly in the darkness.

Through the muslin she could see a ghostly light. The orb was intermittently broken as a shadow passed back and forth before it, and she could hear the sound of soft footfalls and a rhythmic beeping.

Through her confusion and fear, the tiniest flame of hope flickered into life. This could be a hospital. But the darkness and the stale smell in her nostrils seemed out of place, even if this were Gaza or the West Bank. Where were the nurses? Could it be nighttime, hence the darkness? Gaza suffered regular blackouts due to the Israeli blockade. But then, why was she in Gaza?

Fragments of memory spiraled like falling stars through the field of her awareness, briefly illuminating the spaces in her mind before passing on into the darkness. The dig site. She remembered the magnificent specimen, her efforts to retrieve it before . . . before . . .

A flare of recall jolted her. The men who had burst into the site. Balaclavas, black clothes, rough and heavy hands. She recalled running, being tackled from behind, pulling a bowie knife from her shorts and plunging it into the leg of one of the intruders before she was overpowered. Then something being placed over her face, and then blackness. *Christ, what have I got myself into?*

"Pulse is steady."

The voice sounded close, scaring her. Her breathing rasped and she could feel her heart trying to thump its way out of her chest.

"Temperature is rising, seventy-five degrees Fahrenheit."

A figure moved past beside her, the muslin sheet rippling in the draft and parting slightly. Perhaps fifteen feet away was a metal gurney, upon which lay the naked form of a man.

Tubes protruded from his body and she could see his chest rising and falling in slow rhythm, but she could not quite make out his features. An intravenous line rose up to a saline bag suspended above his head, and a series of monitors were arranged behind him recording heartbeat and body temperature. Beside him stood a video recorder on a tripod, aimed at the gurney.

"Seventy-seven degrees."

As she watched, she could see another intravenous line coiling out from the man's left arm, an almost black fluid passing through it. The rhythmic beeping from the machines was slowly increasing in tempo and the body was showing vague signs of movement, crooked fingers twitching sporadically.

"Seventy-nine degrees."

She squinted as she tried to see what was on the monitors, but they were too far away. The figure obscured the screens, leaning over the body to examine it closely.

"Will this one survive?" the voice murmured rhetorically, as though speaking to itself.

A chill rippled down her spine.

"Let us pray that he does. Eighty degrees."

She turned her head and began twisting her wrists back and forth, seeking a weakness in her bonds. The straps were tight, but her wrists were narrow and her hands small. If she could just fold her hand slightly and tuck her thumb in, she might be able to squeeze it through the straps.

She tried first with her right hand, but the pain from the intravenous line in her arm scared her, so she tried with the other. She forced her thumb inward, twisting and pulling against the strap. The thick canvas scraped against her skin, but she felt the edge slipping. Encouraged, she pulled harder, rolling her wrist into a better position before pulling again. The strap slipped farther over her hand, crushing it. She gritted her teeth together, dominating the pain and taking a deep breath before pulling hard.

The strap slipped across her hand and then it jerked free. She clenched her hand a few times before reaching across and loosening the strap on her right wrist.

"Eighty-one degrees."

She sat up in the bed, looking down at the intravenous line in her arm. She reached down to begin easing it free when a strange, unearthly sound caught her attention. It was a distant, feeble whimper, as though someone were crying out for help from deep underwater.

"He's coming round."

She leaned toward the gap in the muslin sheet, watching as the figure, wearing a white doctor's coat, stood back from the body on the table. The body quivered, a shuddering that seemed as though the patient were suffering some kind of seizure.

"Pulse is good," the voice said again. "Hypothermically viable."

The body shivered again as though live current were bolting through the muscles. Another murmur came from deep within the chest cavity, infected with something that sent little insects of fear scuttling beneath her skin, the tones of an endless suffering freed at last.

The body jerked wildly and the man's mouth opened as from within came a ghoulish cry of anguish, of a terror primal, pure, and undiluted that soared from its prison somewhere deep within him to fill the room.

The body flailed wildly, the man sobbing and screaming as he thrashed about on the table.

She saw the doctor reach across to a nearby table and grab a syringe, while struggling to hold the flailing patient's arm and get the needle into a vein, but the man was fighting with insane strength, screaming all the while.

"Can you hear me?"

The doctor's voice interrupted the screams, and in the half-light she saw the crazed patient staring wide-eyed at him, blubbering incoherently, his face stained with tears and his eyes filled with something incomprehensible that caused her bowels to lurch in sympathy. A gabbling torrent of unintelligible noise fell from the man's mouth amid a stream of bile and spittle. His eyes wobbled in their sockets, limbs jerking frantically in the doctor's grip.

"Can you hear me?" the doctor repeated.

The man began frothing at the mouth, choking on his own fluids as his head began slamming violently against the table with deafeningly loud cracks that reverberated around the room.

The surgeon stood up with the syringe in his hand, pinning one of the patient's arms down on the table and jabbing the needle deep into the flesh. The patient continued to flail, and to her horror she saw him suddenly snapping his mouth open and shut. His teeth smashed together with loud cracks, a thick torrent of dark blood spilling across his lips as he crunched through his own tongue. In a moment of sheer terror she recognized the guide who had arrived at her camp, the Bedouin. Ahmed Khan.

Slowly, the sedative began to take effect, and the man's insane thrashings rippled away until he sank back onto the table, his ruined tongue dangling by threads from his mouth and strings of blood drooling away toward the floor. The doctor released the body, the limbs dangling from the table at awkward angles.

"How disappointing," he said into a voice recorder. "I shall dispose of him."

A wave of panic flushed across her body and she reached down, grabbing the restraints around her ankles and yanking them free. As they parted the metal braces clattered loudly against the side of the bed. She sensed the doctor turn toward her and panicked further, yanking furiously at the other restraint.

It was almost free when the muslin sheet was whipped aside and the doctor lunged at her.

"No!"

She struck out, her left fist smacking into his temple, but her weakened muscles were no match for him. The doctor moved into view above her as he pinned her down, his features obscured by the light glowing from behind him so that she could not see his face.

"Not now, Lucy," he said as though admonishing a wayward child. "Your chance to take the ultimate journey will come soon."

Lucy Morgan watched as the doctor reached up and turned the valve on the intravenous drip in her arm.

"Let me go," she begged weakly.

She saw the doctor smile, the shadows around his face creasing.

"Soon, I shall do just that," he said. "And then you will be truly free."

Lucy struggled against the man holding her down, looking at him with pleading eyes blurred with tears of fear and frustration as the room faded to black before her and the pain in her body drifted away into oblivion. With the last vestiges of her conscience, she heard the doctor speak into his voice recorder.

"I must hurry, and prepare her for surgery."

18

HERZLIYA AIRFIELD
TEL AVIV, ISRAEL

T his isn't a good idea."

Rachel sat next to Ethan in the rear of an open-topped jeep as Aaron Luckov drove them alongside ranks of light aircraft parked on the servicing pan of the airfield.

"Trust me, this is the quickest way to find out what happened to Lucy," Ethan said.

"Assaulting our escort and disobeying an order from the Israeli Foreign Ministry?"

Aaron Luckov spoke over his shoulder above the noise of the engine.

"The whole Negev Desert is controlled by the military for training purposes. If there's anything they want to keep hidden, it'll be out there somewhere."

"Not you too?" Rachel asked.

It was Ethan who replied. "There is no real reason for MACE to prevent us from having a look around unless they're afraid of what we might stumble across."

"Maybe they don't want an investigative journalist poking around in their own backyard."

"Possibly," Ethan conceded. "Neither Shiloh Rok nor Spencer Malik like me being here. But what bothers me more is that this is not the first time people have gone missing from the Negev under suspicious circumstances."

Rachel's green eyes locked onto Ethan's, a wisp of her dark hair blowing in front of her face.

"What do you mean?"

This time it was Aaron who replied. "The Negev Desert is a large area, but there are one or two hot spots where people seem to vanish regularly and your daughter was working in one of them. In the past few years several scientists have vanished without trace into the wilderness."

"Somebody," Ethan said, "may have been working out here before Lucy arrived."

Luckov changed the jeep's direction, aiming toward a bright-red-and-white aircraft parked nearby.

"We're going to meet an old friend," Luckov said. "He's a member of the Bedouin tribes living in the Negev, near Masada. A number of Bedouin have also disappeared over the years in the area where Lucy was working, and this man's son was one of them."

Rachel frowned. "That's not quite the same as Western scientists being abducted."

"No," Ethan agreed, "but this Bedouin vanished at exactly the same time as Lucy did."

The jeep rolled to a halt alongside the aircraft, Luckov killing the engine. Ethan turned to see Safiya Luckov clamber from the interior of the plane, smiling brightly.

"Good morning and thank you for flying Luckov Air."

The aircraft was a de Havilland DHC-2 Beaver. A

huge Pratt & Whitney Wasp radial engine powered the fifty-year-old vintage machine, its broad wings sweeping across the top of a boxlike cockpit with simple windows. Aaron and Safiya had flown tourists across the Israeli wilderness for almost a decade, the business their main source of income.

"Are we all set?" Aaron asked, glancing at Ethan and Rachel.

"Let's go," Ethan replied. "I want to be back before sundown."

The interior of the aircraft was filled with canisters of water and a row of seats on either side of the fuselage. Ethan and Rachel buckled themselves in as Aaron and Safiya settled into the cockpit. A few minutes later, and the entire airframe rattled under the torque of the spluttering engine as Aaron taxied onto the runway and applied full power. After a brief takeoff roll the Beaver rotated gently and surged into the hot sky.

Rachel looked out of the opposite window at the city of Tel Aviv in the distance, a chaotic sprawl of metal and glass stark against the hazy blue strip of the Mediterranean. Safiya turned in the cockpit and pointed to headphones dangling from clips against the fuselage wall along with several parachutes, and Ethan and Rachel promptly donned the sets.

"It'll be about twenty minutes before we run south for Be'er Sheva. Then we'll head east for Bar Yehuda airfield," Safiya said, jabbing over her shoulder with one thumb. "The IDF control the airspace very tightly here, and will intercept any aircraft that strays from its flight path. Bar Yehuda is an old airstrip two miles from Masada, and also the lowest airfield in the world."

Ethan listened as Aaron spoke to air traffic control in the warbling dialect of Hebrew. After a few exchanges with the controller, Ethan felt the Beaver bank left, turning to avoid the built-up urban areas and heading out over the broad and rolling hills of Israel.

"You okay?" Ethan asked Rachel as the aircraft banked over.

"Daughter's been abducted, we're flying into God knows what, and you've assaulted our escort—I couldn't be better," Rachel uttered. "Where is Gaza?" she asked Safiya.

Safiya pointed out of her window ahead, toward the starboard wing.

"Out there, to the right and in front of us."

Ethan unclipped his seat buckle, joining Rachel in looking out over the Gaza Strip as it appeared through the haze ahead.

Although there was no singular marker at the edge of the Strip, it was still clearly defined by a band of undeveloped no-man's-land that separated Israel from its entrapped neighbor. Whereas the greenery of Israel was speckled with modern buildings and farmlands, the Strip was a morass of densely packed sandstone, narrow roads, alleys, and derelict buildings baking beneath the sun, like a medieval city stranded in the twenty-first century.

"That small town almost below us is Sderot, a place often hit by makeshift Qassam missiles and rockets fired from within Gaza," Safiya said, gesturing to the little town far below. "If we flew overhead, we'd be intercepted by Israel's fighter jets and shot down within minutes."

"The Gaza Strip looks so small," Rachel commented.

"It feels it too, when you're in there," Ethan replied, moving back to his own seat and tapping Luckov on the shoulder. "Who is the Bedouin we're going to meet?"

"Ayeem Khan," Luckov said, keeping one eye on the skies ahead. "He's a Bedouin elder. Safiya and I have known him for some time."

"Can he be trusted?"

"Absolutely. The guide who went to search for Lucy was Ahmed Khan, Ayeem's eldest son."

The jumbled sprawl of the Gaza Strip and the elegant greenery of Israel fell far behind them into a thickening haze that obscured the horizon. Beneath, the green symmetry of occupied land gave way to the random swirls of desert plains, wadis, gulleys, and canyons that split the epic landscape in winding eddies of erosion. The major roads six thousand feet beneath them vanished, turning instead into lonely threads of dark tarmac winding their way across the vast wilderness of timeless sand and stone. Occasional dusty tracks veered off from the highways into open desert peppered with lonely thorn scrub and isolated trees.

Under Luckov's skilled control the Beaver cruised over the vast desert wastes for almost twenty minutes, Safiya pointing out various towns like Be'er Sheva, an oasis of glittering buildings encrusted like jewels into the ancient desert. Ahead, Ethan could see the broad blue line of the Dead Sea appearing through the haze as Aaron Luckov responded to the chattering air traffic commands and began to descend. Leaning out of his seat, Ethan could see below them a vast canyon system carved by long-extinct rivers, opening out onto a parched floodplain that had probably once fed into the Dead Sea itself. A barely discernable airstrip scarred the terrain ahead of the aircraft, close to the sparkling expanses of the Dead Sea.

"So, Karowitz thinks that Lucy was right about finding alien remains," Ethan said to Rachel. "When do you think that these beings started helping mankind?"

"The Sumerian culture in Mesopotamia is the earliest known civilization," she said. "They began building their cities and mining copper around the same time as Amerindians in what is now Michigan and Wisconsin, around six thousand years ago."

"They were definitely the first?" Ethan asked.

"Sumer was our Eden," Rachel said, "the cradle of civilization. They used agriculture, invented the wheel, centralized government, set up social stratification, kept slaves, and organized warfare. They were experts in astronomy and mathematics and their cuneiform script existed almost six thousand years ago."

"The same time as they were mining for copper," Ethan noted.

"Exactly," Rachel nodded. "Everything happened for them at once, and that's what doesn't fit with the rest of ancient history. At the same time, people here in the Levant were also beginning agriculture, forming a script, mining copper, and attempting to smelt bronze."

"Are there any other legends that match Sumer's?" Ethan asked.

"Plenty. In the Indian Ramayana, the Pushpaka Vimana of the god Ravana is described as a chariot that resembles the sun, that traveled everywhere at will like a bright cloud in the sky."

"You think that they saw a flying vehicle?" Ethan asked in amazement.

"History is full of such records," Rachel explained. "On Kimberly Mountain in western Australia, there are cave walls bearing paintings of several beings with round heads and huge black eyes. Calling the figures Wondjina, the Aborigines consider the beings extremely sacred. The Wondjina were drawn at least ten thousand years ago and bear little resemblance to any known Earth creature."

"Could be just the natives strung out on naturally occurring narcotics," Ethan dismissed her.

"In the Tassili Mountains in the Sahara Desert there are images of towering figures," Rachel continued, "drawn at twice the height of humans and animals drawn alongside them. They also wear strange head-pieces and there are flying discs hovering above them. Hopi Indian petroglyphs tell of 'Star-Blowers' who traveled the universe and visited Earth in the distant past. There is an ancient Peruvian legend about the goddess Orejona landing in a great ship from the skies near the site of the famous Nazca Lines, not to mention Native American 'Thunderbirds,' Arab *djinni*, and one of the first written accounts of a fleet of flying saucers from an Egyptian papyrus of Thutmose III, who reigned around four thousand years ago."

"I had no idea," Ethan admitted.

"Most people don't," Rachel said, "but ancient history is littered with such records, right down to images of flying discs with windows that were painted on rocks thousands of years ago. The extraterrestrial appearance is considered too radical by science, and so other explanations are created despite the obvious implications."

"You can hardly blame them," Ethan said. "The idea that E.T. popped down to teach mankind to brew alcohol and then cleared off doesn't sound like serious archaeology."

"No, but that's the whole point," Rachel said. "I wouldn't have believed it either, but when you look at some of the artifacts, it's virtually staring us in the face. Sumerian and Egyptian gods portrayed as humanoid with animal heads and wings are a good example. In Val Camonica in Italy there's a cave painting of two men in suits holding strange objects that's at least ten thousand years old. In Sego, Utah, there are seven-thousand-year-old petroglyphs of unmistakably alien humanoids drawn alongside ordinary-looking humans."

"Cave paintings are hardly solid evidence," Ethan pointed out.

Rachel shrugged and watched as Luckov made a carefully judged descending turn around the epic heights of Masada as he lined the aircraft up with Bar Yehuda airfield. Set on an isolated cliff in the Judean Desert, Masada's precipices soared more than four hundred meters above the Dead Sea. Ethan could see the immense and seemingly impregnable fortress on its summit, built by King Herod and the site of the last stand of the Zealots against Imperial Rome.

The de Havilland's flaps whined down, the aircraft bobbing and plunging on thermals spiraling up from the hot desert below. Ethan watched with interest as Aaron and Safiya worked together, the scant runway of Bar Yehuda looming up before them as the scrubland whipped past below. Aaron flared the aircraft gently and set it down on the narrow strip as Safiya pulled the throttles back. The engine changed note to a rattling patter as they taxied off the runway alongside a scattering of dilapidated buildings erected from old corrugated iron and sandstone blocks sweltering in the heat.

"This is it," Aaron said, cutting the engine's fuel switch.

The engine shuddered to a stop, and the sudden silence that enveloped them was as deep as the timeless history of the land itself. An elderly man walked toward them from out of the desert as they disembarked, materializing ghostlike through rippling rivers of haze that obscured the horizon. He was dressed in traditional Bedouin garments to protect him from the heat and the winds that moaned across the empty wastes. Behind him walked several young men swathed in similar traditional clothes.

"*Shalom aleichem,* Ayeem," Aaron greeted the elderly man, and they embraced briefly.

"*Aleichem shalom,*" the Bedouin replied, before looking at Ethan and Rachel.

Ayeem's face was lined with crevices and gulleys like those of the desert, his skin scorched a deep mahogany by the harsh caress of a thousand suns. He greeted them warmly, shaking Ethan's hand with both of his own and gently kissing Rachel's cheek.

"I have heard much about you," he said in a surprisingly soft voice. "Aaron has told me only good things. Now we must hurry, if we are to reach the place you seek."

"How far is it?" Ethan asked.

"Perhaps five miles from here, just inside the edge of Israel's controlled zone," Ayeem replied. "It is not safe to travel at night here."

"Why not?" Rachel asked as Ethan shouldered his rucksack.

"Israel does not trust us," Ayeem replied. Anger glittered in his eyes, and for a brief instant Ethan wondered about the Bedouin's motivations. "They fear that they cannot tell between us and those who would harm them. We must find what you are looking for and return here before sundown."

Aaron gestured to a small jeep parked nearby. "Ayeem will drive you to the site. We'll wait here for you."

"What are your friends here for?" Rachel asked, looking at the quiet knot of Bedouin gathered nearby. "They can't all fit in the jeep."

"You will see," Ayeem replied smoothly, the glitter

returning briefly to his eyes as he gestured for them to follow him. "Now, come."

Aaron glanced at Ethan. "Try to keep your nose out of trouble, okay?"

Ethan decided not to respond and followed Ayeem and Rachel toward the jeep. He could hear Rachel and the Bedouin talking as he walked.

"Do you know the spot where Lucy disappeared? Have you been there before?"

"I know the land as I know every line on my hand," Ayeem said with a smile.

Ethan got into the passenger seat of the jeep as Ayeem clambered in and started the engine. As they turned away from the airfield, he saw the little group of Bedouin striking out on foot across the sweltering desert wastelands. Within minutes, they were lost amid the haze as though they had vanished through time itself.

19

MACE HEADQUARTERS
JERUSALEM

Spencer Malik sat in an office overlooking a military compound surrounded by thick concrete walls tipped with razor wire glinting in the sunlight. A slowly rotating ceiling fan did little to alleviate the suffocating heat as he wafted a thick wad of papers across his face.

He stared incredulously at Cooper and Flint standing before him, one with a rapidly swelling black eye and the other leaning on a table, cradling his stomach in one hand.

"We just didn't expect him to do that," Cooper complained.

"You didn't expect me to cut your salary either," Malik said in disgust. "Where did they go?"

"They didn't say," Flint muttered. "They just ran, both of them."

Malik regarded the two men for a moment and then looked down at an open file on his desk, scanning the details with interest. Rafael had worked swiftly.

"Ethan Warner, born 1978, Chicago, Illinois," he murmured. "Former correspondent."

Cooper nodded.

"Warner was an officer in the United States Marines, trained at Quantico, rifleman. Had a reputation for reckless actions in the field and a disregard for political authority. Several commendations for valor in Afghanistan for leading attacks and charges on Taliban positions. He also served in Iraq during the invasion, before working as a war correspondent in Bogotá, Colombia, in the Balkans, and here in Israel."

Malik scanned the areas of the document concerning Ethan's work in the Gaza Strip. His reading came to an abrupt halt as he digested several of the last paragraphs.

"Joanna Defoe," he muttered, glancing out of the window. "His fiancée."

"Disappeared somewhere in the Gaza Strip," Cooper said. "She was presumed abducted by insurgents although no group claimed responsibility. Warner spent two years searching for her before blaming the Israeli government for their lack of assistance in protecting foreign workers. That's why they've been tailing him since he arrived. He left Israel after his outburst, and disappeared off the radar until now."

Malik nodded.

"It says here that Ethan Warner is with this Morgan woman searching for her daughter," Malik murmured thoughtfully. He leaned back in his chair, using the file to waft cool air once more onto his face. "Where is he now?"

"We just heard that both Warner and Morgan were observed boarding a private aircraft leaving Herzliya airfield," Cooper replied.

Malik looked sharply at him. "Destination?"

"Masada. The flight plan is controlled, sir, so they can't fly anywhere within the Negev that is restricted."

Malik's eyes narrowed and he looked again at Warner's file.

"He was a soldier *and* war correspondent," he said softly. "He'll be used to digging around where he's not wanted and he's got nothing to lose. Contact the team at the site and make sure that he doesn't get the opportunity to nose around the area, understood?"

"Yes, sir. And if they're already there?"

Malik glanced out of the window for a moment. "Restrain them until further notice."

The two men turned instantly for the door, limping and shuffling out of sight. Malik stood from his desk and walked across to an open window that looked out over the compound and the city beyond. Men like Ethan Warner were a liability: trained, capable, yet highly unpredictable and with a tendency toward self-destruction.

"Whatever it is that you want, Mr. Warner," he said to himself thoughtfully, "don't cross me to get it."

"Problems, Spencer?"

Malik turned to see Bill Griffiths leaning against the doorframe of the office.

"Just some journalist nosing into things he shouldn't," Malik said dismissively. "Is the excavation complete?"

Griffiths nodded, brushing dust off the broad rim of his hat.

"The specimen will be packaged this afternoon at the site and then transported to Ben Gurion Airport in the morning. I've pulled my team out and they'll return to the States tomorrow. I take it that the remains will be flown out the same day?"

"The jet will be waiting," Malik confirmed. "As far as customs are concerned, the consignment contains medical equipment, brought here by the same aircraft from the United States four weeks ago, being returned to the supplier. All of the paperwork is in order."

Griffiths nodded again. "And the rest of my payment?"

"Sent once the specimen leaves Israel safely," Malik said. "Our administration department will take care of the transfers. Talk to them if you have any issues. My only concerns right now are security and discretion."

Griffiths examined his hat for a moment before speaking. "How did you come about the remains?"

"They were found by men working at the site; it happens from time to time during demolition training," Malik said, shuffling some papers on his desk. "I take it that no further specimens have been found?"

"None," Griffiths replied. "We've dug several areas but the remains appear to be a single burial. Incredible luck, that they should have been exposed by a demolition team."

"They weren't there to play Indiana Jones," Malik muttered. "The sooner this is resolved, the happier I'll be."

Griffiths raised an eyebrow, and Malik instantly regretted his candor as the fossil hunter spoke.

"I'm surprised that the remains weren't destroyed by the explosives your men were using. If enough rock had been shattered away to expose the bones, then I'd have thought that the bones themselves would have been blasted to pieces."

Malik leveled Griffiths with a long, hard look.

"Indeed, and it's your good fortune that we contracted you to excavate them afterward. Perhaps you would prefer us to use another specialist, if you have any doubts about your involvement?"

Griffiths twiddled his hat between his fingers for a moment and then shook his head.

"I'm sure that won't be necessary."

20

NEGEV DESERT
3 MILES NORTHWEST OF BAR YEHUDA

The site where Lucy was working is just on the edge of the floodplain."

Ayeem Khan pointed ahead toward a canyon that sliced through the sandstone cliffs, eroded by the passing of an ancient river. Now parched, Ethan could visualize how the river system would once have streamed from the highlands to spill onto a broad, lush plain.

The Bedouin had parked the jeep inside a nearby *wadi,* hidden behind an outcrop of rock that marked the turning point in the extinct river's course and the entrance to the canyon. Deep shadow enveloped them as they moved into its maw, the sheer walls dwarfing them and the air suddenly cool.

"Do not speak loudly," Ayeem said softly as they moved.

"How much do you know about the security company, MACE?" Ethan whispered.

"They are unpleasant people. They regard us Bedouin as less than human. Our people have been attacked by MACE soldiers for walking their livestock too close to military compounds."

"Private security companies can work almost entirely without fear of legal action," Ethan replied.

"How come?" Rachel asked.

"Governments often contract private security firms to undertake menial work such as guarding military sites. Should anything illegal happen, the government can pass the blame onto the security company, who are privately held and thus cannot be prosecuted by the government. The whole thing goes through the civil courts, and the security companies have become wealthy over the years and can afford the best counsel, overwhelming the prosecution. It happened regularly in Iraq after the invasion."

Ayeem's voice hissed like a knife through the air as he spoke. "Our people cannot afford to take these companies to court for the things that they have done. It is, how do you say, swept under the carpet? And this area is renowned for people disappearing."

"This has happened before?" Rachel asked.

"The Negev Desert is as vast as it is mysterious," Ayeem said. "A number of unwary travelers have disappeared into its wastelands, never to be seen again."

"Like Lucy?" she asked in dismay. "You think that she'll never be seen again?"

"Lucy is different," Ayeem said soothingly. "We have a trail to follow, and it will lead us to her. Be patient."

Rachel was quiet for a moment, and then noticed something on the ground beside her. She reached down and picked up what looked to Ethan like a small piece of stone.

"Pottery," she said, examining it as she walked. "Probably been here for a thousand years. I wouldn't mind betting you'd find worked metals out here if you looked hard enough."

"How old would they be?" Ethan asked.

"There's a Chalcolithic copper mine in the Timna Valley in the southern Negev," Rachel answered, "that was being mined at least six thousand years ago. There are copper axes in museums that are over seven thousand years old in Europe and America. How could man have invented such metallurgy at the same time in so many different places?"

"Silence," Ayeem whispered, climbing up lithely over loose rubble.

As he followed Ayeem and Rachel, Ethan found himself able to study Rachel for the first time unnoticed.

Rachel was attractive in an unconventional way, he decided. Her long dark hair framed her features perfectly, her skin was as unblemished as fresh snow, and he'd seen enough of her clear green eyes to know that he'd liked whatever he'd seen there. Her knowledge of history and her determination to find her daughter attracted him even further. If the situation had been any different, he might have even considered . . . An image of Joanna drifted briefly through his mind and silenced his thoughts. A thin trickle of self-loathing dribbled through his guts as he pictured her suffering somewhere, and he pushed himself angrily up the slope.

"Stay low," Ayeem cautioned, waving them to keep their heads down.

Ethan followed the Bedouin to the lip of the slope, peering over the edge and down onto a broad plain that stretched away beneath a shimmering blanket of heat toward the Dead Sea.

The camp below them consisted of two large khaki tents pitched at the base of the low cliffs amid a scattering of desiccated trees. Beside the tents were parked two Humvees and a small white jeep. On the far side of the camp, six men in black uniforms sat idly on wooden crates playing cards and smoking, assault rifles scattered around them.

"Is this the site?" Ethan asked.

"Yes," Ayeem confirmed. "Several of us saw Lucy's camp while we were traveling out on the plains. You could see her lights for miles at night."

"Probably why she was found so easily."

Rachel looked at Ethan sharply. "She was hardly expecting to be abducted."

"Out here, you need to expect just about anything."

Ethan retrieved a pair of small binoculars from his rucksack and focused them on the camp. He saw shovels, two pickaxes, and a number of buckets scattered on the hot earth near the tent closest to the cliff face.

"Why are they digging?" he asked Ayeem. "They haven't built entrenchments, and if they're guarding a perimeter, then why are they camped against the escarpment?"

"I don't know," the Bedouin said.

Ethan handed the binoculars to Rachel and pulled a camera from his rucksack. "I'm going down for a look."

Ayeem gestured to their right.

"There is a narrow track used by foxes and ibex that leads down to the floor of the plain. You must tread carefully."

"What happens if they find you?" Rachel asked, somewhat concerned.

Ethan checked his camera and then shrugged. "What can they do? Arrest me?"

"If they find you and this is reported back to the Israeli Defense Force, it may stop them from helping us."

"They're not helping us," Ethan said, making for

the track. "That's why we're here. MACE's charter is to guard Israeli assets, not dig up the desert while they're at it."

"Wait," Ayeem said, placing an arm gently but firmly on Ethan's shoulder.

Ethan saw the old man looking out across the desert. There, walking directly toward the camp, a small group of Bedouin men were appearing through the rippling haze. Ethan grinned.

"A distraction, to give us some time," the Bedouin said.

Before Rachel could protest further, Ethan slipped over the edge of the slope.

21

Ethan quietly moved across to his right where a precarious ledge of sandstone jutted out from the main wall of the cliff. Thirty feet below, he could see the MACE tents rippling in the hot wind that scoured the desert plain.

A sense of doubt slithered through Ethan's belly as he hesitated on the slope. Maybe Rachel was right: if the MACE guards spotted him, this would be over before it had begun. Still, *if you've nothing to lose* . . . Ethan took a breath, and moved down the slope.

The sedimentary rock was loose and offered precious little in the way of footholds. Ethan knew that if he dislodged rocks any larger than his fist, he would immediately be detected. Judging every footstep, he edged along the ragged pathway, descending with one eye fixed upon the soldiers.

One of them stood up and Ethan froze. The soldier seemed to be looking almost straight at him as he stretched his arms and scratched the back of his neck with one hand before retaking his seat at the game. Ethan crept forward and began to descend behind the two largest tents. Out of the sight of the camp guards,

Ethan moved quickly down to the foot of the cliff and crouched to listen for sounds from within the camp.

The fabric of the tents rumbled and snapped in the wind. Ethan strained his hearing but could detect nothing. He moved across the rear of the nearest tent and peered across the camp. The soldiers were out of sight, but he could see one of the Humvees and the little white jeep nearby.

Ethan moved slowly out into the bright sunlight and across to the tent's flaps. A fine breeze of sand particles gusted through the camp, whispering against the fabric. He shielded his face, turning sideways beside the entrance to the tent, and peered in between the flaps. Seeing that the gloomy interior was devoid of people, he slipped inside.

It took several seconds for Ethan's eyes to adjust after the blazing sunlight. The interior of the tent throbbed with heat like an oven. Through the gloom he began to make out more digging tools scattered around and, in the center, a deep excavation.

Ethan knelt at the edge of the cavity, looking down at the unmistakable structure of a huge humanoid skeleton imprinted in the rocks of ages. This was where Lucy had discovered the remains, and he wondered why MACE would have gone to such lengths to conceal the site.

He took out his camera, shooting a dozen images of the cavity from various angles before moving back toward the entrance to the tent. If this tent contained the location of Lucy's discovery, Ethan wanted to know what was in the other large tent opposite.

He reached the flaps and eased them aside, and his heartbeat shuddered as he looked straight into a pair of eyes.

"Jesus," he muttered.

"It's in the other tent," Rachel whispered, and jabbed a thumb over her shoulder.

"You shouldn't be down here," Ethan told her, slipping out of the tent.

"Whose daughter is it who's gone missing?" Rachel shot back.

A radio squawked beside him as the trooper laid down a winning hand, directing a hawkish grin at his companions from beneath his thick beard.

"Full house."

A muted chorus of obscenities drifted from his companions as they tossed their hands into the center. The trooper gathered a handful of cash and then picked up the radio.

"Venom, go ahead."

"Venom, this is Sentinel. We have information that your position may be compromised."

The trooper's eyes flicked across the nearby camp. "By whom?"

"A journalist, Ethan Warner. Is the compound secure?"

"My men are patrolling it as we speak," the trooper lied.

"Report back when you can confirm."

The trooper dropped the radio and picked up his rifle. "Spot check. Let's go."

Instantly, the other five men got up, checking their rifles. They were about to disperse when one of them looked out across the desert and raised an eyebrow. "Er, Brad? Boss?"

The soldiers turned to look in the same direction at

a small group of desert nomads strolling nonchalantly across the sands nearby.

"Christ's sake," Brad said angrily. "There's not supposed to be anyone out here; it's a goddamn desert."

"What do we do?" asked one of the soldiers.

Brad glared at him.

"What the hell do you think we do? Go with Kelsey and Archer and check the camp. Saunders, Dev, stay here with me."

Brad walked out to the Bedouin men, confronting them.

"This is a restricted area," he said, raising a hand to halt them.

The six Bedouin stopped and looked at the bearded soldier before turning to look at each other. A swift exchange in Arabic flitted like desert birdsong between them before the tallest man looked Brad in the eye.

"Yes, it is. It is our home, and *you* are trespassing."

Brad glanced across his shoulder at the two troopers behind him.

"Oh me, oh my, so sorry," he uttered before sneering at the Bedouin with undisguised contempt. "Take a walk back the way you came, *Araboosh*."

The Bedouins' faces hardened at the insult and their apparent leader shook his head slowly.

"It is not polite to speak to us in this way," he replied.

Brad grinned coldly, revealing an unsightly gold canine that glinted in the hot sun. "My apologies, let me rephrase it. *Piss off, Araboosh.*"

The young Bedouin hesitated a moment longer and then as one they lunged forward, hands gripping long, slim blades that appeared as if by magic from beneath their robes. Instantly, the two soldiers flanking Brad raised their rifles and the Bedouin came to an abrupt halt.

22

Ethan moved across to the second tent and peered into the shadowy interior as Rachel led him inside.

The tent contained a number of boxes and crates, along with a satellite receiver dish and a small laptop computer. Ethan moved between the crates, glancing at plastic containers filled with brushes and small metallic trowels, a vacuum pump and plastic specimen jars, several of which contained what looked like bones. Ethan peered at one of the tags inside a jar alongside a small bone.

Right metacarpal.

Ethan slipped the small jar into his pocket.

"These are the tools of a paleontologist," Rachel said. "This is Lucy's equipment."

Ethan nodded, taking a picture of the specimen jars and the array of equipment. He wondered why it had not been returned to the Hebrew University in Jerusalem.

Beyond the smaller crates was another crate some nine feet long and three feet deep sitting on a pallet. Ethan moved across to it, reaching for the lid. He shared a glance with Rachel and then hefted it aside, and as he did so he felt a shock wave of surprise hit him.

A huge block of sandstone had been hewn from the living rock, probably using power tools, and placed in the crate. Ethan knew that scientists like Lucy did not use power tools to excavate ancient remains, preferring instead to diligently remove bones one by one and catalogue their type and position as they went along.

Entombed in the rock lay the skeletal remains of an enormous humanoid, nearly eight feet tall and powerfully built. Ethan stared in awe at the figure. At first glance the remains looked perfectly human to Ethan's untrained eye, but he could remember Karowitz's fossils. A gust of hot desert wind moaned through the tent as he stared down at the remains, encased beneath the earth for more than seven thousand years. Now he saw the strangely oval eye sockets in a skull that was far too elongated to be human, the massive chest plate of fused bone splitting into ribs near the spine, the immense arm bones built for carrying muscle far greater than that of a human being.

"I'll be damned," he said.

"You still think Lucy was mistaken?" Rachel asked.

Ethan shook his head, taking photographs as Rachel gestured to the remains.

"Look at the skull cap," she said. "It's elongated, twice as tall as a human's."

"A bigger brain or something?" Ethan asked, snapping a shot of the skull. "Karowitz mentioned infrasound communication, like some dinosaurs."

"That might explain it," Rachel replied, "and there is a human practice going back thousands of years where the skulls of newborn infants are tightly bound, distorting them as they grow into exactly this kind of shape."

Ethan frowned.

"Maybe some kind of religious practice?"

"Not likely," Rachel said. "Such skulls have been found all across the ancient world: Incas in Peru, eastern Germanic tribes, Tahiti and Samoa in the South Pacific, the Atacamero culture, and others. Even the Egyptians practiced it: Tutankhamun, Nefertiti, and Akhenaten all show signs of skull deformation. Hippocrates mentions an entire population, the Macrocephales, who deformed their skulls in worship of ancient sky gods."

"You think they did it to emulate these things?" he asked, gesturing to the remains.

"It's possible," Rachel said. "Why else go to such lengths for something as painful and dangerous?"

Ethan gently replaced the lid, and was about to leave when his eye caught upon several smaller boxes stacked near the rear of the tent. He moved across to them, squatting down and prying the topmost box open as Rachel examined Lucy's specimen jars nearby.

Inside, a small block of a pale-colored material about the same size as a cigarette packet was encased in a transparent sack filled with a gel, the gel packed with ball bearings. A metal rod passed through the gel and into the block. Ethan's eyes traced a wire fused to the end of the rod, running into a small device made from black plastic. From the device a second, thinner wire ran into the bottom of a cell phone.

"IED," Ethan whispered to himself, suddenly feeling cold.

An improvised explosive device—the weapon of choice for insurgent groups across the world—it contained everything required in order to slice, puncture, dismember, or maim its unsuspecting victims. Ethan had seen a hundred such devices while serving in Iraq and Afghanistan. What he had not seen was one so incredibly small and encased in the strange gel package.

Ethan opened the two cases beneath and found several more of the devices, each identical and attached to cell phones of various different types. *What the hell are these people doing?*

Ethan quickly fired off several photographs of the IEDs, before on impulse grabbing four of them from the box at the bottom and shoving them into his pockets. He closed the remaining boxes and carefully stacked them as he had found them, then turned and crept toward the tent flaps.

"Come on," he whispered to Rachel, who got up to follow him.

If he could get these samples back to Jerusalem undetected, then Israel would have to listen to him and—

"Halt!"

The word punched through the silence like a gunshot. Ethan and Rachel froze barely a meter from the tent flaps.

"Come out with your hands in the air! No sudden movements!"

Shit. Ethan checked his pockets for the IEDs and cursed himself for staying too long in one place. He'd disregarded too many of his own golden rules from his days as a journalist working in hostile environments.

"Move, now!"

Ethan sighed and walked to the tent flaps, reaching out and hoping that the MACE soldiers weren't the sort to shoot first and ask questions later.

"Get down on your knees!"

Ethan hesitated at the entrance and looked at Rachel, wondering how the soldier could see him standing in the interior.

"Stay down! Guys, I've got him!"

With a sudden rush of realization Ethan backed up from the tent entrance, listening as heavy boots thundered past outside. Shadows flickered frighteningly close past the tent, and a flurry of curses followed.

"Who the hell is this?"

A voice muffled by the dust of the desert floor spoke out.

"My name is Ayeem."

23

FIRST DISTRICT STATION
M STREET SW, WASHINGTON DC

Lucas Tyrell sat at his desk and twiddled a pen with surprising grace between his bloated fingers in an effort to curb his frustration. That was something he needed to be careful of, so his doctor had warned him: reduce stress and perform moderate exercise frequently. The fact that he was a cop in the murder capital of the United States of America seemed to have escaped the learned physician, as had the futility of exercise in his current condition.

He sighed and took a handkerchief from his pocket, mopping the sweat from his brow. The infernal heatwave cloaking the District made life hard for most all the city's population, but for Tyrell it placed an intolerable strain on his laboring heart. Cardiomyopathy, so they'd said. Should have had it checked out years ago. Why hadn't he seen his physician, his sister had asked him. Why had he not sought help?

Truth was, he'd already known that his clogged heart was suffering. It had gotten to the point where he'd get light-headed just walking up a staircase, so he didn't need some spotty kid with an MD to tell him he was sick. But he hadn't cared then any more than he cared now. Cardiomyopathy had taken his mother decades before, and apart from his sister and her family there seemed little left to hang on for.

Maria Tyrell had borne her husband three children. Lucas Tyrell Jr., named in his honor, was serving as a fighter pilot with the United States Navy, a fact that Lucas Tyrell Sr. would relate with a mighty sense of pride to anyone not already tired of hearing about it. Maria's daughter River was married and living in Michigan with one child, Lucas Tyrell's beloved great-nephew Mitchell Sears, while Maria's third and youngest child, Harriet, was working for a big bank in Manhattan and earning the kind of money that Tyrell had thought existed only in the accounts of Saudi oil princes.

Their family would continue happily after he was gone, his suffering long forgotten. The loss of his own family so many years before might have tipped another man over the edge, but even with a past tinged with such sadness Tyrell had carried on stoically until now.

"Who pulled your chain?" Lopez asked as she glided elegantly toward him and tossed a fat wad of papers onto his desk.

"Powell," he said. "What are these?"

"Results of the ICMP search. Worth a look, if I were you."

Tyrell reluctantly picked up the papers and sifted through them.

"Fourteen possible matches," he observed, scanning images of individuals broadly matching the search criteria he had advised.

"Fifteen, actually, but one of 'em turned up dead

this morning over in Prince George's with a bullet through his skull."

"Any links?"

"Nope, he was a loner and bum," Lopez said. "He's not a match."

Tyrell scanned the rest of the sheets, and then began recognizing images. "That's one of our guys."

"I put the other two with him at the back." Lopez smiled brightly.

Tyrell scanned the next two sheets quickly before looking up at her. "When were they reported missing?"

"All three of them vanished from the DC area in the last three weeks. Two are more or less regular guys, some petty misdemeanors between them. But our man Alpha was straight as an arrow, not so much as a parking ticket on record."

"I'll be damned, abduction. And in this case that means homicide."

"You wanna get ready to give me an even bigger pat on the back?"

Tyrell leaned back in his chair and grinned at his beaming colleague. There weren't many people who could make him smile these days, but Lopez could.

"Go for your life."

"I called the examiner's office and got Fry back on the line, had him run a quick analysis of the hydrogen sulphide he found in Alpha's body. Fry couldn't trace it to an origin because the component chemicals are common enough, so I ran the results of his autopsy through the database instead to see what came up."

"Stop tugging my dick and cut to the chase."

"MPD recorded an identical trace mixture in the blood pathology of a victim who turned up on Fourth District two weeks ago. They were unable to determine anything except that it probably occurred as a result of an unspecified medical procedure."

"Another cold lead?" Tyrell asked.

"Well, the victim doesn't recall much about the procedure itself."

Tyrell almost fell out of his chair. "The victim's alive?"

"He is. He's a twenty-one-year-old former crackhead from Columbia Heights, an African American of Ethiopian descent, apparently. The Heights are not our zone so we don't have any jurisdiction."

"Is he a reliable witness?" Tyrell demanded, ignoring her last comment.

"The kid's not quite all there, Lucas. Whatever he went through must've scrambled his brain. He's been sectioned into a private hospital."

"Goddamn," Tyrell murmured. "You did good, Nicola."

"Maybe," Lopez said. "However, the subject's history doesn't match our victim in any way. He's a first-rate gang color from the Heights, well known to the MPD before this happened."

Tyrell looked back at the three missing-persons sheets. "Who were these guys?"

Lopez frowned as she glanced at the pages.

"Well, all of them had families and, holy of holies, Alpha had thigh surgery in his early twenties after an automobile accident. The serial code matches the titanium pin pulled by Dr. Fry. The families have been informed and Fourth District PD is talkin' to them right now."

Tyrell felt a sinking melancholy as he considered the loss that the families would be feeling.

"What did they do for a living?"

"That's the weird thing," she replied. "Two of the

guys worked construction, but Alpha was some big-shot scientist, a man named Joseph Coogan. He had a PhD in biochemistry and had worked at MIT of all places."

Tyrell took a deep breath before heaving himself out of his chair.

"Let's go and see what our survivor has to say for himself."

NEW COVENANT CHURCH
IVY CITY, WASHINGTON DC

Kelvin Patterson sat in silence in the broad office that dominated the rear of the purpose-built church. Broad windows behind him looked out over the distant rolling plains of New Jersey beyond the surface of the Potomac River, the light reflected off the water shimmering across the wall of the office. The towering chrome crucifix dominated the wall to his right, looming over a small altar, while before him on his mahogany desk a monitor beside a large bronze eagle displayed a newsfeed showing Senator Isaiah Black being interviewed by jostling news crews outside the Capitol.

One of the hacks barged his way past the senator's barrier of bulky security guards and shoved a microphone under his nose.

"Senator, how will you justify your association with the New Covenant Church after the inflammatory sermons conducted by its pastor were condemned by the wider church?"

Senator Black's neon smile flashed like a lighthouse at the correspondent, but his eyes were hard as he spoke.

"Free speech is part of our nation's Constitution. It doesn't mean that I agree with the sermons or that they reflect my party's policies."

Patterson chewed on his lip, a habit born of irritation.

"*Free speech is one thing, Senator,*" the journalist shot back. "*Incitement to hatred is something else. Analysts are saying that you're walking a fine line between policy and popularity that could backfire if your party sees you as a liability.*"

Senator Black stopped on the steps of the Capitol, turning to face the media mob from behind an impenetrable line of secret service agents who turned with folded arms and fixed expressions to bar the journalists' way.

"*I cannot choose who supports me, nor can I dictate what they should or should not say,*" Black intoned smoothly with his hands extended out to his sides. "*That would be a dictatorship, would it not? I can only say that the policies I have placed my faith in include a peaceful resolution to all conflicts in which the United States of America has an interest, and that I put my place in office above my personal beliefs.*"

"*Do you agree then,*" another voice shouted from the mob, "*with Pastor Patterson's views on the Middle East?*"

Patterson leaned forward as the mob suddenly fell silent, waiting for the answer from the senator to the pointed and unavoidable question. Isaiah Black took a deep breath, his hands falling to his sides.

"*No, I do not. Conflict cannot ever be ended by further conflict, that much has proven true for decades, millennia even. War is the easy option, and there is nothing easy in office when it comes to diplomacy between nations divided.*" He fired off a broadside smile again. "*That's why the Senate and Congress exist—to find other ways. We can be influenced by the American people, but not through their rhetoric, only through their vote. Now, if you'll excuse me.*"

Senator Black turned and hurried up the steps and into the Capitol, pursued by a wave of questions that broke against the shore of his security team. Patterson switched off the monitor, chewing his lip until it hurt before picking up his phone and dialing a number. The line connected on the second ring.

"Yes?"

"Black's not going for it," Patterson said simply. "Arrange a press conference for the rally, so that we can get our message out to as wide an audience as possible. We'll take the voters away from that bastard and rip the rug out from under his feet."

"That could be risky, Pastor. There's no guarantee the people will turn away from him, regardless of what we do. He's too well established, too well known."

"So are we," Patterson snapped. "Make it happen."

24

NEGEV DESERT
ISRAEL

Ayeem watched as the three guards encircled him
with their rifles pointed down at his prostrate form.
One of them shouted a command and the old guide got
slowly to his feet, his hands behind his head but defiance
etched clearly into his features. Nearby, Ayeem's Bedouin companions stood under the watchful gaze of the
other three soldiers.

A tall bearded man walked up to Ayeem.

"What the hell are you doing here?" he rumbled.
"Where's Ethan Warner?"

Ayeem said nothing. The soldier smiled cruelly
and then his rifle butt swung around with terrific
speed to smash into Ayeem's temple with a sickening crack that echoed off the cliffs around them. The
Bedouin spun away from the piercing pain, crumpling
onto the earth and clasping his head. Instantly, the
younger Bedouin were shouting, trying to surge forward.

Ayeem felt rough hands grabbing his limbs and half
carrying, half dragging his body away from the tents to-

ward the edge of the camp, where they unceremoniously dropped him onto the dust.

The tall, bearded soldier removed his rifle and pulled off his shirt, his body muscular and his pale skin smothered in purple tattoos. Ayeem struggled to his feet and watched as the soldier raised his fists in a classic boxing stance. A faint ripple of laughter from the encircling guards drifted on the hot wind.

"What were you doing in the camp?"

The bearded soldier's words hissed from behind thick, meaty fists. Ayeem stood before him, ignoring the pain bolting through his skull and the blood dripping from his forehead.

"Walking home."

"This is a restricted area, and we don't allow the unclean to pass here, *Araboosh*."

The surrounding soldiers chortled and nudged each other. Ayeem glanced briefly up at the ridge, above him and to his left. He could just make out Rachel and Ethan watching him from there. He looked back at the soldier.

"This land belonged to my father. You have stolen it from us."

"Screw you."

The soldier jabbed one chunky fist with lightning speed at the Bedouin's face to a cheer from his companions. The cheer fell flat as Ayeem ducked aside and out of range of the punch and nipped forward into the soldier's left side. The Bedouin's hand flicked out in a blur of motion, and with a squelch two bony fingers punctured the soldier's eyeballs like needles through a water balloon.

The trooper screamed out, clasping his hands to his eyes and doubling over. Ayeem spun on one foot before the troops could react and drove his opposite heel hard into the side of the soldier's knee. With a dull crack the man's tendons snapped like dry twigs and the heavy body jerked sideways and slammed into the dust.

Ayeem turned to look at the closest of the soldiers, his voice calm. "What did you do to Ahmed? Where is he?"

The two soldiers glanced at each other, and then as one they plunged into the Bedouin amid a cloud of frenzied blows.

Ethan and Rachel scrambled to the top of the ridge and looked back down into the camp.

"What the hell was he doing down there?" Ethan asked.

"He must have deliberately distracted their attention," Rachel hissed. "Do something!"

Ethan, his camera in his hand, was filming the exchange beneath them. He watched as Ayeem was picked up by two of the soldiers and held in their grasp. A third soldier drove his fist into Ayeem's unprotected belly, the Bedouin guide crumpling over the blow and sinking to his knees. A flurry of cries went up from the other Bedouin.

"For God's sake," Rachel uttered.

Ethan kept the camera on the scene below. "Go and start the jeep, now!"

"What for? Ayeem needs our—"

"Now!"

Rachel hurried away down the slope. Ethan turned to watch as Ayeem was once more dragged to his feet.

"Let him go."

Brad's voice crackled with a rage born of agony. The soldiers holding the guide complied at once, releasing Ayeem and backing away from him.

Ayeem watched as the towering soldier picked up his assault rifle from nearby, cocking the weapon and limping back toward him. Thick blood streamed from beneath his eyes, his features folding in upon themselves with pain.

"Brad, wait."

One of the other soldiers raised a cautionary hand but the bearded man scowled at him. Ayeem took a last glance at the ridge, and then glared at the bearded soldier.

"Coward," he uttered, loud enough for all to hear.

The soldier snapped the rifle up to point at Ayeem, and squeezed the trigger.

"Hey, you down there!" All six of the soldiers and their Bedouin prisoners turned to stare up at the ridge behind them. Ayeem saw Ethan wave at them and point to something he held in his hand. Even across the distance, the shape of a camera was clearly distinguishable. *"See you on the news!"*

With that he turned and fled out of sight.

"Oh shit," someone uttered.

"Get after them!" Brad hollered.

Five of the soldiers turned and dashed toward the Humvees, leaping aboard them and starting the engines amid belching clouds of diesel smoke as the bearded soldier turned his rifle back to point at Ayeem. As the vehicles turned and accelerated away, Ayeem produced from beneath his robes a cruel blade that glittered in the late-afternoon sunlight.

"For Ahmed," he whispered.

As the bearded soldier took aim Ayeem bolted forward, reaching out with one gnarled hand and bashing the barrel of the rifle aside. He saw a ripple of panic flitter across the soldier's eyes as he realized what was about to happen.

Ayeem drove the needle-sharp blade deep into the soldier's chest, sinking it to its delicately carved hilt. The soldier gasped, his eyes bulging and his cavernous pink mouth opening wide in a silent scream of indescribable agony.

Ayeem watched as the man sank to his knees, dropping his rifle and clasping the blade's handle in his hands as dark blood poured from the wound through his thick fingers. The Bedouin turned his back on the dying man, and with a deceptively swift gait strode with his younger companions out toward the sanctuary of the endless plains.

Ethan scrambled down the slope and plunged into the depths of the *wadi*. He heard the jeep's engine turn over as he hit the floor of the canyon.

Rachel was looking nervously over her shoulder as Ethan leaped into the passenger's seat.

"Go!"

"What about Ayeem?"

"He'll be fine as long as we've got this!" Ethan held up the camera. "Now drive!"

Rachel slammed the throttle down, the jeep lurching forward and bouncing violently across the uneven ground. Rachel jerked the steering wheel from one side to the other, swerving around boulders and thorn scrub as they hurtled toward the *wadi*'s entrance and the open plains beyond.

Ethan reached behind him into the backseat, shoving his camera into his rucksack and grabbing his cell phone. He struggled to dial as the jeep leaped and bucked, covering one ear as he listened to the dial tone in the other. Aaron Luckov's voice sounded muted against the roar of the engine through the canyon around them.

"Ethan?"

"Aaron, get the plane started!"

"What's happened?"

"No time to explain, just do it! We're on our way!"

Ethan cut off the connection as the jeep burst from the *wadi* and followed the ancient river course that Ayeem had tracked on the journey in.

"Once we get back to the plane," Ethan shouted above the wind, "we'll be just fine."

"Is this what you call looking for my daughter?" she shot back. "Those people could have helped us for all you know!"

"Those people," Ethan replied, jabbing his thumb over his shoulder, "aren't inclined to help anyone but themselves. The farther we get from them the better."

"They're the authorities!" Rachel protested, swerving the jeep with more violence than was necessary to avoid a scattering of rocks. "If we run away from them, we'll become fugitives."

"If we go back, we'll become victims. They're hiding something out here."

"What on earth would they be hiding from anyone?" Rachel shouted. "This is insane."

Ethan reached into his pocket and produced one of the explosives he had found in the camp's tent.

"Do you know what this is?" he demanded. Rachel glanced at the device and shook her head. "It's an improvised explosive, the type that terrorists use. All you have to do is call the number and boom, people die. You tell me what a company like MACE is doing storing boxes of these?"

Rachel, flustered and confused, shook her head.

"I don't know, but it could be nothing to do with Lucy or what's been—"

"The remains that Lucy found are back there!"

Ethan shouted. "Whatever happened to her, MACE knows something about it. We need to get back and inform the Israeli Defense Force and Ambassador Cutler!"

Rachel turned back to the wheel and squinted in the brilliant sunlight that now streamed across the horizon as the sun began to set in the west. Ethan shoved the explosive devices into his rucksack and held on tightly as the jeep bounced through a shallow gulley and leaped up the other side, Rachel driving at near breakneck speed.

A deafening crack split the air above them like thunder. The windshield of the jeep flared with splintered fractures and exploded inward, showering Ethan with sparkling shards of glass. Rachel screamed, the jeep careening wildly before she brought it back under control.

Ethan turned in his seat, his bowels clenching reflexively as another rifle shot zipped past the jeep. Behind them in the distance, two Humvees bounded along the desert plains, trailing billowing clouds of dust into the evening sky.

"They're shooting at us!" Rachel shouted above the howling wind.

Ethan felt a sudden concern for Ayeem Khan as well as for himself and Rachel as the possibility that he had severely miscalculated how far MACE would go began to weigh on his shoulders.

26

Ethan looked at Rachel as another shot zipped past overhead. Her face was ashen.

"Still want to go back?" he asked her.

Rachel shook her head as Ethan glanced over her for any signs of injury, but all that he found was a creeping veil of shock.

"Get out of the driver's seat," Ethan commanded, moving to try to exchange places with her.

Rachel's head whipped around to look at him, the wind flinging her black hair out behind her. Ethan froze as two clear green eyes glared at him.

"Like hell."

Without another word, Rachel turned back to the barren plain ahead and accelerated the jeep until the engine wailed in protest.

Ethan slid back into his seat, straining to look behind him. Another two shots rang out, both of them striking the earth close to the jeep.

"They're trying to shoot the tires out," he shouted. "Keep swerving to spoil their aim."

Rachel obeyed, drifting the jeep left and right both to avoid obstacles and to evade the shots cracking the wind around them.

Ethan looked at the nearest Humvee, probably a hundred meters behind them but closing fast. The second was another hundred meters farther back and obscured in the dust trail of the first. He turned to look for landmarks from their journey out. The looming bulk of Masada's buttress, crafted by the elements over countless millennia, jutted out above the plains a few miles to their right.

"We've got another three miles to go. We're not going to make the airfield!" he shouted.

Rachel glanced over her shoulder, and Ethan saw the first sickly flash of panic in her expression. The jeep lurched as another shot ricocheted off nearby rocks and whipped past their heads with a metallic twang, Rachel losing control as she flinched.

Ethan grabbed the wheel, steadying it as Rachel recovered. Tears were falling down her cheeks now as she gripped the wheel, her knuckles white as bone.

"Stick with it," Ethan encouraged above the wind, trying to ignore the guilt churning in his stomach.

He looked behind them.

The leading Humvee was within fifty meters now, two men in the front and one in the rear bearing a rifle that seemed to be pointing directly between Ethan's eyes. The wind dashed a spurt of blue smoke from the barrel, and Ethan heard the shot zip past a few feet from his head as he ducked reflexively, banging his forehead on the headrest.

"Jesus!"

The sun ahead flared brilliantly as it sank toward the horizon and the shattered glass on his side of the windshield prevented him from seeing ahead clearly. He turned to Rachel.

"Swerve the jeep more tightly! It'll blind them with dust in the sunlight and spoil their aim!"

Rachel again complied with near-robotic efficiency, jerking the wheel to and fro. Ethan turned back to see thick dust clouds billowing outward behind them, and almost immediately he lost sight of the leading Humvee some thirty meters behind.

He looked ahead and again judged the distance. Too far. Another shot rang out, rocketing by with a supersonic crack somewhere above their heads.

"It's not working!" Rachel screamed, ducking down but this time valiantly keeping control of the jeep.

Ethan looked about the jeep desperately, and saw the water canisters in the rear. Without further thought he scrambled into the back and unstrapped one of the canisters as he shouted above the wind.

"Straighten out, stop swerving!"

Rachel kept the wheel straight, and Ethan hefted the big canister onto the rear of the jeep, looking up through the diminishing clouds of dust behind them. He saw the Humvee surge into view barely twenty meters behind, and instantly he hefted the canister over the back of the jeep. The heavy plastic container bulged as it hit the desert floor, bouncing wildly.

The Humvee's driver glimpsed the canister at the last moment and swerved violently to avoid it as it barreled past his wheels. The rifleman in the rear leaped aside as the canister struck the side of the Humvee and exploded in a dazzling burst of crystalline water that vaporized into spray on the wind.

Ethan unstrapped a second canister, but even as he did so the Humvee changed its position slightly, moving out to the left of the jeep's track and pursuing it from a safer position.

"Damn."

Ethan struggled back into the passenger seat,

glancing over his shoulder at the Humvee, still twenty meters behind but closing, the face of the driver brightly illuminated by the setting sun. He could see that the soldiers were wearing sunglasses and that the man in the rear was reloading his rifle. Another few seconds and he would be too close to miss.

Ethan looked down at his rucksack. An insidious thought crept into his mind, and he pulled out his cell phone before looking across at Rachel again.

"When I tell you, turn hard right, understand?"

Rachel nodded once without taking her eyes off the desert ahead.

Ethan reached down into his rucksack and pulled out one of the explosive devices. Quickly, he pulled the detonating probe from within the plastic explosive, and then turned on the cell phone attached to it. The screen lit up and a simple menu appeared. In Hebrew.

"Christ's sake."

Ethan quickly cycled through the menu as he heard the Humvee's growling engine closing on them. He changed the settings to English and then found what he was looking for. He grabbed his own phone, punching in the number of the bomb's cell phone before resetting its menu and plugging the detonator back into the explosive.

Rachel watched him from the corner of her eye. For a moment he thought that she was looking at him, but then realized that she was looking past him. Ethan turned to see the Humvee drawing alongside, three grim-faced soldiers glaring at them. The rifleman in the rear slowly brought his weapon to bear.

Ethan swallowed thickly as a prayer that he hadn't heard since his school days passed unbidden through his mind. He pressed dial on his cell phone.

"Turn right!"

Rachel yanked the jeep's wheel over and the vehicle surged sideways across the plain, sending up a billowing cloud of dust between them and the Humvee. Ethan hurled the explosive device across the void between the two vehicles, watching it land in the rear of the Humvee as it struggled to match their turn. The rifleman in the rear tumbled backward and out of the vehicle, his shot flying wild and high above their heads. The two soldiers in the front took one look at the tiny device rattling around in the back and instantly leaped from their seats, hitting the desert floor hard amid roiling clouds of dust.

"Straighten out and get down!" Ethan shouted, pointing back toward the sunset.

Rachel jerked the jeep back onto its original course, as Ethan heard the dial tone suddenly beep in his ear. He grabbed Rachel's head and forced it down with his hand.

A crackling blast ripped the sky behind them as the Humvee was torn apart from within. Ethan turned to see the vehicle lurch out of control across the desert floor, hitting an angular chunk of rock and spiraling into the air to crash onto its back amid a cloud of twisted metal and spinning tires.

"Keep going!" Ethan shouted.

Rachel fixed her gaze ahead as Ethan strained again to look behind them.

The second Humvee was pulling up alongside the wreckage of the first, and he could see three specklike figures hauling themselves out of the dust and staggering toward it. He judged the distance to the airfield and allowed himself a brief sigh of relief.

"We'll make it, but only just."

Ahead against the brilliant canvas of the setting sun he could make out the shape of the low stone buildings scattered on the edge of the airfield. He pointed to the left of the runway.

"Head for that part," he shouted to Rachel. "Aaron landed into the wind from that direction, so he'll have to take off into the wind too."

Rachel guided the jeep toward the end of the runway, seeing the familiar silhouette of the de Havilland Beaver sitting on the tarmac with its engine running. Rachel pulled the jeep up alongside the airplane as Ethan vaulted from the passenger seat and grabbed his rucksack, looking out across the desert to see the remaining Humvee trailing a spiraling vortex of sun-gilded dust as it raced toward them.

He grabbed Rachel's unsteady hand as she staggered on legs weak with fatigue and fear.

"Come on!"

Together, they ran around to the port side of the de Havilland, jumping aboard as Aaron shot Ethan a questioning look over his shoulder from the cockpit.

"What the hell happened out there? We heard a blast! Where's Ayeem?"

"I'll explain on the way," Ethan shot back as he slammed the airplane's door shut. "Get us out of here!"

Aaron turned without another word as Safiya pushed the throttles to the firewall. The airplane responded instantly, surging forward and gathering speed along the runway. Ethan held on to his seat, peering through the opposite fuselage windows for a glimpse of their pursuers.

The Humvee had turned to attempt to intercept the aircraft, but Ethan could see that they wouldn't make it. The Beaver swayed and gyrated and then soared into the air, leaving the runway behind them as they climbed out into the brilliant evening sky.

Ethan strained across to peer out of a window, and saw the Humvee slowing down and drawing away from the airstrip, a tiny dot of black against a glowing golden desert tiger striped with long shadows.

Safiya raised the aircraft's flaps and turned around in her seat to look at Rachel, who sat in stony silence, tearstains coursing through the dusty grime coating her face. Safiya shot Ethan a harsh look.

"What the hell happened?"

Ethan wiped the grit from his eyes, squinting against the glare of the sunset blazing through the windshield.

"We got into the camp but the MACE guards caught Ayeem. I think he was covering for us. There was some kind of argument between them and Ayeem's friends, and then the guards started to give him a beating. I managed to film it and then drew their attention away. They chased us out here, shooting all the way."

Safiya glanced at Aaron, and then back at Ethan.

"We'll get you back to Jerusalem and get you cleaned up before we figure out a way of explaining all this."

Beside her, Aaron shook his head. "This isn't over yet. They've got backup."

Ethan looked in the direction that Aaron indicated with a severe nod.

Far out to the north against the darkening skies, the flashing navigation lights of a helicopter blinked toward them on an intercept course.

27

Can we outrun them?"

Safiya's voice was pinched with anxiety as she stared at the distant lights blinking an ominous red against the deep-blue evening sky.

"I don't know," Aaron said. "But whatever happens, they'll be able to land wherever we do."

Ethan moved across to the starboard side of the aircraft and looked at the lights that seemed to come closer with every passing second.

"They want the film I shot," he said quickly. "Footage of atrocities against the Bedouin will see MACE in a Jerusalem court, and a successful conviction could open up a whole legal precedent for Israel." Ethan turned to Aaron. "Ayeem's son disappeared in the Negev and he thinks that MACE has something to do with it."

"Where is Ayeem?" Safiya demanded.

"I left him there," Ethan said. "As long as we've got this footage, there's nothing that they can do to him without further implicating themselves. We have to get it back to Ambassador Cutler in Jerusalem. MACE is in possession of the remains that Lucy discovered and that implicates them in whatever's happened to her."

Safiya looked to her husband, who gripped the controls of the aircraft tighter in his chunky fists.

"We can't land back at Herzliya. They'll be onto us the moment we set down."

Ethan ran a hand through his tousled hair, watching desert sand spill onto the floor of the fuselage.

"How close can you get us to Gaza?"

Both Aaron and Safiya stared at him in disbelief.

"Are you insane?" Aaron uttered. "Gazan airspace is restricted. If we deviate from our flight plan, the IDF will intercept us within moments."

"That's right," Ethan replied. "You'll be forced to land under armed escort and arrested either by the Israeli police or the army." He jabbed a thumb in the direction of the helicopter. "Better that than have MACE's goons waiting for you on the ground."

Aaron shook his head, muttering something under his breath before glancing at Rachel.

"Are you okay?"

Rachel's vacant gaze drifted across to meet the pilot's, and for a moment she did not respond, as though she were a thousand miles away and had only just heard the question.

"I'm fine," she whispered, her voice almost inaudible through their headphones.

Over the engine noise, the rhythmic thunder of the helicopter's blades reverberated through the fuselage. A blinding white light suddenly pierced the interior, sweeping back and forth. Ethan shielded his eyes and looked away. A rush of static hissed and crackled, followed by a commanding voice.

"*X-Ray Uniform Delta Seven One, reverse your course immediately and return to Bar Yehuda. That is an order, over.*"

Aaron glanced over his shoulder at Ethan, who shook his head.

"They beat Ayeem and they shot at us. You don't want to go back there."

Aaron looked across at the helicopter, before reaching down and changing the radio's frequency. "They're speaking in English, so Israeli air traffic isn't on their channel. Hold on."

Ethan barely had time to grip his seat before Aaron yanked back on the control column. The de Havilland surged upward, sweeping up and over the helicopter while falling back as it lost airspeed. The helicopter jerked away, the pilot clearly surprised by the maneuver. Aaron dropped down behind the helicopter, the Beaver's wings waggling in the slipstream. The helicopter pilot swerved left in an attempt to clear the de Havilland from his tail, but Aaron hung on grimly as Safiya deftly adjusted the throttles to compensate.

"Since when are you the Red Baron?" she snapped. "You can hardly shoot them down."

"No, but they can't shoot at us either."

Ethan listened as Aaron began trying to contact Israeli air traffic control, but after several attempts he shook his head, cursing in Yiddish and turning to look at Ethan over the back of his seat.

"They're blocking our radios, some kind of electronic countermeasures."

Ethan felt a sluice of despair flood his guts. Ahead the sun had completely vanished, setting swiftly over the Mediterranean. The horizon was marked by a rapidly fading orange light and the earth below enshrouded in a blanket of darkness, while ahead a thousand tiny lights sparkled across the Gaza Strip and the town of Sderot.

Quite suddenly, the helicopter before them veered

upward sharply in a rapid ascent and braking maneuver that the de Havilland could not hope to match. The sound of the powerful thumping rotors thundered past in the night sky above.

"They're cutting in behind us," Safiya said, straining in her seat to watch the helicopter settle in close behind them.

"They won't shoot us down," Ethan said. "They can't take the risk of us having spoken to the controller before they blocked our radios."

"Yeah, great, Ethan, except that we don't know what they're saying now," Aaron pointed out. "They could be reporting us as having terrorists aboard, bombs, anything."

Ethan felt a new wave of panic flooding his stomach. Faced with the threat of a potential aerial suicide attack, there was no telling what the IDF might do. Without radio contact, they would most likely have a play-it-safe policy of blowing any suspicious aircraft out of the sky before it reached populated areas.

Ethan looked ahead to the sparkling lights of the Gaza Strip. The clattering of the engine and the rhythmic thumping of the helicopter blades reverberating through the fuselage rattled any remaining self-doubt from his mind. You've screwed it up, Ethan. Best thing he could do now was remove any responsibility from Aaron, Safiya, and Rachel before they were all caught.

"How far is it to Gaza now?" Ethan asked.

"Two minutes and we'll be over Sderot," Aaron replied quickly. "We could try for Yasser Arafat Airfield in southern Gaza but it's not great for landing. The IDF bombed it years ago."

"I can't let them get hold of this footage. Take us as close as you dare to the Gaza Strip and turn north when we reach it."

"What the hell are you going to do?"

Ethan reached out to the row of parachutes strapped to the rear of the fuselage.

"I'll get out over the Strip and find my way back into Israel afterward."

"You . . . can't," Aaron stammered. "It's dark out there and you'll have no way of seeing where you'll land."

"Nor will they," Ethan said. "Besides, there's a lot of open ground on the edges of the Strip near Nahal Oz."

"Have you ever even used one of those before?" Safiya asked, gesturing to the parachute.

Ethan managed a meager smile that he hoped convinced them where it failed to convince him. "I was a Marine not an airborne soldier, but how hard can it be? Jump, pull, pray."

From beside him, he could see Rachel watching as he slipped into the parachute harnesses and tightened them over his shoulders.

"This isn't the best way to protect that footage," she murmured. In the darkness, her features were lit only by the soft green glow from the instrument panel. "We could end up losing both you and the camera."

"While I'm in Gaza I can find out if Lucy is being held there, and I know people who can help get me out again."

Rachel got to her feet, swaying as the aircraft rocked through the night sky.

"Are you sure it's Lucy who you're going to be searching for?"

Ethan forced himself to look into her eyes without flinching.

"There isn't anyone else there," he said. "If there was, I would have found her before now."

"How do I know that's the truth?" Rachel said above

the engine noise. "Selby and Woods showed you that photograph of your fiancée, and the first chance you've got you're abandoning me to go running about in Gaza. How the hell is that supposed to help me find Lucy?"

"Israel wouldn't let me into Gaza to find Joanna," Ethan snapped, "just like they won't let us into Gaza to find Lucy. This is the perfect opportunity. Are you willing to throw that away?"

Rachel glared at him, her mouth open to reply but no words coming forth. Ethan turned away and checked his harness before gripping the de Havilland's interior door handle and looking ahead toward the cockpit.

"Ready?"

Safiya nodded, her dark eyes unreadable in the shadowy cockpit. Ethan turned and yanked the door open.

The night air blasted into his face, the aircraft yawing to one side as Aaron fought to overcome the sudden aerodynamic imbalance. Ethan peered over the edge of the fuselage as Aaron gained control and turned swiftly north. Streetlights flickered three thousand feet below, and out to the west Ethan could just make out the surface of the Mediterranean reflecting the night sky like a vast, shimmering mirror.

Aaron had timed his turn well, and was flying almost directly over the unpopulated wasteland between Gaza and Israel. Ethan shouted to Rachel above the buffeting wind.

"I'll try to get back into Israel by the morning through Eraz. Inform the Foreign Ministry of what's happened; they should be able to help me through." Rachel nodded, her face strangely vacant. Ethan fixed her with a serious gaze, trying to assure himself that she understood him. "You'll have to close the door behind me."

Rachel edged across to the doorway. Ethan looked down at the twinkling lights of Gaza far below. He closed his eyes for a moment, taking a few deep breaths. *Get a grip and do it. If you've got nothing, you've everything to gain.*

Ethan crouched and then hurled himself out into the blackened void.

The windblast smashed into him, flailing his body as he spun away into the darkness. The howl of the Beaver's engine and the shuddering blades of the helicopter vanished as he plunged downward. Ethan gripped the cord of his parachute and yanked hard.

The parachute rippled free as the cityscape beneath gyrated wildly through his vision, and then he heard a dull crack in the sky above and was yanked upright as the parachute blossomed open. He swung in absolute silence for a few moments before checking above him. The broad dome of the parachute glowed faintly against the inky night sky above.

He breathed a sigh of relief, and looked down.

The Gaza Strip beckoned, ten thousand darkened alleys and streets populated by a people who had been persecuted for over half a century. A land and a people he knew well, now less than a thousand feet beneath him. For a few moments, he found himself reveling in the silence of the night air, and realized that he had not slept for at least twenty-four hours. Not the first time, he reminded himself, his eyes itching as he became aware of his exhaustion.

The night breeze was blowing him slightly north and west. He began trying to judge his landing point amid the dense rooftops, perhaps half a mile north of where he was now and maybe five hundred feet below. A distant car horn sounded and Ethan looked out across the city. There, rows of headlights drifted in relative silence, but among them, two sets weaved and twisted through the darkness parallel to his course.

The de Havilland and the helicopter would have been an unusual sight above the Strip. As he had feared, he had been spotted. He would need all of his wits about him in order to negotiate a safe passage and not be abducted as Lucy Morgan and countless others had been, for only insurgents would move to intercept him with such reckless speed.

Ethan looked up to check his parachute one last time before his landing, and as he did so something caught his eye floating in the immense night above him. "Oh, for Christ's sake."

A thousand feet above, just visible in the glow from Gaza's feeble streetlights, another parachute blossomed against the night sky.

28

Rachel, close the door!"

Safiya's voice was snatched away on the howling wind as she saw Rachel yank a second parachute from its rack on the fuselage wall, strapping the harnesses over her shoulders in the same way that Ethan had done.

Safiya glimpsed Ethan's parachute billow open behind the de Havilland as she scrambled between the cockpit seats and rushed toward Rachel, grabbing her by the shoulders and holding her back.

"Don't be a fool, *sadiqati*! You can't jump!"

Rachel strained to break free. "My daughter could be down there!"

Safiya wrapped one arm across Rachel's chest, leaning back so that her weight would prevent Rachel from leaping out. "Yes she could, but what good will it do her if you go and get yourself kidnapped, or worse?"

Unexpectedly, Rachel backed away from the opening and turned to face Safiya, gently breaking her grasp.

"You know why Ethan became the way he is?" Rachel shouted above the wind. "He's half a person, isn't he? Nothing like he used to be. I don't want to end up that way."

Safiya stared at her for a long beat, desperately searching for a reply, but she could find nothing. Rachel turned and without further hesitation hurled herself from the aircraft and plunged into the void.

Safiya watched her vanish into the darkness before hauling the de Havilland's door shut, cutting off the noise. She staggered back into the copilot's seat.

"You sure you don't want to go as well?" Aaron uttered. "I don't know how the hell we're going to explain this when we land."

Safiya shook her head slowly, glancing at the helicopter's lights flashing in the darkness off their starboard wing.

"We will tell the authorities that nobody boarded at Bar Yehuda, that it is all a mistake."

"You think they'll believe that?" Aaron snorted.

"They're more likely to believe that than the truth."

Ethan grabbed the guidance cords of his parachute, yanking them sideways as he aimed for a yawning chasm of pitch blackness near a tight knot of apartment buildings. A single, flickering streetlight intermittently illuminated what might once have been a school nearby, now obscured by rubble and litter and hemmed in by two buildings bearing the scars of artillery strikes. On the night air wafted the salty odor of the nearby ocean, tainted with the acrid stench of sewage that ran openly along the gutters of Gaza's streets as dark, thick, and dangerous as the shadows that concealed it.

The inky blackness loomed up swiftly and Ethan braced himself for the impact, pulling down on the cords at the last moment to slow his descent as he belatedly considered the possibility that he could end up breaking either his legs or pelvis. The unforgiving concrete rushed past as his feet slammed into the ground. He managed to run a few paces and then rolled, hitting the ground hard amid a cloud of dust that clogged his throat.

The parachute fluttered down beside him as he struggled to his feet, unclipping his harness and hauling it in. He turned and looked up into the sky. The second parachute was drifting down toward him but clearly wasn't going to hit the same spot. He could detect slight movements as the jumper tried desperately to control their descent.

Voices sounded in the darkness, a flourish of urgent Arabic closing in on him from nearby. Shouts echoed from the main road on the other side of the derelict buildings as a car screeched to a halt and its doors slammed. Heavy feet pounded the earth.

Ethan turned and dashed into the first alley he could see that would take him in the same direction as the parachute above him, his own still bundled under his arm. He plunged into the shadows, tossing the parachute through a shattered doorway as he ran through the darkness, praying he wouldn't break a leg on some unseen obstacle. Something crashed into his shin and he cursed through gritted teeth, staggering onward through the darkness.

The end of the alley broke out into another, larger passage running between two skeletal buildings emaciated by the rigors of war. Ethan checked both ways before sprinting between them. The parachute passed directly overhead, visible barely a hundred feet up in the narrow strip of night sky above, swerving left and right as it plummeted downward.

Ethan ran hard and burst out onto the edge of a dusty wasteland of unused foundations filled with jagged chunks of masonry, razor wire, and abandoned, burned-out vehicles.

The parachute was twenty feet above the center of the clearing, and Ethan knew for sure that Rachel was the jumper. Without real control she would almost certainly break bones if she hit the rocks.

"Rachel! Pull hard on both handles, now!"

He could just make out Rachel's head turn to look at him, her expression of surprise, and then she yanked down on both of the handles. The parachute slowed rapidly and Ethan heard a thump that made him wince as Rachel hit the ground. Behind him, a fresh chorus of angry Arabic erupted from the darkness.

They had heard him.

Ethan dodged between the ragged boulders of concrete, careful not to catch himself on dense webs of rusting steel braces poking out like lances in the darkness. Ahead, he saw Rachel's parachute rippling to the ground and a body lying inert in the darkness.

Ethan sprinted the last few meters and skittered down alongside Rachel's body. To his relief she lay sprawled in the center of a large patch of coarse-grain sand and gravel. She sat upright as Ethan yanked off her harness.

"Are you okay?" he asked.

"I think so," she murmured as though waking from a dream, and she stared at the soft sand beneath her. "That was lucky, wasn't it?"

The shouts behind them became louder, and Ethan glimpsed swiftly moving figures obscuring the streetlight filtering through the alleys nearby.

"I wouldn't call this lucky," he said urgently. "Can you walk?"

With Ethan's help Rachel struggled to her feet, and

he quickly led her away from the pursuing voices, dodging between the rubble and detritus clogging their way. He kept low and headed for the silhouettes of derelict buildings.

"Where are we going?"

"Anywhere but here," Ethan replied. "What the hell were you thinking?"

"I told you, there is nothing that I won't do to find Lucy."

Ethan didn't reply, running instead toward another narrow alleyway that cut between the shattered hulks of the buildings ahead. The voices behind them were calling out to one another, short bursts of Arabic flowing back and forth like gunfire through the night. Another flurry of excited exclamations heralded the discovery of Rachel's discarded parachute.

"Who are they?" Rachel asked.

"I don't know and I don't want to."

"I thought you said you knew people who lived here."

"I don't know everyone! Come on."

They plunged into the safety of the nearest alley, the choking stench of feces overpowering them in the confined spaces and the splash of puddles beneath their feet echoing through the darkness until Ethan slowed. Ahead, a brightly lit road was filled with the sounds of voices. He could hear music playing in the distance from one of the thousands of cafés scattered across Gaza. The figures of people walked past, strangers silhouetted against streetlights.

Ethan turned to look behind. He could hear the voices of their pursuers crossing the open ground, closing in on them. They would reach the alleyway within moments. He turned to Rachel.

"We're going to stand out like a sore thumb. Just walk behind me and try to look normal."

Rachel shot him an uncertain look, but Ethan turned and with a deep breath walked out into the street and turned immediately right.

The street was narrow, with ancient, battered cars and taxis parked haphazardly by the curbs. A cyclist rattled past and looked at them curiously as they made their way along the street, while a young boy sitting in a makeshift carriage being pulled by a mule stared openly at them as they passed. The music from a café on the opposite side of the street became louder, and Ethan could see from the periphery of his vision old men wearing traditional Arab garments sitting outside in the warm evening air smoking hookahs and drinking hot, sweet coffee. They stopped talking as Ethan and Rachel passed by on the other side of the street, watching them with intense gazes.

Ethan searched for a side alley that they could vanish into, and was rewarded with a dimly lit street twenty meters ahead and on the opposite side of the road.

"This way," he motioned, crossing the street with purposeful strides, Rachel struggling to keep up behind him.

The music from the café behind them fell silent.

Ethan glimpsed a car pull into the street, headlights sweeping accusing beams toward them as they walked. The handful of people walking along the street suddenly disappeared in silence, drifting into houses as though obeying some unheard command. He glimpsed shutters on windows closing, saw the old men abandon their hookahs to vanish inside the café.

The car accelerated toward them with a squeal of scorched tires.

"Go, now!

Ethan shoved Rachel toward the alleyway, running after her as the car bore down on them, its screaming engine battering the night air. He looked over his shoulder to see the doors opening as it skidded to a halt ten meters away, men leaping from the vehicle with weapons in their hands. Hoods, boots, bandanas, and balaclavas, dark and glowering eyes filled with hatred and anger.

29

Ethan plunged into the alley behind Rachel, running hard as they dashed between the narrow walls, dodging abandoned litter and leaping the rusting carcass of an old bicycle. Rachel burst out into another street, this one narrower still, looking left and then right as Ethan rushed out behind her.

Another café to their left stood with chairs abandoned outside on the pavement. A pram with a missing wheel lay on its side on the opposite side of the road, and somewhere above them a series of window shutters slammed shut. At both ends of the street, cars accelerated toward them.

Ethan turned and saw the shapes of men rushing toward them through the alley. He felt his guts twist deep inside him as panic fluttered through his chest. The cars screamed up to them, armed and masked men leaping from the interiors with assault rifles in their hands. Ethan moved closer to Rachel, and realized that he had failed to protect her.

"Game's up," he said.

In the abandoned street Ethan raised his hands, watching as a group of fifteen or so men poured out of the alley behind them, AK-47s in their hands and un-imaginable thoughts running through their minds.

Within seconds Ethan and Rachel were surrounded by shouting Palestinians, several of whom began punching the air and firing loud staccato shots from their rifles into the night sky. Ethan placed a hand on Rachel's forearm and squeezed it as reassuringly as he could.

"We'll be okay," he whispered.

From behind him, a gruff voice shouted out in broken English, "Get on the ground, hands on your head!"

"We're American," Ethan said, "and we're looking for—"

Something hard cracked across the back of his legs and he collapsed, his knees smashing painfully on the unforgiving concrete. He had just enough time to see Rachel being grabbed by two men, and then a musty-smelling sack was shoved over his head.

JERUSALEM

"We lost them."

Spencer Malik stood behind a MACE technician operating a computer and two monitors, one of which was filled with the face of a helicopter pilot glowing in the light of his instruments.

"How the hell can you lose a damned airplane?"

"They bailed out," the pilot explained. *"Israeli air traffic control ordered us to cease jamming their signals. We saw two 'chutes go down somewhere in the Gaza Strip. We're tracking them with cameras but they've been grabbed, probably by insurgents. We're having trouble keeping them in sight outside of Gaza airspace."*

"Does air traffic know that anyone has bailed out?"

"Not yet. My guess is that whatever they've been up to,

the pilots are not going to admit anything to the IDF. Best we'll get is a detention and questioning, but we can't prove a thing."

Warner had the camera footage, Malik reasoned, and his priority was getting it back to Israel without MACE being able to intercept him. Now Malik had to find the little bastard before he managed to get to any of the crossing points on the Gazan border. Byron Stone was due to arrive soon, and if Israel got hold of the footage, heads would roll. He had the distinct impression that his would be first.

"Let the aircraft go," Malik said quickly, "stay on the refugees."

Malik looked down at the technician.

"How soon can we have a Valkyrie drone over the Strip?"

"An hour," the technician replied, "but it would have to be cleared by Israel first."

Malik nodded, looking at the helicopter pilot. "Relay the camera's tracking data here."

The pilot said something over his intercom to a crew member in the rear of the helicopter. Instantly, a grainy image from a night-vision camera appeared, following a convoy of four cars through the streets of Gaza.

Malik watched the screen for several seconds before making his decision.

"Track them to their destination. Mark the coordinates and relay them here. I'll organize clearance for the UAV."

"Roger that."

The helicopter pilot's image vanished, and the technician turned to look up at Malik.

"Israel's not going to give us UAV clearance over the Gaza Strip easily."

Malik looked thoughtfully at the screen. Having a foreign-owned, built, and armed unmanned aerial vehicle marauding over Gaza wasn't going to be a walk-over, but Israel's deeply ingrained xenophobia had served MACE well in the past.

"Get all of the video data downloaded to my work-station. All Israel needs to know is that we're tracking terrorists who may pose a threat. Enhance anything that may give that impression from the footage and remove everything that suggests otherwise."

30

EVANGELICAL COMMUNITY INSTITUTE
IVY CITY, WASHINGTON DC

Lucas Tyrell disliked most all medical institutions. But more than that he disliked the clinically insane who haunted them, those who had crossed the line between reality and oblivion. The fact that the Evangelical Institute reminded him of the hospital in which his brother had died so many years ago did nothing to comfort him.

The building was modern, smoked-glass windows stark against white paneled walls blazing in the midday sun, overlooking freshly mown lawns and quiet, shady gardens. He followed Nicola Lopez through a reinforced glass door into the interior of the hospital, more like a rest home than a refuge for the crazies. Gone were the days of iron bars and locks. A sign on a wall in flowing script caught his attention as he passed by.

We do not restrict or restrain. We rehabilitate.

"How many patients do you have here?" Lopez asked the female nurse who met them at the reception desk and led them down an immaculate white corridor.

"One hundred twenty-eight at the moment," came the serene reply, as though even the staff were strung out on sedatives.

"No murderers or other felons?"

"No, although some of our clients are former convicts who suffered breakdowns in the prison system. We analyze them first to ensure they're not playing the mental card to get onto the wards permanently." She smiled. "Many find God while in our care."

Tyrell glanced around as they walked, seeing frail-looking patients who were being guided gently along by orderlies. Soft instrumental music played through speakers concealed in the ceiling panels.

"What's Daniel Neville's history?" he asked the nurse.

"He was brought here four months ago by the MPD after a drug incident over on Logan. He'd been found near death in a crack den and rushed to General Hospital Southeast. They managed to stabilize him, but by then the damage was done."

"What's his condition?" Lopez asked.

"Daniel Neville suffered oxygen starvation to the cerebral cortex as a result of heart failure brought on by his overdose. He has lost some motor function and suffers from various psychological and physical disorders."

"What sort of medication is he on?" Tyrell pressed. "Can he be considered a suitable witness in a court case?"

The nurse frowned.

"Daniel is currently on a prescription of lithium to maintain the chemical balance in his brain, but his concepts of time, space, and judgment are severely distorted. His bouts of depression produce symptoms of mania and extreme paranoia that are difficult to control. I'd imagine most attorneys would reject any testimony from him."

Lopez cast a doubtful glance at Tyrell.

"What blood group is Daniel?" Tyrell asked.

"O-negative, the rarest type."

Tyrell and Lopez exchanged a look but said nothing more as they turned left into another corridor that led to a set of steel gates blocking their path to the corridor beyond. A tall, rangy man in a blue jumpsuit swabbed the floors as they walked past, his face hidden behind a mop of shaggy blond hair. Outside the gates stood a robust-looking man in a security guard's outfit; he moved to meet them.

"These detectives are here to question Daniel Neville," the nurse explained to the security guard.

The guard shook his head.

"I'm afraid Daniel Neville is required to remain in isolation," he said politely.

"On whose orders?" the nurse asked, surprised.

"Chief medical officer," the guard responded calmly. "Doctor and patient confidentiality."

"And you are?" Tyrell inquired.

"Michael Shaw. I'm responsible for security here on the ward."

"We need to speak with Daniel Neville," Tyrell insisted. "We can arrange warrants if we have to, but we'd prefer to do this on a voluntary bas—"

"Mr. Neville signed a confidentiality agreement with his doctor upon his admission," Shaw said firmly. "I doubt that warrants would have any effect."

"We can obtain a subpoena from the district attorney," Lopez challenged.

Michael Shaw looked apologetic but shrugged his broad shoulders.

"I'm sorry. I've got my orders and I just can't let you guys in."

"Lives could depend on what Daniel Neville may know," Tyrell pressed.

Michael Shaw was about to reply, but the voice that Tyrell heard boomed like thunder down the corridor from behind them.

"You get your hands off m'boy!"

31

Tyrell turned to see a formidable bulk of a woman barreling down the corridor toward them. Her huge frame was draped in a bright floral dress that contrasted sharply with her dark skin, her jowls wobbling as she charged. Michael Shaw tried to block her path as his composed expression collapsed into something akin to panic.

"Mrs. Neville, you've already been asked to leave the building and—"

"You get your hands off m'boy!" the woman thundered, raising one flabby arm to point like a shotgun at Tyrell as a pair of nurses leaped out of her way. "You get yo' hands offa him or I'll take that badge o' yours and shove it up yo' ass!"

The woman sent Michael Shaw spinning aside into the wall with one forearm as though swatting a fly. Tyrell glimpsed even the redoubtable Lopez take a cautious step back. He gave Mrs. Neville ample room as she jabbed a finger at the gates behind him.

"You ain't seen enough done t'im yet?" she challenged, glaring at Tyrell and Lopez in turn. "You think m'boy ain't been through enough?"

"Mrs. Neville," Lopez said carefully, "we just came here to ask Daniel a few questions about—"

"Well, he ain't got no answers fo' any of you! I tol' you all before to leave him be!"

Lopez shook her head. "We wanted to find out—"

"Then go ask someplace else!" Mrs. Neville bellowed before rounding on Tyrell. "And I don't care if you a brother or if you ain't, you outta here right now before I—"

"Shut up!" Tyrell snapped.

A humming silence filled the corridor as Mrs. Neville's eyes widened in surprise. Tyrell gave her just long enough for what he'd said to sink in before continuing. "We came here to help Daniel. We think he may have been abused, maybe even the victim of a crime."

Mrs. Neville stared back and forth between them and her eyes narrowed.

"How'd I know tha's the truth?"

"What's your name, ma'am?" Tyrell asked.

"Claretta," she replied cautiously. "And don't give me no horseshit now, y'hear?"

"Daniel is hardly able to commit crimes while inside this hospital," Tyrell pointed out. "We're here because we think he's the victim and we want to know what happened."

Claretta Neville looked at him for a long moment.

"How come none o' you been here askin' about this afore now?"

"Something happened," Tyrell said. "Another victim whose pathology matches your son's. We need to speak to Daniel."

Claretta sighed mightily, reversing her copious frame and parking it on a chair in the corridor that vanished beneath her floral dress.

"There ain't nobody seein' him," she said softly. "He's in quarantine."

Tyrell glanced at Michael Shaw before speaking.

"Quarantine?" he echoed. "You haven't seen him?"

"Only briefly, to bring him his meals," Claretta said. "They say it ain't safe to be about him an' all."

Lopez squatted down and took one of Claretta's hands in her own.

"Can you tell us what happened to Daniel?" she asked.

"His line was crack cocaine," Claretta whispered. "Part of their colors, to run with the gangs they had to be on somethin'. He got too high one night and was picked up by the meds on Fourth. Got a trip in th' ambulance, so they said."

"What happened next?" Tyrell asked.

"He got discharged into the care of the people that run this place—good people, so they said."

"He was brought directly here?" Lopez asked.

"Nah," Claretta said. "They says he was, but I know he was taken someplace else for a few hours. They's been lyin' ever since I came here."

Michael Shaw stepped in quickly.

"We both know that's not true. Daniel was very sick and probably has no idea what was happening to him after he overdosed and—"

"The hell would you know about it?" Claretta snarled. "You just some lily-white shit-fo'-brains security guard."

Tyrell looked at Shaw.

"Just give us a moment here, okay?"

Shaw's skin flushed red, but he turned and strode a few paces down the corridor. Tyrell looked back down at Claretta, who continued while glaring at the guard.

"They took Daniel to someplace in the District along with some other guys he knew, and tripped them out on drugs again."

"What happened next?" Lopez pressed gently. "Did they drug all of the kids there?"

"They's were all gang colors, so Daniel said: Columbia Heights, Trinidad, boys from all over."

"Do you know what they did to Daniel?"

Claretta's features tightened.

"He said they's all crackers about their tests. He said they took their blood, and that some of the kids died in some kind of experiments."

A tear trickled down her face.

Lopez spoke softly to her. "What kind of experiments?"

"The eternal flame, the covenant of God and man, burns for us in our blood," Claretta whispered, as though reciting some medieval verse. "We shall take this bread, for it will sustain us. That was what Daniel said they kept whisperin' to him, that his blood was special and that it would join him to God with the 'men of renown.' What the hell does that mean?"

Claretta's formidable visage was haunted now as she stared into space. Tyrell looked up at the closed doors beside him, and quickly came to a decision.

"Claretta, I want you to get up and hit me," he whispered.

Claretta looked up at Tyrell with widening eyes.

"What the hell's you talking about?"

"Hit me," Tyrell said, "and make a damned fuss about it. I need that guard out of here for five minutes, 'kay?"

Claretta looked at Tyrell for a moment, and then lurched out of her seat and swung a blow that landed under Tyrell's jaw with enough force to hurl him sideways into the metal gates as Claretta's voice thundered out in his ears.

"You goddamn hypocritical motherf—"

Lopez jumped up to restrain Claretta as Michael Shaw bolted back toward them down the corridor. Tyrell staggered upright, regaining his vision as he saw Lopez twist Claretta Neville's arm up behind her back as she ranted and raged. Tyrell gestured to her as he looked at Shaw.

"Jesus, get her out of here! Nicola, help him out."

Michael Shaw nodded, grabbing Claretta's other arm as between them they began hauling her, kicking and screaming, away down the corridor.

Tyrell waited until they were out of sight, wishing he'd figured out another way of creating a distraction as he massaged his throbbing face, then turned to the young nurse who had witnessed the entire exchange.

"I need access to Daniel Neville."

"I don't know what you're doing, but I don't have the authority to let you—"

"If you don't open those doors, right now," Tyrell said, "I'll arrest you for obstruction of justice. Whoever employs Michael Shaw doesn't want anybody to see Daniel Neville, and I need to know why. You can accompany me if you wish."

"But—"

"The keys," Tyrell rumbled. "You're not paid to obstruct the law, ma'am, and I doubt this hospital will pay your court costs."

The nurse was flustered and gasped an expletive in despair, then yanked her keys from her belt before opening the metal gates to the corridor beyond.

"Fourth room on the right," she uttered, and handed him another key. "You'll need this; the door is always locked."

Tyrell slipped through the gates and edged his way down the white corridor, looking in through the plastic windows of each door as he passed. Small rooms, half-darkened, held ghostly forms that stared back out at him with eyes devoid of understanding, as though from other worlds.

Tyrell reached the fourth door, peering into what appeared to be an entirely darkened room, the blinds pulled shut on the window. A figure was just visible lying on the bed.

Tyrell eased the key into the lock, turning it as quietly as he could until the barrel clicked. He gently pushed down on the handle and opened the door, catching a whiff of disinfectant as he slipped into the darkness.

The room was bare but for the bed and a small sink, more like a cell than a hospital room. An intravenous line ran from an IV pole down beneath the sheets where Daniel Neville lay. Tyrell could see the boy's scalp, coils of braided black hair tight against the skin but also scattered across his pillow where they had fallen out. Tyrell edged closer, peering over the top of the sheets to see the boy's face.

Tyrell stifled a gag reflex as he caught the odor of putrefying flesh. The boy's eyes were closed, the lids laced with veins that spread like a web across his face, the once rich black skin now ashen and transparently thin. Forcing himself to overcome his disgust, Tyrell reached out and eased the sheets back.

Daniel Neville's body was a graying mass of decaying tissue, the skin dry and breaking up into plates like the surface of a scorched riverbed. Desiccated slabs of skin and flesh littered the bedsheet beneath him, as though his skin was turning to scales and falling from his body. His abdomen heaved with rapid, hyperventilating breaths. Overcome with morbid fascination, Tyrell leaned closer to one of the boy's scaled lesions.

One hand jerked up and grabbed Tyrell's face like a

gray spider, the smell of the boy's ruined skin thick in his nostrils as he jerked back in horror, yanking the skeletal fingers from his face.

Daniel Neville stared up at Tyrell with eyes as black as night, devoid of iris or pupils as though filled with ink, and a weak but keening cry rasped from his throat.

"Kill me!"

As Tyrell jerked backward in shock, he bumped into the nurse who stood behind him at the entrance to the room. Tyrell managed to find his voice.

"What the hell's happening to him?" he uttered.

"Acute hemolytic reaction," she whispered. "Worst I've ever seen."

Tyrell staggered out of the room and sucked in a deep breath of air as the nurse closed the door behind him. He slowly made his way back to the gates just as Lopez appeared.

"You find him?" she asked.

Tyrell nodded slowly. "What's left of him. Who owns this hospital?"

Lopez retrieved a notebook from her pocket as they turned and walked toward the hospital exit.

"It's owned and maintained by the American Evangelical Alliance."

"Eternal Flame," Tyrell murmured thoughtfully, hearing Claretta Neville's words echoing through his mind. "Ain't that a radio or television show that's got something to do with the alliance?"

"Television show." Lopez nodded. "Got a membership of about eight million. And then there's the same guy who does a radio broadcast out of DC called *This Bread* and . . ." Lopez stopped talking, looking at him.

"Eternal Flame, This Bread," Tyrell repeated. "Who's the pastor who hosts the shows?"

Lopez turned a page in her notebook.

"Kelvin Patterson, pastor of the American Evangelical Alliance. Last showed up on a televised stage rally with presidential candidate Senator Isaiah Black—some kind of charity gig involving blood donors for the city."

As Tyrell walked out of the hospital, Claretta Neville was waiting for him, her defiance and vigor very much back in evidence.

"You give me something t'ave faith in, Detective," she said, pointing a finger at him as he passed. "You give me somethin' to believe in and find out what they did to m'boy."

32

JABALIYA
GAZA STRIP

Breathe.

Ethan sucked in a mouthful of dusty air, trying to overcome what felt like steel bands encasing his lungs. The flustered beat of his heart reverberated through his chest like war drums, his frayed nerves scraping the lining of his stomach like a convict's nails against the stone walls of a cell.

He could see nothing through the coarse sack that was bound with rough cord around his neck, crushing his thorax and filling his nostrils with stale air. His arms were bound behind his back with rope that scoured the skin from his wrists and his knees ground painfully on an uneven floor of bare, rocky earth. He knelt with his head between his knees, kept breathing, and tried to refrain from weeping.

Fear wasn't an emotion that Ethan enjoyed checking out, but it scalded now like acid through his veins. Vertigo from his loss of spatial awareness caused his blackened world to gyrate and pitch around him, further fueling his asphyxia. He had been incarcerated by men who would cheerfully kill him with neither hubris nor regret. And so, in all likelihood, was Rachel. The steel bands around his chest tightened at the thought.

The men who had captured them had wasted no time. His shouts for calm and for Rachel's safety went unheeded, his body lifted by uncaring hands and shoved without ceremony into the back of a car before being driven through Gaza's streets.

His journey had ended with his body being carried from the car and through a doorway. The muted noise of Gaza outside had been brutally shut off with the slamming of a door, and then the cords around his wrists had been mercifully loosened. Any relief he may have felt was swept away as he was forced to clamber blindly down a ladder. He had sensed the closeness of the walls around him, tasted the odors of damp and dust, and felt the warm, heavy air clinging to his skin. He had known then without a doubt that his Palestinian captors were taking him to the only place where they could keep him from any Israeli rescue attempt.

Underground.

Ethan had long known of the network of tunnels that perforated the ancient soil beneath Gaza. The tunnels of Rafah were well known to most, the subject of Israel's wrath on many occasions as Palestinians used them to smuggle contraband from across the border with Egypt. This covert industry might have been left unchecked by Israel were it not for the parallel operations of insurgents bringing weapons and explosives into the Strip. But Gaza City itself was also a warren of interconnecting tunnels used to move men, goods, and equipment beyond the omnipresent eyes of Mossad, Shin Bet, and the Israeli Defense Force.

Ethan's captors had prodded, shoved, and jostled

him for what he estimated was perhaps fifty meters, the heat oppressive and the closeness of the earthen walls amplified by Ethan's blindness until it felt as though the entire world were collapsing in around him. They had then led him to a cavity in the floor where he sensed rather than saw a heavy wooden trapdoor being lifted before he was wedged into the tiny space. The last thing he felt was a boot slammed into his back to jam him down firmly into the hole and then the door shut just above his head.

Breathe.

Ethan focused, and some of the crushing anxiety eased as he forced images of Rachel and Joanna from his mind. He could only guess at how long he had been incarcerated. One, maybe two hours? Christ, he was losing it already. A real man would have controlled himself, maybe even slept a little to conserve energy, but Ethan was barely able to sleep at home in his own apartment with the door double-locked and a gun under his mattress, so the chances of his catching some shut-eye while in the grasp of suicidal militants in Gaza seemed mighty fucking remote. He was buzzing now on nervous energy, the kind that powered the muscles but ultimately drained the mind, poisoning it with paranoia, fear, and hallucinations.

The oppressive heat closed in around him in the darkness. It was joined by a chorus of voices reminding him that he had sallied valiantly forth to free one lost soul and had succeeded only in incarcerating two more. *Moron.* An image of his father appeared unbidden in his mind.

"You should have learned by now, Ethan," the great Harry Warner had said, wagging a thick finger at him, pale eyes glowering above the twisted bayonets of his

broad gray mustache. *"What the hell did you think you'd achieve resigning your commission and gallivanting around the globe with a damned camera? Why didn't you get a proper job like everyone else? You wouldn't have ended up in this goddamn mess!"*

He should have stayed in Chicago and not gotten involved. Doug Jarvis had a lot to answer for. Yet despite everything, somewhere within his tortured soul there remained a spirit that had not yet been extinguished, like a pale candle flame flickering alone in an immense darkness. Maybe he had a bit more of his father's indomitable gumption than he had realized. *If you've got nothing, you've everything to gain.* He could deal with this.

A brief burst of Arabic punctured the silence. *Damn.* The pale flame gusted out.

More voices from somewhere above—muffled, distant. A new and nauseating flush of panic churned within him. Having yearned to be freed, he now feared that they had come for him with murder in their minds. The gumption vanished. A deep thud startled him as heavy wood banged against the roof of his skull, and then he felt a sudden updraft of hot air being sucked from his prison as the trapdoor was yanked open. Rough hands grabbed him and hauled him from the hole. Ethan tried to stand but his legs would not respond and he sprawled awkwardly as unseen hands dragged him across the rough, uneven ground.

"Get up!"

Ethan struggled to his knees and somehow managed to command one of his tingling feet to shift beneath him. He staggered upright, swaying as stars of light sparkled in the darkness before his eyes.

"This way!"

A hand shoved him and he stumbled blindly forward, banging off the walls of the tunnel and dislodging chunks of earth and dust with his shoulders. He heard whispered exchanges from behind him and guessed that two men were following.

The air became slightly cooler, and the tone of the hushed voices changed as he emerged into what felt like a larger space. A hand grabbed his shoulder, turning him around and shoving him downward. Ethan slammed into a wooden chair that almost toppled backward beneath him. Before he could react he felt himself being bound again, this time to the chair itself, and for a brief moment he was almost comfortable as his weary body settled onto the chair.

A long silence ensued and he braced himself for any sudden impact. Something wrenched at the hood over his face and a harsh white light burst into his eyes. He blinked away from it, squinting and struggling to focus on his surroundings.

The room was surprisingly large, about five meters square and braced at the corners and the center by old but sturdy wooden pillars. The earthen ceiling was restrained by a simple latticework of timber beams, from which dangled a single unshielded lightbulb that illuminated the room with an unnatural glow. A handful of scattered crates and boxes lined the walls of the room, and in one corner two AK-47 rifles leaned against a large four-gallon water canister.

"Welcome."

Ethan squinted up and to his right to see a pair of dark eyes observing him. A thick scarf covered the rest of the man's face. He looked about twenty-five years old, his hair thick and black, coarse stubble peeking above the scarf. Ethan looked into those eyes and did not like what he saw there.

"Who are you?" he asked, already knowing the answer but eager to establish some sort of dialogue with his captors. Keep them talking, always keep them talking.

The dark eyes narrowed cruelly. "Are you that stupid?"

Ethan managed to hold the Palestinian's gaze with a thin veneer of bravado.

"You don't look like one of the good guys."

The man leaned close to him. "You parachuted into Gaza from an Israeli airplane at night. You don't look like one of the good guys either."

"Where is Rachel?"

The features creased into a smile that conveyed no hint of warmth or comfort. "She remains well."

"Let me see her."

The man straightened, glancing at his companion before whirling and plunging his fist deep into Ethan's stomach. A surge of air blasted from Ethan's lungs as his eyes almost burst from their sockets. Ethan gagged as he bolted forward over the blow, trying not to vomit as he strained to suck air back into his lungs.

"You may not," his captor said simply, above the blood rushing in Ethan's ears. "Who sent you here and why?"

Ethan sucked in another lungful of air, waves of nausea flushing and tingling like needles on his skin.

"Nobody sent us," he gasped. "We were forced out of our airplane over Gaza."

The Palestinian strolled across the room and grabbed a small chipped mug, dipping it into the open water canister and sipping from it as he returned to stand before Ethan.

"The airplane continued into Israeli airspace," he said quietly. "It was not damaged so there was no reason to escape from it. I will ask you one more time. If you do not answer me properly, I will make you very sorry that you ever encountered me. Who sent you and why?"

Ethan shook his head, slowly gaining control of his breathing.

"Nobody sent us. We're not Israeli. I'm American; so is Rachel. We were forced to jump from the airplane by an organization trying to stop us from reaching Jerusalem."

The Palestinian looked across at his companion, who remained impassive, standing with his arms folded and regarding Ethan from behind a scarf that scarcely veiled a thick beard.

"That, my friend, would seem highly unlikely, would it not?" Ethan's interrogator leaned close to him, the smell of tobacco thick on his breath. "If I were sitting where you are and you were questioning me, would you believe what you have just said?"

Ethan looked at the man and performed a rapid mental calculation.

"I'd wait and see what evidence turned up," he said.

A cruel smile creased the man's features. "Yes, so would I."

He raised a hand and clicked his fingers. Instantly, the bearded man grabbed something from inside one of the nearby crates. Ethan recognized his rucksack. The Palestinian reached inside and produced Ethan's camera, handing it to his companion.

The Palestinian held it to Ethan's face.

"This, my friend, is my evidence."

Ethan saw the screen change as the Palestinian cycled through the camera's menu and selected a video. He felt a deep chill as he saw the film of Ayeem being beaten by the MACE guards out in the Negev Desert, his Bedouin companions held at gunpoint nearby.

33

They weren't with us," Ethan said quickly, aware of the sweat soaking his skin. "The man being beaten was our Bedouin guide, Ayeem. He was captured by those guards in the desert."

The Palestinian's features tightened as sheet lightning danced behind his dark eyes.

"And you filmed it. How do you say? Something for the folks back home?"

"I filmed it and then shouted out to them," Ethan gasped. "If I had film of it, then they couldn't kill Ayeem. They've chased us from that moment onward."

The Palestinian sneered at him and stood upright, handing the camera back to his companion. They exchanged something and then he turned back to Ethan. Ethan saw one of the explosive devices he had stolen from the camp in the man's hands. The Palestinian's head blocked the light from the bulb. His voice was almost a whisper, but laden with an electric charge that crackled as he spoke.

"Each year, Israel attacks our homes with tanks and fighter planes. They kill innocent men, women, and children. They fire mortars at hospitals and United Nations buildings, and they shoot white-phosphorus rounds at fleeing Palestinians, burning them alive. They use remote-controlled drones to attack civilians hiding in buildings and then claim that they were being used as human shields." He set the device down at Ethan's feet and then reached down to his own waistband. From within it he withdrew a long, wickedly curved blade, a crescent of steel that glittered in the light. "My sister, my mother, my father, and two of my brothers were all killed during the wars that Israel has waged upon us, and I am not unusual in this. We all live among the ghosts of our murdered families."

Ethan managed to drag his eyes away from the blade, looking instead at his captor.

"We did not come here to kill anyone," he insisted.

The Palestinian looked at Ethan with an expression that was no longer angry but far beyond such a pitiful emotion. It was the look of a man who had descended through the worst dungeons of horror that mankind's prodigious talent for inflicting pain could offer, and had returned fearing nothing, not even death itself.

"I believe you," he whispered finally. "But I don't care. You see, my dead sister was three months old. They dug her corpse out of the remains of our mother's home. She had burned to death, but they wouldn't show the pictures of her remains on your Western television networks because it might *offend* some people." The Palestinian suddenly grabbed Ethan's hair, yanked it back until it hurt, and turned the blade against his throat. Ethan felt the cold steel touch his skin, felt his pulse throbbing against the blade. "I asked you, my friend, to tell me why you are here."

Ethan peered at the man through the corner of one bleary eye. *Tell him everything, for Christ's sake.* His voice sounded thin in his own ears.

"You asked me who sent us and why. Nobody sent us. We came here looking for someone, but were forced to jump from the airplane to protect that camera and what it contains. The explosives I stole from an American camp in the Negev, owned by the same people who pursued us. Check the photographs in the camera!"

The Palestinian raised the blade in his grip. "Who were you looking for?"

"A scientist who went missing in the desert: Lucy Morgan, Rachel's daughter."

The Palestinian's left eyelid twitched erratically.

"Why would you be here and not the mother alone?" he snapped.

"I was asked to help her by the American Defense Intelligence Agency. They're afraid that Lucy's abduction might be an attempt by insurgents to derail the peace efforts out here." Ethan let what felt like an unconvincing glare settle on his strained features as he hissed. "They think that you took her."

"Why did they ask you?" the Palestinian shouted, spittle flying into Ethan's face.

"Because I know Gaza!" Ethan yelled back as a sudden and unexpected anger surged through him. The pale flame flickered back into life. "Because you bastards took my fiancée away from me and I spent years searching for her in this shit hole! If I could have my way, I'd blow every single one of you terrorist bastards to hell for what you've done!" Ethan glared at the Palestinian for a moment longer, felt hot tears scalding his own face and running down across the hands of the man about to kill him. The anger faded, lost amid a turmoil of despair, regret, and helplessness. "So go ahead and do it, because like you, I've got nothing left to lose."

An unexpected void of calm descended upon

Ethan's shoulders, the fear suddenly purged from his veins as he realized that he meant every word. The Palestinian held the blade still, his expression riveted on Ethan, and then from the deep silence another voice spoke softly.

"That is enough, let him be."

The Palestinian looked past Ethan, then lowered the blade and stood back without another word.

Ethan struggled to look over his shoulder and saw that another narrow tunnel led away from the chamber into some unknown darkness. A figure moved out of the shadows, thin and bespectacled, his features drawn and lightly touched with graying stubble. He moved to stand before Ethan.

"Who are you?" Ethan rasped, his throat parched.

"My name is Dr. Hassim Khan. I was working with Lucy before she disappeared. I am truly sorry for your suffering, Mr. Warner, but these men had to be sure you were who you said you were. Rachel has told us everything." He turned to Ethan's captor. "Release him; he is telling the truth."

Ethan blinked in confusion as the Palestinian moved behind him and began loosening the restraints from his wrists.

"We thought that you'd been abducted by insurgents," Ethan said to Hassim.

The doctor shook his head. "No, Mr. Warner. These men are not insurgents. They are protecting me."

Ethan's mind reeled as he tried to assimilate what he'd heard.

"Protecting you from what?"

34

BEN GURION INTERNATIONAL AIRPORT
ISRAEL

Byron Stone stepped out of the sleek Gulfstream V550 jet and onto the tarmac, catching the commingled odors of aviation fuel and distant deserts on the night air. He might have briefly reveled in the unmistakable, aromatic scent of the Middle East, were it not for the pall of displeasure that enveloped him. A ring of uniformed soldiers surrounded the aircraft as Spencer Malik strode out to greet him.

"Good trip?" Malik saluted Stone, his back ramrod straight and his expression unreadable.

"What news?" Stone asked without preamble. Malik dropped the salute and joined him as they walked toward a parked car nearby.

"The preparations are continuing as planned, and the remains will be here by tomorrow and flown back to the States. Customs won't be a problem; I've handled that."

"What else?" Stone demanded.

Malik squirmed uneasily.

"Our site in the Negev was compromised earlier

today by a journalist." Stone ground his teeth but remained silent as Malik spoke. "The man's name is Ethan Warner. He's got history in Gaza going back a few years."

"So I've heard. What was he doing at the site?"

"We're not sure, but he wasn't alone. He was led in by a Bedouin guide whom we captured but who subsequently escaped. Warner also escaped, along with Rachel Morgan."

Stone hissed a breath from his lungs as he stopped beside the car.

"Go on."

"The pair fled in a private aircraft that was intercepted by the IDF at Ben Gurion. Warner was not on board, nor was the woman. The owners of the aircraft claim they took off alone and were then harassed by a MACE helicopter in a case of mistaken identity, a story that the IDF appears to believe, and they have no apparent interest in Warner or the woman. The pair must have jumped out over the Gaza Strip, in which case they're now almost certainly trying to return to Israel with the evidence."

Stone cast a fearsome glare in Malik's direction. "Evidence?"

Malik carefully formulated his response.

"The Bedouin guide was involved in an altercation with the guards at the site that resulted in an unfortunate incident. It would appear that Warner was able to film part of the altercation and escape with the footage."

"Your purpose was to ensure that MACE maintained a low but professional profile," Stone growled. "What kind of imbecilic morons have you employed here?"

"My men were guarding a site on the border of the Negev's training area," Malik replied quickly. "They had no knowledge of what the site contained, as we agreed. Our people are told only that which they absolutely need to know."

"What happened to the soldiers at the site?" Stone snapped.

"One was killed, another two injured. They're being treated in a field hospital in Jerusalem. The dead man's family have been informed. We can use his demise to illustrate the aggression faced by our team at the site."

Stone forced his chest to expand and suck in air, calming himself by force of will.

"How long ago did this man Warner infiltrate Gaza?"

"Two hours at most," Malik said. "We have narrowed their position down to a small area of Jabaliya."

"What of the IDF?"

"They remain convinced that we were pursuing terrorists of one kind or another. The pilots of the civilian aircraft have not made any statement to the effect that they flew by choice over Gaza or allowed people to parachute into the territory: to do so would render them liable to prosecution for violating any number of Israeli aviation laws."

Stone thought for a moment.

"Then we must ensure that Warner does not make it back into Israel with this evidence of his. MACE cannot afford an investigation here in Israel, financially nor professionally, especially at this time. We've only just closed the litigation against us in Iraq."

Malik nodded. "I will deal with it personally."

"You will do no such thing," Stone snapped, and glanced over his shoulder.

Rafael walked slowly across the tarmac toward them, dressed in a traditional Arab shawl that couldn't conceal his powerful frame.

"We don't need Rafael," Malik uttered quickly, his authority suddenly under threat. "If he learns of our activities in Gaza, he could become a liability and—"

"Right now, you're the goddamn liability," Stone snapped.

"This way," Stone gestured toward an SUV parked nearby as Rafael joined them.

The three men climbed aboard and closed the doors. Rafael regarded Stone for a moment before speaking. "What would you have me do?"

Spencer Malik sat in frigid silence as Stone spoke.

"I require you to infiltrate the Gaza Strip, locate and retrieve explosives and a camera stolen from one of our encampments, and ensure that you are not identified."

Rafael nodded silently in response. Malik, mastering his humiliation, spoke up.

"When should we implement this?"

"Immediately," Stone said. "I will speak to the IDF in Jerusalem. You will provide me with any and all evidence supporting the infiltration of the Negev site by insurgents crossing the Sinai. Provide tracking evidence and have it ready for presentation within the hour. I will then request clearance from Israel's Northern Command to use Gazan airspace. Once Rafael has located and recovered the evidence, we will use one of our Valkyrie drones to vaporize the problem. Understood?"

Malik twisted his features into a crooked smile as he glanced suspiciously at Rafael.

"I know that we need this situation contained, but the more people we bring into this the more complicated everything becomes. This should remain an internal affair and—"

"If you'd done your job, we wouldn't be having this conversation," Stone snapped.

"What evidence am I looking for?" Rafael asked Stone.

"Photographic evidence," the Texan drawled. "A camera and film."

Malik looked at the Arab. "You don't need to know any more than that, *Araboosh*." He took the word, twisted it, and shoved it into Rafael's face.

Rafael regarded the soldier in stony silence, not rising to the provocation.

"Do whatever you feel necessary to obtain that equipment," Stone said to Rafael, then looked directly at Malik. "Let me down again and I'll have you guarding illiterate drug dealers queuing for bread in Chechnya, understood?"

Malik winced but said nothing as Rafael climbed out of the vehicle. Stone waited until he was out of sight before leaning closer to Malik.

"I would prefer that the evidence is destroyed rather than recovered during this mission, along with all witnesses."

In the darkness, Malik's grimace twisted into a cruel smile.

35

M STREET SW, WASHINGTON DC

What do we got?"

Tyrell drove out of the MPD Headquarters onto Delaware Avenue, his headlights illuminating the colorful murals painted on the walls of the station claiming "We can" and "We will" as Nicola Lopez read the files she had downloaded from the Metropolitan Police Department's servers.

"Kelvin Patterson, born 1954, Huntsville, Alabama. Married to Julie, no fewer than six kids. The guy's an evangelical fruit loop, the type who appears on TV after every disaster and claims it was the hand of God. Last time he got major news coverage was after Hurricane Katrina, claiming the storm was God's wrath for the American tolerance of homosexual marriages and abortions."

"Criminal activity?"

"The guy's as clean as a pastor could be. Earned a degree in theology from the University of Phoenix in Austin, Texas, before joining a revolution in political religious activism in the early eighties. Moved to the District and attached himself to the hard-right political parties before starting his own ministry. Was a million-aire within five years and now heads a congregation of around thirty million Americans gathered under a fed-eration of evangelical churches across several states. He has his headquarters in the District in a purpose-built megachurch he had constructed four years ago."

Tyrell changed lanes.

"What about these radio and TV shows that the kid mentioned?"

"Patterson does a weekly radio piece called *This Bread*, an ad for various faith leaders pushing the boat out for bringing God into the public sphere. Apparently, they either don't know or don't care that to do so would be against the Constitution. The TV show is the vehicle that made him a millionaire, with regular tithing events and requests for viewers' money donated for charitable causes."

"Like the hospital?"

"Among other things," Lopez noted, scanning through the files. "It would seem that the good pastor manages to cream off a holy slice for himself. Three houses, plenty of cars. This guy's big and he's well con-nected. He's allied to the current opposition front run-ner for the primaries, Senator Isaiah Black. They were college friends, apparently." Lopez put the file down. "It's hardly a lead, though. This guy recruits from prison populations through his charities and hospitals, but he has no direct contact with them."

Tyrell massaged his temples with his free hand, wip-ing the sweat from his forehead. The car was hot but his skin felt cold to the touch and a dull nausea infected his stomach.

"There'll be something," he said. "We've got enough here to at least make some inquiries, provided I can get it past Powell."

"There's no way he's gonna let you harass this guy. Everything we've got is circumstantial and none of it actually points to a homicide. Where are we goin' anyway?"

"General Hospital Southeast. I've got an appointment with a doctor there."

"Great." Lopez smiled brightly. "It's about damned time."

"The appointment's not for me," Tyrell countered. "Suppose that Claretta's recollections were all correct. This kid was pulled from the AEA's institute and subjected to medical experiments. What the hell do you think would be the point of that?"

Lopez shrugged.

"There's no point in killing someone just to bring 'em back. You want a mark to stay down, not get up and start wanderin' around looking for the cops."

"Unless there was some reason for keeping them dead," Tyrell said quietly, "even just for a while."

"What do you mean?"

"That's what we're going to find out."

Tyrell found a space in the hospital's parking lot before he and Lopez entered the crowded ER. Tyrell was directed to a small room overlooking one of the operating theaters.

The windows were of smoked glass, allowing people to look in from the viewing platform without distracting the attention of the surgeons below. A man stood on the platform with his arms folded, observing the surgery going on within the theater below as Tyrell and Lopez joined him.

"Dr. Holloway?"

Dr. Graham Holloway was shorter than Tyrell and armed with quick, alert blue eyes and an aura of supreme confidence.

"Detective Tyrell," he said, shaking Tyrell's hand.

Tyrell introduced Lopez before looking down into the theater below. Eight surgeons surrounded a patient on the table, the theater filled with computers and complex-looking devices all connected to each other and the patient with a web of wires and tubes.

"What can I do for you?" Holloway asked.

"I understand that you're the senior surgeon here," Tyrell said, transfixed by the surgery below them.

"I'm the most experienced by years but there's no real order of seniority."

"Okay," Tyrell said, opening his notebook. "When you perform surgery on your patients, how often is it necessary to put them into a *homeostatic* state?"

"Only when we're required to perform deeply invasive brain surgery in hemorrhagic brain injuries or aggressive melanoma cases."

"Cancer?" Lopez asked from one side.

"Yes. Very occasionally patients will be referred to us suffering from malignant tumors close to the brain stem or deep in the cerebral cortex."

"And if you are required to perform such a procedure, you might bring the patient's heartbeat down to a crawl," Tyrell suggested. "How would you go about that?"

"There are several methods," Holloway said, "but the principal ones include chemicals that relax the major organs. Another is via induced hypothermia."

Tyrell caught Lopez's look of surprise. Dr. Holloway didn't miss the silent exchange. "It might help if you were to tell me what the problem is," he suggested.

Tyrell nodded.

"We noticed some unusual pathology in the autopsies of three bodies discovered yesterday morning. All three had suffered from the early stages of hypothermia."

Tyrell saw Holloway raise his eyebrows at that. "You're aware that it's been nearly eighty degrees across the District over the past few days."

"Go on," the surgeon said quietly.

"The medical examiner confirmed that all three individuals showed excessive hydrogen sulphide in their blood."

"Anything else?"

"All of the victims were of the same blood group, O-negative, but originally their blood had been AB, suggesting a transfusion." Tyrell took a breath. "Given what I've just told you, what would be your best estimate of the kind of procedure that these individuals were subjected to?"

Holloway let out a long breath before speaking.

"It's possible that a human body cooled using a saline solution to transfuse blood could suffer effects somewhat like frostbite if the procedure was poorly conducted."

"They were actually frozen?" Lopez asked, mortified.

"Yes, it's a common procedure developed to make open-heart surgery easier and is being enhanced for battlefield trauma victims and automobile accidents. By rapidly cooling the body using a chilled saline solution, a form of controlled hypothermia can be induced in the victim, slowing their metabolism to clinical death."

"How does it work?" Tyrell asked.

"The patient is anesthetized, hooked up to a heart-bypass machine, and receives heparin, which is made from cow's gut, to prevent blood clotting. The heart is then stopped via intravenously administered potassium chloride. The body is cooled over a period of about one hour to a temperature of around sixteen degrees Centigrade, essentially as cold as a corpse. We then drain the blood from the body and replace it with a chilled saline solution. By this time the patient is clinically dead, with no heartbeat, no blood, and no brain activity. Surgery is undertaken and when the work is complete the process is reversed, ending with a small electrical charge applied to the heart to initiate rhythm."

"And this is done on a regular basis?" Lopez asked.

"Only in extreme cases to allow prolonged access to the brain or heart," Holloway admitted. "Long-term hypothermic methods have only been conducted so far on dogs and mice in an experimental manner. The method was reported as having a success rate of better than eighty percent. The dogs even answered to their own names."

"Eighty percent," Lopez repeated softly. "And the other twenty?"

"Hard to tell in animals," Holloway said, "but probably a condition similar to posttraumatic stress or schizophrenia. Mood swings and evidence of depression were noted, along with motor deficiency."

Tyrell nodded, thinking furiously now.

"What about the altered blood group of the victims?"

"Entire blood transfusions are not uncommon," Holloway said, "but would only occur to prevent rejection of foreign organs."

Tyrell nodded, gathering his thoughts. "We have a survivor."

"A what?"

"A twenty-one-year-old who survived this procedure. He's suffering from paranoid schizophrenia and will be on antidepressants for the rest of his life. His mother told us that he and others were experimented on by physicians who, among other things, were attempting to extract and replace their blood. Many of the victims died. When we spoke to the medical examiner who examined the bodies we found, he said that the blood in their bodies was genetically unrecognizable, not human. One of the victims had suffered the extraction of reproductive tissues."

Dr. Holloway's face drained of color, turning almost as pale as the white of his coat. He looked from Tyrell to Lopez and back again.

"I can't imagine what that would mean."

"Try."

"If you were to put a gun to my head and force me to suggest something, then the only thing that I can think of is that somebody was trying to use humans as incubators, perhaps to generate blood lines or stem cells for a chimera."

Tyrell looked at Lopez, who had also paled. "What's a chimera?"

Holloway spoke quietly.

"A species that is a combination of the genetic codes of two preceding species, a hybrid if you will." Holloway paled again. "Whoever conducted those experiments is using human incubators in order to bring something back to life."

36

What do you mean, bring something back to life?"

Lopez watched as Dr. Holloway removed his spectacles and cleaned them as he spoke.

"With the recent advance of genetic science, it's been possible to cross-breed two distinct species in order to create a half-breed, a chimera. It happens in nature quite a lot, but the more separated the two species are from their common ancestor, the less likely they are to be able to produce offspring."

"But it's been done," Tyrell guessed.

"Oh yes. Sheep and goats produced a chimera, the so-called Geep. Such interspecies are made in the laboratory by transplanting embryonic cells from an animal with one trait into the embryo of an animal with a different trait. This practice is common in the field."

"So why would somebody want to conduct that procedure on humans?" Tyrell pressed.

"I really don't know," Holloway said. "But whatever the aim, the procedure would be highly illegal. In 2003, researchers at the Shanghai Second Medical University in China successfully fused human skin cells and dead rabbit eggs to create the first human chimeric embryos. The embryos were allowed to develop for several days in a laboratory setting, then destroyed to harvest the resulting stem cells. But from what you're suggesting—"

"They're using unwilling victims," Tyrell said. "Which means that they're probably taking things further than stem cells."

"Could they produce another species if they had the required materials?" Lopez asked, clearly appalled by the thought of such genetic engineering.

"Absolutely." Holloway nodded. "Though there would be a number of obstacles to overcome."

"Such as?" Tyrell pressed.

"Well, the immune system would need to be repressed, which could explain the hypothermic cooling. Then there's the fact that sperm and eggs of differing species won't recognize each other, and the number of chromosomes won't match, which will prevent effective fertilization. They would need to acquire stem cells from the species they're trying to clone, or at least culture cells from existing material in order to produce viable embryos using host or donor cells, which could explain the surgery marks on some of your victims and . . ."

Dr. Holloway suddenly trailed off. Tyrell saw the doctor's expression sag and his eyes fill with horror.

"What is it?" Tyrell asked.

Holloway shook his head, his voice throaty as he spoke.

"If they fertilized human eggs that had had their nucleus replaced with foreign stem cells, they could possibly create an embryo that could then be implanted into a host."

Lopez winced.

"They can do that?"

"They could use bone-marrow stem cells," Holloway said, "from the species they are trying to clone. From those cells all the various types of blood cells are descended, and using a laboratory can give rise to even non-marrow cells."

"Like embryonic stem cells," Tyrell suggested.

"It's cloning, in effect." Holloway nodded. "Whole cell or animal cloning occurs through the transfer of the nucleus of an adult cell into an enucleated egg. This can result in the reprogramming of the adult cell DNA to produce a cloned animal. They could create an extinct species, for instance, from the nucleus of a cultured mammary gland cell or similar that is then fused to a human egg cell that has had its own nucleus removed. The fused cell can then be implanted into a female human host. Nuclear transfer has been applied to produce cloned animals like cows, goats, pigs, mice, cats, and so on."

"What, you mean impregnated in vitro?"

Holloway nodded, his features twisted with distaste.

"In the 1920s, Joseph Stalin sent an animal-breeding expert to Africa in hopes of creating an army of half-man, half-monkey soldiers. They tried to inseminate women with monkey sperm and impregnate female chimpanzees with human sperm. All of the attempts failed. But now we have genetic control over the donors and recipients, which is why they might be harvesting rare O-negative blood via transfusion, to reduce the chances of immuno-shock in the impregnated female if the source species carried the same blood."

"Why is that type of blood so rare?" Tyrell asked.

"Evolution," the doctor said. "Most blood groups can be traced back to our evolutionary cousins via proteins, and human blood reacts with the blood of rhesus monkeys as a result of our shared antibodies. Some ninety percent of people have the rhesus antibody in their blood, hence our shared common origin."

"But some don't," Tyrell said.

"About ten percent of people have rhesus-negative blood, which means that the antibodies are not present. That's good for other people as they can receive the blood from O-negative donors without fear of rejection. The problem is its heritage: O-negative blood constitutes less than seven percent of the world population. We just don't know where the hell it comes from, as it's the purest form of human blood and the only type that cannot be cloned. Most believe that it's something like our original human blood before the mixing of populations, but nobody's really sure."

Tyrell tried to understand what the doctor was saying.

"So this blood type has no apparent origin in human evolution?"

"It evolved all right, it's just that we can't tell how or where it started. Our species evolved in Africa, yet only one percent of rhesus-negative people are of African descent. That means it must have appeared after our dispersal from Africa millions of years ago. The highest concentration of people with rhesus-negative blood live in the Basque region and Israel."

"When did it appear?" Lopez asked curiously.

"Our best estimate is around five to six thousand years ago, roughly the time that human civilization began."

"The dawn of recorded history," Lopez said. "Didn't Claretta mention something about that, something she'd heard from Daniel?"

Tyrell nodded.

"Men of renown," he murmured. "Some kind of

quote. And our pastor at the Evangelical Alliance has been running blood-donation charities across the District."

Tyrell thanked Dr. Holloway before turning and walking away with Lopez, who produced her notebook.

"I want you to get me a list of every surgeon who has ever served in the District, Virginia, New Jersey, and Maryland. Start with people who have worked for the Evangelical Alliance's hospitals."

Lopez nodded, scribbling as she did so.

"Then get me everything you can on the American Evangelical Alliance's activities over the last ten years, specifically those that involve drug rehabilitation and blood work. Make sure that you learn everything you can about Kelvin Patterson: how he works, where he works, who supports him, who hates him, and why."

"Wait one," Lopez looked at Tyrell. "You can't just build a case here and then get in his face. It might send a warning to whoever is responsible."

"I don't give a damn if he turns out to be God's right-hand man and can turn shit into gold just by looking at it. If he's the owner of this hospital, then he's got some responsibility for it, and if he's innocent of any crime, then he should have no problems assisting us."

Lopez sighed, brushing a thick lock of black hair from her eyes. "Run any of this by the district attorney and I'll be impressed."

"My guess is that there aren't all that many neurosurgeons out there and even less who have had their medical licenses revoked. We have one survivor, and that means whoever did it was competent enough not to kill everybody they tried it on."

Lopez nodded, but remained unconvinced. "It'll take a lot of man-hours."

"Not if we're on the right track already. Dr. Holloway said that these people with rare blood originated somewhere in Israel, so make your search in particular for surgeons with any kind of connection to Israel."

"What about Daniel Neville? He's in a hospital owned by the people we're investigating. Don't you think we should get him some kind of protection?"

Tyrell nodded.

"Get on it, and don't let Powell talk you down. I want an officer guarding that hospital ward until this case is solved."

37

AMERICAN EVANGELICAL ASSOCIATION
NEW COVENANT CHURCH, WASHINGTON DC

Casey Jeffs stood alone and immobile in the office of Kelvin Patterson, a towering hulk of a man dressed in blue overalls, his face half hidden by a mop of lank blond hair. Reverentially, he knelt down in front of the small altar and looked up at the towering chromed cross as he clasped his hands before him.

"I din' mean to cause trouble," he whispered. "I din' mean it."

Jeffs knelt for a long time, grinding his hands before him and closing his eyes tightly, as though the mere action of doing so could wipe away his anxiety and fear.

"I din' mean it," he whispered again.

"I know you didn't, Casey."

Casey's head jerked up as he gasped and leaped to his feet, and Patterson saw the flare of alarm in his bright blue eyes, the feeble mind behind them unable to account for Patterson's sudden materialization. Patterson stepped from behind the altar and shook one of Casey's giant hands in his. Casey stooped when upright, partly because of his height and partly because he had long taken to hiding from an uncaring world behind his fringe of hair. He glanced behind him at the office door, still closed, and then looked at Patterson.

"Where'd you come from?" he asked, his tone rigid with awe.

"The Lord works in mysterious ways, Casey," Patterson said. "Now, you have something to tell me?"

Casey's blue eyes flickered anxiously. "They're not comin' here, Pastor? That right? The police ain't comin' here for me?"

"No, Casey, they're not coming here. Let's sit down, shall we?" Patterson suggested.

The pastor lead Casey to the magnificent mahogany desk that dominated his spacious office, a large bronze eagle mounted on one edge and a small American flag on the other. The sunlight flooding the office from beyond the rolling hills and valleys of Virginia flared off the giant chrome crucifix, sending reflections flickering around the room.

Patterson poured Casey a cup of water from a cooler near the window before sitting down opposite him and watching as he sipped.

"So, did something happen today at the hospital?"

Casey's features were cast in simple slabs, the round blue eyes gazing at Patterson from behind the floppy blond hair.

"The police were at the hospital askin' questions, though I din' hear all of it."

Casey Jeff's voice was monotone, as though somebody had removed the soul from his chest and replaced it with a recording. Complex potions conspired to quell the wayward neurons of Casey and his fellow patients, stifling their psychosis in a frozen fog of sedatives and binding their self-destructive urges in chemical chains. In the case of Patterson's loyal protégé, they served well enough to keep him occupied as a useful source of information within the institute, at least until anything unexpected spooked him into fleeing.

"The police weren't there to speak to you, Casey," Patterson reassured him. "Just you tell me what you did hear."

"I couldn't get close," Casey mumbled, "but they was talkin' about experiments of some kind, that Daniel Neville may have been hurt. What does that mean, Pastor?"

"It means that Daniel has suffered," Patterson said, "and that we should pray for him."

Casey nodded robotically. "We could help him."

"Do you think that we should, Casey?"

Casey's rudimentary features twitched into a smile for the first time since entering the office. Entrusted with a decision, Casey felt secure again. Patterson smiled back on cue as little insects of loathing scuttled across his skin.

The truth was that Kelvin Patterson despised Casey Jeffs. Casey was a psychotic shambles who would be unable to walk the streets were it not for the advances in medical science over the past forty years. But Patterson was also fascinated by the mentally afflicted. How did their minds work? What did they see? Hear? Taste? For Patterson, the conscience of the mentally ill represented a simple and yet unreachable unknown every bit as unfathomable as the nature of God Himself, and the similarities bothered him immensely. Narrow was the line between genius and insanity. Was it not true that the savant was also vulnerable, a genius shackled to the unstable foundations of a crumbling mind?

He looked down at his desk to a drawer where he

kept his own medications, those that he took when even
the brightest of days seemed overcast, shadowed with
dense and bottomless pits of despair that seemed to draw
him in with powerful gravitational fields.

"Yes, I do. How should we help him?"

Casey's voice made the pastor jump. He had briefly
forgotten that he was there.

Since his gradual recovery from terminal psychosis,
when medical science had plucked him from oblivion,
Casey Jeffs had been employed as a handyman undertaking menial tasks at the institute. The employment
served as a valuable psychological anchor amid a strange
and often hostile world. In these modern days of empow-
erment to the weak and support of the needy, Casey's apparent success in leading a near-normal life was held by
the institute as a symbol of the power of rehabilitation.
The meek shall inherit the Earth, Patterson reflected as
he looked into Casey's innocent features. But the meek
needed those who could lead the way, the shepherd to
their flock. Patterson knew that he himself represented
the closest thing to a father and a family that Casey had
ever known.

"We should ease his suffering, and help him to find
God," Patterson responded. "Daniel has suffered enough,
hasn't he?"

Casey nodded seriously. "We all have, Pastor."

Patterson wondered where Casey might have picked
up the reply, doubtful that it could have tumbled unbidden from the confused miasma of his own mind. Daniel
Neville had been allowed to live in order to study why he
alone had survived the experiments, but now he was a
liability that Patterson could not afford.

"Did the police officers actually see Daniel Neville?"
he asked.

"One of them did." Casey nodded. "They let him into the room for a moment."

Patterson nodded slowly, and made his decision.

"You remember what we spoke of, Casey? That we would do it just like we did before?"

The blue eyes twinkled. "Yes, boss, I know what to do." A flicker of doubt appeared. "Will it be like last time? The police made me think about the last time, about how—"

Patterson overcame his revulsion as he reached out and patted the back of Casey's hand.

"It won't be like last time, Casey, and even if it is, I will protect you when you need me."

The childlike relief in Casey's eyes contrasted with the lumbering movements of his body as he stood from his chair and loped out of the office. Patterson leaned back in his chair and looked down at his desk. There a broadsheet was emblazoned with an image of Senator Isaiah Black alongside the results of the most recent polls. Patterson bit his lip as he read.

Black's popularity had increased in spite of, or perhaps because of, his distancing himself from the American Evangelical Alliance. Patterson felt his eyeballs surging briefly in their sockets, and he forced himself to remain calm. The polls weren't any more psychic than he was, and could change almost literally overnight. As for the police at the institute . . .

Patterson dug out his cell phone from his pocket and dialed a number, waiting for the line to connect. The digital warbling of advanced security functions assured him that Byron Stone was leaving nothing to chance in Israel.

"*Yes?*" came the drawling Texan voice as the line picked up.

"There has been a complication," Patterson said briskly. "One of the bodies may have been identified, and detectives are snooping around. Ensure that the surgeon is close at hand. We may require him to void any investigations."

The pastor could almost hear Byron Stone's irritation down the line.

"Your amateurs should never have been employed to transport the remains. Just make goddamn sure you give us enough warning, Pastor, understood?"

Somehow, Patterson managed to rise above the Texan's imperious tone.

"Of course."

38

**JABALIYA
GAZA STRIP
AUGUST 26**

How on earth did the two of you come to be here?" Dr. Hassim Khan asked.

Ethan struggled out of the chair to which he had been tied. As he stood, he saw that his hands were trembling. He flexed them a few times as Rachel appeared from the tunnel behind him.

"Are you okay?" Ethan asked.

"I'll be fine," she muttered coldly, passing by him to perch on the edge of a crate nearby.

Ethan could hardly blame her for being pissed with him, considering the situation they were now in, but it wasn't like he'd pushed her out of the goddamn airplane. He turned to Hassim Khan and explained how MACE had pursued them, and their escape with the camera footage into Gaza.

Hassim asked Ethan's captors, "You know of this MACE company?"

"Private contractors," the younger one said, his features twisted with disgust. "They infect our land like a parasite."

Hassim gestured to the Palestinian who had questioned Ethan.

"This is Mahmoud. He and his companion, Yossaf, have been protecting me here."

Ethan wasn't sure how to acknowledge the men who had moments earlier been threatening to slit his throat. He decided simply to ignore them, keeping the focus of his conversation on Hassim.

"Protecting you from what?" Ethan asked once more.

"From abduction, ironically." Hassim chuckled.

Rachel frowned as she glanced at the two burly men.

"But insurgents are sworn to Israel's destruction, and have the most to gain from abductions."

It was Mahmoud who spoke, his arms folded and his gaze brooding.

"Most Palestinians are not terrorists. Your Western media portrays us all as brutal, killing in the name of Allah, but most of us do not support terrorism. We want our homes and our lives back, but we don't want to kill people any more than you do."

Ethan turned to Hassim.

"Who's orchestrating these abductions then? A splinter faction?"

Hassim shook his head.

"Mahmoud and Yossaf have spoken to everyone they know and nobody is aware of the abductions."

"Unlikely," Ethan said, turning to Mahmoud. "Who do you think is abducting Westerners?"

"The company you call MACE."

"What would they want with my daughter?" Rachel snorted. "What could they gain from abducting people when they're responsible for *security*?"

"Maintaining war maintains profits," Mahmoud replied darkly. "And business here is booming."

"Profits over peace?" Rachel gasped.

"Why not?" Hassim said. "It wouldn't be the first time."

"It doesn't make sense," Rachel said, looking at Ethan for support. "If any organization wanted to abduct people, then they would target high-profile individuals like politicians or television stars, not a group of scientists. Nobody would even notice they were gone."

Hassim nodded.

"Indeed, unless you had other motives that remain out of the public eye."

"What do you mean?" Ethan asked.

Hassim spoke softly.

"MACE is a powerful supplier of arms and technology to Israel, but is owned by a large church."

"You're kidding me?" Ethan said in surprise.

"No," Hassim replied, "and the church bought them for good reason. There are many in the United States who would like to see their interpretations of biblical prophecy fulfilled, of an undivided Jerusalem as capital of Israel heralding the supposed Second Coming of Christ."

Ethan sat down on a crate near Hassim and looked at his watch.

"The peace accord is due to be signed in fifteen hours' time," he said. "Who else was involved in Lucy's work?"

"Four of us that I know of," Hassim said. "Hans Karowitz, Lucy Morgan, myself, and another American—Joseph Coogan—a biochemist from Washington DC. He was to receive any remains that Lucy found and attempt to identify them."

"We need to contact them," Ethan said. "Get the word out about what's happening here."

Hassim smiled bitterly.

"That's what I was trying to do when my friends here were able to bring me to safety before I too was abducted. All of the other scientists involved in the project have either vanished or been silenced ever since Lucy found the remains out there in the Negev."

Ethan thought about Hans Karowitz and his reluctance to speak of what had happened in front of the MACE bodyguards.

"Lucy made a brief radio call about her discovery to the museum in Jerusalem. Do you think it likely that she was tracked because of those communications?"

"It is possible," Hassim agreed. "But the Negev is a very large desert and Lucy was digging in a restricted area where few people travel. To have found her, somebody was most likely watching her movements all along and followed her out there."

"Which means either the IDF or MACE," Ethan said, turning to look at Rachel, "and given what we've seen so far today I know who I'd put my money on."

39

EREZ
ISRAEL

Spencer Malik watched as Rafael approached from the shadows, gliding silent as a ghost before stopping a meter away from where he stood. The darkness obscured his features; the broad face, the skin darkened by the passing of endless suns in countless countries. A thin silken scarf covered the lower half of his face, shielding him effectively enough to prevent identification.

"Information," Rafael demanded in his husky accent.

"I don't take orders," Malik hissed. "You do."

"A shame, then, that you so often fail to carry them out."

Malik flashed a brittle grin in the darkness, but said nothing.

"I will contact you with the coordinates as soon as I have them," Rafael said. "Try not to screw up this time."

Malik's grin did not budge.

"Just get the job done." Malik produced a small set of folded papers. "These will get you past the security at the crossing. Israel closed it some time ago, but there . . ." Malik stared as Rafael walked past him without another word, ignoring the papers. "Where are you going?"

Rafael turned back to face him.

"Fool, you would have me approach a guarded crossing? I will make my own way into Gaza. There is always a way in and out for those who know. Be gone."

Malik whipped his pistol out of its holster, strode forward, and jammed the metal barrel against Rafael's head.

"Who are you calling a fool?"

Rafael stared up at Malik for a long moment before speaking in a soft whisper, his shoulders slumping. "Forgive me, I did not mean to offend."

Malik felt his features melting into a grin of deep satisfaction, and with his free hand he tapped Rafael's stubbled cheek a few times for good measure.

"Run along, little man."

Rafael nodded obediently before turning and walking away. Malik watched him stride into the night, then basked in the surge of adrenaline that coursed through his veins. Rafael was just big talk, dominated as easily as a whipped dog. A euphoric sense of well-being enveloped him as he looked down and slipped his pistol back into its holster.

It was only then that he saw the small tear in the fabric of his shirt, just below his rib cage. He tugged at the material, saw the clean cut, and cursed. The bloody Arab had held a blade to his ribs and he never even noticed.

He looked up, but Rafael had vanished.

40

IDF NORTHERN COMMAND (PATZAN)
NEVE YAAKOV, JERUSALEM

This had better be important."

Byron Stone stood inside the doorway to the office of Lieutenant General Benjamin Aydan, a craggy, broad-shouldered veteran of the Six-Day War.

"It is."

The Israeli Defense Force was never off duty, even in the small hours of the night. In a country surrounded by populations violently opposed to its very existence, it had long been learned by both the government and the military that letting one's guard down was tantamount to submission and an invitation to destruction.

Within just a few years of its independence, Israel had been subjected to a joint military invasion by all three of its neighboring enemies, Arab states infected with the divine certainty that to destroy Israel was to enact the will of Allah. Israel had fought back, repelling even this concerted assault on its statehood, and had done so alone.

"Enter."

Byron Stone walked into the office and closed the door. Benjamin Aydan stood and was courteous enough to shake Stone's hand before gesturing for him to sit in the chair opposite.

"What may I do for you?"

"We have a situation in the Negev," Stone said briskly. "Several hours ago one of our encampments in the Negev was infiltrated by what we believe to be a terrorist cell. Several items were stolen from the site and smuggled into Gaza."

General Aydan sat in silence for a moment, regarding Stone through icy eyes that had seen untold horrors. "Value?"

"High," Stone replied crisply. "We're not sure of the insurgents' intentions but we were able to track them into Gaza just after sundown."

"What do you want us to do?"

Stone took a deep breath. "I'd like to conduct an air strike on the insurgents' lair."

Aydan's eyes narrowed.

"How can you be sure that the target will not incur civilian casualties?"

"I have a man inside Gaza as we speak. He'll identify the insurgents and their locations and be ready to provide coordinates."

"You've a man on the ground right now? That's beyond your remit."

Stone maintained a neutral expression.

"Sensitive data was stolen that concerns both MACE and Israeli Defense Force operations in the Negev. Exposure of that data to insurgent networks could be catastrophic."

Stone saw the general's fist clench on his desk as he spoke.

"What could they have taken from a little company like MACE that might possibly cause such a disruption?"

Stone didn't miss the jibe.

"It isn't just data that they've stolen," he uttered. "They murdered one of my men and injured several others. Whoever they are, they're serious enough to kill."

The general offered Stone a dispassionate stare. "In fifty years, thousands of Israel's sons have lost their lives defending us. Your men know the risks of service here and are paid considerably more than our conscripts. Live with it."

"They also have footage of Israeli troops beating an unarmed Bedouin."

The lie fell out of Stone's mouth as though it had been waiting there all along.

"What?"

"Almost five minutes' worth," Stone went on without missing a beat. "I've been assured that it was immensely brutal." He leaned forward on the desk, staring hard at the general. "It could cause a crisis should the footage be released to the media. The northern Negev battalions are under your command, are they not, General?"

Benjamin Aydan glowered at Stone.

"Do you have copies of this supposed footage?"

"No, the cameraman escaped before he could be apprehended."

"Incompetent."

Benjamin Aydan remained silent and still as though hewn from a vast chunk of granite. Stone maintained what he hoped looked like an expression of confidence. For several seconds it seemed as though neither he nor the general was actually breathing. Then Aydan exhaled.

"How accurately can your man identify where these individuals are located?"

"He'll report in from the location itself. I suspect that it'll be within one of the tunnels that the Palestinians use to smuggle goods across the city. The destruction of the evidence is my aim here, not the taking of lives."

Aydan frowned.

"Then why doesn't your man on the ground simply recover the footage for himself and avoid the need for an air strike?"

"Simply?" Stone echoed. "What's simple about entering a heavily guarded insurgent network and escaping with your life? My man is doing enough as it is to locate the evidence showing your troop's brutality. I'd hoped that you'd be good enough to meet us halfway and avoid a firefight on the ground. Unless you'd rather send your own men in to clear the insurgents out of the tunnels?"

General Aydan's eyes glittered like the points of twin bayonets.

"I would lead them myself, but I can't commit the Israeli Air Force to an attack on Gaza without good reason. Our own Heron TP drones are for reconnaissance only."

Byron Stone resisted the urge to smile as the general wandered into his trap.

"A MACE Valkyrie drone carries Hellfire missiles and cannon. It's the perfect opportunity for our drone to be tested in combat conditions, and the ideal means for us to bring this unfortunate episode to a close."

"It'll have to be cleared with Southern Command," Aydan growled.

"Israel's involvement in this incident will be minimal," Stone insisted. "Everybody wins."

"Except anyone caught in the line of fire."

Byron Stone chose not to respond, allowing instead

the delicacy and danger of the situation to weigh on the general's shoulders. Aydan reached down and opened a drawer at the side of his desk. He produced a card and handed it to Stone.

"Call me as soon as you have the coordinates, and I'll clear the flight."

Stone took the card as he stood.

"Thank you, General."

He walked out of the office and closed the door behind him. Spencer Malik stood waiting in the corridor.

"Well?"

"Prepare the Valkyrie for flight, and ensure that all of our loose ends are vaporized when you receive the target coordinates. Then find the surgeon. We may need him soon."

41

JABALIYA
GAZA STRIP

Ethan Warner sipped water from a chipped mug as he listened to Hassim Khan.

"The American Evangelical Alliance owns MACE, is run from Washington DC, and has consistently sought to alter the course of American history by distributing false information to schools, colleges, and universities throughout the country. It was partly responsible for the attempted insertion of 'Intelligent Design' into the education curriculum, which was thwarted in 2005 by state courts as being no different from creationism. Their efforts were exposed after a leaked document called 'The Wedge Strategy' reached the mainstream media, revealing their plan to put a wedge between science and the public through a campaign of deliberate disinformation in order to generate doubt in scientific endeavor."

"They're willing to play dirty," Ethan murmured, thinking about the MACE troops shooting at them in the desert.

"They are," Hassim agreed. "You can see how such an organization might react to Lucy's discovery out here."

"They'd do anything to cover it up," Ethan said. "Even kill."

"When you believe you're doing God's work, anything is justifiable."

"But what if they've got it all wrong?" Ethan said. "Those remains could be something else, a freak of nature or a deformed species of some kind. Even someone as experienced as Lucy could have got it wrong. What's the chance of there being life in space at all for that matter?"

Hassim Khan seemed surprised.

"Life is known to be everywhere in the universe."

"No, it's not," Ethan said. "Nobody knows if there's intelligent life out there."

"I didn't say *intelligent* life," Hassim said. "I said life."

"How would you know that for sure?" Rachel demanded. Mahmoud and Yossaf were also frowning uncertainly at the scientist.

Hassim shrugged as he looked at her.

"The origin of life, *sadiqati,* is the formation of the chemical elements themselves, the very things from which we are made. Each and every form of life and structure on our planet and every other planet in the known universe were conceived in the hearts of giant stars: everything that we see, everything that we breathe, touch, taste, and are physically made of. All life on Earth is quite literally built from the chemical ashes of dead stars. We are stardust."

Ethan experienced a fleeting bout of vertigo.

"Ashes? You mean life is, like, the leftovers?"

Hassim Khan nodded.

"All life as we know it is quite literally debris, nothing more. Lucy knew this, and understood its connection to what she found out here in Israel."

42

NAHAL OZ
GAZA STRIP

The night was a blessing that shielded his movements and deadened the sound of his footfalls. Car horns sounded from a main road nearby, voices responding in a babble of angry Arabic and Urdu, then fell silent as the whisper of a vehicle's tires faded into the distance. The Gaza Strip slumbered beneath a heavy blanket of heat as Rafael drifted through alleyways and across rubble-strewn ground.

The Gaza Strip was never silent. Voices carried on the warm breeze from the coast, sometimes seeming almost upon his shoulder, as though the entire population were watching him. Sound travels farther at night, and among the densely packed buildings it seemed to turn corners, taunting his movements as idle conversations spilled from darkened houses onto the night air.

It was not the first time that Rafael had been required to infiltrate the Gaza Strip. From time to time he had been paid by Byron Stone to eliminate trouble-some figures that haunted this land and the innumerable wretches who scratched out an existence from its unyielding soil. He had few qualms about lancing such abscesses of violence. Men killed. It was not cultural, tribal, or even a family thing. As a young soldier he had witnessed both the horror of conflict and the macabre euphoria of taking a life in the defense of one's own.

Rafael killed only those whom he judged unworthy of life, and killed silently and quickly no matter how grotesque the crimes of his victims. Once they were dead, that was the end of it. The flatulent wittering of psychologists and philosophers did not interest him, especially since killing had earned Rafael far more money than he had ever earned in the service of his country.

He slowed and crouched like a cat in the darkness as a small knot of Palestinian teenagers sauntered past nearby. The tips of their cheap cigarettes glowed like beacons in the night, flaring into life and illuminating dark faces scarred by years of hardship.

Rafael had earned his battle honors in a dozen conflicts, the last of which had been fought amid the derelict streets of Chechnya. Working as a mercenary in the north of the country, he had been caught in the midst of a brutal firefight between Chechnyan rebels and Russian Spetsnaz forces. Rafael had killed a Russian radio operator and captured his set. Fluent in Russian, as he was in so many languages and dialects, he had quickly called in an air strike against a militant position while giving the coordinates of the Russian forces.

Somehow, the coup failed: the Spetsnaz had foiled his plan, probably possessing a backup radio set within their team. The air strike arrived and decimated half of his fellow fighters. Instantly, the hard-core fanatics suspected betrayal, and the *mujahideen* were upon him. Overpowered by men of his blood and his lands and yet ignoring his explanations, he was bound and taken to a place in the bleak eastern hills where he learned the true nature of faith and what it made men capable of.

There was no Geneva Convention for those held by men who opposed the very society that created it. Rafael was stripped naked, beaten with hoses and batons, and then drenched with ice water before being locked in a tiny basement cell, the stones in the walls worn smooth by the clawing of desperate fingers from time immemorial. The militants wanted to know for whom he had been working, where they were based, and how to obtain access to them, for they believed that his mind had somehow been violated and that Allah had sent him to them for what they euphemistically referred to as "cleansing." When Rafael was unable to provide them with suitable answers, they attached electrodes to his genitals and cranked them from the mains, searing his body with white pain that left him weeping. When that failed to bring forth the answers they required, they severed two of his fingers with jagged, rusty knives and abandoned him in his cell, accompanied by crippling cold and the raging infections that coursed through his body.

Somewhere in the bleak hours between life and oblivion he was liberated by a small handful of his captors who opposed his detainment. From within the depths of his suffering, Rafael realized that even in the presence of utter barbarianism some souls harbored morsels of humanity, like lonely flowers blossoming amid smoldering plains of ash. Having correctly deduced that Rafael could not have endured such torture unless innocent, and at great risk to themselves, his saviors had spirited him away and placed him in a safe house until he recovered.

Since then, Rafael had been a man on a mission

for both himself and for humanity. His work had carried him around the world in the pursuit of criminals and terrorists; Mafioso henchmen in Palermo, Sendero Luminoso assassins in Peru, corrupt police organizing abductions in Colombia, and al-Qaeda cells all over the globe. Ironically, taking out the terrorists had turned out to be far safer than working as a soldier. Hatred of extremists seemed a universal theme. Rafael had realized that nobody cared if an al-Qaeda operative was found facedown in a sewer conduit in Berlin with a crowbar lodged in his skull, or in flames by the side of a lonely desert road in Kashmir, or hanged from the roof beams of a church in Santiago. Rafael's work was the only perfect murder: one where nobody gave a damn about finding the perpetrator, and he was proud to serve MACE in eliminating terrorists.

The sound of a distant car jerked him from his reverie. The kids had vanished, and Rafael moved out across the open ground and disappeared into an alley. At the end of the alley was a narrow street faintly illuminated by a light somewhere off to the left. Few of the streetlights in this part of the Strip worked with any reliability, a further aid to his movement.

Opposite the alley was a four-story building, one side of which hung in chunks of tattered masonry and steel shattered by countless mortar rounds and aerial incendiaries. The other side of the building was intact but clearly abandoned.

It was a common tactic of insurgents to occupy recently bombed buildings. The Israelis, having blasted them to pieces, would consider their job done and move on to other more interesting targets. Insurgents would occupy those shattered hulks and use them as storage depots, hideouts, and, in this case, entrances to tunnels dug beneath the foundations of the abandoned buildings. It was much harder for Israel to spot tunnels that began beneath buildings than it was to identify those that fed from the Gazan border into the smuggling network beneath Egypt.

The building was the third such location that Rafael had checked since slipping into Gaza an hour previously. The first two had been empty, a fact quickly confirmed by Rafael's observation that they sat unguarded. This one was different. Sitting on a doorstep outside the building, a watchful Palestinian teenager smoked a cigarette. The building had no visible lights and indeed was unlikely to have any running water. Therefore, the foot soldier was guarding something that lay within. Insurgent groups used a network of teenage layabouts to run errands or keep an eye on sensitive locations, far too many for Israel's intelligence organizations to run tabs on or interrogate.

Quietly, Rafael slipped out of the shadows and sauntered with his hands in his pockets across the road. Although he looked directly at the young man, his senses scanned like radar up and down the street on either side of him. The area was deserted, as he had expected at this time of the night. Gaza was not so much governed by Hamas's police as ruled with an iron fist, and anybody out at night was likely to attract their attention. For that reason, he would have to be quick.

The teenager saw him the instant he emerged from the shadows, suddenly trying to look tough rather than bored. He flicked the butt of his cigarette away.

Rafael, having removed his scarf, revealed a set of neat white teeth.

"*Salaam*," he said softly.

The boy nodded once, looking Rafael over. "You should not walk the street at night. It is forbidden."

"I'm on my way home," Rafael replied easily, producing a packet of his own cigarettes. "Would you care for one?"

The youngster looked at the proffered packet, and then at the butt he had flicked onto the street before him. "I just had one."

"Ah." Rafael nodded. "But these are American, Marlboro. Have one for later."

The teenager's eyebrows lifted in surprise and he reached out for the cigarette that poked from the open pack.

There was no haste in Rafael's movement, even though it happened in a blur. As the teenager's fingers settled on the cigarette, Rafael let the packet go, gripping the boy's left hand in his own and twisting it sideways across the palm, yanking it hard as he stepped in.

The boy's shoulder turned in sympathy with the pain as he struggled up onto one foot, his mouth gaping open to cry out. Rafael's right hand whipped between them, a blade glittering in the streetlight before he slammed it hilt deep into the young man's throat, slicing into his windpipe and snatching the call from his lips.

The boy lurched but Rafael picked the body up under his arm with immense strength and rushed across the street into the darkness of the alleyway opposite. He crouched down and clamped one hand across the boy's mouth before turning the blade in his throat and pulling it hard to one side. A crisp sound like splitting fresh lettuce issued as the blade left the boy's throat, followed by a deep gurgling as blood flooded his lungs. Rafael closed his eyes, holding the boy and gently stroking his hair until he stopped struggling, only the occasional twitch of his limbs betraying the last vestiges of life. A final gush of blood onto his grubby T-shirt and the boy fell limp.

"Go in peace, my young friend, *ma'assalama*," Rafael whispered softly, and set the body gently down in the darkness.

He turned and walked back across the street, slipping the blade into his jacket and pulling the scarf up across his face before reaching the door of the building and quietly slipping inside.

43

"That's ridiculous."

Rachel Morgan gazed at Hassim Khan as though he had just grown horns. Ethan too found himself intrigued by Hassim's casual degradation of the miracle of life.

"Life is debris?" he asked.

"And nothing more," Hassim replied. "It is a scientific fact that was uncovered decades ago. It concerns the fabric of our entire cosmos, everything that we are and everything that we're made of, changing over time."

"Then how come we don't all know about it?" Ethan challenged.

"A question that I too would like answered. If all people were educated about the fundamental origin of life, then there would be far more understanding in the world."

Rachel shook her head.

"How can life be everywhere and be debris? It doesn't make sense."

Hassim shrugged.

"When our universe was born in the Big Bang, it consisted of about three-quarters hydrogen, a quarter helium, a smattering of lithium and deuterium, and nothing else."

"How do you know that?" Rachel asked.

"Because it still does," Hassim said. "The rest of the universe's mass is made up of dark matter and dark energy, substances about which we know very little indeed."

"And we're the debris?" Mahmoud asked.

"Absolutely," Hassim said. "Look at yourself. Look at the room you're in, the earth that we're standing on, the air that you're breathing. Think about anything chemical at all in this universe. Then think about what you've just learned. A universe filled with swiftly cooling hydrogen and helium gas, unknown dark materials, and *nothing else at all*."

Ethan thought for a moment.

"We must have been created after the Big Bang."

"Exactly," Hassim said. "People think that the universe came into being containing everything within it and that stars, planets, and life evolved thereafter over immense periods of time. This is basically correct but it misses a most important point: that the young universe contained no heavy elements like carbon, oxygen, silicon, iron, and so on—nothing that makes solid matter like planets, trees, oceans, or people."

"So where did it come from?" Ethan asked.

"Stars," Hassim replied. "They all form from interstellar clouds of hydrogen gas that collapse under their own gravity, creating pressure and heat within. When the core of the cloud gets hot enough, it shines with nuclear fusion, just as our sun does now. What's happening inside is that the hydrogen fuel is being converted into heat and light as atoms of hydrogen fuse together under the immense gravitational pressure: fusion. The thing is, when this occurs, only a small percentage of the mass of each atom is released. The rest remains within, and so the two nuclei fuse and create a new element, helium."

"Which was already present in the universe," Rachel said.

"Yes," Hassim agreed. "From this process, a helium core grows inside the star, and when it's big enough, it too begins burning with nuclear fusion, creating carbon. In stars, the deeper you go, the heavier the elements you find being created, all the way up to iron, if the star is large enough. When these stars exhaust all of their fuel, they blast their material out into space in supernova explosions to become part of the interstellar medium from which new stars are made. As the heavier elements build up in space after each generation, so the next generation of stars has an abundance of heavy elements that form planets and comets and asteroids in orbit around them: the things that we're made from."

Rachel blinked in surprise. "That's where the Earth came from?"

"Yes," Hassim said. "The process is called nucleosynthesis. This is where you get the sodium in common salt, the neon in fluorescent lights, and the magnesium in fireworks, not to mention the zinc in your hair, the calcium in your bones, and the carbon in your brain. The iron in the hemoglobin in your blood shares the same origin as the iron in the rocks of our planet. In your body there's enough iron to make a three-inch nail, enough carbon to make nine hundred pencils, enough phosphorous to make two thousand match heads, and enough water to fill a ten-gallon tank. We are all chemical beings."

"And all of this is 'old news'?" Ethan asked.

"The physics behind all of this was worked out in the 1950s and early 1960s, using Einstein's general relativity," Hassim said. "Scientists like Fred Hoyle, Geoffrey and Margaret Burbidge, and William Fowler did all the calculations long ago, and they've all been proven right with further actual observation of the stars using spectroscopy. William Fowler won the Nobel Prize for Physics in 1983 for the work done. But it's generally unknown within the public domain, and powerful faith movements prefer it to remain so. Their beliefs are all based upon a human-centric view of the universe, but nucleosynthesis proves that all life is merely a product of natural processes and not unusual or even unique to our world, their disinformation just a smoke screen to deceive the public."

"But why does that make Lucy's discovery so important to you?" Rachel asked.

"For two reasons," Hassim explained. "Firstly, if genetic material from the remains that Lucy found can be extracted and analyzed, it may show what evolutionary path life has followed through natural selection on other worlds. And secondly, it proves what we already suspect: that life is as common as the stars that fuel its existence."

"Several hundred billion stars in our galaxy alone," Rachel murmured, "and hundreds of billions of galaxies in the universe."

Ethan began to realize the scope of what Hassim was saying, and suddenly the existence of extraterrestrials didn't seem quite so ridiculous after all.

44

Rafael slipped through the door of the building and closed it behind him. An archaic iron lock protruded from the door. On an impulse he turned the key, locking the door from the inside, and slipped it into his pocket before taking in his surroundings.

Musty odors of dust and desiccated soil stained the air; chunks of dislodged masonry and shattered bricks littered the floor. Letting his eyes adjust before daring to move, he saw the faint outlines of a crumbling stairwell leading up and away to his left, and a narrow corridor ahead of him that led into the gloomy depths of the building.

He was about to venture forward into the corridor when he noticed a single door to his left, just before the stairwell. It stood ajar, and he crept toward it, reaching for his knife before swinging the door open.

A large gib frame stood in the center of the room. Atop the frame was a barrel-sized coil of thick rope, from the end of which dangled a heavy iron hook. To Rafael's right, an unused diesel generator crouched above patches of fuel staining the dusty floorboards.

Rafael edged forward, and in the dim light he saw a large rectangular hole hewn from the living earth, an impenetrable blackness that plunged to unknown depths beneath the city. On the far side of the hole, a rope ladder was tied to two stakes driven deep into the earth, the ladder vanishing down into the darkness.

Rafael squatted at the edge of the tunnel entrance and listened intently.

No sound emanated from within, although he could feel the hot air from the underground tunnels wafting toward him as though the ancient soil was breathing. He knew that there would be other entrances and exits from this tunnel, providing some meager ventilation to those hiding or incarcerated within.

He closed his eyes, orienting himself within the building to the street outside, picturing the layout of the nearby streets. He recalled the single glowing streetlight perhaps a hundred yards to his left. Power was intermittent in Gaza and electricity cables were often run directly down the tunnels by insurgents, using either the grid or generators to supply light to the depths. This tunnel would most likely pass close by the streetlight, an easy point at which to tap into the electricity supply. From there, he suspected that a row of buildings on the opposite side of the street provided a likely termination point, an escape route for Hamas fighters fleeing an Israeli assault.

Rafael pocketed his blade and moved around to the ladder, carefully testing its strength before lowering himself into the darkness.

45

The remains Lucy found were similar to humans," Rachel said. "You think that life on other planets is like life on Earth?"

Hassim Khan shook his head.

"That's unlikely. Life on other planets will endure differing environments. If a planet orbiting another star was more massive than Earth, then its gravity would be correspondingly higher, resulting in species of a more muscular build to counter their increased weight on such a planet. That could match the physicality of the species Lucy found."

"But it looked almost human to me," Ethan said, "just a lot bigger. Surely that can't be possible on an entirely different planet?"

"Evolution often follows certain paths," Hassim explained. "There are facets of biological species that often appear as a result of natural selection, especially in predatory species. Limbs, eyes, ears, grasping hands, and so on appear frequently in the fossil record. There is no reason to think that this would not occur on other planets too."

Ethan sat in thought for a moment.

"Do you think that genetic material could be extracted from Lucy's find?"

"Almost certainly." Hassim nodded. "Researchers have successfully extracted intact blood cells from a *Tyrannosaurus rex* bone some sixty-five million years old. The remains that Lucy found were only seven thousand years old. I wouldn't be surprised if they were able to recover organic material from it, maybe even intact DNA."

"Which would confirm the idea of life forming on a universal theme," Ethan guessed.

Hassim smiled.

"The origin of life among the stars as a universal and not a local event," Hassim agreed. "It's known as *panspermia.*"

"You mean that we didn't evolve on Earth?" Rachel stammered.

"Oh, we evolved here all right," Hassim corrected. "But the very things we are made of did not, and that may include life in all of its self-replicating glory. It has been known for some time that when giant stars die in supernova explosions, the material they release in the cooling conditions contain carbon grains, and that particles of other chemical elements attach themselves to the tiny grains and react enthusiastically with each other. These carbon grains were given a name: stardust."

"Grains?" Ethan asked. "Like sand?"

"Much smaller," Hassim said. "Spectroscopic studies of these star-remnant molecular clouds have found there the presence of methanimine, formaldehyde, formic acid, amine groups, and long-chain hydrocarbons caught within their veils. These are the building blocks of life: methanimine is an ingredient in amino acids; formic acid is the chemical that insects use as venom and is also the stinging ingredient in nettles. Both are polyatomic organic molecules that combine to form the amino acid glycine, which has since been seen in molecular clouds in deep space and found in comets by NASA in 2009, and amino acids are one step away from life itself."

"And that's without planets forming?" Rachel asked.

"Yes," Hassim said. "Ultraviolet radiation bathes the clouds, heat from other nearby stars warms them, and all manner of chemical reactions occur. Frozen water, methanol, and ammonia rapidly form around the grains as the heat from the supernova fades. Trapped within these tiny cores the elements react and produce various polyatomic molecules. Experiments carried out in 2001 at NASA's Ames Research Center confirmed these processes, when silicate grains covered in this kind of material were chilled to the temperature of deep space and suspended in ultraviolet light. When the organic compounds produced were immersed in water, membranous cell structures appeared spontaneously, as they may well have done on the young Earth: life, without supernatural intervention. All life on Earth is based on cells such as these, biological material encased in a membrane."

"It all fits together," Ethan said, genuinely amazed.

"That's what science does. In 2002," Hassim went on without missing a beat, "further experiments conducted with water, methanol, ammonia, and hydrogen cyanide found in molecular clouds discovered that three amino acids called glycine, serine, and alanine arose spontaneously within the containers. In another similar experiment, no less than sixteen amino acids and other organic compounds were produced under the conditions that exist between the stars using nothing more than the ingredients of molecular clouds. The proteins of all living things on Earth are composed of combinations of twenty amino acids."

Ethan grasped where Hassim was going just before Rachel did.

"All life might be very similar in a fundamental way," he said.

"Yes," Hassim agreed, and tapped his own chest. "The chemical reactions that support metabolism in all of our bodies involve just eleven small carbon molecules such as acetic and citric acids. These eleven molecules would have been sufficient to produce chemical reactions that led to the development of biomolecules such as amino acids, lipids, sugars, and eventually early genetic molecules like RNA on Earth. Metabolism came first, the fuel for life, before cells or replication or anything else. Life then followed as a natural result of chemical metabolism. If it happened here on Earth, then it could happen anywhere on suitable planets harboring liquid water, and life might follow a similar path of evolutionary development that leads eventually to intelligence."

Rachel caught on quickly.

"And if an intelligent species evolved on a planet reasonably close by, and was only ten thousand years more advanced than us . . ."

"Even a thousand years more advanced might do it," Hassim said. "In two hundred years mankind has gone from wooden sailing ships and witchcraft to landing on the moon and nuclear power. Think what we could be like in another thousand years."

"It would look like magic," Ethan said, remembering Arthur C. Clarke's *Third Law*. "Or God. But could they be that much more advanced than us?"

"The universe has been producing stars for over thirteen billion years," Hassim explained, "and the elements required for life have been in place within galaxies for at least eight billion years. By our planet's timeline of evolution, it's quite possible that advanced, intelligent life has existed in our universe for the past

four billion years or so. The technology of such civilizations could be advanced on a scale completely unimaginable to us."

"If so," Ethan challenged, "then why would they
bother with us at all?"

"We can only speculate," Hassim admitted, "but
such civilizations may well have been forced to travel
through space as their parent stars aged and became unstable: the window in which our own Earth can support
complex life is surprisingly short in cosmological terms,
ending as the sun grows hotter and Earth is no longer
able to harbor liquid water. However, although life may
be common in the universe, intelligent life will be much
rarer, and if you were an advanced race traveling the
stars and found early humans struggling to survive after
a climatic disaster, wouldn't you be tempted to stop and
help them or at least investigate?"

Rachel stood up, pacing again as she struggled with
the consequences of her newfound knowledge.

"But if this actually happened, surely our ancestors
with their newly acquired skills might have recorded it
better, in more detail?"

"Perhaps they did," Hassim said. "But we haven't
learned to recognize the signs for what they are yet."

"How do you mean?" Ethan asked.

"Imagine," Hassim suggested, "that you're living
in ancient Egypt, before the pyramids or technology,
and down from the skies come beings that reveal great
knowledge to you and then vanish again. As you struggle
to capitalize upon this new knowledge, would you not be
tempted to beg them for help, to make contact again?"

"I guess so," Ethan agreed.

"And how would you do that?" Hassim asked.

"I'd make a sign," Ethan said cautiously, "in the

ground or something." Then he got it. "A big sign, big enough to see from the air."

"Exactly," Hassimm nodded. "You'd create mega-structures, hoping that your mysterious flying benefactors would see them and return."

Rachel seemed bemused.

"You're talking about the pyramids, aren't you?"

"Not just the pyramids," Hassim replied. "Almost every major ancient megastructure, and I can prove it too. Have either of you heard of something called a cargo cult?"

Rachel was about to answer, but Mahmoud got up from the crate upon which he had been sitting and looked at her.

"Whatever your daughter was dabbling in, it is better left alone. There are some things we weren't meant to see," he warned before looking at Yossaf. "Time to check the tunnels."

Ethan watched as the two Palestinians went in opposite directions.

"Why would MACE abduct Lucy when they could just have taken the remains and left her there?" he asked Hassim.

"The reason for that, my friend," Hassim said, "is almost too horrific to speak of."

46

Rafael crouched at the bottom of the ladder, enveloped in near pitch-blackness but for the glow of a low-watt lightbulb flaring some ten meters down the narrow, craggy walls of the tunnel.

He crept away from the ladder, careful to avoid the electrical cables secured with lengths of string that ran along the upper-left corner of the tunnel. The smuggling tunnels were periodically bombed by Israel, and as a result the Palestinians bothered little with such trivial concerns as electrical insulation.

The heat clung like a blanket to Rafael's skin as he edged forward, holding his knife in a loose grip. He had no idea how many men might be hiding down in the tunnels, nor how they were armed. If he encountered anyone, they would have to be dispatched quickly and silently.

The harsh light of the bulb ahead obscured the tunnel beyond, preventing Rafael from seeing more distant threats. A small fly buzzed lazily around the light, entrapped beneath the earth. Rafael kept his gaze downward, sensing for movement ahead on the upper periphery of his vision as he ducked beneath the bulb. He crouched to avoid casting long shadows down the tunnel, and then peered ahead into the gloom.

Perhaps five meters or so ahead the tunnel turned right, to where a faint patch of light glowed from some unseen source. Rafael observed a particularly large cable entombed in the wall of the tunnel and guessed he was beneath the streetlight he had seen, the tunnel's electrical supply spliced into the mains. That would mean that the tunnel indeed terminated beneath the houses at the opposite end of the street. He recalled that several were abandoned buildings, the skeletal remains of Palestinian homes and businesses pounded into oblivion by Israel.

He crept toward the curve in the tunnel and was halfway there when a flicker of a shadow drifted across the patch of light. Rafael froze and crouched down again.

The shadow began moving toward him.

Then he heard the footfalls. Urgent synapses fired across his brain, thoughts too rapid to process yet crystalline in their clarity. *The shadow moved toward me. Footsteps, heavy, male. Moving slowly.*

A chunky figure with broad shoulders and a thick neck appeared in the tunnel, the unmistakable shape of an AK-47 rifle cradled loosely in his grip. Rafael crouched down, concealed in the darkness between the two light sources. *Don't move. Movement is much more dangerous than staying still.*

The figure lumbered closer, the footfalls growing louder and heavier, thumping rhythmically with the rolling beats of Rafael's heart. *Move without fear, without tension, without compromise. Breathe.* The body now blocked the light from beyond completely, looming to fill Rafael's field of view.

He relaxed his body and mind, exhaling a ghost's breath as he did so.

Rafael lunged upward and forward even as the

man's eyes registered the form crouched in the tunnel before him. Rafael's blade flickered in the weak light and plunged into the man's throat with a quiet, crisp rasp.

The man's cry gargled somewhere below his thorax, lost forever as the blade crossed his windpipe and severed his spinal column just above the third vertebra. Rafael caught the man as he fell, his body crumpling onto the ground in the center of the tunnel. He quickly slammed his hand over the man's bearded mouth, slipping the blade out of his throat as he yanked the head to one side and jabbed the steel upward into his skull. A faint crackling of splintered bone just behind and below the ear, and the body jerked with a series of diminishing spasms before falling still. The undignified odor of spilled feces tainted the hot, stale air as Rafael slipped the blade out of the lifeless skull.

He stood quickly and forged ahead through the tunnel. There was nowhere to hide the body, and it could be discovered at any moment. Time was of the essence.

Ahead, somewhere beyond the turn in the tunnel, the sound of voices reached his ears.

47

What do you mean horrific?" Rachel asked, concern stretching her skin tightly across her features.

Hassim Khan massaged his temples. "You say that you went to Lucy's dig site?"

"That was where I got the images on my camera." Ethan nodded.

"I saw them," Hassim said. "And the specimen that Lucy discovered was in a crate."

"Yes, but it hadn't been sealed yet."

Rachel looked at Hassim. "What are you thinking?"

"We know that the remains alone are not reason enough for your daughter's abduction: as you said, they could have left her there."

"What about money?" Rachel said. "A ransom."

Hassim shook his head.

"A sale of such remains would be almost impossible to coordinate without being detected by enforcement agencies, and a ransom would come with demands that we haven't had."

Ethan leaned back against the wall. "Bill Griffiths is a fossil hunter and he holds the only key to exposing this abduction for what it really is: a theft. He walked away from me when I offered him five million dollars."

"What then, if not money?" Rachel asked Hassim, her fists clenched by her side.

Hassim stood, pacing as he spoke.

"Your daughter was one of several people to have vanished from that area of the Negev Desert. No remains have ever been found. All of those disappearances have occurred since MACE began working out here in Israel under the AEA's control."

"You think that the church is really behind it all?" Ethan asked.

"Their leader, a powerful pastor named Kelvin Patterson, has been a vocal proponent of using science to prove the existence of God, using his television and radio stations to promote his views. He believes that faith has proven itself impotent without knowledge, and is known to have conducted various experiments in the past with volunteers from his church in an attempt to discover the nature of the divine."

"Experiments?" Rachel asked nervously. "What kind of experiments?"

Hassim's voice was low, as though he regretted having to speak at all.

"The kind that require live volunteers. But if there are other experiments he wishes to conduct that are illegal, and he requires live bodies, then there are ways to acquire them."

Rachel seemed to Ethan to be having difficulty breathing as she spoke.

"What might they do to Lucy?"

"I don't know," he admitted. "But after what has happened to you both they'll be keen to get the remains out of Israel before you can inform the authorities. Even a fossil hunter as well connected as Bill Griffiths will have difficulty in achieving that without some kind of specialist help."

Ethan nodded. "He'll need a company trusted by the Israeli government, just like MACE. I need to make a phone call."

Hassim looked at Mahmoud as he emerged from one of the tunnels. The Palestinian shook his head.

"You can't make a call from down here; we're too deep for a signal and we can't risk moving at night. We can get you to the Erez crossing at dawn."

"What time is it?" Ethan asked.

"Two-thirty in the morning," Hassim said, glancing at his watch.

"That makes it the middle of the afternoon in Chicago. If I can make a call, I can smooth the way for us."

A look of displeasure creased Mahmoud's features. "We should wait until Yossaf returns from checking the building."

"As long as Yossaf is between us and the other exit, we have nothing to fear."

Mahmoud glanced at Hassim, then sighed and nodded.

"We can use the opposite end of the tunnel and make the call from there. It leads to a building on the far side of the street."

Rafael, crouched in the darkness, listened intently.

He did not need to see the faces of the people talking a few meters away, hidden from sight by the curving tunnel walls and the shadows. Arabic and American voices left him in no doubt that he was in the right place. The name of a man, Bill Griffiths, drifted to within earshot of his position, and he thought of the fossil hunter employed by Byron Stone and Spencer Malik.

Perhaps aid workers were secretly assisting in-surgents? Or maybe journalists had gained access to the tunnels, an event not unknown near Rafah on the Egyptian border.

Either way, Rafael would have to work swiftly and without endangering innocent lives.

Slowly, he edged back into the deeper darkness be-hind him, still with his knife clasped in one hand in case the possessor of the more threatening voice he had heard should choose to wander in his direction.

He turned, moving swiftly past the corpse of the man whose name he now knew had been Yossaf, and moved as swift as a leopard through the darkness toward the distant light ahead. He reached the ladder, pausing only for a few moments to listen for pursuers or for anyone lingering above him at the tunnel entrance before scaling the ladder and emerging into the building above.

He squatted down and reached into his pocket for a small device, the blue glow from the screen lighting his features with a peculiar radiance. The GPS device showed an image of the Gazan streets at the point where he had entered the tunnel. Rafael oriented the device to point north, read the coordinates at the top of the screen, and added two seconds latitude to the west and one to the north for the building the Palestinian had referred to.

Rafael reached again into his pocket for his cell phone, accessing the text menu, and typing in the coor-dinates from his GPS device. He quickly added a line of text to the message.

TARGET LOCATED, COORDINATES ABOVE.
STRIKE IN TEN MINUTES!!!

Rafael pressed the Send button, waiting until the message was confirmed as sent before pocketing the device and his GPS receiver.

Turning, he gripped the ladder and once again descended into the tunnel.

48

RAMON AIR BASE
NEGEV DESERT, ISRAEL

Twinkling like a galaxy amid the immense black universe of the Negev, the lights of the sprawling air base glowed blue and orange as they traced the lines of taxiways and a broad runway stretching out into the dark wilderness. Cavernous hangars loomed against the night sky, one of them with its immense doors open. Within, small groups of men worked feverishly with fuel lines and sensors, cables and satellite communication dishes.

In their midst sat an aircraft with a sleek triangular shape, looking like a fighter plane and coated in matte black paint. But there was no space for a pilot, the cockpit replaced by a sharply angled nose sheathed with dark glass that contained a multitude of cameras and sensors. The legend MACE was stenciled down the fuselage in stealthy graphite gray, and beneath it a single word: VALKYRIE.

"Clear for engine start!"

Technicians and soldiers alike backed away as the unmistakable whine of a turbine engine issued from the aircraft's exhaust. It reached a crescendo and then settled down to a steady whistle, a series of navigation lights flickering on the wing tips as the unmanned aerial vehicle rolled out of the hangar toward the huge runway nearby.

The men watched as it turned onto the airstrip as though guided by an artificial intelligence. With a sudden howl from the engine it lurched forward, accelerating and lifting off into the darkness. The whine faded as the gently blinking lights rose up into the night sky, and then even they were extinguished.

Utterly invisible and with its small turbine engine almost inaudible as it climbed above two thousand feet, the UAV turned toward the distant Mediterranean.

MACE
JERUSALEM

Spencer Malik watched as the technicians operated the controls of the Valkyrie, one flying the aircraft and the other monitoring the weapons and guidance systems. A large screen in the office before him showed a pixelated, green-tinged image of ramshackle buildings and dusty streets illuminated by sporadic streetlights. The image jerked and lurched under the high zoom of the camera as the Valkyrie bobbed and bounced on wind currents.

"We have the coordinates," Malik said, watching over the technician's shoulders and reading the figures from his cell phone to them. One of the young men tapped the coordinates into a computer, and the image on the screen snapped briskly to the right.

"It's in Jabaliya, sir," the technician reported. "Four buildings at those coordinates."

"Get into position," Malik ordered. "We will launch as soon as we've identified the most likely target."

"Do we have assets on the ground?" the other technician asked.

Malik stood for a moment, an image of Rafael materializing in his mind. By now the Arab would almost certainly have infiltrated the required building in order to have sent the coordinates. With only empty or incomplete apartment blocks and shattered concrete hulks visible on the screen, it stood to reason that the prisoners were being held beneath ground. Nowhere to run.

"Our asset will have left the scene by now," Malik replied with a grim smile. "Strike as soon as you have the target in sight."

49

JABALIYA
GAZA

The cool caress of the night air was the sweetest thing that Ethan had ever experienced as he clambered from the tunnel. As he stood in the center of a shattered apartment block and sucked in a lungful of that air, surrounded by ragged towers of masonry that had once been the home of Palestinian families, he noticed a vast panorama of stars glittering in the heavens above him.

For the first time in his life, Ethan realized he was looking at those stars in a totally different way. The ancient pagan cults had got it right after all, worshipping nature and the heavens without ever realizing how close to the truth they'd actually been. Mankind was not alone.

"You can make your call from there."

Ethan turned in the direction Mahmoud indicated, toward a concrete ramp that had once been the upper floor of the apartment block and now lay at a steep angle against the surface of the last remaining upright wall.

Ethan picked his way between blocks of rubble that

littered the earth around him. He stepped up onto the ramp, climbing until he was some ten feet above the ground. He looked at his cell phone and glanced back at Mahmoud, giving him a thumbs-up. Mahmoud made no response, simply standing guard in the darkness.

Ethan sat down on the ramp and dialed a number into his cell phone, waiting for the line to connect. From his elevated viewpoint he could see the low roofs and haphazard streets of Gaza stretching away to the south between the skeletal remains of the building.

"Hello?"

"Doug? It's Ethan."

"Ethan!" It sounded as though Doug Jarvis had fallen out of bed. *"Where the hell have you been? What happened to the daily call?"*

"Things got complicated and we were compromised before I could contact you," Ethan said quickly. "I don't have much time, so just listen."

"Go ahead," Jarvis replied.

"Lucy's disappearance isn't just to do with fossil hunters: it's got something to do with an American security company called MACE: Munitions for Advanced Combat Environments. They've been operating out here for some time and have the ear of the Israeli Defense Ministry. It was their people who stole Lucy's discovery and they presumably know what happened to her and her team."

"MACE," Doug echoed. *"Haven't heard of them."*

"There's more," Ethan said quickly. "They're responsible for atrocities against the indigenous population of Bedouin in the Negev and I have it on film. Unfortunately, they know this and have been trying to recover the incriminating evidence, and they're not shy of shooting first and asking questions later."

"Christ, Ethan! Is Rachel okay? Where are you?"

"Rachel's fine," Ethan assured him. "We're in Gaza. We were chased here by MACE operatives and we're trying to get back into Israel. I need you to contact the IDF and clear us a passage through the Erez crossing by dawn our time."

"You're in Gaza?" Ethan could hear the concern in Doug's voice. *"Who are you with?"*

"It's a long story," Ethan replied. "Let's just say that we know that insurgents did not abduct Lucy or anyone else in her team."

There was a pause on the line before Jarvis spoke again. *"Look after my daughter, Ethan."*

"I'll have her out of Gaza by dawn, I promise. I need you to look into MACE, see if you can find out what connections they have to the fossil black market, or anything that might give us some perspective on what the hell they're *really* doing out here. Look for any connection that you can find with something called the American Evangelical Alliance, a church in DC that owns the company."

"Consider it done," Jarvis said.

Ethan was about to speak when he noticed Mahmoud leap with feline agility onto the edge of the ramp and stare up into the night sky. The Palestinian's face contorted as though he was straining to hear something, and then with an urgent grimace he waved at Ethan to follow him.

"Doug, I've got to go," Ethan said, standing and running down the ramp.

"Why, what's happenin—"

Ethan had barely managed to shut the phone off when Mahmoud grabbed him and hurled him toward the tunnel entrance. For a brief moment Ethan heard a strange humming noise.

"What's happening?"

"Get down!"

In an instant the entire area around Ethan lit up in a blinding flare of unimaginable brightness. His eyes automatically shut, an image of ruined buildings seared onto his retina amid blazing light as a blast of super-heated air slammed into him like a freight train.

50

Ethan felt his body propelled sideways through the air as an enormous explosion radiated out from a nearby building. He slammed into the ground backward, felt the breath blasted from his lungs as he crashed into a slab of shattered brickwork. He rolled away instinctively from the painful assault on his eardrums as the darkness plunged down around him once more.

He lay for several seconds with his arms over his head, curled into a fetal ball in the rubble as the pain in his ears subsided to a torturous ringing echo of the infernal blast. He rolled over, lifting his arms from his head and trying to force his eyes to focus.

The entire adjoining building had been obliterated, a burning wasteland of vaporized rubble and debris cast wide by the explosion. The few shattered walls that remained standing looked like the carcasses of rotting animals burning from within. From the stygian darkness above fell a rain of glowing embers that spiraled down around him.

Ethan blinked into the flames, and saw a figure moving with them, the flames curling around her body like snakes. For a moment he thought Rachel had been caught in the blast, but then he saw blond hair shining in

the light of the fires, saw Joanna standing on the edge of·
the darkness. Ethan staggered to his feet as his legs quivered beneath him, and struggled toward her, the searing
flames ahead stinging his eyes.

"This way!"

Mahmoud leaped from nowhere through the clouds
of cement dust and falling embers, his hair and face
caked with dust. He grabbed Ethan's shoulder and
yanked him away from the fire.

"What are you doing?" the Palestinian demanded.

Ethan saw the phantom image of Joanna spirited
away on the crackling flames before him. Above the
humming in his ears he heard the cries of Palestinians
fleeing in the darkness, the screeching of women and the
haunting cries of children awoken by the blast. Nausea
poisoned his innards and swelled into his throat, and he
jolted forward as a thin stream of bile splattered into the
darkness at his feet.

"Come on!" Mahmoud shouted.

Ethan staggered along with him, trying to ignore
the acid burning his throat as they stumbled across the
broken remains of the building, illuminated now by the
shimmering flames.

"Hurry, there will be more," Mahmoud said as they
reached the entrance to the tunnel.

Ethan clambered down the ladder on legs weakened
from shock, Mahmoud following him underground once
again into the cloying heat. Ethan reached the tunnel
floor and turned to his right, regaining his senses as he
jogged along the passage. He emerged into the subter-
ranean chamber to see Hassim and Rachel looking panicked and confused.

"What happened?" Rachel asked.

"I don't know," Ethan said, guzzling water from

his mug and turning to see Mahmoud join them in the tunnel.

"Air strike," the Palestinian said urgently. "Somebody knows that you are here."

"We have to get aboveground," Rachel said, her features pale as she looked at the earthen walls surrounding them.

Mahmoud, his pistol held at the ready, gestured with a nod of his head to Hassim.

"Go, there is nothing more that we can do for you here. You must seek protection from Israel."

Hassim was about to leave when the sound of thunder blasted through the tunnel.

Ethan had no time to react before the shock wave rushed down into the chamber, solid and unstoppable. Ethan felt himself hurled sideways as though clubbed by a giant baseball bat, saw Rachel flung to the ground in a blaze of confusion and noise. Hassim slammed sideways into a wall and crumpled to his knees. Mahmoud crouched before the blast, rolling over as dust and debris filled the chamber in a dense, choking cloud.

Ethan's knees connected with the earth with a dull crack as grime filled his nose and throat. Fighting an instinctive panic, he struggled to get to his feet as the lights in the chamber flickered around him.

Rafael charged forward, his scarf wrapped across his face to protect him from the thick dust that swirled in diaphanous eddies down the tunnel toward him. Like a demon flitting through the catacombs of hell, he sprinted toward the light of the chamber as the second detonation thundered through the darkness, the walls of the tunnel shuddering beneath the blow. The light ahead flickered as the shadows of tumbling figures were cast through the glowing veils of dust.

Rafael rushed on with scarcely a pause, reaching into his pocket and producing a small pair of bolt cutters. As he reached the chamber he glanced left and right, then reached up to his left and with a single swift crunch sliced through the electrical cables running along the ceiling.

The light vanished, and he heard shouts of alarm from the chamber as the occupants were plunged into complete darkness.

51

The tunnel's collapsed!"

Ethan heard Mahmoud's voice shouting out to them, but in the darkness he could see nothing as grains of grit scratched across his corneas. His exhaustion suddenly overwhelmed him as he lost his balance and staggered, his darkened world gyrating and pitching. His voice when he called out was choked and raspy.

"Rachel? Hassim?"

For one long, terrible moment he heard no reply as he fumbled in the darkness with his hands outstretched. Something brushed his fingers, someone moving past him, and he heard the sound of rapid footfalls in the darkness.

"Rachel?"

"I'm here," came her voice from another direction in the inky blackness.

Ethan flailed to his left, trying to stay upright.

"There's a flashlight," Mahmoud's voice called out, "in the wall by the entrance."

Ethan turned, guessing roughly where the entrance to the chamber was, and felt his way there with his arms outstretched. His fingers touched the walls of the chamber as he fumbled until he felt the wall vanish into the tunnel. Something brushed past him again in the darkness, disappearing almost before he had registered its presence.

"I can reach it," he said, turning sideways.

Ethan struggled across to the opposite wall and groped in the blackness for several seconds until he found the recess where Mahmoud must have stored the flashlight. Quickly, he reached inside and grabbed a cylindrical object, turning as his thumb found a switch on the barrel. The beam burst into life, cutting a swathe of light through the cramped chamber.

Ethan blinked the grit from his eyes, sweeping the beam in Rachel's direction. He saw her crouched beside the crates with Hassim, the scientist's arms wrapped protectively around her.

"Get out of here, both of you!" Ethan shouted, pointing the flashlight beam down the tunnel to guide them.

Hassim lurched to his feet and hurried out of the chamber, with Rachel close behind.

"Mahmoud?" Ethan called, sweeping the beam to his left.

"Get out of here," Mahmoud called, "they'll hit the building again! Go now!"

Ethan was about to turn and run when he remembered his rucksack.

"My camera," he said, rushing forward and directing the beam at the chair where his belongings had been deposited. He stopped dead in his tracks as he saw that the rucksack had vanished. Mahmoud appeared through the dust clouds, his face wracked with anger.

"Go, now! To hell with the rucksack!"

Ethan remembered his fingers brushing across someone in the chamber before he'd found the flash-

light, and a shiver rippled down his spine. He turned
the beam around the chamber before pointing it down
the tunnel. In the light, he saw a severed electrical cable
dangling from the tunnel ceiling. Before either Ethan or
Mahmoud could say a word, a scream echoed down the
tunnels toward them.

"Rachel!"

Ethan sprinted out of the chamber toward her voice.
He was almost halfway down the tunnel when he saw
something large crumpled on the ground before him. He
leaped over the body, glimpsing Yossaf's bearded face
slick with blood.

Mahmoud skidded to a halt beside the body, and
then shouted after Ethan.

"Wait! We're not alone!"

Another scream came from the darkness ahead and
Ethan ran toward it, all thoughts of his own safety suddenly vanquished by the fear that something was happening to Rachel. He rushed into the small antechamber
halfway down the tunnel, the bouncing flashlight beam
illuminating Hassim and Rachel as they fled down the
tunnel ahead, and then something slammed into Ethan's
stomach with immense force, voiding the air from his
lungs. The flashlight spun from his grip as he fell to the
ground, chunks of dust and grit filling his mouth.

He heard a shout of fury as he rolled onto his back,
struggling against the pain swelling in his abdomen
while he fought to regain his feet. In the diffuse, shifting
light of the rolling flashlight beam he saw Mahmoud and
a stranger locked in a furious exchange of blows, primal
growls of rage and fear filling the tunnel as though wild
animals were fighting for their lives.

Ethan struggled to his feet and rushed forward as
Mahmoud was beaten back into the darkened tunnel

beyond by his assailant. Ethan could see his rucksack on the attacker's back and a bolt of fury coursed through his veins. He grabbed the bag and yanked the man backward with all of his might.

The attacker turned, shifting his balance with lightning speed and unstoppable force as he gripped Ethan with hands sheathed in black leather gloves. Ethan felt his body being propelled backward as the attacker turned Ethan's advantage into his own and hurled him into the wall of the antechamber. Ethan's skull smacked into the wall, jarring his vision as his teeth clashed in his jaw with a sharp crack. The man released Ethan as he fell, twisting so that Ethan felt his grip on the rucksack weaken and the fabric slip from his fingers. In an instant, the attacker vanished into the adjoining tunnel.

Ethan struggled to regain his balance, but almost instantly the tunnel was rocked as another blast slammed into the earth above his head. The walls of the tunnel crumpled around him, the light from the flashlight almost completely lost as the main chamber collapsed, clouds of dust billowing thickly through the tunnel. He heard a splintering sound as the desiccated timbers supporting the ceiling fractured beneath the blast, followed by an anguished cry from somewhere in the darkness.

"Mahmoud?"

Ethan's own voice was feeble, his throat parched like the deserts above as he groped for the flashlight. He found it and turned the beam to see Mahmoud facedown before him in the mouth of the antechamber, shattered timbers and chunks of rock and earth piled high across the backs of his legs.

"Go!" Mahmoud spluttered angrily. "Get out!"

The ceiling of the chamber rippled, rocks and thick lumps of earth falling to shatter around Ethan's feet as the timbers above his head groaned. A jagged crack in the ceiling snaked its way above his head and spilt streams of dust like dark water from its depths.

Ethan tossed the flashlight to one side and grabbed Mahmoud beneath his armpits, hauling with all of his strength. The Palestinian cried out as Ethan pulled, his teeth gritted and his eyes shut tight.

A timber as thick as Ethan's thigh split above them, a cascade of crumbling dirt spilling onto Ethan's head and shoulders. He ignored the falling debris, gagging for air as he repositioned his feet and pulled again on Mahmoud's torso.

The earth trapping the Palestinian shifted and then suddenly his body slid free, Mahmoud kicking back against the debris as Ethan hauled him clear and toppled over. Mahmoud scrambled to his feet and grabbed the flashlight, pulling Ethan upright by his shirt and shoving him down the tunnel ahead.

The timbers behind them plunged down with a terrific crash as Ethan ran through the darkness, the tunnel ahead lit only by the wavering beam of Mahmoud's flashlight. He lurched to the ladder, grabbing the rails and hauling himself upward on legs that were quivering with fatigue.

Ethan finally reached the top and dragged himself out onto the concrete, and Mahmoud followed him up and out of the tunnel. Ethan, his lungs sore and aching, coughed heavily and saw clouds of fine dust puff out of his chest. He barely had the strength to get onto his hands and knees, and as he did so he felt his stomach plunge in dismay.

"No."

Rachel was sitting with her back to the wall and her hands over her mouth. She was staring at a body lying on the opposite side of the hatch from Ethan, just in front of the open door of the building. Ethan wiped the grime from his eyes with the back of his hand, and realized that the body belonged to Hassim Khan.

Ethan struggled to his feet and joined Mahmoud, who crouched down next to the scientist and searched for a pulse. Ethan looked down and saw Hassim's eyes vacant and empty. Behind his head, thick blood leaked into cracks in the concrete.

Rachel looked at Ethan.

"Someone stabbed him," she said, alternately angry and horrified. "A man had locked the doors. Hassim fought him for the key."

Ethan felt a bleak sense of desolation overwhelm him.

"Whoever he was, he took my camera and the explosives."

Mahmoud gently closed Hassim's eyes and then stood, turning to face Ethan.

"His death will not be in vain. Allah willing, he will be in paradise, but we must get outside. They may bomb this building too."

Ethan helped Rachel gently to her feet and followed Mahmoud in an unsteady run out into the night air.

To their right across the street a large building burned. Palestinians milled about in the light from the flames and pointed at Ethan and his companions. Before Ethan could orient himself to the world around him, a humming sound drifted through the streets from somewhere above. Palestinians immediately scattered in all directions as the sound reverberated between Gaza's crumbling walls.

Mahmoud grabbed his shoulder.

"They are coming, run!"

Ethan took Rachel's hand in his and turned, breaking into a run. Behind them, the humming sound became louder, as though some unspeakable prehistoric creature was swooping down from the inky blackness above.

52

JERUSALEM

There are too many people."

Spencer Malik watched the large screen before him showing a blazing building in garish shades of yellow and orange. The shapes of fleeing Palestinians littered the scene, some running away from the burning building, others paradoxically running toward it.

"They'll come out of one of the adjacent buildings," Malik said. "Just keep the camera steady."

The technician flying the Valkyrie struggled to keep the aircraft in position.

"We're running out of airspace; I'll have to turn."

Malik watched the screen intently, and spotted three figures sprinting away from the burning remains of the building. He squinted at the image, seeing the clothes that they wore, the way that they moved. For a brief moment, as the Valkyrie turned gracefully through the sky above them, he caught a glimpse of a pixelated but recognizable face.

"There they are." Malik pointed to the small group of running figures, their forms blurred and indistinct through the sensitive night-vision cameras. "Take them out."

The technician shook his head.

"We can't be sure at this range."

Malik smashed a clenched fist down on the table beside him.

"Kill all of them. That's an order!"

The whine of the turbine engine howling behind Ethan and Rachel was suddenly broken by a loud clattering noise that echoed off the densely packed buildings around them.

"Get down!"

Ethan hit the ground behind Mahmoud as bullets whipped and cracked around them, churning the dust in wicked little bursts. Rachel slammed down alongside him, her long hair smothering his face. The sound of the turbine howled past overhead and vanished.

"This way!" Mahmoud said. "We must get out of sight!"

Mahmoud scrambled to his feet and turned right down a narrow alley. Ethan dragged his protesting body up again, Rachel struggling alongside him as they plunged down the alley in pursuit of Mahmoud. The Palestinian halted at the end, craning his neck to look up into the sky and listening intently.

"It's coming back; you can hear it."

Ethan strained, but could hear nothing save for the cries and shouts of alarm from around the burning building far behind them.

"We can't keep running like this," he said wearily. "There's nowhere to hide."

"They've used all of their missiles and have only bullets remaining now. In Gaza, there is always somewhere to hide from bullets." Mahmoud smiled grimly. "Come, this way."

They ran out into the street together, sprinting toward where the road ended in a T junction, splitting left and right and the way ahead blocked by a wall pockmarked with impact craters from artillery fire and bullets.

"There is another tunnel in the building at the end, on the left," Mahmoud shouted as they ran. "It goes under the wall and comes out in open ground beyond."

"They'll see us emerge!" Ethan shouted.

"We have only to wait until their fuel is exhausted."

Ethan turned, looking over his shoulder as the sound of the turbine whined back toward them.

"We're not going to make it!" he shouted.

Mahmoud reached the door of the house at the end of the street and promptly slammed into it as it failed to open before him.

Ethan slid to a halt alongside Mahmoud, who banged against the heavy door with his fist.

"Don't suppose you have a key?" Ethan muttered.

"It's coming back!" Rachel called, and pointed back down the street.

In the faint glow of the flickering flames from the adjoining street, Ethan saw the Valkyrie descending toward them, its inky fuselage silhouetted against the hellish inferno beyond.

"There's nowhere to go," he uttered helplessly.

The Valkyrie howled down the street toward them, and Ethan turned to shield Rachel from its view, waiting for the crackling sound of its guns and the unimaginable impact of superheated bullets slamming into their bodies.

The sudden howl of a rocket deafened Ethan as a trail of white smoke screeched past their heads from behind the battered wall nearby. Ethan glimpsed a slender shape whistling up into the sky and then the Valkyrie vanished amid a blast of boiling flames and smoke before falling in ungainly flaming spirals into the street below.

Mahmoud stared in shock at the shattered UAV as a growling mechanical roar filled the air. Ethan sheltered Rachel against the locked door as the wall nearby suddenly crumbled, chunks of masonry and clouds of cracked cement spraying out over the street.

"Israel is coming," Mahmoud muttered darkly, and placed one hand firmly on Ethan's shoulder. "I must leave, but know this: I owe you a debt, *sadiqi,* that cannot be repaid with words. *Ma'assalama.*"

Ethan opened his mouth to reply, but before he could speak Mahmoud had sprinted away and vanished into the chaotic sprawl of Gaza's alleys.

The roar intensified as an enormous tank rolled over the wall and onto the street, crunching over debris as its immense diesel engine snarled and smoked. Ethan stared at the troops wearing body armor and carrying assault weapons who were amassed around the vehicle. In the light of the distant flames, Ethan could see white discs marking the tank, each with a blue star in its center: the Star of David.

The tank drew up in the street and an Israeli soldier bearing the epaulettes of an officer moved quickly forward, his rifle pointed at them.

"We're American," Ethan called.

The Israeli officer hesitated, his expression alert and cautious. Ethan saw his eyes scan their bodies for any sign of explosive devices, a grim reminder of the threat to Israel from suicide bombers. Ethan's ripped shirt betrayed the presence of no suspicious packages, however, and the officer waved them forward.

"Ethan Warner?" the officer asked briskly.

"How the hell did you know we were here?" Ethan stammered.

"We got a call from Washington," the officer said. "Follow me."

Ethan led Rachel past the tank, its huge diesel engine idling now in the darkness, and knew that they would be safely escorted from Gaza. Doug Jarvis had come through once again.

"I need a direct line to the office of the commander of the Israeli Defense Force," Ethan told the soldier as he directed them to an armored personnel carrier parked nearby. "There's a lot I need to tell them."

"There's a lot the Ministry of Foreign Affairs needs to tell *you*," the officer replied, turning and pressing a pistol to Ethan's chest as another soldier grabbed his wrists and bound them in handcuffs.

"What are you doing?" Rachel demanded.

"Ethan Warner, you are under arrest," the officer said briskly. "I suggest that you reconsider your alliance with him, Ms. Morgan. He won't be in this country by the morning."

53

ROOM 517, HART SENATE OFFICE BUILDING
CONSTITUTION AVENUE, WASHINGTON DC

Kelvin Patterson stared at his appearance in the smoked-glass windows of Senator Isaiah Black's twin duplex suite in the Senate building. He looked tired, older than his years. Maybe the late nights were wearing him down, but this one was important enough to justify. He straightened his tie and smoothed his hair before retaking his seat.

In years gone by, men like Senator Black would have flocked to his church, eager to be seen to worship with the vigor of earlier times. No more. Now, such men considered themselves more powerful than him, more powerful even than God. From his viewpoint he could see the marble facade of the Hart Senate Office Building that led into a cavernous ninety-foot-high central atrium populated by milling crowds of diplomats, civil servants, and tourists. Walkways bridged the spaces above the atrium on each of the building's nine stories. Dominating the ground floor was a fifty-foot-high sculpture in black aluminum, *Mountains and Clouds*, suspended from a ceiling above that allowed natural light to illuminate the building.

A monument to power, and all of it before the eyes of a God they sullied with their arrogance. Patterson had been forced to cancel his press conference in light of the changing polls, and now found himself waiting on Senator Black's doorstep like any other citizen, begging for a chance to be heard.

As Patterson watched, a long black limousine pulled up outside the building and a tall man in a dark suit got out, surrounded by staff wearing earpieces and sunglasses. Senator Black strode into the Hart Senate Building surrounded by a maelstrom of journalists, broadsides of camera flashes and salvos of questions bombarding the senator's entourage as they wound their way through the atrium below.

Greater than God, Patterson thought to himself as Senator Black dismissed the wolves of the press with a bright smile, a wave, and a slick one-liner that dispersed the journalists with a trickle of laughter.

Patterson stood, and watched as the elevator nearby signaled the senator's imminent arrival.

"Pastor," the senator greeted him as he stepped from the elevator, his staff on either side of him, "I didn't expect to see you before the rally tomorrow."

Patterson shook his hand, following Black into the suite and closing the door behind him.

"Something came up."

They sat down on opposite sides of the senator's desk.

"What can I do for you?" Black asked.

"I take it that you have seen the news?"

Senator Black smiled at the pastor. "It would appear that the opinion polls have shifted considerably."

Patterson concealed a sudden ripple of displeasure that twisted deep within his belly.

"In our favor, Senator?"

Isaiah Black leaned back in his chair. "In mine."

Patterson watched as the senator tossed a newspaper onto the desk to face him. It was folded so that the opinion polls were uppermost. Patterson scanned them with a renewed sense of dismay.

"The polls are unreliable, the people fickle."

Isaiah Black shook his head. "Yesterday they were reliable, according to you."

Patterson felt his features twist into something between a smile and a grimace.

"It would be unwise to act with haste on such dismissable statistics."

The senator shook his head slowly.

"The people are voting with their feet, Pastor. New York, Pennsylvania, Maryland, and others are placing economic concerns, foreign policy, and climate change far above any theological interests. The mood of the nation is changing."

"Do you think that Texas, Alabama, and Ohio will do the same?" Patterson challenged.

"No," the senator responded. "And I don't give a damn if they do or not, because the conservative vote remains in the minority. The point, Pastor, is that I'm in a dominant position in the primary campaign with or without your support."

Patterson lost the ability to maintain the grin slapped across his face.

"Do you really think that you can afford to lose the voting block that I control? Can you afford to spout your arrogance when I could block your campaign in a half-dozen swing states? This is the voice of God that you're turning your back on."

"It's the people of America who are turning their backs, Pastor," Black responded. "On you."

Patterson struggled to prevent himself from clenching his fists.

"Go down to the Reflecting Pool, stand before the granite wall there, and see the images of our soldiers—Americans who fought for the ideals we preserve, who fought for God and for country and for us to be here in this land fighting for what we know to be true. Read the words imprinted there."

"'Freedom is not free,'" Black recited the inscription.

Patterson spoke softly, trying to let the weight of his words carry their importance.

"'If you abide in Me, and My words abide in you, you will ask what you desire, and it shall be done for you.' John fifteen seven."

Senator Black smiled without passion.

"'Whosoever will, let him take the water of life freely.' Revelation twenty-two seventeen."

The ripple of despair stirred painfully now within Patterson's belly. The senator before him may be poised upon the brink of a victory that could see him in just a few short months become the most powerful man on the Earth, an ally that Patterson could not afford to lose. Unfortunately, the senator was clearly aware of that.

"Do not quote so carelessly the words of the Good Book," Patterson said, "if you are not prepared to follow them."

"It's not my choice." Senator Black smiled with supreme confidence. "My purpose is to serve the people of this country, and if they are supporting policies that you disagree with, then it is up to you to change, not the people you claim to represent."

So, it was naked power play. Patterson found himself pinned between second and third base with a ball in the air, nowhere to run, and not really sure how it had happened.

"A man of true principle stands rigidly by his beliefs," he muttered.

"As have I," Senator Black replied evenly, before sighing and offering his trademark ultraviolet smile. "Kelvin, we're not moving forward here. You need me now, not the other way around. You might be able to swing voters down in places like Oklahoma and Arkansas, but not enough to influence the whole country. And what would you gain if you did? A presidency even more opposed to your moral convictions. Compromise is what you need."

"Conviction is what we all need," Patterson said through gritted teeth, his eyes bulging as he strained against his disbelief at the senator's ignorance. "How can I stand against my own congregation?"

"You'd be standing with them, Kelvin," Black soothed. "They're the ones doing the voting, remember? They're the ones who are setting the polls. Like it or not, they're speaking for their nation, and if you believe that they're wrong, then perhaps it is you who knows nothing of God." Black smiled again. "You've said it yourself, many times, that what happens here on Earth is God's will. Maybe He's trying to tell you something."

Patterson squirmed beneath the senator's patrony. How such a man could dare to speak with any authority on the Almighty was beyond him. How could any mortal man know the mind of God when . . .

Patterson's vision blurred. The impact of his thoughts slammed through the field of his awareness like a scimitar through crystal. Suddenly, he sat in a sphere of perfect loneliness as he considered what his mind's eye had seen. Everything seemed clearer than it ever had. Ignorance. It is I who knows nothing.

I know nothing of God. No man knows anything of God. Blind faith is empty.

"Pastor?"

Patterson blinked at the sound of Black's voice, looking up and remembering that the senator was still there, watching him now with a concerned gaze. "Are you all right, Pastor?"

"I just need a while, to think."

"Of course," Black said, standing.

Patterson stood on weakened legs and shook the senator's hand, barely hearing his words and trying to ignore the nausea twisting his throat. He turned, leaving the suite and closing the door behind him to stand in the corridor outside.

I know nothing of God. Nothing. He closed his eyes. *I must learn of God. I must learn of God.* If ever he had been at a crossroads in his life, then this was it. For the first time in history man had the chance to reach out and touch the divine, and he, Kelvin Patterson, had the power to do so in his hands. Now was the time. There would be no other, ever. Lives were being lost in order to achieve a greater good.

Patterson looked at his watch, straightened his tie, and lifted his chin in defiance of himself. There would be no further delays, no further hubris or doubt.

"If you can't find your way to God, Isaiah, then I'll make sure God finds His way to you."

EVANGELICAL COMMUNITY INSTITUTE
IVY CITY, WASHINGTON DC

Officer Leon Gomez sat in an uncomfortable wooden chair at the end of a long corridor, staring at the featureless white wall before him and cursing silently, as he had done for the past three hours.

Assigned to guard a goddamn mental case. He had been given some tough assignments in his time, scouting through the District's meanest neighborhoods in the dead of night for gang leaders and homicide suspects, but he'd have taken any one of them over sitting on his ass waiting for nothing to happen. Like most all cops, boredom was Gomez's worst enemy. No doubt he'd been stuck with this shit because he was a Latino. Wouldn't have seen the lily-whites sending one of their own down here with his thumb shoved up his ass to sit around and—

Gomez broke his reverie to smile at a cute nurse who glided past into an office to his left. To his right, the corridor extended down to a dead end and housed twelve private rooms in which the patients spent their lives painting, drawing, licking windows, or doing whatever the hell it was they did. *Jesus,* he could have been on patrol. The weather was good and it made the girls get their long legs out, strutting around in shorts and miniskirts or power suits, depending on where you were patrolling.

A movement caught his eye as a tall, loping, blond-haired man appeared, carrying a tray with a dozen foam cups of juice. Gomez glanced him over, recognizing him as an orderly he'd seen earlier leaving for his lunch break. As he strolled past he looked down at Gomez.

"Evening, Officer."

Gomez nodded and smiled dutifully, watching as the orderly walked down the corridor to pause at each door and knock politely. The patients usually dropped a small latch on their doors for some semblance of privacy, although all of the doors were paneled with a plastic window through which an observer could maintain a watchful eye on the patient within. Most all of them were low risk, which made Gomez wonder why he was being asked to guard them. One by one, the doors would open and a patient's furtive hand would appear to take the juice from the blond man, and then he would move on.

Gomez, bored already, turned to look back at the nearby office where the cute nurse was chatting with a colleague. Something about a local restaurant. Gomez focused on the conversation, trying to catch the name of the place. Benson's Grill? Barnie's? He leaned forward in his chair to hear better.

A crash from the corridor caused him to whirl to see the tray of drinks on the floor, the blond orderly pointing and shouting at him.

"Fetch the nurse! Fetch the nurse!"

Gomez leaped up, shouting for the nurse as he dashed down the corridor toward where the blond man was trying to force open one of the patient's doors. As Gomez ran, the man leaned back and swung one thickly bunched fist, smashing it through the plastic window of the door. The plastic snapped in half and the orderly reached in and yanked open the latch from the inside. Gomez skidded alongside the orderly as he bolted into the room and then came to an abrupt halt.

Inside, a young man lay flat on his back on the bed, a slick of vomit across his vein-laced face, his jet-black eyes staring wide and empty at the ceiling. A waft of putrefaction choked Gomez's throat as he stared at the horrific lesions scarring the kid's body. Across his chest were a scattering of pills, more of them on the floor and an empty pill bottle lying on the tiles. Gomez glanced at the name plate scrawled on the open door: *Daniel Neville.*

The blond orderly, his features blanched and pale, reached down and picked up the bottle, showing it to Gomez. As the nurses flooded into the room, Gomez saw that the drug bottle was empty.

54

JERUSALEM

The Israeli Humvee in which Ethan sat handcuffed to a door handle was hardly a luxury vehicle, but in his exhausted state the rolling of the chassis on the road and the hum of the engine was almost comforting. He wound down a window and let the cool night air blow away some of the weariness aching through his bones.

Along with Rachel he had been safely escorted across the Gazan border at Erez; the Israeli troops there were forewarned of their passing. Now the glittering panorama of Jerusalem glowed against the horizon while above a thousand stars glistened like jewels adrift on a black sea. Ethan stared at them, hearing Hassim's words whispering across the empty void above, of gargantuan stars and broiling elements, of supernovas and embryonic solar systems, of the cycle of life replayed endlessly across the tremendous ages that had passed and were yet to come, long after he had been cast back into the dusts from which he had been forged. Life, everywhere.

Somehow, the traumas of his life seemed suddenly trivial against the epic backdrop of the universe. Even Joanna's shadowy presence, her unknown fate looming over everything that he did, seemed inconsequential. *Nothing matters.* One day he would be nothing more than a footnote in history, or an image in a photograph, dead and forgotten along with his woes. Maybe he should just quit and get out of Israel before his time came to a premature end.

But then he looked at Rachel, and remembered that science didn't have an explanation for the human spirit, for courage, fortitude, or love.

She sat beside him, her head nestled against a jacket folded up against the opposite window frame. She had fallen asleep within minutes of crossing the border an hour previously, and despite the hardship and trauma that she had endured over the last few days, her sleeping face was an image of serenity. *No regrets.* Her inner demons, doubts, fears, and insecurities were temporarily silenced by the solitude of a sleep that still eluded Ethan.

He turned away and looked into the blackness of the Israeli night. Far out to the east, the first faint line of dawn was creeping toward them, broken ribbons of distant cloud black against the deep blue. He looked at his watch: 5:26 *a.m.*

He looked again at Rachel. Ethan's past was full of regrets packed, jammed, and shoehorned into every crevice of his existence until some had inevitably spilled out to contaminate his present. He regretted not attending college, regretted resigning his commission in the U.S. Marines and the animosity that had developed between himself and his father as a result, regretted becoming a journalist, regretted the risks he had undertaken and the risks he had exposed others to, and he regretted most of all losing Joanna in this brutal and uncaring corner of the world.

And now he had let Rachel down too.

Rachel yawned, sitting upright and peering out of the window. "Where are we?"

"About ten miles from Jerusalem," Ethan said.

"You haven't slept," she observed.

"Didn't want to," Ethan lied, and immediately wondered why.

Rachel's eyes narrowed slightly, almost playfully, and then it was as though she suddenly recalled where they were and why, and her features sagged. She looked at her makeshift pillow, probably wishing she could return to oblivion.

"Hassim," Ethan said to her in an effort to distract her. "Before he died he mentioned something called cargo cults. You know what they are?"

Rachel ran her fingers through her long black hair and sighed.

"There's a few of them, mostly in the Pacific," she said. "They're Melanesians who encountered Westerners for the first time during World War II when U.S. Marines were advancing on the Japanese. What's that got to do with Lucy?"

"Just bear with me for a moment," Ethan said. "Why do they call them cargo cults?"

"Well, the occupying American forces built runways on the islands, brought in supplies using aircraft loaded with weapons, radios, medicine, and suchlike. They had a good relationship with the islanders. But when the war was over they left, taking their equipment with them and leaving the islanders alone again. What happened was that the islanders built mock runways complete with air control towers, hangars, and aircraft made of straw. They even sat in them wearing wooden radio earpieces, trying to make contact with the great gods and their powerful sky machines. They would have flaming torches at night on the runways to guide down the 'airships,' or march up and down with either salvaged or wooden rifles like parading troops, mimicking American dress styles and behavior."

"And all of it to bring the Americans back?" Ethan asked.

"Pretty much." Rachel nodded. "The practices eradicated any existing religious observances they previously had. The leaders of the cults promised their people that if they did all of this, then the 'gods' would return. It got the leaders power, and it gave the people hope that they were not alone anymore, that they were special."

Ethan shook his head in wonder.

"Hassim Khan was right. The ancients didn't have extraterrestrial help in building their megastructures: they built them themselves in an attempt to reestablish contact with their godlike visitors." He looked at her. "How many cargo cults could there have been?"

"In history? Thousands," Rachel said. "The Nazca's lines in Peru, depicting animals on such a scale that they're only visible from the air, would be among the most likely candidates."

"Right," Ethan agreed. "I've heard about them, and as icons visible from great heights they'd be perfect."

"Most of the pyramidal structures built by civilizations around the world could have served a similar purpose," Rachel agreed, "and they're everywhere, not just in Egypt. Mesopotamian ziggurats that were once colorfully painted, Nubian pyramids in Sudan, the Sula Temple in Java, the granite temples of the Chola Empire in India, others in Samoa and Greece and those of the Maya and Aztecs at Teotihuacán in South America. The pyramids in Egypt are the most famous, but few people realize that there is not a single hieroglyphic anywhere suggesting that they were burial sites for pharaohs, or that they were once covered with smooth white sandstone: they would have shone like beacons in sunlight, perhaps brightly enough to be visible from space. Virtually every religion on Earth could have started out as a sort of cargo cult and just grown from there."

"And pyramids would make sense as they're a stable structure," Ethan said. "I've read that we know they were built by human hands because the graves of the builders were found near the pyramids themselves in Egypt, complete with hieroglyphics recording their achievements."

"Stability is one reason," Rachel said. "But we're used to seeing pyramids from the ground. If you fly directly above one, you see a big X in a box." She smiled. "Sometimes, X does mark the spot."

Ethan grinned ruefully.

"What are you going to do when we get back to the city?" Rachel asked him.

"Meet with Ambassador Cutler, Shiloh Rok, or anyone in the Knesset who'll listen and tell them what's happened. We need them aware that MACE is involved in this."

Rachel sighed. "We still don't know that for sure. They were at Lucy's dig site and they pursued us, violently, but that doesn't necessarily mean that they abducted Lucy."

"MACE," Ethan said carefully, "whoever they are and whatever they're doing here, has no interest in Lucy's survival."

"They were at the site. It doesn't mean they abducted Lucy, only that they found and were excavating the remains. We can't lay blame without proof; that's not how the law works."

Ethan felt disbelief sluice through his gullet. "You're living in denial."

"Tell me what happened to your fiancée."

Rachel's unexpectedly direct question stumped Ethan.

"It's not worth the telling."

"It is, to me."

Ethan turned away from her and looked out of the window even though there was nothing to see but the inky blackness. He looked down, and saw his hands trembling in the darkness. Nervous exhaustion, lack of sleep. More hallucinations would come next, probably, like the one in the market square in Jerusalem. He folded his hands tightly together, looking out the window and seeing Rachel's reflection watching him in the glass as she spoke.

"Since we came here I have trusted you, relied upon you, and taken risks with you because my father told me that if anyone could find Lucy, it was you. I think I have a right to know why that is."

"I haven't found your daughter yet and I never said that I could," Ethan murmured.

"No," Rachel admitted. "That's why I want to know the truth. I may have to spend the rest of my life wondering what happened to her. I might end up like you."

Ethan shot her a sideways glance. "End up like me?"

"Cynical," Rachel said, "aloof, nihilistic, thinking that nothing is worth anything. I want to know why you're like you are so I can try to be something else."

Ethan looked outside again for a long moment before whispering a name as though he were speaking of a ghost.

"Joanna." He could see Rachel staring at him in the window's reflection. His own face was illuminated starkly on one side by the glow from the city ahead, the other half lost in deep shadow. "Joanna Defoe was my fiancée. We met while I was serving in the Marines and she was covering the invasion of Iraq, embedded with our platoon. We fell in love, the usual crap. I resigned my commission and worked freelance with her after my unit pulled out of Iraq, traveling together to wherever the news was: New Orleans, Aceh, Afghanistan, Africa, you name it."

Having started, Ethan let the words fall from his lips, not looking at Rachel but staring out into the shadows sprawled like slumbering demons in the desert darkness.

"While everyone else was covering the war on terror, we decided to change tack and cover the smaller stories, human stories, things that were forgotten in the wake of the obsession with terrorism."

"Where did you go?" Rachel asked in a whisper.

"Bogotá, Colombia," Ethan replied. "We'd uncovered a lot of reports there of abductions, criminal syndicates that owned the police forces, a hostage-ransom industry, not to mention the trade in drugs coming from South America. After exposing a number of corrupt officials within the Colombian government, we decided to do the same again, this time in Gaza. During that time we gained a reputation for being able to locate missing people as a result of our investigations."

Ethan did not feel as though he was speaking, the words drifting through his awareness as though he was picking up a faint distress signal on an archaic radio.

"We wrote several articles about atrocities against Palestinians in Gaza City by both Hamas and Israel that made the international press, but I suppose somehow we dug too deep or pissed off too many people who were making too much money to see their dirty little industries shut down.

Joanna Defoe vanished from Gaza City on the afternoon of December 14, 2008, abducted by persons unknown. No ransom, no contact, no information or evidence. Nobody knew a thing about it except that a cleaner said she'd seen someone wearing clothes that matched Joanna's being dragged from the back door of the hotel we were staying in, with a bag over her head, and that the person was dumped into a car that disappeared. No plates, maybe dark blue in color, she thought. Maybe."

Ethan's voice trailed off as though he was miming the words, watching in his mind's eye as the past replayed itself once again on an endless, miserable loop.

"I spent the next two years searching for her. I used up all of our savings, sold everything we possessed, spent months scouring the alleys and back streets, the refugee camps and villages for her. I printed thousands of pictures of her and put them up all over Gaza City." He shook his head. "I never heard a word."

Rachel waited patiently as he went on.

"When the money ran out I thought I'd just curl up and die, that there was no point in going on because there was nothing worth going on for. It was Amy O'Hara, a journalist friend who had covered our stories, who helped me from Chicago to find Joanna. I'd done a piece on missing journalists in the hope of raising awareness. Amy read it, hated what had happened, and decided to help me out. She actually came out to Jerusalem in the end, lent me some money, and told me to get out of the city and find the world again. That Joanna was probably dead and gone, and that even if she wasn't, there was nothing more that I could do. That if I didn't leave I'd just destroy myself."

Rachel remained silent, Ethan speaking without thought or conscious planning.

"So I did. I went back to Chicago, back to work. I did okay until the pointlessness of it all hit me. I resigned my job, gave up on whatever it was I had left. The thing about it was, I didn't care, didn't give a shit. I might just as well have been dead already."

Ethan fell silent, caught in the web of his own memories, of months and years lost in a paralysis of grief. Rachel's voice spoke softly from nearby.

"What happened next?"

Ethan roused himself.

"Nothing happened next," he said. "I've been fully unemployed ever since. Posttraumatic stress, they call it, makes me medically unable to work. I don't sleep much, maybe an hour here, an hour there." Ethan shrugged to himself, felt her penetrating gaze on him but went on talking quietly. "She was a great person, Joanna. You'd have liked her. She loved life. Always full of energy, always quick with a joke. Bright. Cheerful. One of those people that you can't help but like."

Ethan's voice started to become strained as though his vocal chords were being twisted.

"You've got some idea, now, of what it's like when someone you love so much just vanishes, completely and utterly, without explanation or information. What it's like when you have no idea if they are safe or not, suffering or not, alive or not. I have images of people harming her, and of going and finding those people and skinning them alive, or having them fed to sharks or lowered feetfirst into wood-chipping machines." He saw Rachel wince and shook his head. "It brings things out in you that you can't imagine."

Ethan glanced out of the window, fatigue amplifying his grief.

"I send her parents flowers on her birthday, every

year. They always return them unopened. I still don't feel right alone in bed at night unless I wrap her T-shirt around a pillow next to me. Can you believe that?"

He lowered his head, not willing to let Rachel see what he knew she already must have seen. His voice when he spoke sounded strained in his own ears.

"I wanted to find out what happened to her, and to find Lucy for you. I thought maybe I could put this all right, but I can't. There's no such thing as a hero when there's no way to solve a case. There's nothing more I can do for you here except tell the authorities about MACE's involvement."

Rachel's reflection was pinched with remorse.

"You've done enough," she said quietly. "It took a lot for you to come out here after all that's happened. I wouldn't have come this far alone."

Ethan was still unable to bring himself to look at her.

Rachel squeezed his arm and rested her head against it, while Ethan continued to stare out of the window at the pale strip of light now slicing across the eastern horizon.

55

WADI AL-JOZ
WEST BANK, PALESTINE

Lucy Morgan awoke, struggling to overcome her drug-induced lethargy and reach the shore of consciousness just ahead.

She tried to move her body but her wrists and ankles were still firmly bound and a thick leather strap encircled her waist. Cold metal touched her skin. She turned her head and saw the room about her, enshrouded in darkness, and with a bolt of panic she realized where she lay.

"Good morning."

The voice, somehow familiar, hovered somewhere beyond the periphery of her vision. A face appeared and gazed down at her, hollow-looking eyes, a flare of white hair illuminated like a halo by the bright light, and wearing what looked like a surgeon's gown. She realized that semi-opaque adhesive patches had been attached to her face to protect her eyes, obscuring her vision.

Lucy Morgan swallowed thickly, trying not to tremble.

"Murderer," she whispered. "You killed Ahmed."

Again, that excruciatingly compassionate smile.

"No," the surgeon replied. "A discoverer, a journeyman, a seeker of the truth."

Lucy's addled brain struggled to comprehend what the man was referring to as he moved around the gurney upon which she lay. As he spoke, she realized that her body and forehead were covered with electrodes attached with adhesive patches. Small wires ran from the pads to the monitors alongside the gurney.

"You don't know what you're doing," she muttered with forced contempt. "You're dabbling in things that you can't possibly comprehend."

The surgeon looked at her in surprise, and nodded happily.

"You're the first patient to say that, Lucy. I'm impressed, truly I am."

Lucy saw him adjust dials on one of the monitors before turning to look down at her again. She was naked but for a small pair of white briefs and a bra, not her own, she realized. He must have dressed her, tended to her as she lay comatose beneath the anesthetics that he had forced into her unwilling body. The knowledge sent a bolt of nausea through her.

"Don't worry," he said quietly, as if sensing her discomfort. "You have been cared for without violation of any kind."

Lucy looked at him, radiating hatred. "You don't call *this* a violation?"

The surgeon chuckled. "It is for the greater good, Lucy. Not just yours, not just mine."

Lucy remembered what she had seen here previously, the image of Ahmed Khan's bucking, writhing, salivating madness filling her with horror.

"Maybe nobody can survive whatever you're doing."

He shook his head again.

"It was their brains. The arteries could not withstand the rise in blood pressure nor the oxygen bubbles reaching the brain during transfusion. The drug addicts developed cerebral aneurisms. I should have tilted their bodies to raise the head, preventing oxygen bubbles in the blood from reaching the brain. But that matters not; now I have you."

Lucy felt a mounting sense of horror.

"That might not be enough!"

"There is always a way, Lucy. You of all people should know that, as a scientist. The gathering of data, over time, leads to evidence, hypothesis, and eventually to theory, and that theory, based on fact, must be accepted by the observer regardless of their own prejudices. I have examined every single patient, every single procedure, and thus have seen the error in my thinking. They might have survived had I been more adept."

Lucy shook her head.

"Your errors cost them their lives. Murder is murder no matter how it comes about, when it is done against the will of your so-called patients." Lucy covered her fear with a thin smile. "What goes around, comes around."

The blurred figure shrugged.

"My fate is irrelevant, Lucy. Only the results matter, and when they are published, the cost will be far outweighed by the value of the discovery, of the evidence."

"Evidence of what?"

The surgeon moved toward her, and she realized he was carrying a syringe. He reached up for the saline tube that ran into her left arm.

"Time for you to go to sleep, my dear," he said softly.

"You don't have to do this," Lucy said, her voice quivering now.

"But, Lucy, of course I do."

"*No.*"

Lucy's voice was a weak whisper, but a deeper voice growled from the darkness.

"Wait."

A figure lumbered out of the gloom to stand over her body. Thick stubble and bulky features, squinting piglike eyes, wearing combat fatigues and boots.

"Time for you to see the light of day," the soldier said to the surgeon.

The surgeon looked at the soldier, frustration building in his body until he trembled and with one hand thumped the metal desktop beside him.

"Damn! Now? Can it not wait another hour?"

"No, it can't. You'll be back here by midday."

The surgeon gathered himself together and put down his syringe, looking at Lucy.

"A pity," he said. "I was looking forward to this."

"You'll be able to continue within a couple of hours," the soldier assured him. "Right now, we've got to move."

"I take it that Patterson's little game is starting to unravel at the seams?" the surgeon asked.

Lucy saw the soldier glare cruelly at the surgeon.

"You mention a name one more time and I'll put that syringe somewhere that will silence you for good."

The surgeon, slipping out of his lab coat, chose to ignore the threat and instead walked to a locker. Lucy saw him open it and lift out an old, battered and torn gray jacket. The surgeon looked at her, as if remembering that she was there at all. He strolled over as he slipped into the jacket, and twisted the little dial on her drip.

Lucy felt the darkness slowly enveloping her again.

56

FIRST DISTRICT STATION
M STREET SW, WASHINGTON DC

Tyrell listened to Lopez as he drove onto M Street
Southwest, joining rivers of headlights flowing
south.

"Okay, this guy was born in Israel and raised with
dual nationality in Huntsville, Alabama," Lopez read
from a report nestled on her lap. "Got a degree in neu-
rological sciences at the University of Alabama, before
settling in Israel in 1978 and conducting clinical studies
on the suspended animation of mammals using methods
involving cryogenic cooling."

Tyrell glanced at her. "Something like what we saw?"

Lopez sifted through the file and pulled one sheet
out that she'd marked in red pen on the corner. She read
through a couple of lines.

". . . replacing the blood using a controlled saline
solution cooled to thirty degrees Fahrenheit, introduced
to the subject intravenously. The body of the subject
will experience hypothermia with the complete cessa-
tion of all major organ activity, rendering the subject
clinically dead and in a state of controlled homeo-

stasis. Here, the immune system becomes drastically hindered, allowing otherwise toxic alteration of a given biological system."

Tyrell blinked. "And he's done this legally?"

"On animals," Lopez noted. "He was denied the opportunity to perform the procedures on humans."

"He actually tried to practice this on people legally?"

"Applied to the Medical Ethics Board of Maryland upon returning to America, for hospital patients suffering from terminal illnesses to undergo the procedure as part of a proposed medical trial. His application was unanimously denied."

"No shit," Tyrell murmured. "When was this?"

"Three years ago," Lopez said. "After that he was employed by a company called Munitions for Advanced Combat Environments, MACE, out of Maryland, doing research into battlefield trauma surgery techniques. He recently resigned his post and took to performing charitable work, splitting his time between Israel and America."

Tyrell nodded, pulling out his badge and flashing it at the attendant guarding the parking lot. He drove through as the barrier was raised and quickly found an empty space.

"What about those hymns that Claretta Neville mentioned, or whatever they were?"

"The men of renown?" Lopez asked, and read from her notebook. " 'When men began to multiply on the face of the ground, and daughters were born to them, the sons of God saw that the daughters of men were fair; and they took to wife such of them as they chose . . . The Nephilim were on the Earth in those days, and also afterward, when the sons of God came in to the daughters of men, and they bore children to them.' "

"The Bible," Tyrell said, recalling his Sunday school. "The Nephilim were the product of human women and angels and were referred to as giants both physically and intellectually, just the kind of thing Kelvin Patterson might be interested in pursuing. This guy's got to be the one," he said as he turned off the engine. "Maybe he's doing some kind of Frankenstein experiment or something. It all ties in."

"Correlation does not always mean causation," Lopez pointed out. "You taught me that."

Tyrell grinned as he opened his door.

"True, but that doesn't mean you can't follow up on a lead, especially when there are three dead people to think of."

"Okay, you got me," Lopez conceded. "Pastor Kelvin Patterson currently owns the controlling share of MACE, and we have this surgeon on the record as having performed charitable work for the Evangelical Alliance. It's how he and Kelvin Patterson must have met."

Tyrell climbed out of the car. Almost immediately, the world went dark as flashing points of light dazzled him. He staggered backward against the rear door, toppling over as vertigo sent his world reeling. His left knee cracked painfully against the unyielding tarmac as he went down.

"Lucas?"

He heard rather than saw Lopez rush around to his side of the car. Slowly, the sparkling lights obscuring his vision faded as a clammy wash of nausea flushed through him.

"I'm okay," he mumbled, righting himself against the car and smiling feebly.

"Like hell you are—you've lost your color."

Tyrell dredged up a chuckle. "What, you mean I'm white now?"

"I'm bein' serious, Tyrell; you look like shit."

"That ain't changed for a decade or two, honey."

Lopez's dark eyes narrowed. "You gotta get this checked out, Christ's sake."

Tyrell sighed, regaining his vision fully and feeling the nausea slide away.

"In the morning," he said finally. "I'll do it first thing."

Lopez jabbed a finger at his chest.

"Just make sure you damn well do. I don't wanna see yo' fat ass sprawled on a mortuary slab, okay?"

Tyrell managed to smile, and with Lopez walked slowly through the lot and into the main building itself. They had barely gotten inside when a young lieutenant by the name of Reuben crossed their paths. Fresh out of college, Reuben delighted in his own sense of humor.

"You've been summoned by the High and Mighty," he said with a cheerfully mocking smile. "God knows whose chain you've pulled, but half the First District Department's waiting for you in the briefing room."

Tyrell noticed Lopez glance with concern down the corridor to their left. "What's the score?"

"Got me beat," Reuben admitted. "Bureau's involved though, so your chances are about as good as the Yankees at the bottom of the ninth 'gainst the Red Sox."

Tyrell sighed. "Cain."

He led Lopez to the main briefing room, knocking and entering. A large table dominated the room, more than half of the two dozen available spaces filled. A disconcertingly large number of the officers present bore chunky epaulettes, and an equal number of faces were pinched with disdain as he and Lopez entered the room and closed the door. Special Agent in Charge of Investigations Axel Cain and another FBI agent stood briskly.

"Tyrell." Cain grinned without warmth. "Thought we'd seen the last of you downtown yesterday."

"So did I," Tyrell murmured, noting that for once Cain wasn't grinding his chops around a piece of gum. "What brings the Bureau here?"

Captain Powell, sitting at the head of the table, gestured to the two agents.

"Agents Cain and Denny want the Potomac Gardens case shut down due to lack of manpower. Commissioner Cathy Devereux wants to know what your handle on the investigation is."

Tyrell nodded at the commissioner, a high-flying and well-respected officer who had begun her career as a beat cop. Before he had a chance to speak, Cain had a stab at grabbing center stage.

"We've uncovered some anomalies with the case but don't consider them worthy of investigation."

"*You've* uncovered?" Lopez uttered beside Tyrell, and before he could intervene she pointed a finger at Cain. "This joker would have shut us down yesterday if it weren't for our work at the scene."

A shadow of displeasure creased Cain's features. "Charming."

"What's your angle here?" Cathy Devereux asked Cain.

"The case has crossed state lines as one of the victims was from Maryland. That makes it a federal case, not a district one. Not to mention the near fatality this morning at the medical examiner's office. We're here to find out exactly what's been happening and what the Bureau can do to bring this to a close."

Tyrell considered Cain to be a card-carrying member of the asshole club but he realized that he was now in a particularly delicate position. He had the tricky job of defending the validity of his case in front of Powell and the brass, while at the same time preventing it from passing into Cain's jurisdiction or being shut down. Cathy Devereux turned to look at him expectantly.

Tyrell gestured to the file Lopez was holding. She passed it across the table to Cain, who leafed through it as though it were a travel brochure while Tyrell spoke.

"Three victims of an apparent group overdose. One of the victims was a respected scientist by the name of Joseph Coogan, a biochemist working in the District with no history of substance abuse of any kind. Autopsy shows that he underwent a medical procedure before having his blood contaminated with crack cocaine to approximate the appearance of an overdose."

Cain frowned as he flicked through the file. "Meaning?"

"That his true cause of death was disguised amid crack-addict overdoses."

"The medical examiner hasn't even been able to confirm a time of death," Cain said, scanning the last page of the file before closing it.

"What's to say that it just looks that way and that this guy did indeed die from an overdose?" Commissioner Cathy Devereux asked.

"Pathology from the lab reports," Lopez said. "The examiner's on the record as saying that the victim's blood had been entirely transfused, meaning that the drugs had to be administered after the procedure not before, as his blood type had changed. Either that or he decided to shoot up about a half hour after dying."

"Maybe," Cain said offhandedly.

"Maybe?" Tyrell muttered. "Either we've got a homicide or the city's first case of zombie drug abuse. What's the problem?"

"Occasionally," Cain said with a smug smile, "an individual's blood type can change as a result of antigens in infection, malignancy, or autoimmune disease. It's been known to occur after liver transplants. We've done the research."

Commissioner Devereux spoke quietly to Tyrell.

"Why do you think that you have enough information to produce a prosecution?"

"The fact that we have both a possible perpetrator and a motive." Cain raised an eyebrow, but Tyrell kept going. "If you'd looked at the file more carefully than you looked at the crime scene, you'd have noticed that it names a suspect, a neurologist. He's got a history of experimental procedures on mammals going back years, involving research into homeostasis and the use of induced hypothermia to treat victims of trauma."

Cain squinted at Tyrell's advanced terminology, but did not reach again for the file.

"Go on," Devereux encouraged.

"This surgeon is central to all of this. One of the victims of these procedures survived and remained lucid enough to inform his mother of the basic details, which jibed with the assessment of a clinical surgeon at General Hospital. These people were experimented on illegally and against their will, and those experiments led to their deaths and the scene downtown yesterday morning."

"What kind of experiments?" Cain demanded impatiently.

Tyrell took a deep breath. In for a penny . . .

"We talked to a surgeon, and he said that the only possible reason for conducting this procedure would be as part of an attempt to create a chimera, the genetic fusing of two distinct species into one. The victims we found were being used as human incubators, live test tubes providing or receiving rare O-negative blood."

Commissioner Devereux stared at both Tyrell and Lopez for a long moment. "And this, chimera? Who, or what, exactly is it?"

"We don't know yet," Tyrell said. "Once we've got further pathology we'll push for the district attorney to grant us a prosecution."

Cain smirked in bemusement as Captain Powell unexpectedly chimed in from his seat.

"We'll need something more than this for the DA to get involved, Tyrell."

Commissioner Devereux looked at Cain. "What's your take on this?"

"I've got real crimes to investigate," Cain muttered. "The Bureau doesn't have time to be chasing around the District after Lucas Tyrell's mad fantasies."

"Since when was homicide not a crime?" Tyrell asked.

"Since it was suicide," Cain shot back and stood from the table, Agent Denny alongside him as he turned to Commissioner Devereux. "What are the chances that this is an international conspiracy involving genetic experiments, against those that it's an ordinary overdose of three drug abusers in a downtown hovel? I recommend that this case be closed and our time spent on more fruitful avenues of investigation."

"We have a suspect!" Tyrell almost shouted in disbelief.

"Damon Sheviz?" Cain uttered airily.

Tyrell felt his heart skip a beat and his jaw hang open. "Where did you get that name from?"

"Interpol," Cain murmured with a sly grin. "I did in fact read your report properly, and I also checked our data on Dr. Sheviz's whereabouts. Turns out he was liberated from a terrorist cell in the Gaza Strip barely an hour ago, where he's been held for several days. The chances of him being your supposed deranged surgeon would appear somewhat diminished, Detective."

Before Tyrell could reply, Cathy Devereux made her decision.

"I suggest that we close the proceedings forthwith."

"Close the proceedings?" Tyrell uttered as the commissioner stood from her seat.

"Yes, Detective. This case has grown disproportionate to the value of its potential convictions."

"You think I'm exaggerating the extent of the crime?" Tyrell demanded.

"And not for the first time."

"The surgeon we believe is involved has dual Israeli and American citizenship and hasn't been seen or heard of in the District for several weeks, until now."

Cathy Devereux sighed heavily, searching the ceiling as though for inspiration.

"You're connecting yesterday morning's case with abductions halfway across the world."

"No surgeon in the United States would dare carry out a procedure like this unless the patient was at death's door," Tyrell insisted. "If I was this guy and I wanted to both escape a murder charge and continue my work, I'd go somewhere that would have me."

Powell rubbed his temple with one hand.

"You realize that if you're right, then this is indeed an international crime and an FBI matter?"

"If it's crossed international borders," Tyrell said, "then it can go to Interpol first. Extradition could follow."

Devereux chuckled out loud and shook her head.

"From Israel? Do you honestly think they'll give up

one of their own, especially a respected surgeon, on a charge as thin as this?"

"The charge isn't thin," Tyrell insisted.

"It's all circumstantial," Devereux shot back. "You won't get extradition."

"The file says he was working in a charitable position for the American Evangelical Alliance," Lopez cut in, "who have strong links to the Israel lobby in Washington and to the government of Israel itself. The AEA owns the hospital that he worked for and where we found our survivor. Not only that, but according to our research, the AEA's owner Kelvin Patterson has a long-standing interest in using experiments on humans to prove the existence of God."

Commissioner Devereux leveled Lopez with an uncompromising gaze.

"Do you have any idea how it would look if I put that in front of the district attorney? I'd be laughed out of the damned office. Do you even have a witness to any of this?"

"We have a single witness, Daniel Neville, under assessment now," Tyrell replied, deciding not to elaborate on the patient's mental capacity. "Hopefully, we'll be able to—"

"Would Daniel Neville be an inmate at the hospice in Ivy City?" Powell asked.

Tyrell blinked in surprise. "Yeah. How'd you know that?"

"I can't give you any more resources," Powell said quietly, almost apologetically.

"Why the hell not?"

"Because your witness is lying in the city morgue."

Tyrell felt his world tilt as he processed what he had heard. "The morgue?"

"Suicide," Powell said. "Little over an hour ago."

"That settles it then," Commissioner Devereux said with brisk finality. "Whatever case you may have can wait until forensic evidence is available."

Tyrell stared at Devereux, well aware that his own jaw was hanging open. "It could take months for forensic tests to be completed."

"Time that can be spent pursuing more viable cases," Devereux snapped, turning away from the table and casting Tyrell a final glance. "You're to close the case. That's an order."

Tyrell and Lopez both remained silent as Commissioner Devereux strode out of the briefing room, a smirking Cain following her. As they left and closed the door behind them, Captain Powell retook his seat and regarded the two detectives.

"I'm sorry, Tyrell, but it's gone cold, just let it go for now."

"Doesn't the fact that a key witness has just died in a secure institute, and the key perpetrator has conveniently reappeared with an alibi, strike you as just a tiny bit goddamn suspicious?"

"Yes, it does," Powell conceded, "but there's nothing that I can do about it, and the kid you're talking about was a former drug addict with a history of mental problems. You won't get anywhere near a prosecution with what you've got. Go and check out what happened at the hospital, then go home and get a good night's sleep. We'll talk about this in the morning."

Tyrell stared at him for a long moment, and then turned away and strode from the briefing room in disgust, Lopez hurrying after him.

57

EVANGELICAL COMMUNITY INSTITUTE
IVY CITY, WASHINGTON DC

"Suicide."

The word fell from Tyrell's mouth to the floor with a thud.

"Two hours ago," a nurse said as she stood with him in the corridor. "We attempted resuscitation, but it was too late."

Tyrell stared at the tape cordon blocking access to Daniel Neville's room. The door was propped open by a small wastepaper bin. Inside, the bed looked recently used. There was no sign of a struggle except for the broken plastic of the door window. Nearby, a tall man with blond hair sat sullenly in a chair with his back to the wall.

"What happened?" Tyrell asked the nurse, feeling numb.

"Daniel was guarded constantly by the police officer you assigned to him. Daniel ate food that was brought here by his mother from the kitchens, and she left once he was tucked up in bed. The police officer remained at the end of the corridor after she left."

"Who found him?" Lopez asked.

"The handyman, Casey Jeffs. He was walking down the corridor with drinks for the patients when he saw Daniel lying on his bed in a pool of vomit. He shouted for the keys to the room but the duty nurse wasn't quick enough, so he punched through the plastic window and unlocked the door. Your police officer went with him to help, but Daniel had already passed away."

Tyrell looked across at Casey Jeffs and recognized him as the man who had been swabbing the floors when they'd first arrived to speak to Daniel Neville. Casey's hand was bandaged, a soft pink stain betraying where the plastic had cut into his knuckles.

"Casey is a former patient," the nurse said softly to Tyrell. "He was kept on here as an assistant to help him get on his feet. Daniel's death has hit him pretty hard."

As they spoke, the young Latino beat cop assigned to protect Daniel appeared from down the hallway. Tyrell gestured him to join them.

"Officer Gomez," the cop introduced himself as he shook Tyrell's hand. "Listen, I don't know how this happ—"

"Forget it," Tyrell said. "I just need to know how you found the kid."

Gomez pointed into Daniel's room as he spoke.

"Right there, layin' on his back. Looked like he'd choked on his own vomit. There were pills around him on the bed and on the floor, and one o' those small bottles they come in. Thing is, the kid was a mess and couldn't have smuggled anything in there if he'd tried. The staff are real strict about drugs and the patients get their meds hand-fed to them once or twice a day."

"Who was the last person to see him alive?" Lopez asked.

Gomez thought for a moment.

"I guess I was, an' before that you were, along with Mrs. Neville and Michael Shaw, one of the orderlies here. Michael wasn't in the building at the time of death, as his shift had ended. We've checked the security cameras and nobody entered Daniel's room between the time he was left here and when he was found by Casey."

"What about Casey? Where was he?" Lopez asked.

"Was just back off his break," Gomez said, and then called out, "Hey, c'mere, Casey."

Casey got to his feet and shuffled across to them. Tyrell judged him at about six-three and at least two hundred forty pounds. A pair of listless blue eyes shyly met his. Tyrell extended his right hand and Casey reached out for it, the shake limp and damp.

"Can you tell us what you saw, Casey?" Tyrell asked.

"Nothin'," Casey said in a whispering Texan accent. "I just happened by, doing my drinks rounds when I saw Daniel. He'd been sick, his eyes were open but he wasn't looking at anythin', and there were a lot of pills around him. I couldn't open the door, so I went in through the window instead." He shrugged. "Din' know what else t'do."

"You did good, Casey," Gomez said reassuringly.

Tyrell frowned, looking back into the room.

"How does a bedridden former drug addict in a controlled hospital gain access to enough drugs to overdose?"

The nurse beside them sighed softly.

"There is only one way," she said, and gestured down the hall.

Walking toward them, flanked by two police officers, was Claretta Neville. Gone was her defiant bravado. Claretta walked with shoulders slumped, staring at the floor, her huge arms dwarfing those of the officers' looped through hers.

"You're kidding?" Lopez snapped. "There's no way."

Claretta came to a stop in front of Tyrell, looking up at him. No psychologist was needed to see that the events of the day had entirely sapped her of her will.

"You know what happened here?" he asked her simply.

Claretta shook her head once.

"I told 'em everythin'." Glistening pools appeared beneath her eyelids. "I don't know why he'd have done somethin' like this. I din' give him no pills."

Tyrell looked into the empty room where Daniel Neville's short life had come to an end, and then looked at the nurse and Officer Gomez.

"Daniel Neville was suicidal with pain," he said softly before looking at Officer Gomez. "A locked room, no way of getting contraband in or out, cameras on the corridor. You're absolutely sure all of those criteria were met by the hospital staff?"

Both Gomez and the nurse nodded without hesitation.

"Couldn't have got in any other way," Gomez said sadly.

Tyrell nodded, and turned to Daniel's mother. "Claretta Neville, I'm arresting you on suspicion of first-degree murder. You have the right to remain silent, you have the right to an attorney . . ."

From the corner of his eye he saw Lopez's jaw drop. Claretta Neville stared at him with drops of liquid quivering in her eyes as he read her her rights, the two officers flanking her remaining stonily silent.

Claretta held his gaze for a few seconds.

"This one's for real," she hissed at him.

One powerful arm snapped free and whipped across Tyrell's face with a sharp crack.

Bright pain stung his face but he did not respond, watching silently as Claretta was brusquely handcuffed by the officers and led away down the corridor.

"Go with them," Tyrell said to Gomez, gesturing after the other officers. "Keep an eye on Claretta for me back at the station."

As Gomez moved off with Casey and the nurse, Lopez moved to stand in front of Tyrell. "The hell d'you think you're doing?" she whispered.

"Buying us some time," he said quietly.

Lopez pointed abruptly down the hall. "You just booked her, for Christ's sake! This isn't a mercy killing; she wanted us on Daniel's case!"

"I know," he replied. "Daniel might have overdosed but he still had to get hold of the pills somehow."

Lopez eyed Tyrell testily, but he saw her forcing herself to consider the possibilities.

"They said the cameras saw nobody enter or exit the room," she said, "so he was definitely alone. The security door at the end of the hall was locked, Officer Gomez was beside it and Daniel couldn't even feed himself let alone overdose. So if Claretta didn't provide him with the pills, who could have?"

"Call the morgue," Tyrell said quietly. "I want Daniel Neville's body tested for foreign DNA samples: hair, skin, blood, anything. There was one thing we never learned about Daniel: why he alone survived these experiments."

"Even if forensics found DNA samples, there's no guarantee that they belong to a murderer, and how could the perp have gotten into the room without being seen on camera? Even if we could find a way, it doesn't mean that they were in the room at the time of death."

Tyrell nodded.

"I know, but we need everything we can get." He hesitated, looking thoughtfully back down the corridor. "Find everything you can on Casey Jeffs, Michael Shaw, and Claretta Neville just in case."

"What for?" Lopez asked.

"Just do it," Tyrell said as they started walking. "Anyone who's a witness is a suspect right now. Then I think that we need to pay a visit to the great pastor himself."

"If he's involved in this, he's not going to just open up," Lopez pointed out as they walked down the corridor. "And Claretta's arrest might not be enough to let them drop their guard, whoever *they* are."

"We'll play it as though it's just a routine questioning," Tyrell said. "He's bound to be expecting something along those lines after what's happened here."

"If Powell finds out about this, he'll hit the goddamn roof."

"Sure he will," Tyrell agreed. "But if we find the link we need, he'll be forced to keep the case open. What was the name of that surgeon again?"

58

JERUSALEM

Byron Stone watched as Malik strode with a casual gait to the glossy black SUV parked by the roadside, opening the rear passenger door and climbing in beside him. The tinted windows gave the world outside a peculiar polarized light. From his vantage point, Stone could see the blocky walls of the Israeli Parliament's Knesset building glowing in the sunlight.

"Well?" Stone drawled, closing the partition between him and the two MACE operatives, Cooper and Flint, in the front seat.

"The building in which Warner and the woman were hiding was completely destroyed. There are Palestinians on the scene clearing rubble, but we can rest assured that the tunnels beneath have collapsed."

"What of Rafael?" Stone asked.

"The Palestinians have found one dead Arab in the rubble," Malik murmured with an unconvincing tone of regret. "Rafael must have been killed in the blast."

Stone looked out of the windows toward the Knesset.

"One of our two Valkyrie prototypes was shot down," he hissed furiously. "Warner and the woman must have convinced Israel to help them out of Gaza."

"The evidence is long gone," Malik repeated, "buried under tons of rubble, and we have another Valkyrie standing by."

Stone turned back to face Malik.

"Perhaps the two million dollars it took to build that prototype should come out of your salary then, if it is of such little consequence?"

"The drone proved its capability," Malik said defensively. "It hit a target in a hostile and densely populated environment with no collateral damage. What do you want me to do about Warner?"

Stone jabbed a thumb over his shoulder at the Knesset building outside.

"We'll go in there and clear up this mess once and for all."

Rafael sat in cross-legged silence at the corner of a street that looked out across the Knesset, peering through the folds of traditional Bedouin attire that shielded his features from view.

Byron Stone and Spencer Malik strode arrogantly toward the Knesset with their two MACE escorts, showing their papers to the gate guards before being admitted inside. Rafael watched them as contempt seethed like acid through his veins. He looked down into his lap, where a digital camera that had once belonged to the American journalist lay. Rafael watched again the images of the Bedouin man being beaten, looked once more at the images of the strange bones and of the explosive devices in the MACE encampment.

Stone had betrayed him—that much was obvious. The wounds on his body caused by the Valkyrie drone's blasts served as a constant reminder of it. But what fired Rafael's rage was that MACE was supplying arms to terrorists in Palestine. The exotic nature of the devices in Ethan Warner's rucksack left Rafael in no doubt that whatever MACE was up to, it was designed to continue the conflict in Palestine. Profits over peace. Yet that alone was not sufficient reason for their destruction of Ethan Warner's belongings: the images on the camera, however, might just have been. Rafael was no scientist, but he guessed that whatever the skeleton in the crate was, it was valuable. His mind turned to Bill Griffiths, the fossil hunter hired by Stone a few days before, and the woman with Warner whom he had overheard in the tunnels, speaking of her search for her daughter who had vanished after discovering something in the desert. Griffiths was the man who connected everything, and Rafael knew *exactly* where to find him.

Rafael turned to the rucksack beside him and opened it, lifting out one of the explosive devices and looking again at Byron Stone's car as a dark plan began to blossom in his mind. Then he got up and hurried toward the SUV.

THE KNESSET
JERUSALEM

The sky was bright and hot as the Humvee pulled into the heavily cordoned security of the Knesset building, the fortified home of the Israeli Parliament. Ethan peered through aching eyes out of the window at razor wire, metal fences, and hefty concrete blocks arranged to obstruct suicide bombers from hurtling vehicles into the building. The defenses contrasted sharply with the elegantly formed Shrine of the Book that dominated the entrance to the Israel Museum nearby.

Armed guards checked the vehicles through and then they drove up to the Knesset building itself, a large and heavily glazed box-shaped structure. It looked to Ethan like a cross between a castle and a giant greenhouse. As the vehicle came to a stop a trooper promptly opened Ethan's door for him and almost caused him to fall out after his cuffed hand. Ethan dragged his aching legs out of the vehicle and stood in the fresh morning air, dizzy with exhaustion as his cuffs were unlocked from the door and refastened around his wrists.

"Ms. Morgan?"

An officer approached them.

"Yes?"

"Would you come with us, please?"

Ethan turned to follow the officer, but a soldier blocked his path. "Only Ms. Morgan may proceed, sir," the soldier intoned robotically. "You're to be taken for questioning."

"He's with me," Rachel cut across him in a tone that brooked no argument. "He's innocent of any crime and I can prove it."

Ethan watched as the soldier took in Ethan's battered appearance and decided that he represented a threat only to himself.

The officer led them through the Knesset to a series of conference rooms, opening the door to one and gesturing for Rachel and Ethan to enter. Ethan's tired eyes took in the circular table in the center of the room, the wood-paneled walls decorated with a large image of the Negev Desert and the broad windows aglow with the golden light of the rising desert sun. As Ethan followed Rachel through the door he saw the Foreign Ministry's Shiloh Rok sitting at the large table.

"Ms. Morgan, are you all right?" Shiloh asked in concern.

Rachel nodded. "We're okay, just tired."

"I can imagine," Shiloh said, turning a suspicious eye on Ethan, "after what you've been dragged through during the past few hours."

Ethan felt a bolt of anger twist his innards as a pair of Knesset Guards flanked him.

"Which wouldn't have been necessary if you'd helped us."

Ethan was taking his seat when a familiar voice spoke from behind them.

"Had you not broken the law, nothing would have happened to you."

Ethan whirled around to see Spencer Malik enter the room. "What the hell is he doing here?"

Malik raised his hands defensively, but it was Shiloh who spoke.

"He is here to help, Mr. Warner."

"We've already seen what that help has done for us."

Shiloh raised a placating hand. "Please, let us be seated and discuss this."

"Where is Ambassador Cutler?" Ethan demanded.

"He is unavailable at this time," Shiloh said. "I can speak for him."

Ethan was about to protest, but he caught a glance from Rachel and managed to swallow his anger as he took a seat alongside her. Shiloh retook his seat and looked at Rachel.

"What on earth happened?"

"MACE pursued us in the Negev and into Gaza," she said.

"There was a pursuit of a group of insurgents who infiltrated one of our perimeter camps in the Negev," Malik interrupted. "We didn't know who they were."

"We were shot at by your personnel," Ethan snapped.

"Please, gentlemen," Shiloh said, and looked at Rachel. "Tell us, Ms. Morgan, what happened."

Rachel spoke quietly.

"We went out to try and find out what happened to Lucy at her dig site. We were taken to an airfield near Masada, where a tracker led us out into the desert."

"Whose idea was this?" Shiloh asked.

"It was Ethan—Mr. Warner's," Rachel admitted.

"To take you into what you already knew was a restricted area," Malik muttered. "After Warner assaulted the escort we assigned to protect you."

"Mr. Malik," Shiloh cautioned, shooting him a severe look before motioning for Rachel to continue.

Rachel outlined the altercation between Ayeem and the MACE soldiers, and their subsequent flight across the deserts.

Shiloh leaned forward on his elbows as he spoke. "This Ayeem, your guide, where is he?"

"He escaped," Malik replied from across the table, "after killing one of my men."

"Probably in retaliation for the murder of Ahmed Khan," Ethan said.

Shiloh shook his head in confusion.

"You must slow down; these accusations are getting us nowhere fast. What does this Ahmed have to do with anything?"

"Ayeem told us that his son Ahmed disappeared in the Negev after being asked to search for my daughter," Rachel explained.

"As a matter of fact," Malik said, "if I remember correctly, the body of a young Bedouin man named Ahmed Khan was autopsied recently in Jerusalem after being found in the desert by the IDF."

Ethan and Rachel exchanged a glance.

"I was not aware of this," Shiloh said.

"The Bedouin are a complicated people," Malik said conversationally. "Their traditional ways have given over to a more modern lifestyle as a result of their inability to provide for themselves in the desert, and that's exposed them to alcohol, drugs, and crime. It's not that uncommon for us to find Bedouin corpses in the desert."

"What was the cause of death?" Shiloh asked.

"I don't know," Malik admitted, "but there was evidence of drug abuse, needles and suchlike. It's possible that he was a wounded insurgent and had received some kind of rudimentary medical attention."

"I want a copy of that autopsy report," Ethan insisted.

Spencer Malik ignored Ethan, looking at Rachel.

"Why did you jump out of the aircraft over Gaza?"

"To protect the footage of the incident that Mr. Warner had filmed. If we had landed at Herzliya, we feared that the footage would be confiscated by MACE. We were hoping to find Lucy while in Gaza, as Mr. Warner has contacts there."

"And did you find them?"

"No," Rachel said sadly.

Shiloh looked at Ethan curiously. "Why did you not contact us directly?"

"We couldn't make contact with anyone from Gaza," Ethan explained. "The best I could do was contact an associate at the Defense Intelligence Agency. It was he who contacted Israel. Without Israel's protection I feared that MACE would get hold of the footage, which unfortunately is exactly what happened."

Shiloh sat back in his chair. "What was this footage of?"

"MACE soldiers beating Ayeem," Ethan said, "and of cached improvised explosive devices used by terrorist groups. I also shot footage of the remains that Lucy Morgan was excavating before she disappeared. They were being prepared for shipment under the protection of MACE."

Malik clenched his fists on the table.

"That's ridiculous, a complete fantasy of the type I told you to be aware of from this man. Warner will concoct anything he can to make a story."

Ethan fumed silently in his seat but managed to remain silent.

"What happened to this footage?" Shiloh asked Rachel.

"We were attacked by a MACE drone," Ethan replied for her. "During the attack the footage was stolen, along with the explosive devices I found in the MACE encampment."

Malik blurted out a laugh. "How convenient, and the meddling of your friend in America cost MACE a two-million-dollar drone, one of only two in existence."

Shiloh remained silent for a moment before turning to the soldier.

"How do you explain your attack?"

Malik spread his palms upward.

"It was an unfortunate misunderstanding. Our encampment was infiltrated by Mr. Warner, who seems hell-bent on exposing something that just isn't there. My men tell me that they found the Bedouin sneaking around the camp and arrested him; that much is true. But there was no beating and certainly no shooting."

Ethan slammed his fist on the table.

"That's a lie. It was all on film."

"Then where is it?" Malik inquired calmly. "My men thought that they were under attack and that equipment from the camp was being stolen by insurgents. They pursued, and you fled. They understandably believed that you needed to be stopped. Everything that has happened is a product of the moment that you ignored our advice to stay out of the Negev."

"You used an air strike against civilians in Gaza," Ethan stammered.

Shiloh looked at Malik severely but the soldier appeared unfazed.

"We tracked Mr. Warner's movements via our aerial drone after he escaped into Gaza. Of course we didn't know who it was, only that we were tracking someone we thought was a terrorist. In the early hours of this morning the image of an individual matching the features of the man at the campsite was spotted, and the air strike was requested on those coordinates."

Ethan leaned forward on the table.

"And what was MACE doing with improvised explosive devices in the first place?"

Malik stared blankly at him, and Ethan sensed in his dazed expression the realization that he had been cornered.

60

"The explosives are irrelevant," Malik muttered dismissively. "This is about your intrusion into a restricted area."

Shiloh was watching Malik suspiciously. "I think that the presence of such weapons is anything but irrelevant."

Ethan nodded in agreement. "I recommend that you investigate the MACE encampment immediately. Whatever the hell they're up to, it's got nothing to do with protecting Israel."

Shiloh was about to speak, but the voice that replied came not from him but from behind them all in a broad Texan accent.

"That won't be necessary, Minister."

Ethan turned to see a tall, gaunt figure stride into the conference room, flanked by MACE operatives Cooper and Flint. The Texan crossed the room to stand at the other end of the table, his icy gaze boring directly into Shiloh's.

"The explosives were recovered from a cache that we found in the desert. Insurgents often infiltrate Israel through the Sinai to carry out rocket attacks and other atrocities on towns like Be'er Sheva. They bury their weapons throughout the desert. Part of our remit is to use technology to locate these caches and remove them from play before ambushing the insurgents when they return to collect their horrible little packages. It is a ploy that has served us well, until Warner here dug his grubby little hands into a box of them."

"Who the hell are you?" Ethan asked.

"This," Shiloh said, "is Byron Stone, the CEO of MACE."

"There's more to this than he's saying," Ethan snapped. "It doesn't add up."

"No, it doesn't," Stone agreed, "unless you're a journalist with a chip on his shoulder looking for someone to blame for losing his fiancée."

Ethan lurched out of his chair toward Stone, only to find himself restrained by strong hands. The pair of Knesset Guards had locked his arms in theirs to prevent him from moving.

"Is there actually any evidence to support Warner's claims?" Byron Stone asked Rachel.

She shook her head slowly.

"None."

Shiloh reached out and squeezed her arm gently.

"It's not your fault. It's a tragedy that you were there to witness it at all."

Byron Stone's voice filled the room as he spoke.

"A tragedy indeed, brought about by Mr. Warner's decision to steal equipment and dangerous explosives before fleeing from the MACE site, destroying one of my company's vehicles and killing one of my men in the process. I now have the unenviable task of informing that man's wife and children of his demise." Byron Stone took a deep breath before continuing. "I understand that the desire to locate Ms. Morgan's daughter may override certain concerns for personal safety, but it does not justify compromising the security of Israel as a whole. In short, Minister, it's a wonder that Mr. Warner is even here and alive at all."

"You're behind this," Ethan growled, his fists still clenched. "I know it."

"*We're* behind it?" Stone echoed, and turned to the still-open door of the room before beckoning someone inside.

Ethan watched as a tired-looking old man trudged into the room, his baggy suit crumpled and dusty.

"This," Stone drawled, "is Dr. Damon Sheviz. He was abducted at the very same moment as Lucy Morgan."

Rachel shot bolt upright out of her chair, ignoring Ethan's expression of disbelief as she dashed past him to grab the old man's hands.

"Dr. Sheviz, have you seen my daughter? Have you seen Lucy?"

Ethan watched as the old man took Rachel's hands in his, a kindly but regretful smile warming his features.

"I'm sorry, my dear," he said in a weary voice. "It all happened so fast, and we were kept apart from each other by the insurgents in Gaza. All I can tell you is that she was alive when I last saw her, after they found us at the dig site."

Byron Stone, his arms folded as he towered over the old man, looked at Ethan as he spoke.

"And who abducted you, Doctor?"

Sheviz's expression hardened somewhat.

"Palestinian insurgents," he uttered, "terrorists. They were heavily armed and threatened me." He closed his eyes for a brief moment. "Had Mr. Stone's men not found me when they did, I hate to think what might have happened."

Rachel nodded understandingly, and released She-viz's hands. Byron Stone gestured for Malik to accompany Sheviz, and the soldier went to guide the old man out of the room with one arm draped protectively over his shoulders but waited for Byron.

"I hope that this brings an end to these baseless accusations," Byron Stone rumbled.

"This doesn't mean a damned thing!" Ethan snapped. "Your company has done nothing but obstruct us!"

"And you are nothing but incompetent!" Stone fired back. "You've disobeyed warnings, endangered lives, and now you sit here trying to justify it." The Texan gestured to Cooper and Flint. "These are the two men that you assaulted, are they not? The very men I tasked to protect you. If you want to search for Lucy Morgan, then go ahead, but don't put the lives of others at risk while you're at it."

Ethan glared at him but could find nothing to say in response, his exhausted mind filled with a haze of frustration. Byron Stone looked at Shiloh.

"Sir, I have a great deal to do and I need Mr. Malik to assist me."

"Of course," Shiloh agreed, to Ethan's dismay.

Malik offered Ethan a sly grin from the corner of his mouth before striding confidently out of the room with Stone, Cooper, and Flint.

Shiloh turned to Rachel.

"MACE has offered a permanent escort for you, despite everything that has occurred, and they believe that it still may be possible to locate your daughter."

Rachel nodded. "What about Ethan?"

Shiloh glanced in Ethan's direction.

"Mr. Warner will be escorted from the country this morning," he said.

Ethan stared at the minister in disbelief.

"Do you really think that I'm lying about all of this? One of the men with us in the tunnels was Hassim Khan, a scientist who had worked with Lucy. We thought that insurgents were holding him, but Hassim himself said that they were friends protecting him from the same fate that Lucy is now facing."

"Where is Hassim Khan now?" Shiloh asked.

"He's dead," Rachel said softly. "He was killed by the same man who took Ethan's video camera." She looked at Ethan. "Too many people have died here; we can't handle this alone anymore and we're running out of time. If Lucy was here, she'd probably be telling me to do this, before the peace process renders her useless to her captors."

"You don't know that," Ethan said. "We can't just give up and—"

"We've achieved nothing!" Rachel insisted. "We're no further now than we were yesterday, except that I'm exhausted and have spent much of my time being shot at."

Ethan sighed, rubbing his temples with one hand.

"I know, but even if this *is* the work of politically motivated insurgents, Israel's in no better position to search for Lucy than we are. We can't abandon the search."

"It's my decision," Rachel said, "not yours. I'm leaving this in the hands of Israel. Go home, Ethan; there's nothing more we can do here right now."

Ethan held her gaze for a moment, surprised by her sudden conviction, and then sighed.

"Fine," he said, looking at Shiloh. "In that case, can you remove these damned things now?"

Shiloh looked at the handcuffs, and nodded for one of the guards to remove them.

"Come," Shiloh said to Rachel, taking her arm, "we can discuss our next move over coffee."

Ethan watched as Rachel was led away by Shiloh, desperately scouring the recesses of his tired mind for some way to deter her. He was about to call after her when his cell phone buzzed in his pocket. He took it out and listened for several seconds as a pulse of excitement whizzed through him.

"I'll need a little help to get there," Ethan said. "I'm at the Knesset. Call this number." He recited a cellphone number from memory, and then rang off.

"Who was that?" Rachel asked over her shoulder.

Ethan hesitated. "No one."

Moments later, he was being prodded from the room by the Knesset Guards.

61

The Knesset Guards pushed Ethan into the back of a government sedan as soon as he'd finished his phone call. As he got into the vehicle the two men took their places in the front seats.

Ethan glanced at the doors as the sedan rolled out of the Knesset compound. Both were locked and controlled from the front seat by a panel of switches on the center of the dash.

As the vehicle joined the main road away from the Knesset, Ethan saw a white jeep pull in alongside. He refrained from looking directly at it, but could see Safiya Luckov driving, her long black hair billowing out behind her as the jeep passed the sedan and gently eased into place in front of it.

Ethan tensed, waiting to see what would happen next.

Ahead, a set of lights turned red at a junction. He could see Safiya braking gently as she eased up to the lights. The sedan began to slow. Ethan lifted one arm up and braced it against the back of the passenger seat.

In an instant, Safiya's jeep suddenly braked hard and then flew into reverse, accelerating backward. Ethan's escort yelped in alarm as the jeep smashed into the sedan with a crunch of shattering plastic and rending metal, and instantly two impact bags billowed out from the dashboard as the windshield imploded with a tinkling avalanche of glass chips.

Ethan lurched forward between the seats, reaching out and hitting the two lowest switches in the panel on the dashboard. He heard the whine of the central-locking system as he pushed his door open and dashed out, running round to Safiya's jeep and leaping aboard as the two escort drivers floundered behind the safety cushions.

Safiya crunched the jeep into gear and accelerated away from the red light, swerving briefly to avoid a couple of startled motorists before clearing the junction.

"This had better be worth it!" she shouted above the hot wind.

"It's worth it, trust me," Ethan said. "MACE has gotten things all neatly packaged up and Rachel's fallen for it, but the whole thing stinks. Something just doesn't add up."

Safiya drove two blocks before turning right, then left, then right again, and pulling up alongside a red pickup parked by the sidewalk. Ethan jumped out of the jeep and climbed into the pickup to see Aaron Luckov grinning at him from behind his thick beard.

"Three years of peace, Safiya and I had, before you came back here. Three whole years."

Ethan smiled grimly as the pickup pulled away.

"Safiya going to be okay?"

"She's pretty damned sore with you, Ethan," Luckov said, "but she'll come round. It's not like we're doing this for fun. Not entirely anyway."

"Where's Griffiths?"

"Not far," Luckov said. "He phoned you?"

"Yeah," Ethan said. "Whatever he's got to say, it had better be good, because Israel's going to be on my ass for this."

62

AMERICAN EVANGELICAL ASSOCIATION
NEW COVENANT CHURCH, WASHINGTON DC

Lucas Tyrell had never failed to be impressed by the fabulous scale of the monuments erected by the faithful.

"It is more blessed to give than to receive," he murmured as he tossed a handful of biscuits into the backseat of the car, Bailey crunching them noisily.

"What?" Lopez asked from beside him.

"The church," Tyrell gestured. "How'd you suppose it got so wealthy if it really was giving and not receiving?"

The New Covenant Church dominated an entire corner of the block, a broad white building with narrow smoked windows shaped like medieval stained glass. The central portico was a vast triangular affair of steel and more glass, the central panels mirror-finished in the shape of a huge crucifix that reflected the early-morning sun's rays.

"We shouldn't be here, Tyrell," Lopez said.

"Guess this is how much it costs to have God on your side," Tyrell continued as they walked toward the vast portico. "Lucky *He* takes dollars."

"Tyrell," Lopez muttered sternly.

"It's your call," Tyrell said with a hefty sigh. "I'm not quite ready to put this case aside. Are you in or not?"

Before Lopez could reply, her cell phone buzzed in her jacket pocket. She pulled it out, listening intently for a few moments before ringing off.

"What is it?" Tyrell asked.

"We just got the files on Daniel Neville," Lopez said, switching to her PDA and opening an e-mail. "Claretta Neville came up clean, no criminal record or history of any kind with the police except in connection with Daniel's gang activities. Turns out that her African heritage is Ethiopian."

"As would be Daniel's," Tyrell said thoughtfully. "Aren't there tribes in Ethiopia who are said to be the descendants of Israel, lost tribes or something?"

"Maybe, I saw something on TV about that once." Lopez nodded. "Michael Shaw, the hospital orderly, is also clean, nothing but a couple of parking violations. Casey Jeffs is . . ."

Lopez broke off for a moment as she read.

"Is what?" Tyrell asked.

"Is of interest. He's been an employee of the institute for the past sixteen years. However, prior to that he was a patient, long-term psychosis. His name flagged up in relation to a homicide charge from back in 1984."

"You're kidding? He killed someone?"

"Went to trial." Lopez nodded as she read. "A late witness testimony caused the case to collapse amid accusations of fraud and Casey was acquitted. The full file's at the station."

Tyrell rubbed his chin with one hand. "What about DNA from Daniel Neville's room?"

"Dozens of them," Lopez said. "It'll take weeks to

obtain profiles, and we haven't got a suspect in custody to match them against. Besides, we know that Casey was nowhere near Daniel when he died."

Tyrell let out a long sigh. "Powell will piss all over it. What else do we know about him?"

"Orphaned young. Mother was a hooker working San Antonio, died back in 1984 from a heroin overdose . . ." Tyrell frowned and looked at the pixelated image on Lopez's PDA. A straggly haired blond woman, her features creased with the passing of the years. "Casey was arrested for killing her; attorneys filed for manslaughter charges and got a prosecution. He got taken in by the institute for treatment after the trial collapsed."

"Who was the benefactor for his treatment?"

"It doesn't say," Lopez replied. "He's been in and out of private rehabilitation clinics ever since. Doesn't make any sense though. He's never held full-time employment except at the institute, so where'd the money come from?"

"The father?" Tyrell guessed as he opened the door to the church foyer.

"Father's unknown, according to this."

Tyrell led the way to a broad reception desk overlooked by a brightly painted mural of a crucifix atop a hill, the sun casting beams of light upon it and the sky emblazoned with three inspirational words:

Rehabilitate. Rejuvenate. Rejoice.

Resurrect, Tyrell thought, but didn't say.

The receptionist in the entrance foyer was a petite, slim, and bespectacled woman in her forties who seemed perturbed by the presence of two police detectives and their need to speak to Kelvin Patterson himself.

"I'm afraid the pastor is preparing for tonight's presidential rally," she said politely, "but I can arrange an interview for tomorrow if that's convenient?"

Tyrell smiled tightly.

"It's not. We need to speak to Mr. Patterson urgently, regarding the death of a patient."

The receptionist frowned and turned away without another word, moving across to a phone and dialing a number. Tyrell watched her body language become defensive as she spoke. Finally, she set the phone down.

"If you'll follow me this way, please."

She led them through a myriad of corridors, many of them bearing vast canvases on the walls depicting biblical scenes. Tyrell struggled to remember his Sunday schooling as he noted images of the crucifixion, of the Garden of Eden, and what he guessed might have been the destruction of Babylon. Or was it Babel?

"Mr. Patterson is a very busy man, you know," the receptionist said over her shoulder.

"As am I," Tyrell replied.

"He has an immensely important rally tonight with a presidential candidate."

Tyrell felt a squirm of irritation. Lopez hurriedly spoke beside him.

"Which candidate?"

"Senator Isaiah Black, Texas."

Tyrell looked across at Lopez, who raised an eyebrow.

"Isn't Kelvin Patterson the man who said New Orleans was destroyed by God because it hosted a Gay Pride rally?" Tyrell inquired.

The receptionist raised her chin as she walked, not looking back at him. "Who is to say that He didn't?"

Tyrell chose not to reply.

They reached a large set of ornate double doors at the end of a long corridor that seemed to orbit the church's main hall to their left. The receptionist knocked briskly on the doors before opening them and calling into the room.

"Pastor? The two police officers are here to see you."

There was a muffled response, and then the receptionist backed out of the doorway and gestured for Tyrell to enter.

63

The expansive office, dominated by a huge chrome crucifix on one wall and by towering windows on the other, seemed to make Kelvin Patterson more diminutive than he actually was. He turned and smiled regally as the receptionist closed the door behind Tyrell and Lopez.

"Detectives," he greeted them.

Patterson was wearing an expensive silk shirt and dark trousers, and a navy blazer hung from a chair nearby.

"I understand you have a big night ahead, Pastor," Tyrell said.

"It is a big night for America," Patterson replied. "Much hangs on how the crowd views us tonight." *Us,* Tyrell thought quietly as they followed him across to his broad mahogany desk, complete with bronze eagle and the Stars and Stripes. "What can I do for you?"

"The Evangelical Institute," Tyrell said. "You own it?"

"It is owned by the alliance."

"And it is used as a rehabilitation site for drug addicts."

"The hospital provides a place for the poor to gain access to free health care, food, and accommodation,"

Patterson said as he picked up his tie. "Only a small part of the hospital is dedicated to long-term patients."

Tyrell nodded. "Your staff there, how are they recruited?"

Patterson tucked his tie under his collar and began tying the knot.

"We advertise for volunteers. Why do you ask?"

Tyrell ignored the question.

"What background checks do you have in place when recruiting them?"

"All of our procedures follow recruitment laws," Patterson replied without elaboration.

Lopez sensed her moment instinctively when Tyrell let a silence hang in the room.

"Do you have records of all members of staff?"

Patterson began fastening his cuff links. "The hospital's records are very thorough."

Tyrell spoke quickly, giving Patterson no room for thought.

"Where do the funds come from to finance the hospital itself?"

"From our congregation. We have almost thirty million members across the United States."

"It is more blessed to give than to receive," Tyrell ventured.

Patterson appeared surprised, and smiled. "It is indeed."

There was a long pause when neither Tyrell nor Lopez said anything, simply looked around the sumptuous office.

"I don't mean to pry, Officers, but what are these questions referring to?" Patterson asked. "Has a member of my staff committed a crime?"

"No," Tyrell said, "a member of your staff has not committed a crime."

Another long pause. Patterson appeared bemused. "What then?"

"There was a patient in your hospital by the name of Daniel Neville," Tyrell said.

"There are so many," Patterson said. "I have no knowledge of individual patients."

"You weren't informed of the circumstances surrounding his death?" Lopez asked in surprise.

"I'm sorry," Patterson said, "but the AEA manages dozens of charitable organizations. I was informed that a death had occurred, and that a police officer was present at the scene."

"Daniel Neville," Lopez continued smoothly, "claimed that he was taken to a laboratory where tests were conducted on him and other patients."

Patterson's smile did not slip as he reached out for his jacket.

"One does not end up in a drug rehabilitation center for no reason. Many of our younger patients have issues facing up to their addiction, and construct fantasies to justify it."

"So there were no experiments conducted on institute patients?" Tyrell asked.

Patterson frowned as he slipped into his jacket.

"None that I know of."

"We need to be certain," Tyrell said, and let the bombshell drop. "It would help us to understand what happened to the bodies we found yesterday morning."

Patterson froze in motion. "Bodies?"

Lopez produced a series of photographs of the dead men they had discovered and handed them to Patterson. The pastor stared down at the images in his hand as though he were handling poisonous insects.

"Poor souls," he said finally.

"All three of these men were found with high levels

of crack cocaine in their blood, indicative of overdose. The problem is that one died from hypothermia induced by a medical procedure, and the drugs were administered after death, not before."

Patterson did not look up from the photographs for a moment, leafing through them.

"What are you suggesting?" he asked, still without looking up.

"You have carried out experimental procedures into consciousness at the institute, is that correct, Pastor?" Lopez asked.

Patterson stared at her for a long beat, caught up in the tangle of unexpected questions.

"Yes, we have a history of such work."

"We consider this to be a homicide investigation," Lopez said. "Daniel Neville provided enough information for us to follow leads connecting his experiences with the fate suffered by these three men, and those leads have led us here."

Patterson's eyes widened. "Here?"

Tyrell took the photographs from the pastor.

"We believe that these men died while undergoing a medical procedure administered by one of your staff."

"Which one?" Patterson gaped in astonishment.

Tyrell handed him another printed image. "Do you know this man?"

The pastor looked down at the image and shook his head.

"No. He is a member of my staff?"

"We believe he was," Lopez said. "His name is Damon Sheviz."

"I understand that your alliance has been heavily involved in experiments involving human volunteers," Tyrell said.

Patterson slowed his button fastening, leveling a calm gaze at Tyrell.

"It is my opinion that churches around the world have been too long hoarding their finances and trying to force their followers to believe in the unbelievable, to have faith in emptiness. There can be no knowledge without study."

"How are these experiments conducted?" Lopez chimed in.

"We use noninvasive means," Patterson said. "Hypnotherapy, meditation, the study of near-death experiences in cardiac-arrest patients," Patterson replied warily. "Where are you going with this?"

Tyrell took the plunge.

"We believe that Damon Sheviz is harvesting live victims to conduct illegal experiments involving the genetic creation of a chimera between a human and an unknown species."

Patterson's eyes flickered.

"That's . . ." he began. "That's ridiculous. Such procedures do not even exist."

"Actually, they do," Tyrell went on. "We have gathered detailed files on this man, and we have people working on finding out where he is obtaining the equipment necessary to conduct these experiments."

"But he wouldn't be able to do things like that without other staff members knowing about it and stopping him," Patterson said.

"I didn't say that the procedures were conducted *here*," Tyrell said, and then decided to take a chance. "We also need to know about Casey Jeffs."

Tyrell caught another tremor of apprehension in the pastor's demeanor.

"Who is he?" Patterson asked.

"A janitor who works at the institute. You said that you run checks on your members of staff?"

"Of course, all members are carefully vetted."

"Mr. Jeffs was tried for homicide," Tyrell pointed out. "Isn't that something that would have been a cause for concern?"

Patterson remained rooted to the spot as he spoke.

"Perhaps, but if Mr. Jeffs is one of our rehabilitated patients, then his employment will be a part of our rehabilitation program."

"For sixteen years?" Tyrell inquired.

"I wouldn't know how long Mr. Jeffs has been in treatment or employment," Patterson said quickly.

"Of course," Tyrell replied. "We have evidence that Casey Jeffs has received private clinical treatment for most of his life without apparent financial means. Do you know anyone who may be providing this support to him?"

Patterson stared directly into Tyrell's eyes. "No, I'm afraid not."

Tyrell forced a bright smile onto his face as though nothing untoward had passed between them.

"Thank you for your time, sir."

Tyrell turned and walked to the office door, letting Lopez through first before looking back into the office to where Patterson stood as though stranded.

"Pastor? Daniel Neville."

"Yes?"

"You said that you did not know him."

"That's right."

"You also said that many of your younger patients create fantasies to cover their addictions," Tyrell said quietly. "I did not tell you that Daniel Neville was young."

Patterson's eyes quivered in their sockets.

"Most all of our addict patients are young males," he said. "That is a demographic of substance abuse."

Tyrell turned and closed the door behind him.

"He's covering something," Tyrell said as he walked away with Lopez. "The only other route we've got is Senator Isaiah Black."

Lopez stared at him as though he'd turned blue.

"You can't just stroll into a senator's office, Tyrell. They'll call District or headquarters to confirm your identity and Powell will string you up by the balls long before we get through the damn door."

"Look, if we can get Isaiah Black to give us an angle on Patterson, then we've got a lead we can follow. He might have heard or seen something. I can't just tell Powell that we think Patterson's covering something up; it isn't enough to convince Commissioner Devereux to reopen the case."

"This one's cold, Tyrell, maybe we should do what Powell says and let it go until forensics turn in their data."

"It ain't over till it's over, Lopez. Sometimes you just gotta do what you don't want to."

"That's right," Lopez said. "And I'm tellin' you it's too far. At least get a subpoena or something?"

Tyrell stopped, looking down at her for a long moment.

"Look, just do some digging into this Casey Jeffs and see what you can come up with. The money for his treatment had to come from somewhere. Patterson and Jeffs may be connected and we need to know how."

"I'll do what I can," Lopez replied disconsolately.

"You're losing it for this, aren't you?"

"You've only just noticed?" Lopez asked. "We're chasing a pastor around a church while talking about surgeons conducting insane experiments on abductees, trying to turn them into frickin' angels. The hell you think I'm doing?"

Tyrell nodded, rubbing his temples again and feeling a slick sheen of sweat lacing his skin with beads of oily liquid.

"I know it's crazy, but that's what the evidence is telling us. You think that by following me everyone else will think you're nuts too?"

Lopez sighed and spoke softly in the deserted corridor.

"Where I come from, there's a place up on the foot-hills above the town called Pateon Cemetery. The people who have family members interred there have to pay a tax for the land. Anyone defaults, then the officials dig up the remains and put them on display in the Museo de las Momias, the Museum of the Mummies." She looked briefly at the floor as she spoke. "Nobody goes there at night because there's all kinds of bad shit goin' down. Disembodied voices, things movin' about on their own, you name it. So no, I don't think we're nuts, but Powell sure as hell will and I'm not willing to put my career on the line for this. It just isn't big enough."

Tyrell gave her a long look before speaking.

"Powell isn't going to start blowing sunshine up your ass for playing the good girl," he muttered. "Look where playing by the rules got him."

"Yeah, and look where breaking the goddamn rules got you."

A deep silence filled the corridor.

"Cheap shot, Lopez," Tyrell observed finally.

"I'll let you know what comes up on Jeffs."

With that, Lopez turned and left him standing in the corridor.

64

JERUSALEM

This has got to be stopped."

Ethan sat opposite Bill Griffiths on the veranda of his rented villa overlooking the city, trying to stave off his exhaustion.

"Why didn't you tell me before that you were a journalist?" Griffiths asked.

"It was none of your business," Ethan replied. "Now it is and I need your help."

"I don't know how to help," Griffiths said, looking him up and down. "Look at the state of you—you're dead on your feet. What the hell difference can you make?"

"You called me, Bill," Ethan reminded him, "and I've just escaped Israeli custody to get here, so tell me what's happened."

Griffiths closed his eyes for a moment before speaking. "One of the guards at what may have been Lucy Morgan's dig site, a MACE soldier, was killed by a Bedouin yesterday afternoon." Ethan kept his expression neutral. "Turns out that when the soldier was autopsied, his buddies reported that the Bedouin had claimed he was searching for his son, an Ahmed Khan.

The surgeon who autopsied the soldier recognized the name, as he'd autopsied this Ahmed just the day before."

"So? He was supposedly found dead in the desert, drugs or drink or something."

Griffiths shook his head. "Ahmed Khan worked for the university as a guide for some years. I met him several times. He didn't take drugs and he didn't drink." Griffiths leaned forward on the table. "Point is, Ahmed's body was poisoned with something like cyanide. It was in his lungs and nearly wiped out the surgeon who autopsied him."

Ethan reached into his pocket. From within, he produced a specimen jar with a label stuck to the outside.

"Lucy Morgan excavated several bones for DNA analysis before returning to the field, and this is one of them. Another is in Chicago's Field Museum. No matter where you or MACE take those remains, police forces will be able to genetically match it to these bones. There'll be no place to hide and no way for you to extricate yourself from your involvement in what is now a crime."

Griffiths slammed a balled fist down on the table.

"MACE directed us to that site three days ago! If there's a crime that's been committed, then go to them with your accusations!"

"Israel and the United States won't see it that way," Ethan said simply.

Griffiths shook his head.

"Why would MACE abduct her? They only needed the remains, not the scientist."

"We don't know, but she's being held against her will and MACE has no reason to keep her alive. The question is, Bill, what are you going to do about it?"

Griffiths still refused to look at him and Ethan made full use of his discomfort.

"Think about it. You've told me that you were directed to the remains by MACE. Why the hell would they have found the site and excavated the remains without informing the authorities of what they'd found or Lucy's absence? It's your call, Bill. Are you really the sort of guy to profit from death?"

Griffiths sighed heavily.

"If I help you, what are you planning to do?"

Ethan grinned. "Go for a jaunt with some friends."

RECHAVIA
JERUSALEM

"They're onto him."

The voice was distorted by digital scrambling devices fitted to Byron Stone's SUV. Bright sunlight from the rising dawn beamed in shafts between buildings outside and flickered through the interior of the vehicle as it cruised through the narrow streets.

"When?" Stone asked.

"Half an hour ago, two MPD detectives. They've tracked down Sheviz's connection to the pastor but they're still fishing around for something usable."

"Patterson's a moron," Stone spat into the phone, "another fundamentalist who's climbed so far up God's ass he can't see where he's going anymore. The police will work it all out eventually, and when they do Patterson's pious little fantasy will collapse."

"We need to break the link between DC and Israel before the Bureau gets involved," the voice cautioned. *"If Patterson is investigated, he'll sing like a canary once they threaten him with a cell and I can't hold them off forever."*

Stone considered this for a moment. Kelvin Patterson was one of the most outspoken conservatives in all of America, making the most outrageous statements while hiding behind a thin veneer of compassionate faith. But most all such men fell victims to their own bigotry and hypocrisy: homophobic pastors found to have indulged in gay relationships, anticorruption pastors arrested for embezzlement and fraud, countless others arrested for child molestation and other unspeakable crimes. Robbed of his power and his influence, Kelvin Patterson would become the man he had always been: weak, timid, and afraid.

"Then we must prepare for the worst," Stone said.

"*Understood,*" the voice replied. "*What about the detectives?*"

Stone gripped the phone tighter.

"They must not make a connection between MACE and Sheviz," he said firmly. "Find a weakness and exploit it. Keep them at bay until tomorrow and all will be done."

"*I'll do what I can. What about the boy?*"

"He's as much of a liability as the pastor," Stone growled. "Do whatever is required."

Stone set the phone down, and looked up to see Spencer Malik watching him expectantly.

"What's happening?" the soldier asked.

Stone settled himself into the plush leather seat, thinking for a moment before replying.

"Change of plan. It's time to start clearing up this mess and get on with the business of looking after ourselves."

Malik nodded, and the Texan turned his head to watch the sun rising over Jerusalem's Old City.

"Are the surgeon and Lucy Morgan still in position?" he asked.

"They haven't moved," Malik confirmed.

"Good, then we bring this to a close right now. Organize your men and have them conduct a rescue operation. Ensure that Patterson's imbecilic surgeon suffers an unfortunate accident while you're there."

"I'll take care of that personally. What's happening in Washington?"

"Patterson's losing control of Senator Black, but I don't give a damn now we have a chance to close the deal on the Valkyrie drones. What about Warner?"

"He's escaped Israel's custody. We can't be sure, but my guess is that he's going to try to rescue Lucy Morgan."

"Not if we destroy everything first," Stone growled. "Let Warner enter the area and then have your men engage him; send Cooper and Flint to lead the defense. I want no trace left. Have the remaining Valkyrie drone launched to cover the operation, then vaporize any evidence."

Malik nodded and climbed out as Byron sat back in his seat and ran everything through his mind one more time. As long as Malik could ensure that every loose end was destroyed and every loose tongue permanently silenced, then there was no longer anything to fear.

A shame, Byron reflected, about Lucy Morgan.

65

FIRST DISTRICT STATION
M STREET SW, WASHINGTON DC

Lopez stood outside the door of Captain Powell's office and hesitated, her knuckles touching the cheap wood. She could hear the captain talking on his phone and it gave her a moment to reconsider.

Tyrell was going too far; she couldn't deny that. There were political channels to consider, etiquette to ensure a senator's compliance with any investigation. Tyrell's crusade would get Lopez far deeper into the shit than she was prepared to accept, and though she'd struggled with the decision for two hours, it was time to make a stand.

Warring against her determination to avoid a catastrophic black mark against her name was a sense of loyalty to Tyrell. It felt as though she was ratting on a classmate, a stool pigeon butt kissing her way into—

"Are you coming in or are you going to stand there all goddamn day?"

Powell was off the telephone. Lopez opened the door and stepped into his office.

"What is it?" Powell demanded, surrounded by teetering mounds of paperwork.

Lopez took a deep breath.

"Tyrell is headed for Senator Isaiah Black's offices in the District. He's looking for help to link a pastor named Kelvin Patterson to the homicides at Potomac Gardens yesterday."

Lopez expected Powell to spontaneously combust in fury. Instead, the captain leveled her with a somber expression.

"When did he leave?"

"A couple of hours ago, but he doesn't have an appointment."

Powell set his pen down.

"Let me take care of it," he said. "I'll head down there and have the Capitol Police pick him up before the damned fool can do any more damage."

A weight lifted from Lopez's shoulders at the same time as an unfamiliar self-loathing churned deep inside her.

"Tyrell wanted me to run a few checks on some of the leads we were chasing. I'm going to head down to see Larry Pitt and try to figure out what Casey Jeffs might have to do with all of—"

"You'll do no such thing," Powell growled, standing up behind his desk and leaning forward with his balled fists resting knuckle-down before him. "You've wasted enough time on this."

"It ain't right to leave it."

"It's not right," Powell agreed, "but it's necessary. Tyrell's crusade's getting in the way of the department's work. You've done the right thing, Lopez. I don't want to see your name dragged down with Lucas Tyrell's charades."

"He's onto something," Lopez said.

"Yes, he is," Powell admitted, "but we've been here

before. The guy can't investigate anything without think-ing it's the work of a secret cabal of nymphomaniac vam-pire zombies." Lopez shot him a curious look. "You know what I mean."

She sighed.

"I've worked with him for three years and he's never been wrong about anything. Sure, he gets big ideas about small fry but what's the deal with that any-how? There's too much about this case that doesn't fit without the players being somehow connected, and I can't see the sense in letting it all go just 'cause Tyrell's going off the range."

"Off the range?" Powell repeated. "Walking into the Capitol and laying into a senator? Tyrell can't walk around here thinking he's DC's fat-assed answer to Jack Bauer."

"All the same," she said, "I think we should keep playing his hand here and see what comes up."

"And if you come up with nothing?" Powell chal-lenged.

"Then all we'll have wasted is my unpaid overtime and the world will be safe again."

Powell sighed, grabbing his jacket and folding it over his arm.

"Just sit back from it for a couple of days then look at it afresh. Christ's sake, Lopez, your shift ended four hours ago. Take a break, okay?"

"But the links," Lopez said. "Maybe there's some-thing else behind all of this and we can—"

"The district attorney isn't going to start handing out warrants on something as slim as correlating but obscure medical procedures. Look at what happened in Peru, people being murdered for body fat that was sold in Europe for cosmetic surgery purposes. At the same time there's a black market for spare body parts in Asia and India, but nobody's suggesting the two are connected."

"Is anyone suggesting that the two are legal?"

Powell shot her a severe look over his shoulder as he turned and strode from the office.

"Go home. That's an order, Lopez."

66

WADI AL-JOZ
WEST BANK, PALESTINE
AUGUST 26

Ethan sat in silence as Bill Griffiths parked his car near the entrance to a narrow street and glanced in his rearview mirror before climbing out. Ethan followed him to the corner of the street and peered along its length.

At the opposite end of the street stood a warehouse nestled against a small grove of acacia trees that rustled gently in the morning breeze. Outside, two MACE operatives stood in their distinctive black suits and sunglasses.

"That'll be the one then," Ethan said quietly.

"It's one of six buildings used by MACE to store equipment. We were ordered to bring the remains here to be packaged for shipment." Griffiths looked about nervously. "There could be more of them. Are you sure this is a good idea?"

"It's the only idea I've got left."

"Fantastic."

The sound of a car engine behind them caused Ethan to turn in time to see Aaron Luckov's jeep pull up nearby. The towering Israeli climbed out and Ethan and Griffiths joined him.

"You bring everything we need?" Ethan asked him.

Aaron grinned beneath his beard, leading them to the rear of the jeep and yanking off a canvas cover. Inside lay several weapons, including a sawed-off shotgun, pistols, and two flash-bang grenades. Luckov picked up the sawed-off.

"Gentlemen, meet my good friend, Old Painless."

Griffiths balked.

"Jesus Christ, who the hell do you think you are? Steve McQueen?"

Ethan grabbed a pistol, checking the mechanism.

"MACE is serious," he replied evenly. "No sense in handing them the advantage."

Griffiths looked at the pistol handed to him by Luckov.

"I'm not a soldier," he said quietly.

"Neither am I," Luckov replied. "Let's get this over with."

Rafael sat silently with his back to the wall of an alley, watching as the three men lifted their weapons from the back of the truck. Griffiths, Warner, and the big Israeli strode off toward a series of low warehouses opposite an apartment block near where Rafael sat.

He looked up at the building, at the vantage points offered by a number of the higher apartments, and settled in to wait. It would, he was sure, not be long before his quarry would arrive, especially now that the fool American was launching his own attack. Now, at last, he was fully prepared.

Quietly, Rafael pulled out his cell phone and dialed a number.

67

IDF NORTHERN COMMAND (PATZAN)
NEVE YAAKOV, JERUSALEM

General Benjamin Aydan sat in silence for a long moment before speaking.

"He escaped custody?"

The two Knesset Guard soldiers before him nodded, one of them speaking in clipped tones.

"He had help, at least one and probably two vehicles. We lost sight of them after he damaged our vehicle to prevent any pursuit. We were assured that he was considered low risk, sir, and unlikely to cause problems."

General Aydan rubbed his temples wearily.

"That would not appear to be the case now, gentlemen, wouldn't you agree?"

The two guards remained silent as General Aydan considered the case of the man before him. A former journalist, he had lost his fiancée to an insurgent abduction in Gaza. Now he was back in Israel supporting a similarly bereaved American, Rachel Morgan, an individual for whom Aydan held considerable sympathy.

He was about to pick up his phone when it rang loudly, startling him.

"Aydan."

"Sir, we've just received a call from an anonymous source revealing the whereabouts of Dr. Lucy Morgan."

Aydan blinked in surprise.

"Veracity?"

"Likely to be genuine, sir. We've been unable to trace the cell from which the call was made, but it was from within two hundred meters of the alleged abductee. Sir, the problem is that it's a privately held compound of Munitions for Advanced Combat Environments, and guarded by their private security forces."

General Aydan felt his jaw tightening.

"Gather an assault team immediately. Privately held or not, if Dr. Morgan is there, we're going in to find her, understood?"

68

The brilliant sun blazing above the Old City had risen far enough to scorch the morning air, flaring up off the stone flags of the military compound as Rachel was led to where a small IDF convoy was preparing to leave.

Lieutenant General Aydan joined her from the other side of the compound.

"We've had a tip-off," Aydan said.

"From whom?"

"We don't know but it's evidently somebody who knows a great deal about what MACE has been up to," Aydan said. "Clearly an insider of some kind and they're in the West Bank. They've told us that Lucy is being held in a warehouse in Wadi al-Joz. You mentioned to Shiloh that Mr. Warner found explosives in the MACE camp in the Negev?"

"They were taken from us," Rachel said. "IEDs, he called them, encased in a sort of gel."

"Triacetone triperoxide, or so we've been told by the informant," General Aydan said. "It's been used by terrorist organizations because it's extremely difficult to detect, can be formed at room temperature, doesn't contain nitrogen compounds, and has an explosive force eighty percent greater than TNT."

"Can you find them?" Rachel asked.

"MACE has a Valkyrie drone that is equipped with infrared sensors," Aydan said quickly. "Now we know where to look, we can seize the craft and use its abilities."

"What if Lucy's there? If her abductors have explosives, they could . . . use them!" Rachel stammered. "Do we know if she's alive yet?"

"We don't know anything yet," Aydan said.

"Contact the informer," Rachel said quickly. "Offer me as a trade for Lucy."

General Aydan looked down at Rachel for a long moment, a new respect in his eyes.

"I won't let it come to that. Let's concentrate on finding Lucy." Aydan gestured to a tall, lean-looking officer who joined them. "This is Lieutenant Jerah Ash. He will be leading your team and will protect you with his life."

Rachel looked at the officer, who seemed quiet but confident, and the general looked at her seriously.

"Ma'am, where is Ethan Warner?"

"I don't know," she said quickly. "He hasn't made contact since escaping from custody. I don't know what he's doing but if this tip-off is correct, then he was right about MACE."

General Aydan turned to Lieutenant Ash.

"If what I've heard about this Warner is true, he's probably attempting a rescue of his own. Tell your men to watch their fire."

Aydan hurried away toward a waiting car near the compound entrance. Lieutenant Ash turned with Rachel and clambered up into the troop transporter, taking their seats alongside soldiers loaded down with weapons, radios, and body armor.

"Put this on," Lieutenant Ash said to her, handing her a heavy blue body-armor kit. "Just in case."

Rachel complied, and then the vehicles started their engines amid clouds of diesel fumes before pulling out of the compound and turning north toward the West Bank.

69

WADI AL-JOZ
WEST BANK, PALESTINE

Lucy lay adrift on a sea of delirium when a voice broke through the silence surrounding her.

"It is time."

A figure moved into view as she opened her eyes, gray eyes gazing down at her and the white hair glowing in the light. The serene expression on that face chilled her even more than the cold surface upon which she lay.

"Sheviz."

Damon Sheviz mocked her with an excruciatingly compassionate smile and turned to a bank of monitors.

"What happened to you?" she gasped in despair. "You were a scientist, once."

"I still am," Sheviz said without looking at her. "And I am on the verge of the greatest breakthrough in the history of mankind."

Lucy felt horror caressing her senses like lice crawling under her skin.

"You're a killer, nothing more. Whatever you're doing, it's not worth it."

Sheviz looked at her seriously.

"The return of the Nephilim to the realm of mankind is my only remaining goal."

"What's a Nephilim?"

Sheviz's face twisted into a grimace. "A pity that you understand so little, but don't worry, everything is about to become crystal clear. I'll explain what I'm going to do, and how you're going to help me."

"I'll die before helping you," Lucy spat.

"The process is simple," Sheviz said as though he had not heard her last retort. "I will anesthesize you and connect you to this heart-bypass machine. I'll then begin the process of cooling your core temperature down to around ten degrees Celsius before replacing your entire blood volume with a chilled saline solution."

Damon Sheviz showed her a small test tube as he went on with delight.

"At the point when you are clinically dead, without a heartbeat or brain function, I will insert this fertilized egg into your ovary. With your body in hypothermic suspension, your immune system's ability to reject foreign tissue will be hindered sufficiently for the egg to take hold on the lining of your uterus."

Lucy felt a bolt of nausea lodge deep in her throat.

"Whose fertilized egg?"

Sheviz smiled.

"That of a Nephilim, a fallen angel. The specimen that you found will rise once again, cloned by me and carried by you, and God's kingdom shall return."

Lucy blinked, unable to comprehend the madness infecting Sheviz's mind.

"Those remains are of a species not of this Earth," she said slowly, carefully. "They're not of an angel; they're of an extraterrestrial species that—"

"Pah!" Sheviz sneered. "Only someone poisoned by

secularism could be so blind to the truth. This, Lucy, is our history becoming our future. Imagine, the blood of God running in the veins of men once more, this godless age of filth and despair eradicated once and for all."

Lucy lay back on the gurney, shaking her head. As a scientist she had no fear of dying, for there was nothing to fear in the unknown, only something new to be discovered. Blind faith instead feasted upon the bloated carcass of ignorance, gorged itself on fanaticism and dogma, and Sheviz was its ultimate creation.

"So this is what you did to the others?" Lucy uttered, trying to conceal her revulsion.

"No," Sheviz said. "They gave their lives to span the ages that have passed since Genesis, to overcome the genetic divide between our ancestors and modern man. They made possible this chimeric linking of man and God, so that our holy covenant may be complete."

Lucy realized that Sheviz's mind had truly gone, entirely devoid of any sense of responsibility for the deaths that he had caused.

"You're insane," she said softly.

"The word of our Lord was spoken in this very land," Sheviz insisted, "and science has done nothing but endorse the word of God."

"How's that?"

"Our common origin with the Nephilim, the children of God, as recorded in our bloodline. Think about it, Lucy: all of this time we have searched for evidence of God, and all of this time it has run in the veins of a lucky few, the descendants of the inhabitants of the Garden of Eden, of Adam and Eve themselves. How else can such pure blood, O-negative, have appeared without precedent six thousand years ago?"

Lucy spat out a cackling laugh.

"Evolution," she said in terminal delight. "It's rare because it's a line from a common ancestor not diluted by genetic drift and random mutation. There's nothing godly about it!"

"Evolution by natural selection is impossible," Sheviz spat. "It is the same as a whirlwind passing through a junkyard and assembling a Boeing 747—pure chance. Design by God is the only alternative."

Lucy slowly shook her head.

"It's nothing to do with chance and everything to do with time. You cite your God as the designer of everything because you say complex life can't exist without a designer, yet who designed your designer? If everything complex that exists requires a designer, then your theory collapses beneath the weight of its own contradictions: it fails miserably because it cannot explain the origin of your designer, who must be complex to have designed everything in the universe in the first place. Your God, by your own definition, cannot exist."

Sheviz's eyes flew wide and spittle flew from his lips as he seethed, too lost now in the throes of fervor to speak. He reached across to a table nearby and produced a syringe tipped with a wicked-looking needle.

"Time for you to make history, my dear," he intoned. "You will help me because if you don't, then the experiment might fail and you'll lose your life. For your own sake, Lucy, let's work together."

"Like hell," Lucy muttered.

"We have cloned the blood of a Nephilim, but it has been rejected by all previous subjects, despite their being universal recipients carrying the AB blood group. Why is this?"

Lucy remained silent, staring at the ceiling. Sheviz smiled coldly.

"Allow me to motivate you further," he said, and held out a photograph above her head.

Lucy gasped as she saw a black-and-white shot of her mother. Sheviz didn't give her the chance to speak.

"Your mother, my dear, is in the company of my associates. If you do not comply with my demands, perhaps she will become the next subject of these experiments."

Hot tears stung Lucy's eyes.

"Leave her alone," she hissed.

"Then tell me what I need to know."

Lucy squeezed her eyes shut, struggling against the tide of despair that washed over her.

"It's not just about blood groups," she uttered. "The species you've cloned has evolved on a different planet. It isn't a Nephilim; it's an alien species and its tissue cannot be grafted onto any species on Earth. There is no way to do it without killing the patient!"

Sheviz slowly shook his head, tutting as he slipped the needle into her arm.

"One more time, Lucy. I want you to imagine this needle slipping into your mother's body. Now, tell me how to overcome the cellular rejection."

Lucy swallowed, blinking away tears and with them her resolve.

"You need to induce donor nonresponsiveness using hematopoietic chimerism," she whispered harshly. "That's how real scientists have cloned donor cells in the past."

"Go on," Sheviz said.

"Introduce the donor stem cells into the bone marrow of the recipient, where they will coexist with the recipient's stem cells. Bone marrow stem cells give rise to cells of all hematopoietic lineages."

Sheviz gasped, slapping his forehead with his spare hand.

"Of course," he uttered. "Through the process of hematopoiesis. We were using leukodepletion of the blood to remove the recipient's white blood cells to reduce alloimmunization, but it wasn't enough to prevent immunoshock."

"Lymphoid progenitor cells are created," Lucy continued in a whisper of self-loathing, "and move to the thymus where negative selection eliminates the reactive killer T cells. The existence of the donor stem cells in the bone marrow causes donor reactive T cells to be considered native to the body and undergo apoptosis, or programmed cell death. There is no further rejection of the new genetic material."

Damon Sheviz smiled down at Lucy as she looked away in disgust.

"Congratulations, my dear," he said, shaking his head. "You've solved the mystery of why one of my patients in Washington DC survived: his lineage came from Ethiopia, and there are some tribes living there who originated in the Levant. He was already carrying native T cells, and they protected him long enough for the genetic material we inserted to begin taking effect. Now the next subject will not die from the procedure, but shall be our crowning glory."

A sudden crackling noise erupted from beyond the darkness of the room, like hailstones hammering on a tin roof. It was a moment before Lucy realized that it was the sound of gunfire coming from outside.

Sheviz withdrew the needle from her arm, and Lucy realized that perhaps someone had finally found her.

70

WADI AL-JOZ
WEST BANK, PALESTINE

Keep low and stay behind me," Ethan said to Griffiths.

The fossil hunter grunted in reply as they hugged the side of a low wall. Aaron Luckov, the sawed-off shotgun cradled in his grasp, led the way.

Even as they were coming within firing distance of the two MACE guards, Ethan saw one of them press his finger to his ear and frown in concentration as he listened to a message presumably coming through an earpiece he was wearing. Ahead, Aaron Luckov moved out to the right as Ethan saw the two guards suddenly reach for their weapons.

"They've made us!" Luckov hissed.

Ethan saw the guards turn to face them, both handling machine pistols with military efficiency as a burst of semiautomatic fire shattered the hot morning air. Ethan flinched and ducked aside as from the corner of his eye he saw a parked vehicle's windshield smashed into a web of cracked glass.

"Aaron, covering fire!"

Luckov popped up from behind the parked car and unloaded two rounds in the general direction of the MACE troops, who leaped desperately down into cover as a hail of buckshot hammered the warehouse doors.

Ethan lunged forward, reaching a low wall no more than twenty feet from the warehouse before he took aim and fired off four rounds at the brickwork behind which the guards had disappeared. Bullets whipped past in response, zipping and twanging as they ricocheted off the car beside him.

"Keep them down!" Ethan shouted to Aaron.

The Israeli popped up again, letting both barrels fly this time before rushing forward and ducking into a narrow alley almost opposite the warehouse. Firing by sections, Ethan and Aaron edged closer to the two men, flanking and pinning them down.

Aaron fired again, causing both guards to remain out of sight. Ethan was about to fire and advance when the doors to the warehouse suddenly burst open and four suited figures rushed out into the sunlight, firing as they moved. Ethan cursed, ducking back down as bullets shattered masonry all around him.

"Balls."

Griffiths shot Ethan a dirty look.

"Cover Aaron!" Ethan shouted. "Try pulling the trigger!"

Griffiths angrily let fly a half-dozen rounds in the general direction of the warehouse as they began falling back.

"We're outnumbered."

Ethan cursed, retreating alongside Griffiths and firing as he went. Aaron Luckov was coming back toward them between bursts of automatic fire when the MACE vehicle appeared behind them, tires screeching as it pulled into the street.

"Enemy rear!"

Luckov's warning was audible even above the clattering automatic fire.

Ethan whirled, firing off three rounds at the vehicle as it skidded to a halt and a half-dozen MACE troops dispersed from within and took up firing positions on either side of the street.

"We're surrounded!" Griffiths shouted, his voice high in alarm.

"Stay low!" Ethan countered, shouting out across the street to Luckov. "Where does that alley go?"

Luckov fired a single shot that burst one of the front tires of the MACE vehicle before shaking his head at Ethan. Clearly, there was no escape to be had down the alleyway.

"Glad you thought this through!" Griffiths shouted.

Another hail of raking fire swept the street, and then suddenly everything fell silent. Ethan, crouched with Griffiths behind the crumbling bricks of a low wall, heard a voice call out.

"You're outgunned and outnumbered. Step into sight with your hands where we can see them!"

Ethan looked across the street at Luckov, who held his gaze for a moment and then nodded slowly.

"They'll kill us if we give ourselves up now," Griffiths hissed.

"They'll kill us if we don't."

Slowly, with one hand holding his pistol high for the MACE troops to see, Ethan stood up from the wall in plain view. One of the MACE guards shouted out again.

"And the other one, the bastard with the shotgun!"

Reluctantly, Luckov stepped out, his shotgun held

above his head. As Ethan stepped out into the street, Griffiths stood and followed him until the three of them were standing in a row.

"Drop your weapons, slowly!"

The MACE guards came out into view, machine pistols pointed at the three men standing before them. Ethan recognized Cooper and Flint, the MACE guards he'd incapacitated the previous day, as he laid his pistol down, Luckov and Griffiths doing the same on either side of him.

"Now stand back three paces!"

Ethan and his companions did as they were ordered, acutely aware of the four MACE guards now standing behind them, having moved out of cover from the warehouse.

Agent Cooper walked forward, and a brittle smile cracked his jaw as he reached up and keyed his earpiece microphone.

"We've got them. What do you want us to do?"

There was a short pause, and then Cooper's smile grew broader. He nodded, and then raised his machine pistol once again and pointed it at Ethan. His next order went out to the men standing behind Ethan.

"You four, get back into that warehouse and kill the surgeon and everyone else in there."

Ethan felt a sudden chill as the MACE soldiers dashed back toward the warehouse. He watched as Cooper and Flint raised their weapons to point directly at him, hungry for revenge.

71

Ethan inhaled once and closed his eyes.

A second passed.

Then another. Ethan felt himself drift into a weary oblivion, asleep on his feet.

"Hands in the air, nobody move!"

Ethan flinched and his eyes jolted open as the bellowed voice echoed loudly off the walls around him, and saw Cooper and Flint standing with their hands and weapons in the air, staring wide-eyed past Ethan. Ethan turned to see dozens of IDF troops tumbling down the street toward them, weapons trained on the MACE soldiers. Farther back, a huge troop transporter thundered into view.

The four soldiers running back to the warehouse dashed for the door and opened fire in unison at the massed Israeli soldiers. Ethan, Griffiths, and Luckov instinctively dove to the ground as the Israeli troops opened fire. Ethan watched as Cooper, Flint, and their companions flailed and jerked as bullets tore into their bodies, hurling them onto the road.

Ethan grabbed his pistol, rolling over and firing at the retreating MACE troops as they vanished into the warehouse. He sat up and shouted at the advancing Israeli soldiers.

"There are civilians inside the warehouse!"

The troops veered off en masse and plunged into the building in pursuit. To his surprise and horror, Ethan saw Rachel sprinting behind them as he struggled to his feet and rushed in after her.

"Rachel, get down!"

The bright sunlight vanished as Ethan plunged into the darkened warehouse.

Flashes of gunfire illuminated the shadows as though Ethan was trapped in a Hadean catacomb filled with warring demons. Figures ran with juddering strides in the muzzle flashes, weapons spitting flames and crashing like thunder around them.

Ethan glimpsed an IDF trooper toss something small between partitions of thin wood being shredded by the passage of supersonic bullets. He covered his eyes and saw a brief but brilliant flash of light that glowed red across his retinas, accompanied by a crack like a firework. He opened his eyes again and saw the IDF soldiers lunging between the partition walls, the flash-bang grenade having stunned the MACE troops. A single round burst through the splintered wooden partition and caught an IDF soldier clean in the center of his chest, hurling him backward into his companions.

The rest of the troops plowed onward. Ethan heard a scream of agony as a hail of bullets thudded into a MACE soldier's body, his arms flailing like a grotesque puppet as he was hurled sideways into discarded pallets to lie with his limbs contorted at impossible angles. Ethan looked desperately about for Rachel, unable to pick her out in the confusion.

Suddenly, like the last rumble of a passing storm, the firing stopped. Ethan's ears hummed in the silence as a high-pitched whistling echoed through his skull.

He looked ahead toward where a narrow doorway separated another partition wall, light that glowed from beyond spilling through the warehouse in a shaft filled with whorls of smoke and dust. Then a woman's voice called out.

"Lucy?"

Ethan rushed through the darkness and dropped down behind Rachel, keeping a grip on her body armor as a determined-looking officer hurried to their side.

"All contacts down except one male in that room," he whispered into his microphone before looking at Ethan. "Ethan Warner?"

Ethan nodded once.

"Lieutenant Jerah Ash," the officer said by way of an introduction. "Thanks for starting World War III out here."

A sudden cascade of bullets clattered all around the partition walls, leaving holes through which light beamed into the darkness surrounding them.

"Stay out of here!" a frail-sounding voice shouted out.

"Kill him!" screamed another female voice.

"That's Lucy!" Rachel cried out. "Don't shoot!"

From the corner of his eye Ethan saw one of the IDF troopers train his weapon through the open doorway and take aim. A single round shattered the silence as it passed through his skull, flicking his head at right angles to his shoulders and snapping the spinal column like a twig.

"Stay the hell out of here! Get out of my laboratory!"

Rachel tugged at Ethan's hand. "Let me go."

"He'll shoot you too," Ethan hissed.

Lieutenant Ash called out toward Sheviz.

"You're surrounded; it's over. Come out with your hands up and we can talk about this."

"You're here to kill us both," Sheviz hissed. "Do you take me for a fool?"

Rachel looked at Lieutenant Ash. "Let me go; he'll know who I am."

The lieutenant glanced at the doorway and reluctantly nodded.

Ethan let go of Rachel's body armor as she stood and walked into the light, her arms outstretched. As she moved, Ethan edged along beside her, careful to keep out of the surgeon's field of vision.

"Mr. Sheviz, my name is Rachel Morgan. I'm Lucy's mother, and these men are not here to kill you. Please, we need to talk."

"Mom?" A frantic and disbelieving voice called.

A long silence ensued. Ethan listened intently as Damon Sheviz replied from somewhere within the room beyond.

"I want immunity," he demanded. "I want a written letter signed by the prime minister."

"You're in no position to make demands!" Lieutenant Ash snapped.

"You're in no position to give me orders!"

Rachel stood in front of the doorway, her arms outstretched.

"At least take me instead," she called to Sheviz. "Whatever you're doing will work just as well on me as it would on Lucy. Just let my daughter go!"

Ethan shifted position, raising his pistol as he heard Lucy shouting.

"Like hell! Shoot this bastard!"

Ethan, his hands trembling with fatigue, took a chance.

"You can't win, Sheviz—it's over," he shouted. "If you don't surrender now, you'll die here."

"Who is that?" Sheviz shouted back. "Who do you think you are to—"

Ethan fired three shots straight at the sound of the voice through the chipboard wall in front of him as Rachel dropped to her knees and covered her ears. He heard a sudden burst of automatic fire and a female scream coming from within the room as Lieutenant Ash thundered past with his troops, and he realized that he had missed.

72

A bright flash of light burst from the room as the IDF troopers tossed in a flash-bang to blind Sheviz. Ethan, his arms trembling, shifted position and peered through the doorway.

A man in a white coat lay beneath the writhing bodies of two IDF troopers, one of whom had wrestled a pistol from the man's hands. Ethan glanced up as Lieutenant Ash reappeared in the doorway.

"God knows how but Sheviz is down and Lucy's okay," he said quickly.

Ethan felt a flood of relief as he lowered his pistol. Damon Sheviz glared at him with a fanatical expression, thick blood staining his shoulder.

"This is God's work!" he spat in fury.

"We need him to tell us everything he knows and then get back to Jerusalem," Ethan said.

Sheviz shook his head, his teeth gritted against the pain of his wound.

"I'll die before I'll tell you anything."

Ethan watched as Lucy Morgan was carefully lifted from the gurney by two soldiers who set her onto unsteady legs in time for Rachel to fold her arms around her daughter. From somewhere deep within,

Ethan felt a warmth radiate from the abscess of pain he harbored, and his shoulders sagged with relief as his eyes closed.

A hand clapped him on the shoulder, jolting him alert.

"I never thought I'd say this, but good work," Lieutenant Ash said. "That was a hell of a shot."

Rachel looked at him as she held her daughter and smiled as tears flowed like rivers from her eyes. Ethan could see that the spark of life had returned within them, glowing brightly once more.

He turned his attention to Sheviz.

"This man," he said to Jerah Ash. "What do we do with him?"

Lieutenant Ash considered the surgeon before them.

"I want to know everything," he said. "Now."

"Go to hell," Sheviz shot back.

The lieutenant took a pace toward him and slammed his hand around the surgeon's neck, lifting him off the floor.

"Now."

Sheviz choked for a moment until the soldier released him. Coughing, Sheviz shook his head.

"My allegiance is to God," he rasped. "Anything you do I'll report to the Court of Human Rights."

"Like your victims could?" Ethan snapped. "What is MACE's connection to all of this?"

Sheviz remained silent. Ethan turned to Lieutenant Ash.

"You're answerable to the Court of Human Rights, as a soldier," Ethan said. "But I was never here."

Ash thought for a moment, and then looked at his fellow soldiers.

"Didn't see a thing," one of them said.

Sheviz looked at the troops, and his defiance crumbled into panic.

"You'll never get away with it!" he stammered.

The soldiers silently filtered out of the laboratory, leaving Sheviz, Lucy Morgan, Ethan, and Rachel. Lieutenant Ash remained, glancing at a pile of videotapes stacked on a counter nearby.

"What are those?" he demanded.

"We taped the procedures," Sheviz said.

"Did you tape what you did to Ahmed Khan?" Ethan asked.

The surgeon's eyes widened briefly.

Ethan moved to stand in front of him, reaching down beside him and picking up a scalpel that lay on a bench. He examined the cruel little blade as he spoke.

"If you fail to tell us everything, then I'll make damned sure you lose your life. But I won't have you killed, Sheviz. I won't let them put you on trial or go through any legal process. I have a friend—Ayeem Khan—a Bedouin man who lives out in the deserts near Bar Yehuda. His son disappeared at the same time as Lucy, and from the same place. His name was Ahmed. You remember him, don't you, Damon?"

Sheviz's eyelid twitched. "I remember him."

"Good," Ethan said softly. "Ayeem is a popular man, with friends among the best and the worst of all Palestine. I promise that these soldiers and I will take you to Ayeem and show them that video, and he will take you to his Bedouin family." Ethan paused for a long moment, letting the information sink in. "What they will do to you for weeks and months and years will be worse than a thousand deaths. Do you understand what I'm saying?"

Sheviz stared at Ethan, taking in his uncompromising expression before speaking.

"I will help," he said quietly.

Ethan nodded slowly. "Start talking."

"I work for an organization in the United States called the American Evangelical Alliance. They called me some months ago to conduct experiments in America using DNA extracted from the fragmentary remains of a Nephilim, a fallen angel, that I discovered in Iraq three years ago. I had tried in the past to conduct genetic transfer studies, requesting through normal channels permission to conduct the procedures, but the Ethics Board of the American Medical Association refused me. I was due to return to Israel when the AEA stepped in and provided me with a cover for my work."

"What connection does MACE have to all of this?"

"MACE provided me with security and equipment under the guise of experiments in battlefield trauma prevention. They did so in Washington DC at first and then here in Israel after it became too difficult to maintain secrecy."

"The reason why scientists like Lucy disappeared from the Negev," Ethan realized. "You abducted them when they found useful remains. What's MACE's endgame?"

Sheviz's features screwed up in distaste as he spoke.

"They are bent on procuring the profits of war. MACE is here to sell their unmanned aerial drones to Israel. In order to assure their success, they are supplying explosives to the insurgent groups here to continue the war."

"And the church provides the finance for your gruesome little experiments?" Ethan asked.

"Money," Sheviz agreed, "equipment and premises from which to operate. We conducted several tests in America on drug addicts who were less likely to be reported missing, but they were unsuccessful. Only one subject survived but he was severely impaired afterward."

Ethan felt himself recoil inwardly at the surgeon's choice of clinical words. *Tests. Subjects. Impaired.*

"Go on."

Sheviz spoke quietly.

"After the fourth patient succumbed it was decided that we could no longer use drug addicts and so I was secretly flown here by MACE in their private jet. We needed new material from which to extract fresh DNA. I had heard from contacts at the Hebrew University about Lucy Morgan working in the Negev and had followed her work closely. I advised that she might find fresh remains near Masada, where once Neolithic villages had existed. When she succeeded, I called in MACE to abduct her and secure the remains. I then used the finds as leverage to effect further abductions and obtain clean bodies."

"And killed them in the process," Lieutenant Ash snarled.

"What about the remains that Lucy found?" Ethan asked.

"Ah, yes," Sheviz said, "a fine specimen of a Nephilim, a fallen son of God. I've found fragmentary remains in Iraq and India before now, but never a complete specimen. They are aboard a MACE jet at Ben Gurion Airport, bound for the United States."

Lucy Morgan eased herself away from her mother.

"You've found other remains?" she stammered.

Sheviz smirked at her despite his pain.

"You scientists, you think you know everything but you miss so much. Remains of Nephilim have been found before but discounted by science as aberrations or lost to history. My team and I have excavated such remains in the ruins of ancient cities several times in the past. We searched for years in the deserts, the jungles, and the mountains, only ever discovering fragmentary bones, but the DNA we extracted from them was unlike any terrestrial signature, the genetic code of God locked into them for all eternity. The evidence of angels, of the Nephilim on Earth, litters our earliest civilizations. They are out there right now, just waiting to be found by those of sufficient faith to locate them."

"Those remains aren't the result of some biblical fantasy, no matter how much you want to believe it," Lucy snapped. "That's why your sick little experiments don't work."

"What's a Nephilim?" Lieutenant Ash asked. "What's this about?"

Ethan answered before Sheviz could speak.

"It's just a fossil that has black-market value," he said quickly. "These lunatics think it's the remains of an angel. How were you doing this, Sheviz?"

"We used stem cells extracted from the Nephilim, reverse engineered to their embryonic state, to replace the nucleus of egg cells provided by Lucy Morgan. Our intention was to place those fertilized eggs in vitro into Lucy, inducing a viable pregnancy. She would carry the son of God in her womb, launching the Second Coming and the final solution to the covenant between man and God."

"What the hell would MACE have to do with all of this?" the lieutenant asked.

Sheviz sneered at Lieutenant Ash as he spoke.

"MACE has been abducting people for years and hiding them away, before negotiating their release for ransom. They've made a tidy sum for themselves all over the world, mimicking insurgent groups and corrupt police forces, and use an assassin to erase any trace of their deception. I have heard them refer to him as Rafael."

Ethan shook his head in disbelief. "I might have known."

"That's insane," Lieutenant Ash said. "They'd never have gotten away with it."

"Yes, they could," Ethan said. "Desperate, wealthy parents make an easy target for predatory companies like MACE. They needed the extra income when the supply of arms contracts dried up in the United States after the Iraq War fiasco." Ethan shook his head, amazed that he hadn't thought of it before. "They wouldn't have to worry about a damn thing unless someone looked into it and got too close, and then they'd have to . . ."

Ethan's voice trailed off.

"Ethan?"

Rachel's voice reached him as though from the other side of the universe. Ethan stared vacantly as an image of Joanna appeared in his mind's eye, clearer and sharper than ever before, her face watching him from a crowded but blurred street. Her gaze was boring into his, driving into and through him with an unshakable, unbearable certainty.

The world shifted beneath his feet and he collapsed sideways, grabbing the edge of the gurney for support as his legs quivered beneath him. Rachel jumped up to his side, holding his shoulders.

"How long has MACE been working in Gaza and Israel?" Ethan asked Lieutenant Ash in a feeble voice.

"Four years, maybe five."

Ethan looked at Damon Sheviz.

"Where else has MACE done this?"

"South America, maybe North America too."

The doctor's voice trailed off as Ethan spoke.

"Joanna was tracking the movements of hostage takers and guerrilla groups in Colombia, writing reports on the corruption of governments and police forces. We barely got out of the country after receiving anonymous death threats. Shortly afterward we came to Israel and Joanna began working on the same thing in Gaza and the West Bank." Ethan looked at Lieutenant Ash. "She was sure that someone was behind the abductions, but she never got to the bottom of it."

Rachel put her hand on his shoulder. "Maybe she did but never got the chance to tell you."

Ethan's voice was a whisper in his own ears as he looked at her.

"MACE. The Defense Intelligence Agency must have suspected them before we even left Washington. You were right. They weren't interested in finding Lucy or Joanna; they just wanted the remains found and MACE investigated without arousing the suspicions of Congress."

Rachel nodded slowly.

"MACE has strong connections with the administration," she said. "The encumbent president's campaign could be derailed if any evidence of MACE's activities here were leaked to the press."

"All lies lead to the truth," Ethan murmured. He looked up, shaking himself from his sudden torpor. "We need to stop them—now."

Lieutenant Ash nodded.

"We were tipped off," he said to Ethan. "Someone let us know where Lucy was."

"If that's so," Ethan said, "then MACE's operation may be collapsing. We need to find Byron Stone."

"I'll radio General Aydan and let him know about this," Lieutenant Ash replied. "Do we know where he is?"

Ethan looked at Bill Griffiths, who had walked into the room with Aaron Luckov.

"MACE has a private jet, a Gulfstream V550, waiting to leave Ben Gurion International."

"Then let's get out of here," Ethan said. "I need to stop that jet from taking off."

"What about him?" Lieutenant Ash asked, jabbing a finger at Sheviz.

Ethan turned to the lieutenant and whispered in his ear.

"Ayeem Khan lives near Bar Yehuda," he said simply. "Don't forget the videotape."

Lieutenant Ash turned and called to his men.

"Time to move out!"

Lucy Morgan moved to stand before Ethan.

"I'm coming too," she said.

"This could be dangerous," Ethan said, "and I don't know if—"

"I wasn't asking," Lucy snapped. "I want to see these bastards go down, understood?"

73

Spencer Malik strode into Wadi al-Joz even as the distant sound of small-arms fire echoed off the ancient stone walls around him. He quickened his pace, and saw IDF cordons ahead near the entrance to the quiet little street where the MACE warehouses stood.

The Israeli Defense Force had moved swiftly. Malik didn't know how the operation had become exposed, and could only assume that everything had unraveled in Washington somehow. It mattered little. Soon, it would all be over.

He carried a bag filled with vegetables bought from a local market nearby, and he wore traditional Palestinian dress that helped to conceal his features and detract attention from himself. Among the vegetables in the bag was a large pistol, just in case anyone attempted to stop him in his mission.

Malik turned, entered a familiar apartment building, and climbed up the stairwell, slipping the pistol out of the bag and setting the safety catch to Off. The stairs opened out onto a single corridor that held four doors, two on each side, marked with hastily scrawled numbers on bits of paper tacked to the cheap wood.

He moved silently between the doors, seeking the

first on the left, and hugged the wall alongside it. He looked down at the thin strip of daylight beneath the bottom edge of the door for several moments, waiting to see any telltale moving shadows crossing the light. None came.

"Rasheed, *keef halak?* How are you?" he whispered through the door.

There was a brief pause before a reply came.

"*Salaam.* Enter."

Malik opened the door and entered the apartment to see a Palestinian standing over a sniper rifle mounted on a tripod facing a broad open window. The weapon was pointing down to the MACE warehouse visible below on the street.

"*Salaam,* Rasheed," Malik said. "You have done well."

Rasheed nodded and backed away from the rifle as Malik put his pistol into a shoulder holster and lay down behind the rifle, sighting through it. Even as he did so, he saw the doors to the MACE warehouse open and figures appear in the bright sunlight, escorted by IDF troops. Malik settled in behind the weapon, gripping the trigger and controlling his breathing.

He saw Ethan Warner and Rachel Morgan lingering just inside the building, along with surgeon Damon Sheviz. Malik smiled, and aimed carefully at Ethan's head. He heard Rasheed's footsteps behind him.

"Time, Mr. Warner, for you to become another tragic statistic," Malik said. "Which one shall I kill first, Rasheed?"

Malik flinched in shock as Rasheed's face smashed down onto the tiles alongside him, his nose exploding in a burst of blood as the Arab's eyes stared lifelessly into his. Malik reached down for his pistol, yanking it from its holster as he jumped to his feet and turned to see an Arab in traditional Bedouin dress flash toward him in a blur like a phantom, the apartment door still swinging open from where he had slipped silently inside.

An iron-hard forearm clubbed Malik's pistol to one side, and before he could react the equally hard edge of one hand scythed across his throat. Malik felt his eyes bulge as he staggered backward and tripped over the sniper rifle, crashing down onto his knees.

Malik, choking and his eyes flooding with tears, scrambled for the door of the apartment. A tiny, sharp pain pierced the underside of his elbow and Malik gasped as his body twitched and jerked uncontrollably as though electric currents were rocketing through his tendons. Another hand clamped across his face, yanking him up before pinning his back to a wall.

The Bedouin glared at him, and Malik's bowels flipped as he stared into Rafael's eyes. A blade flickered in the light as Rafael whipped it up against Malik's neck, the cold steel resting on the pulsing thread of an artery.

"*Salaam*," Rafael whispered. "We shall work together, you and I."

74

"P lease," Malik said, "we can work something out."

Malik struggled like a trapped insect pinched between Rafael's finger and thumb, the assassin twisting the pressure-point grip on Malik's elbow. Malik felt himself spun around again and marched to where the sniper rifle lay by the window. A knee slammed hard into his legs and dropped him with a crack onto his knees. Rafael shoved him over onto his front and drove a knee into his back, grinding his ribs against the tiles. Malik's hands were yanked behind his back and bound tightly with electrical cord.

"This was Stone's idea," Malik said desperately. "He's lost his mind."

Rafael said nothing.

"You don't have to do this."

Rafael remained silent, binding Malik's ankles and then removing his shoes and socks.

"Stone is out of control," Malik said, "but we can stop him."

"You can plead, bargain, and beg all you want," Rafael said softly, "but rest assured that you'll not be leaving this room alive, and your passing will not be pleasant."

Malik struggled to control himself.

"You don't have to do this."

"No, I don't have to do this," Rafael agreed. "But I am going to, I'm going to enjoy every moment of it and there's nothing you can do about it."

Something trickled out onto the tiles beneath Malik's body as he felt hot fluid spilling down his legs.

"Please," he gasped.

Rafael moved across and squatted down beside him.

"Tell me," he whispered, "what is MACE really doing out here?"

Malik, wracked with dread, dribbled as he blurted out an explanation.

"They are trying to resurrect some kind of alien that they found out in the deserts. We wanted nothing to do with it, but Patterson insisted that he be allowed to—"

"Who is Patterson?" Rafael demanded.

"Kelvin Patterson, the head of the American Evangelical Alliance," Malik spluttered.

Rafael slowly reached down and from his waistband produced a slim, long blade with a needle-sharp tip. Malik whimpered and shivered as he caught a whiff of a pungent odor staining the breeze, that of his own feces and urine.

"Now," Rafael said quietly, "you're going to tell me everything, from the very day you joined MACE. If you hide anything or fail to answer any of my questions, I will kill you. Begin."

Malik told him. Everything. Of Byron Stone's plan, of the fossils and the girl, of Bill Griffiths and the Bedouin and Israel and the profits from weapons and abductions. When he was done, Rafael looked at his watch.

"Let me go," Malik begged, still trembling and with tears now blurring his eyes.

Rafael looked down at him and nodded. "Very well."

A pitiful wave of relief and gratitude flooded Malik as Rafael turned and reached out for his wrist bonds. The assassin suddenly pressed down hard, and Malik's breath caught in his throat as he felt something pierce the base of his neck, a quiver of motion that was gone as soon as it had arrived. Malik's body stopped trembling as though a switch had been flicked. The assassin leaned back on his haunches.

"I would pity you, were you not such a coward."

Malik managed to crane his head around to look at him. "What have you done?"

Rafael leaned forward, raising one hand and revealing the blade now smeared with dark blood. Malik heard a pitiful sound crawl from his own larynx as Rafael spoke.

"You are paralyzed for what little remains of your life. I've severed your spinal cord between the fourth and fifth vertebrae. Enough remains intact for you to breathe and speak, but little more."

Malik tried to move his body. Nothing happened. Tears scalded his face as he cried out in despair, only for Rafael to shove a pungent-smelling sock into his mouth.

Malik watched helplessly as Rafael reached down, searching his body and retrieving his cell phone. Then Rafael turned to the sniper rifle, pushing it forward to poke out of the window and tying a length of thread to the trigger, unwinding it as he backed away. Malik could see that the rifle would be easy to see from outside the open windows, as would his body lying prone behind it.

Malik screamed through the sock lodged in his

mouth as sweat streamed down his face and prickly heat stung his skin. Rafael looked down at him for a few moments, an expression of absolute calm on his dark features, and then he turned and walked out of sight.

Moments later, the apartment door closed behind him.

75

Byron Stone settled into the plush leather seat of the SUV and picked up the phone, dialing a number and listening as the line clattered with digital activity, the scramblers coding and decoding the signal before allowing the line to connect.

"General Aydan," came the gruff voice on the line, sounding as though it were coming through a microphone rather than a mouthpiece.

"General, how are you?"

"I have been looking for you, Mr. Stone." Byron felt a ripple of alarm twist his guts. *"Where is your remaining Valkyrie UAV?"*

"Airborne, somewhere over Jerusalem, I believe. We have identified a potential insurgent target in Wadi al-Joz that we think should be neutralized with a—"

"We've taken control of the Valkyrie," the general interrupted sharply. *"Where are you?"*

"What the hell are you talking about?" Stone muttered. "That UAV is private property and you have no right to—"

"Our men are on site in Wadi al-Joz and we have it on the authority of one Dr. Damon Sheviz that MACE

is responsible for the security of illegal experiments there. Where are you, Mr. Stone?"

Byron Stone sat in dumbfounded silence for a long moment, staring wide-eyed at the city passing by outside.

"The man is insane," he stammered. "I have no idea what you're talking about."

"We have also found explosive devices like those described by Ethan Warner in the possession of your men," the general muttered angrily down the line. A long pause followed. *"Where are you, Mr. Stone?"*

Byron Stone sat for a moment in catatonic silence and then promptly put the phone down. He leaned forward in his seat, tapping a button on a console beside him that activated the intercom with his driver.

"Get us to the airport at Tel Aviv immediately."

What the hell's happened?

One of the cell phones next to him rang loudly and he almost jumped out of his skin. He picked it up, half expecting to see the number of Israel's Shin Bet or, worse, Mossad. Instead, Stone recognized the number as Malik's and quickly answered.

"What the hell is going on?" he shouted down the line. "Is Rafael dead yet?"

There was a long silence, and in a moment of something that he might have considered precognition, a dread swelled in his belly.

"No, Mr. Stone, he is not yet dead."

Ice water sluiced through Stone as he recognized Rafael's voice.

"Where is Malik?" he asked, veiling his panic with feigned outrage.

"He is enjoying a ringside view of your downfall, one that is about to become much better."

Stone turned cold as he realized the breadth of Rafael's revenge, and through his fear probed a thin spark of fury.

"You'd better start running, Rafael. I'm going to make damned sure that my men and the IDF hunt you down. By the time they're done with you there'll be nothing left to—"

"I'm afraid that you have no time left for that."

Stone was about to reply, but then heard the car phone ringing. He looked down at it in confusion. The screen wasn't glowing, and the noise sounded somewhat muted as though it were coming from beneath the seat on which he sat.

Before he could even consider what was about to happen, Rafael's voice spoke again.

"There were four missing IEDs taken by Ethan Warner from the encampment, Byron. I've returned them to you."

"No!"

Stone lunged for his door handle as suddenly everything turned a bright and brilliant white before him and the universe ripped itself apart in his ears.

Rafael lowered a pair of cell phones from his ears as their signals were abruptly cut off by a sharp crackling noise. From somewhere outside in Jerusalem he heard a rolling boom that reverberated gently through nearby windows, rattling the shutters in their panes.

Casually, he turned to glance at the apartment door beside him. He gripped the roll of thread he held in his hand and yanked hard on it.

A shockingly loud report crashed out as a high-velocity round burst from the rifle within the apartment. Three more shots crackled on the hot morning air as Rafael yanked the cord, each seeming louder than the first and rolling in echoes across the ancient city.

Rafael snapped the thread off and sprinted down the stairwell, turning for the rear exit of the apartment block as distant shouts from apartments above pursued him. As he burst out into a narrow paved area and vaulted over a wall, he heard a whining sound drifting ghostlike through the hard blue sky above.

76

Ethan flinched instinctively outside the warehouse as three sudden gunshots crackled out from somewhere above them.

"Sniper!"

Ethan heard Jerah Ash's shouted warning as he grabbed Lucy and pulled her back into the building, huddling beside the door as he glimpsed a burst of blue smoke spurt from the uppermost window of an apartment block on the opposite side of the street.

"Any other way out?" he shouted back to Lieutenant Ash.

The officer leaned in and spoke into his microphone.

"Ground force six, under fire, Wadi al-Joz! Repeat, we're under fire, requesting support!"

NORTHERN COMMAND (PATZAN)
JERUSALEM

"Shots fired!"

The Israeli technician's voice was edgy as he looked at the unfamiliar controls in front of him. "Building visual, quarter of a mile, camera ready."

The operator of the Valkyrie drone turned the UAV toward the stacked buildings near the edge of the West Bank, spotting the tall apartment block on the corner of the street.

"Zoom in," General Aydan said quickly, watching as a second operator manipulated the UAV's camera controls, zooming in to the top level of the apartment block. One of the balconies was wide open. "There, zoom in there," the general added.

The operator zoomed the camera close on the balcony, and instantly the shape of a man lying prone behind a smoking rifle wavered into view.

"Sniper in sight!"

"Fire! Fire now!"

Malik lay with his chin resting against the stock of the sniper rifle, his face feeling dry and sore as he stared at the shimmering heat haze cloaking the city. The acrid smoke from the rifle barrel had drifted away in the breeze after stinging his eyes and burning his throat, and he could see a distant pall of oily smoke rising where a car bomb had exploded.

He could hear sirens far away, and in a last moment of hope envisioned soldiers finding him trapped and paralyzed behind the rifle, which had clearly been fired not by his hand but by the thread Rafael had attached to its trigger.

He could feel nothing but could smell the stale odor of excrement soiling his legs as he lay helpless. He barely noticed the droning sound as it drifted on the breeze, but when he did he looked up and saw a faint glint of metal flashing in the sunlight against the stark blue sky above.

"Oh no," he mumbled, "please no."

The drone shuddered and a streak of white smoke accelerated toward him.

"Please, God, no," he uttered, closing his eyes as something silvery flashed through the sky before him, and then everything vanished into a terrible inferno of flames and agony. Malik's body was hurled through the air as the flesh was seared from his bones.

Rafael glanced over his shoulder as the apartment vanished within a roiling ball of flame, heard shouts of alarm from neighboring buildings, and saw thick coils of ugly black smoke spiraling upward from where once there had been a balcony.

A few of the IDF soldiers guarding the nearby cordon watched as the Valkyrie drone zoomed over their heads and disappeared. Rafael turned to survey the jumbled skyline of Jerusalem for a few moments before hurrying away down the street.

77

Ethan propelled Rachel in front of him as the sound of the exploding Hellfire missile silenced the sniper, and they dashed for the cover of the vehicles in the street outside.

"You sure they got him?" Ethan asked Lieutenant Ash as they ran.

Ethan looked up at the apartment building that was now billowing smoke as Lieutenant Ash spoke into his microphone. A man in traditional Bedouin clothes appeared on the street outside the apartment building and looked up at the billowing clouds of smoke.

"He's dead," Lieutenant Ash said to Ethan. "The UAV got him."

"A good sniper would change positions," Ethan pointed out, tucking his pistol into his belt.

"They saw him on camera before the missile hit," Ash insisted grimly. "They got him."

Ethan frowned and shook his head, one eye on the distant Bedouin.

"He fires his shots and then sits around to get blown to pieces?"

Ethan watched as the Bedouin turned toward a narrow alley. He glanced over his shoulder at the IDF

cordon before looking briskly away, a red scarf concealing his features and black gloves on his hands. Ethan
recalled the man in the tunnels beneath Gaza, wearing
black gloves when he had stolen Ethan's rucksack. For
a brief moment, a spectral image of Joanna drifted into
Ethan's field of view. He gasped softly, losing his balance
and trying to blink the hallucination away. She stood on
the sidewalk, watching him intently, superimposed over
the Bedouin man hurrying away from him and beckoning Ethan to follow.

"Get your men together," he said impulsively to
Lieutenant Ash as the bizarre vision faded away.

"What the hell for?"

"I doubt you've got the man you think you did,"
Ethan shouted over his shoulder as he broke into a
sprint, aiming for the Bedouin.

Ethan looked to where the man was vanishing into
the side alley. As he did so, Ethan saw him peer sideways
again in his direction from beneath the veil of his head-
dress, and in that moment he knew that the Bedouin
was the man MACE would have tasked with abducting
Joanna: Rafael, the assassin. Ethan shouted back at the
lieutenant.

"Get some backup and meet me on the other side of
the block!"

Ethan didn't give the officer a chance to reply, con-
centrating on the alley into which the Bedouin man had
disappeared. He plunged headlong into it, the shadows
enveloping him as he ran, his footfalls echoing off the
narrow walls. From somewhere in front of him he heard
a dog howl in alarm.

Ethan burst out into a square enclosed on all four
sides by featureless apartment buildings. A skeletally
thin dog stood on scrawny legs near a long-dry fountain,

having clearly just picked itself up off the dusty earth. Ethan felt the skin on the back of his neck tingling and staggered sideways as his balance failed him, his hands trembling freely now and his knees weak with fatigue.

Ethan guessed that the man he had seen would keep heading directly away from the scene of his crimes, so he hurried across the square to an alley that led off toward the east, running hard and splashing through puddles of dirty brown water.

An open area of wasteland appeared as he reached the end of the alley, while on his left was a main street filled with scattered pedestrians and cars parked outside cafés. To his right, a narrower street that seemed devoid of life led between tall apartment blocks.

Ethan headed down the narrow street, running hard as he found his stride again, looking left and right into dingy alleys passing between the blocks. At the third he glimpsed someone moving out of sight at the last moment and he plunged through the shadows in pursuit.

A bright rectangle of light at the end of the alley was blocked by a low, mangled chain-link fence. Ethan took three long running strides and leaped up, vaulting over the fence. As he arced through the air he glimpsed abandoned apartment buildings that overlooked another square in greater disrepair than the last.

The blow came from his right as he landed hard, a whisper of movement in the air, and in an instant Ethan realized that he had vaulted over the fence without regard to anyone waiting for him out of sight against the walls.

The Bedouin slammed into him, his face obscured by the red scarf above which dark eyes blazed with unrestrained fury. Ethan threw his hands up in desperation as a rusty length of scaffolding pole whipped toward his skull. The cold metal smashed into his forearm, a dull but terrible pain shuddering along the length of the bone. Ethan cried out, the ragged edge of the pole barely deflected from his face as he was driven backward.

The man lunged forward with the point of the pole and Ethan twisted aside, swinging a wild left hook that connected with the Arab's temple but barely checked his movement as he ducked aside and turned, swinging the pole up.

Ethan jerked left and raised his right arm, catching the pole under his armpit. He closed his arm around it and yanked his left knee up into the assassin's rib cage. The man grunted and Ethan felt brittle bones somewhere in the man's chest crunch against his kneecap. The Arab lost his grip on the pole as he fell sideways, and Ethan saw that the index finger of his left hand was missing.

Ethan grabbed the pole from under his arm and swung wildly for the man's head but the Arab was too fast, ducking low and leaping back up, a fist flashing into Ethan's vision and smacking across his cheek. Ethan reeled away, managing to hang on to the pole and his balance, but before he could regain his advantage the assassin slammed one foot into the inside of Ethan's left knee. The leg buckled with a lance of bright pain that bolted up his thigh as he crashed down onto the unforgiving concrete.

The assassin swiveled expertly on one foot, driving the other toward Ethan's chest. Ethan struggled to bring the pole up in both hands to deflect the blow, but the Arab's foot smashed into his chest and hurled him onto his back, chunks of gravel painfully driving through his shirt and into his skin. Somehow he managed to keep the pole defensively in his hands as the assassin whipped a slim, glittering blade from his waistband and plunged down toward him.

Ethan brought one leg up against his chest and pushed out with the pole, catching the Arab in free fall with the blade a hairbreadth from his throat. Dull pain throbbed through Ethan's skull as he struggled against the weight and insane strength of his assailant. He pushed hard on one end of the pole and thrust out with his leg, rolling the assassin off balance. The Arab toppled over and onto his back as Ethan rolled with him and forced his way on top, pinning the pole across the assassin's throat while trapping the man's arms beneath his knees. Ethan saw the Arab's thorax collapse beneath the weight, his dark eyes bulging and something rattling deep in his esophagus.

Ethan felt a sharp jab in his flank. He looked down to see the blade held with its tip nestling under his rib cage. Needles of ice prickled Ethan's skin as he realized that they were in a stalemate.

The assassin looked up at him without mercy as though he were examining a peculiar form of insect. Ethan shook his head. "It's over, Rafael."

The assassin gritted his teeth in a brutal smile, raising the blade as he rasped a few short words. "It is for you, my friend."

Ethan grunted with effort, twisting away from the blade as he felt the tip lance him with a stab of exquisite pain. He pressed down on the pole, crushing the Arab's throat further, and managed with one hand to retrieve a crumpled photograph from his pocket.

"Joanna Defoe," he gasped above the supreme effort of keeping the killer on the ground. "Disappeared from Gaza, thirty-one, a journalist."

Rafael smirked over his pain.

"Go to hell."

Ethan felt a surge of anger course through his veins. He jerked away from the blade and shoved down hard on the pole. An agonized rattle escaped from Rafael's mouth amid a spray of spittle. He looked up at Ethan through the pain.

"Release me, and I'll tell you."

"Not a chance."

"Your loss."

The assassin whipped the knife across Ethan's exposed flank, causing him to jerk farther away from the bright pain. Instantly, Rafael's right leg hooked up and curled around Ethan's neck, arching his back and slamming him down onto the rocky earth. Before Ethan could respond, the Arab was upon him, the knife pressing against his throat.

He squinted up into the bright blue sky above and saw Rafael looking down at him.

"I am not a dishonorable man," the Arab said softly, "but you should have let me leave. Without me, you and your friends would be dead."

"You stopped it?" Ethan asked.

"Who do you think tipped off the IDF and disposed of Byron Stone? MACE deceived all of us, and I was making amends. Now you have again forced my hand, Mr. Warner."

"Joanna," Ethan said, twisting the photograph of her in his left hand and holding it up to Rafael once more. "Please."

The assassin considered the picture for a moment.

"Joanna must have gotten too close to the truth long before I did, in Colombia and then again here in Gaza. She learned that MACE was abducting wealthy civilians and then negotiating their release with their own agents in order to reap the ransom payments. I learned this only today from a man named Spencer Malik, recently deceased."

Ethan stared up at him. "Where is she?"

"I don't know," Rafael muttered. "The only man left alive who will know now is an American, a pastor named Kelvin Patterson. But I do know that she was not killed."

For a brief moment in Ethan's awareness, time ground to a halt.

He stared up at the man who had so casually erased the pain that he had harbored for so many years. He felt something released from his chest, the dense and festering abscess suddenly lanced. He closed his eyes, not feeling the hot tears that rushed down his cheeks and spilled onto the ancient earth.

Rafael stared down at him, surprised.

"You have fought bravely," he said in a somber tone, "but now I must protect myself. And for that, you have to die."

Rafael leaned his weight into the blade.

And Ethan fired the pistol in his right hand.

The bullet slammed upward through Rafael's hip, shattering bone and plowing through his internal organs before bursting from his shoulder in a fine mist of blood. Ethan smashed the blade aside as Rafael shuddered from the blast, pushing him away and leaping to his feet as Rafael collapsed onto the dust.

Ethan looked down at the assassin as he lay on the ground, blood leaking from his wounds.

"Remember Hassim Khan?" he asked rhetorically, and saw a shadow of recognition flicker behind the pain in the assassin's eyes. "You're done, asshole."

Ethan aimed between Rafael's eyes and pulled the trigger once. The assassin's head quivered and the life in his eyes vanished as quickly as the bullet punctured his skull and buried itself in Gaza's baked soil.

A swarm of Israeli soldiers burst into the courtyard around Ethan.

"What happened?" Lieutenant Ash demanded, looking down at the corpse.

"I found your informant."

Lieutenant Ash shook his head, a disapproving look on his face. "Well done, he's useless to us now. What do we do?"

"We find Byron Stone."

"That could prove a problem," Lieutenant Ash said. "We just heard on the radio that the vehicle he was traveling in has been hit by an explosive device. Byron Stone is dead."

"What about the MACE jet? Can we ground it?"

"I don't know."

Ethan thought furiously for a moment, and then turned to the lieutenant.

"Can you get me to the airport, quickly?"

"Why should I?"

Ethan wiped his dirt-stained face with his sleeve, trying to stave off the exhaustion that was now tilting the earth beneath his feet as though he were standing on a boat on a rocky sea.

"Because it's the last chance I have to end all of this. They abducted my fiancée, Jerah, might even have killed her, and I don't want to see a single one of them get away with it."

Jerah Ash looked at Ethan's bedraggled form.

"I'll call it in. Come with me."

"I'll need to pick up some friends along the way," Ethan added.

78

BEN GURION INTERNATIONAL AIRPORT
ISRAEL

The late-afternoon sun flared off the hot asphalt as Lieutenant Jerah Ash guided the jeep to a manned barrier on the edge of the airport. In the rear of the jeep sat Aaron, Safiya, and Rachel, while Lucy Morgan sat next to Ethan, guzzling water from bottles and gorging on Israeli Army ration packs.

"You shouldn't be here," Ethan said to Lucy. "You need a hospital."

"Like hell," Lucy shot back between mouthfuls. "Do we know if they've taken off yet?"

Ethan shrugged as Lieutenant Ash signaled to the guards manning the barrier and drove through. As they reached the gates where rows of private aircraft were parked, Ethan could see several large jets with towering T-tails, shiny white fuselages, and chrome fittings.

Lieutenant Ash stopped and climbed out of the jeep to scan the airfield for one aircraft among dozens.

"There, that one," Ethan said, spying a distant sleek jet with a blue MACE logo emblazoned across the fuselage. "It's taxiing out right now."

Lieutenant Ash nodded, keying his microphone and speaking quickly. Ethan didn't wait to hear what he said, leaping instead into the driver's seat and gunning the engine as the MACE jet taxied to the edge of the runway.

"Hey!" Lieutenant Ash shouted.

Ethan barely heard him as he accelerated directly toward the runway, yanking the wheel to avoid clipping the tails from a line of parked training aircraft.

"Jesus, Ethan!" Aaron Luckov shouted. "Take it easy!"

Ethan ignored his friend as he forced the jeep into a hard turn around one plane, the tires screeching on the tarmac and the chassis shuddering. Ahead, the whine of the MACE jet's engines suddenly climbed to a deafening roar, the jumbled city horizon behind it blurring in clouds of heat.

"They're taking off without clearance!" Lucy shouted, hanging on desperately in the rear of the jeep.

The jet suddenly sprang forward as it released its brakes, accelerating down the runway.

Ethan turned the jeep, mounting the taxiway with a thump before surging onto the open grass alongside.

"That's a twenty-five-ton aircraft!" Rachel shouted as she realized what Ethan was about to do. "Are you suicidal?"

Ethan turned a pair of cold, gray eyes to her. "Almost."

Rachel sat back in silence. The jeep bounced violently as it left the grass verge and skidded onto the dark tarmac of the runway. Ethan struggled for control of the jeep as it swerved into the path of the oncoming jet, wrestling the wheel back into his grip and steering the jeep to the edge of the runway and leaping out.

The Gulfstream jet roared toward him, a cloud of

translucent brown haze billowing behind it as it accelerated. Ethan dashed to the center of the runway, the Sig
pistol in his hand as he took aim at the undercarriage
of the jet rushing toward him and filling the sky. Ethan
aimed carefully and fired three times, the sound of the
pistol drowned out by the roar of the jet's turbofan engines.

The second bullet punctured the left nosewheel tire,
the third piercing the right as the jet swerved violently.
As the Gulfstream thundered past in a crescendo of jet
blast, Ethan hurled himself to one side, rolling and looking back to see the plane's air brakes pop open and the
thrust-reverser buckets close over the engine exhausts.

"She's disabled!" Ethan shouted, as Lieutenant Ash
jogged breathlessly to the edge of the runway, joining soldiers in two other vehicles as they accelerated in pursuit
of the rapidly slowing jet.

Ethan leaped back into the jeep as the Gulfstream
taxied off the main runway and came to an ungainly
halt nearby. The three vehicles converged on the aircraft
even as the boarding steps unfolded and three men
scrambled out in a desperate attempt to flee.

"Freeze!" Lieutenant Ash bellowed, drawing his pistol and aiming it at the men. "Hands in the air!"

Ethan watched as the crew members came to a
standstill and were surrounded by a dozen armed troops.
Lieutenant Ash waved two of his men forward, and they
cuffed the crew before leading them away. Ethan looked
up the steps of the aircraft, and then at the lieutenant.
Without hesitation, the Israeli officer led the way into
the interior.

The jet had been heavily modified, with plush
leather couches and a minibar, but none of that interested Ethan as much as the large crate lashed down in

the center of the fuselage. Lieutenant Ash checked the consignment numbers on the side.

"Listed as medical supplies and equipment," he said. "The package is for a private residence in Washington DC."

He tore open a consignment note stuck to the side of the crate, and raised his eyebrows in surprise as he read the address.

"It's for a Kelvin Patterson."

"The man behind everything," Lucy Morgan hissed as she looked at the crate. "I'll bet a year's salary that the remains I found are in there."

Lieutenant Ash looked at one of his men. "Open it."

The soldier produced a digging tool from his webbing, lodged the hook under the lid of the crate, and pulled hard. The wooden lid splintered as the nails popped out, and Jerah Ash reached over and pushed the lid clear.

Ethan stared down into the crate to see a rectangular block of sandstone. Inside, illuminated by the interior lights of the aircraft, lay the skeletal remains entombed in rocks that had held its body for millennia.

"That's the one," Lucy Morgan said as she joined him beside the crate.

Lieutenant Ash stared at the remains, apparently caught between relief and alarm. "And this . . . thing. It's—"

"Some kind of ape," Ethan said, shutting the lid. "First things first, this isn't over yet. There's still Kelvin Patterson. He must be involved and he must have people waiting for this to arrive in DC. Let's fly this plane over there and see who turns up."

"Not a chance," Lieutenant Ash snapped. "You can't fly this plane anyway."

Aaron and Safiya Luckov, standing behind the officer, spoke together as though prompted.

"We can."

Lieutenant Ash looked over his shoulder at them in mild surprise, but shook his head vigorously as he turned back to Ethan.

"These remains belong here in Israel, and I've already risked enough bringing you here. This ends now."

"It won't if you don't let this aircraft travel back to the United States," Ethan said calmly. "If we repair the aircraft's tires and leave now, then you're in the clear. You found and protected Lucy Morgan and you ensured that I left the country, as ordered to by Shiloh Rok. You're the hero of the hour, Jerah. If you don't, there's going to be one hell of a diplomatic spat over these remains. We only have Sheviz's testimonial evidence against Patterson, but people have died in America as a result of these experiments and neither I nor the United States of America want to let that go unpunished. Do you?"

Lieutenant Ash stared at Ethan for a long moment, and then a bitter chuckle erupted from his throat. He shook his head and rubbed his temples wearily.

"If I do this, will you promise that I'll never, ever see you again?"

Ethan grinned.

"That, I can promise you."

Jerah Ash sighed, and turned to the troopers standing behind him.

"We wouldn't have time to offload that . . . thing anyway. Seal the crate and repair the damage to the aircraft's tires."

As the soldiers hurried to do their work, Lieutenant Ash turned back to Ethan.

"And what exactly are you going to do in Washington?"

Ethan wiped the exhaustion from his eyes with one trembling hand, and looked longingly at one of the Gulf-stream's plush leather couches. Suddenly, for the first time in years, he desperately wanted to go to sleep.

"I'll figure that out when I wake up."

Rachel looked at Ethan, but said nothing.

"Not like you to be at a loss for words," Ethan said.

Rachel smiled, shrugged. "I don't know what to say. You were right."

"I'm making the most of it—doesn't happen that often."

"I don't believe that for a moment," Lucy Morgan said from one side. "I owe you one."

"You owe me two," Ethan said, and gestured to the crate. "Why did these things leave one of their own behind, do you think?"

"Everything dies," Lucy said sadly.

"Unless what?" Ethan encouraged her. "There's a reason. Sheviz said it himself: he couldn't find as many remains as he felt sure were out there. Why would that be?"

"Sheviz said that he found similar remains in India and Iraq," Lucy replied, looking at him curiously. "Both are part of what was once Mesopotamia, the cradle of civilization and the origin of many claimed instances of extraterrestrial influence on mankind in ancient history."

"And Hans Karowitz told us about the change in climate at the end of the Younger Dryas, which affected sea levels," Ethan said. "That would alter certain conditions."

Lucy paced up and down in deep thought.

"He said something about experiments in Washington DC too, something to do with blood groups?"

Ethan nodded.

"They think that O-negative blood stems from these beings, as it has no apparent origin in human evolution and can't be cloned."

Lucy looked at the crate for a moment longer.

"Blood groups, DNA, climate," she murmured softly to herself. "Why would they try to—"

"Think about it," Ethan said with a brief smile. "There may be one in every ancient city."

Rachel gasped, her eyes flying wide.

"My God," she said. "They left it here on purpose. It's a Rosetta stone."

hat the hell's a Rosetta stone?" Lieutenant Ash asked, dumbfounded.

Lucy gestured to the remains.

"It's a stone tablet that recorded a decree issued in Memphis by King Ptolemy over two thousand years ago. The decree was in three texts: Egyptian demotic script, ancient Greek, and Egyptian hieroglyphics, and allowed archaeologists to decipher hieroglyphics for the first time. Don't you see? They must have left behind one of these skeletons at the site of every early civilization they encountered; that's why Sheviz found fragmentary remains in different countries."

Jerah Ash shrugged.

"Why bother?"

"Because it was the best way for them to leave us a message," Lucy gasped, turning a full circle on her feet and holding her hands to her head. "My God, I can't believe I didn't realize it before."

"You think that's what really happened?" Ethan asked.

"Of course," Lucy replied. "For years we've wondered, if they visited us in the past, why they hadn't left markers or evidence of their presence. We know the ancients expended enormous effort, materials, and even lives on building temples and pyramids when the time would have been better spent building fortifications instead, so whatever the reason it must have been important. So why would such visitors just leave our ancestors to build ambiguous megastructures, maintain oral traditions, or carve figurines that could be interpreted in any number of ways? But we've been looking at the problem the wrong way round, thinking in terms of our own technology, not theirs."

Rachel frowned.

"You think that the answer is in the burials?"

"Not the burials," Lucy said, "but the bones, the mitochondrial DNA. That's why the blood could be so important. O-negative blood could have had its origins in these beings. If so, the fact that it remains today means that it could be traced via people with O-negative blood using mitochondrial DNA that's been passed down the feminine line from seven thousand years ago."

Ethan thought for a moment.

"Could they actually do that? Leave a message in the remains?"

Lucy nodded enthusiastically.

"It would be like a message in a bottle," she said. "The bottles are living cells and the message is encoded in mitochondrial DNA. Viruses are designed to infect organisms on Earth and upload their DNA into the genomes of those organisms, so there is a well-understood pathway for getting information into DNA. Our own genomes have got huge amounts of this junk that has climbed on board from viruses over evolutionary history. Now there could be a message encoded in it, maybe in a string of nucleotide bases."

Ethan caught on to her train of thought.

"We wouldn't be able to decipher the message until we'd reached a certain technological standard."

"Exactly," Lucy agreed. "And the climate change since these beings were on our planet has hidden the evidence from view."

"How?" Rachel asked.

"Virtually all of the megastructures that appeared during the Bronze and Copper Ages can be considered as cargo cults," Lucy said, "but we can't see all of them anymore because so many of them are underwater."

"Underwater?" Rachel repeated.

Lucy nodded.

"All of the world's religions have their global flood myth, like Noah in the Bible. About a decade ago divers off the coast of Japan found an enormous city complete with its own pyramid. It's called the Yonaguni Formation, and is around eight to ten thousand years old. Sea levels were much lower after the Younger Dryas when these cities were first flourishing, and like today people built on rivers, floodplains, and coastal estuaries. When the planet warmed, the glaciers melted, and sea levels rose and swallowed entire cities in a matter of years, burying them forever. Many of mankind's earliest megastructures are to be found not on land but underwater."

"How sure can you be?" Ethan asked.

"Yonaguni isn't the only one," Lucy said. "There are others: Dwarka, off the coast of India, and Poompuhar, in the Bay of Bengal, a submerged city that may be Kumari Kandam, where local fishermen are often forced to dive to free their nets caught on underwater temples with columns, pyramidal pagodas, and buildings with doorways."

"So there may be other humanoid remains like the one you found, marking the locations of ancient settlements," Lieutenant Ash said, trying to keep up.

"Exactly," Lucy said. "It all fits, and even explains why in the ancient past it wasn't male gods who were worshipped but female deities, with men honoring the fertility of the female form. Perhaps they understood something of the importance of the way in which the visitors regarded fertility and hereditary mitochondrial DNA."

"Could the messages in the remains you found still survive?" Ethan asked.

"Probably," Lucy said. "I was careful not to contaminate the remains in any way. The bone marrow should contain preservable genetic material, provided Sheviz's goons haven't tampered with it. I should get to work on this immediately and find out what—"

"Not a chance," Rachel said, gripping her daughter's shoulders. "You're coming home first, and there's no way I'll take no for an answer. You need rest before you start playing around in the dirt again."

Lucy was about to protest when Ethan spoke.

"This has to go into the hands of the DIA," he said. "Part of the deal to get you out of Gaza."

Lucy sighed, but nodded reluctantly.

"I thought as much," she said, and then on sudden impulse stepped forward and wrapped her arms around him. "Like I said, I owe you."

Ethan returned the embrace, and as she released him, he pulled a small plastic jar from his pocket and handed it to her. Lucy saw the label and smiled. *Right metacarpal.*

"Like I said," Ethan corrected her. "You owe me two."

Rachel stepped up to Ethan as Lucy turned to leave, and kissed him on the cheek.

"I hope you find Joanna, wherever she is."

"Me too," Ethan said.

With that, Lieutenant Ash led Rachel and Lucy off the Gulfstream. Aaron and Safiya looked at Ethan expectantly.

"Let's go," he said.

80

NEW COVENANT CHURCH
WASHINGTON DC
AUGUST 26, 8 P.M.

Pastor Kelvin Patterson sat at his desk and listened to the call coming in on his secure line as his heart seemed to stop in his chest.

"*. . . there's nothing left. Dr. Sheviz apparently managed to escape the raid but was abducted by the Bedouin relatives of his victims and vanished into the deserts, so whatever he learned out there has disappeared with him. All MACE assets have been seized by Israel and what's left of Spencer Malik and Byron Stone is being collected in small bags in Jerusalem. Their jet is on its way here, however, with the remains on board.*"

Patterson tried to speak but found himself unable to form coherent words. He swallowed and cleared his throat.

"Is there any chance that the connection between MACE and the Evangelical Alliance has been made by the authorities?"

The voice on the other end of the line was grim.

"*Everyone is dead so nobody's talking now, but we can't take any chances.*"

Patterson sat in catatonic silence for a long beat before slamming a clenched fist down on his desk. The sound made the two MACE guards standing by the door of the office glance across at him. He forced himself to calm down.

"Then this is damage limitation. We must hold them off for as long as possible. Intercept the jet when it reaches Dulles and ensure that the remains on board are safely locked away before the FBI or anyone else can seize them. Destroy everyone and everything that may betray our involvement, is that clear?"

"That may involve people, not just material."

"Do what must be done, for the greater good."

Patterson put the phone down and looked at his two guards. "Gentlemen, Senator Isaiah Black will be attending his primary rally in the District this evening. I am going to request that he call in here beforehand. Please ensure that the church is secure, that all church employees are sent home, and all security staff are at their posts."

One of the guards frowned.

"We heard that Byron Stone is dead," he said uncertainly. "We're not sure who should be giving us our orders if—"

"Byron Stone is indeed dead," Patterson snapped. "Which means you do as I tell you. Unless you'd rather be unemployed?"

Both of the guards nodded curtly and left the office.

Patterson waited until they were gone before rubbing his face with his hands, struggling to maintain his composure. He walked across to the towering chrome crucifix, standing before the altar and falling slowly to his knees.

"Give me strength, Father, to do what must be done."

Slowly, he stood, and with one hand moved the bronze eagle on his desk. Moments later, and he was walking down a narrow passage concealed behind the walls of his office, descending in silence to where a door opened into a chamber where the sound of his footfalls sounded dead, as though soulless and without form.

He flicked a switch on the wall, and a single fluorescent tube illuminated an operating theater complete with heart-bypass machine, monitors, glass cabinets filled with vials and serums, and a single, T-shaped operating table.

He checked that everything was in order and ready for his guest before returning to his office. He picked up the phone and began to dial Senator Black's personal number.

81

ROOM 517, HART SENATE OFFICE BUILDING
CONSTITUTION AVENUE, WASHINGTON DC

"Please wait one moment, Detective."

Tyrell stood in a plush corridor and considered the opulence around him as a young aide hurried into one of the Senate offices. He'd already waited two hours, but then he was a mere mortal walking among the most powerful men on Earth.

The United States of America was built upon the policy of all Americans being equal. The American Dream was supposedly their future, yet too many were born into unimaginable squalor and hardship, their lives expiring from a cocktail of drink, drugs, and sickness, like his older brother. The American Nightmare. It didn't much matter whether you were black or white, Mexican or Latino; for the Phillies or the Knicks, a Fed or a Yankee. Life was gonna be short and would likely end much as it had begun: feeble, dependent, and flat broke.

"Detective, this way, please."

Glass doors at the entrance to the two-story duplex suite were flanked by dark-blue flags bearing the Texas

State emblem. Senator Isaiah Black extended a hand as Tyrell entered the suite, a bright smile painted across his perma-tan features. Tyrell relaxed a little as he looked into the senator's eyes and judged that smile to be genuine.

"My apologies for arriving unannounced, Senator."

"It's no problem," Black replied, gesturing to a chair. "But I'm due out in about ten minutes so this may have to be a little rushed."

"That's fine, sir," Tyrell said. "I'll be brief."

Tyrell reached into his jacket pocket and retrieved the images of the dead bodies from the Potomac projects, fanning them out across the senator's desk before he sat down. Black froze with hands flat on the desk and legs half-bent.

"Three young men whose postmortems suggest they were murdered, the killings made to look like a drug-related act of misadventure."

Black slowly sat down. "Do you know who they are?"

"All three have been identified. Two of them were petty criminals but the one in the middle was a respected scientist working in the District with no history of drug abuse. Do you know him?"

Senator Black shook his head, still looking at the gruesome images. Tyrell swept the photographs out of sight, eager to judge the senator's expressions as he continued.

"The victims all suffered an illegal medical procedure designed to alter their genetic structure by contaminating them with foreign DNA."

Senator Black's jaw dropped like a stone. "You're not serious."

"Yes, sir, I am."

"Why are you here?"

"We believe that the procedures were financed by

the American Evangelical Alliance, with the knowledge and consent of Pastor Kelvin Patterson, who believes the DNA to be that of angels known as Nephilim."

Black's face collapsed like a pile of granite slabs.

"Kelvin Patterson?" he repeated, his mouth moving slowly as though wrapping itself around the name. "That's not possible. The pastor is a man of God."

"Many have committed terrible crimes with God's name on their lips," Tyrell said. "That has been true for all of human history."

"What does this have to do with me?" Black asked.

"I am trying to connect the events in the District with those in Israel. We believe that there is a link and we think it may be this man." He handed the senator a picture of Dr. Damon Sheviz and decided to twist the screws a little. "I don't want to expose you to any negative media at such a sensitive time in your campaign by applying for a subpoena from the district attorney. I thought it best that we should be able to speak privately about this first. Do you know or recognize this man?"

Senator Black looked at the picture and shook his head.

"Never seen him before in my life."

"He's a surgeon of some repute. He was here in DC at the time the murders were committed, working for one of the Evangelical Alliance's churches, and has since traveled to Israel."

Senator Black nodded slowly. He looked at the picture again.

"You remember something?" Tyrell prompted.

The senator shook his head. "No, I've never seen this man before, but . . ."

"Anything, no matter how trivial, may be worthwhile knowing."

The senator looked out of his office window, trying to remember.

"Kelvin has spoken publicly of his support for Israel based on a biblical interpretation of history. I've tried to distance myself from his comments, and his association with other companies involved in such lobbying."

"Which companies?"

"MACE, a security and arms company, owned by a man named Byron Stone."

Tyrell frowned. "This MACE is involved with the alliance?"

"Yes, and they're one of the companies supporting my campaign," Black said.

"Why would an arms company ally themselves to an evangelical church?" Tyrell asked.

"MACE is owned by the church," Black explained. "They've invested large sums into advanced aerial drones and cryogenic battlefield trauma surgery to save lives that otherwise would be lost to . . ."

Tyrell didn't hear the rest. Four words rolled through his mind. *Cryogenic battlefield trauma surgery.*

82

What kind of surgery?" Tyrell asked. "How were they doing it?"

Isaiah Black seemed momentarily stumped.

"Something to do with a kind of advanced suspended animation, I think." Tyrell felt a shiver down his spine as the senator spoke. "They rapidly freeze people with severe injuries to prevent death and then thaw them out once surgery is complete. Quite remarkable, although I don't really understand the details of it all."

"I'm beginning to," Tyrell murmured thoughtfully. "Senator, the battlefield surgery could be a cover for these experiments."

Senator Black looked at him for a minute as his brain processed the allegation.

"That's ridiculous," he stammered.

"Ignoring the connection would be ridiculous, Senator, for more reasons than one."

"This could be detrimental to my campaign," Black uttered as he made the same connection, then rubbed a hand across his face. "I should disassociate with them. I should have done it years ago."

"That might be premature," Tyrell said. "It might

alert either Patterson or his accomplices to our investigation. We've already had one witness die under suspicious
circumstances."

"Suspicious?" the senator echoed in alarm.

"I would seriously suggest that you do not approach
Patterson in any capacity, Senator," Tyrell cautioned.

The senator sat for a moment, and then shook his
head.

"I can't let this get out to the American people," he
said finally. "It could upset the entire primary campaign
and throw the party into confusion. If we lose our way
now, we'll never get our momentum back before the elec-
tion."

Tyrell saw his chance slipping away.

"We could preempt any political fallout, Senator,
if we act now. Would you be willing to accompany me
to the district attorney's office? With you there I feel
certain that I can obtain a prosecution, which would
alleviate any pressure on your campaign, but alone I'm
not able to present a case."

Senator Black sat for a long moment and then
looked at a copy of the United States Constitution af-
fixed to the wall nearby.

"You're sure that your case is sound, that the DA
will be open to a prosecution? It's a hell of a chance for
me to take."

"I'm sure," Tyrell said. "All it needs is your support."

The senator took a breath and was about to speak
when the glass doors to the office burst open behind
Tyrell with a loud crack, and he whirled in his seat to see
four Capitol police officers rush into the office.

"Detective Tyrell, would you come with us, please?"

Tyrell struggled to his feet as the officers surrounded him. "What the hell's this?"

Before the police could answer him, Captain Louis Powell swept into the suite.

"This comes to an end, now," Powell growled.

Tyrell felt a plunging sense of dismay sink through him. "Lopez," he said softly.

Powell turned to Senator Black.

"My apologies, Senator, but your time has been wasted."

"I'm not wasting anybody's time!" Tyrell shot back at the captain.

Senator Black raised his hands.

"Gentlemen, please. What the hell is going on here?"

Captain Powell gestured to Tyrell.

"Detective Tyrell has been ordered off this case by the District commissioner herself. It's based on dubious evidence, unconvincing methods, and has been dismissed by every single authority involved, including the FBI."

Tyrell struggled to keep himself under control.

"People have died and the case has been closed despite the evidence, not because of it."

"The evidence you've acquired is inadmissible," Powell said before turning again to the senator. "With your permission, Senator."

Senator Black looked from Tyrell to Powell and back, and his survivalist political instinct took over.

"I'm sorry, Detective, but I can't help you."

Powell grabbed Tyrell's arm, pulling him out of the suite. Tyrell looked over his shoulder at the senator.

"Stay away from Patterson," he said as he was manhandled out of the suite.

Powell released him as the suite doors closed behind them.

"What the goddamn hell do you think you're doing here?" the captain demanded.

"It's something to do with a security company, MACE," Tyrell said quickly. "They and the Evangelical Alliance are planning something in Israel. Get in touch with Interpol and—"

"The hell I will," Powell said, cutting Tyrell off. "Your badge and your weapon."

Tyrell felt the bottom drop out of his world. "You're kidding me?"

Powell held out his hand.

"You looked at where we're standing, Tyrell? You thought about the fact that it might not be your ideas that are crazy but your way of following them? Hand them over or I'll have departmental charges made against you through Commissioner Devereux."

"You're making a mistake."

"Maybe," Powell said. "But you've already made yours by putting yourself where you shouldn't damned well be."

Tyrell was about to say something when his train of cognition slammed to a halt. *Putting yourself where you shouldn't damned well be.* An image of Daniel Neville's room at the hospital drifted through the field of his awareness and he gasped as a flood of revelations rushed through his mind.

"Damn, I've been an idiot," he said out loud.

"Smartest thing you've said all day," Powell snapped. "Badge and weapon."

Tyrell focused again on Powell and handed his service pistol over as an image of Claretta Neville flashed through his mind. *You gimme somethin' to have faith in.*

"There's no way I'm going to walk away from this. I know how the kid died. It ain't over till it's over, and the key to it all is Casey Jeffs."

Captain Powell rubbed his temples with his free hand.

"You want to keep chasing rainbows, Tyrell, then go ahead, but make damned sure neither I nor the commissioner hear a damned thing about it till you can prove something. As far as the department's concerned you're suspended until further notice."

Relieved of his weapon and badge, Tyrell strode past Powell toward the Senate building's elevators.

Senator Isaiah Black watched as Detective Tyrell was stripped of his badge and gun before he and the remaining police officers strode away to the elevators. He was thinking deeply about what he had heard when he felt his cell phone vibrating in his pocket. He lifted it out, and saw the name flashing on the screen. K. PATTERSON.

The senator took a breath, and answered the call.

"Kelvin."

"Senator," the pastor replied formally down the line. *"I hope that I'm not interrupting anything?"*

"No, Pastor, but I'm just on my way out to the rally. What can I do for you?"

The senator heard a sigh down the line before the pastor spoke.

"You were right, of course. I can't afford not to bridge our differences, especially not at such a critical time in your campaign. America needs you as much as I do, and we will be stronger unified. Perhaps you could stop by the church on your way through? I'd be delighted to join you at the rally, and proclaim our support for your campaign."

Senator Black struggled to control the broad grin that spread across his face as he glanced at his reflection in the suite's glass doors, an image of the White House appearing unbidden before him. Detective Tyrell's image materialized before the reflection, his warning echoing around the senator's brain. Two guards, that was all he'd need, and he could slip out of the Hart Senate Office Building's tunnel entrance and avoid the army of journalists camped outside the building.

"I'd be delighted, Pastor. I'll be there in half an hour."

83

FIRST DISTRICT STATION
M STREET SW, WASHINGTON DC

Lopez tossed her case files onto her desk like a spoiled child discarding an old toy and picked up her jacket and car keys. She couldn't bring herself to hate Captain Powell but she sure as hell hated herself. If she hadn't reported Tyrell, then none of this would have happened. By now he'd probably be having his ass whipped by Commissioner Devereux, and Lopez herself was headed home with her own tail between her legs.

From where the files had fallen, a picture of Damon Sheviz stared out at her in black and white, his eyes a mischievous cross between those of the enlightened and the fanatic. There was something about the image that made her feel uneasy, something primal.

Beside her Lucas Tyrell's phone rang suddenly, making her jump. She reached across and picked up the receiver.

"Yeah?"

"Hello," came a voice that Lopez guessed was probably from the Windy City. *"Is Detective Tyrell there?"*

"He's"—Lopez picked her words with care—"off

duty right now. Let me take your name and number and I'll get hold of Tyrell."

"Of course," the voice said, *"my name's Douglas Jarvis, Defense Intelligence Agency."*

"And what's it regarding?"

"It's regarding a report filed with the ICMP. I've been trying to reach Detective Tyrell but he's been away from his desk."

Lopez looked at the file in her hands and felt an almost supernatural tingle rippling down her spine.

"I posted information to the ICMP about a man found dead in the capital two days ago, a scientist by the name of—"

"Joseph Coogan?" asked the voice.

"How did you know that name?" Lopez asked in surprise.

"What's your connection to this?"

"Lucas Tyrell is my partner. We've been working on this case for the past forty-eight hours or so."

There was a pause on the line. *"What sort of case?"*

"Homicide that looked like an overdose but the pathology didn't figure."

"What was the discrepancy?"

"Too complicated to go into without the paperwork, but Coogan appeared to have died after some kind of unexplained medical procedure performed by a Damon Sheviz."

"Was that analysis obtained during autopsy, something to do with traces of excess hydrogen sulphide in the blood?"

Lopez stood bolt upright.

"It was, along with signs of hypothermia and altered blood groups."

The voice on the other end of the line became equally agitated.

"I think that we need to talk. I've been in touch with our embassy in Israel. It would appear that wherever Mr. Sheviz goes he leaves a trail of bodies behind him. We've also got some evidence of a company owned by the American Evangelical Alliance called MACE, purchasing and importing medical equipment into Israel that doesn't correspond with their stated research programs, things like heart-bypass machines."

Nicola Lopez could barely suppress the smile that broke out on her face as she grabbed a pen.

She quickly wrote down Jarvis's details and hung up. Before she had even a chance to think about what had just happened, Larry Pitt, one of the junior officers in her division charged with administration duties, walked up to her desk and tossed a file in front of her.

"History on Casey Jeffs that you asked for," he said casually. "Didn't have enough time to grab all the files for your PDA earlier. Interesting guy."

Lopez picked the file up as Pitt strolled away, opening it to find two pages of information, the first filled with what she already knew. As she read the second, however, her jaw fell slack and a sudden premonition of doom swamped her like a heavy blanket.

Lopez reached into her pocket for her cell phone, quick-dialing Kaczynski's number, but the engaged tone cut her off. She rang off and tried Tyrell instead. Another recorded message droned in her ear.

Lopez leaped out of her chair and ran through the office until she caught up with Pitt.

"Larry, you seen Kaczynski?"

"He left about an hour ago," Pitt said, jabbing a thumb over his shoulder.

"Shit."

Lopez knew that she had to get to Tyrell before he did something he would regret.

"Get on a terminal. I need Casey Jeff's home address!"

84

ANACOSTIA, WASHINGTON DC

Casey Jeffs shook Tyrell's hand and regarded him with a serene expression as they sat down opposite each other in the living room of Casey's small apartment.

"What can I do f'ya, Detective?"

The apartment was devoid of excess furniture or trinkets. A simple crucifix dominated one wall of the lounge, and there was no television or music system in the room.

"You've a nice place here, Casey," Tyrell said, looking around. "Been here long?"

"Sixteen years," Casey replied, "ever since I've worked at the hospital."

Tyrell retrieved a photograph from his pocket. "Do you recognize this man?"

Casey looked down at the black-and-white image.

"No."

"His name is Damon Sheviz, and we believe he is responsible for a number of murders in Washington DC and in Israel."

The Texan shifted as though he were being prodded with hot needles.

"What's this got to do with me?"

"We think that there may be a connection between this man and Pastor Kelvin Patterson."

"The pastor?" Casey asked, frowning.

Tyrell looked at the man's expression and judged his apparent confusion to be genuine. He would need a different tack, and with Casey Jeffs he reckoned that brazenly revealing his knowledge might tease out a confession more quickly than more surreptitious means.

"How come you work at the hospital, instead of for your brother, Casey?"

"He runs a big corporation," Casey said proudly. "Byron's in Israel signing a big deal right now."

"Is he now?" Tyrell replied, lifting one eyebrow.

Casey's expression quivered as though he had woken from a brief nap. "How did you know about my brother?"

"I know a lot of things, Casey," Tyrell murmured. "Byron keeps you a secret. Have you ever wondered why?"

Casey's expression remained stoic, as though he were unable or unwilling to consider the complexities the question provoked.

"I ain't given it much thought," he replied awkwardly.

In truth, Tyrell hadn't been sure of the family connection and maybe Casey wasn't aware of the truth himself, but it explained everything. Bradley Stone had been a whiskey-drinking, cigar-smoking philanderer with a taste for younger women, and he was both willing and able to pay any amount for the company he sought. Casey was the orphaned son of a Texas hooker who had overdosed under suspicious circumstances, and his whole life had somehow been financed by persons unknown. Tyrell had suspected that Bradley and now Byron Stone were behind Casey's covert financial security, probably to avoid scandal or more likely a lawsuit. Moreover, Casey had been on the stand for killing his own mother, but the case had collapsed due to witness testimony and the defense arguing that Casey was mentally incapable of both premeditated homicide and the deluding of detectives investigating the scene. That, of course, did not mean that the young Casey had done either the planning or the deluding. Nor did it mean that his mother had overdosed.

"How often does Byron fly to Israel on business?" Tyrell asked.

"Maybe twice a month."

"And he flies with scheduled airlines?" Tyrell baited him.

"No. He has a private company jet."

Tyrell nodded and smiled an ingratiating little smile. The gesture had the desired effect as Casey squirmed.

"We believe that the AEA is actively involved in illegal medical experiments, which have resulted in the deaths of at least three American citizens."

Casey blinked, taking a few moments to absorb the information.

"Experiments?"

"Medical experiments on live people, only one of whom survived."

"There was a survivor?"

"You know about that, Casey?"

Casey's expression quivered.

"I think it'd be better if we had this conversation with a lawyer present."

Tyrell sat back on the sofa, casually placing one hand in his jacket pocket to rest on a can of pepper spray nestled within.

"Can you tell me your whereabouts this afternoon?"

"I've been at work all day."

"And you had a particularly busy day, didn't you, Casey?" Tyrell saw the Texan's larynx rise and fall silently in his throat. "You were in the hospital kitchens."

Casey's blue eyes flared brightly in surprise. Tyrell didn't give him the chance to speak.

"We have your DNA, Casey," he lied. "We know how you did it."

Casey Jeffs shook his head. "No, you don't, else you'd have arrested me already."

"So you admit that you were involved?"

"I din' say that. I din' go nowhere near the boy."

"I didn't say that you went anywhere near him."

"The boy was found with the pills; they were there in his room!"

"Seemed like the perfect crime, didn't it?" Tyrell continued. "A mentally impaired boy enduring great suffering commits suicide by overdose in a locked and drug-free room. We find the pills and bottle on the floor, but nobody else went near the room and nobody saw him except his mother, who's arrested for being the only person who could have given the drugs to him. Neat, Casey."

Casey Jeffs stared at Tyrell with an impassive gaze that the detective recognized as the visage of the guilty, struggling to conceal emotions behind a facade of indifference.

"I had nothin' to do with that boy's murder."

"*Murder,* Casey?" Tyrell echoed. "So you're saying that it was murder now?"

Casey slammed a clenched fist down on the table between them.

"I didn't kill the boy! He overdosed, locked in his room!"

"Didn't you kill before, Casey?" Tyrell asked.

"I din' kill no one!"

"The pill bottle on the floor, that was the key," Tyrell went on. "He couldn't have gotten them into his room—past all that security and all those checks and a police officer—in clothes that had no pockets. He could barely walk at all. Had to be his mother, didn't it?"

"Suppose," Casey muttered.

Tyrell watched Casey's blue eyes transfixed on his own, unable to tear himself away from his own terminal demise.

"Actually, Casey, I don't think there were any pills in that room at all."

85

I don't know what you're sayin'," Casey rasped.

Tyrell leaned back on the couch.

"Daniel Neville, a survivor of Kelvin Patterson's experiments, was a liability. Easy enough to slip a lethal dose of his own medicine into his food and let it leak toxins into his bloodstream. Especially easy if you happen to be on your lunch break in the kitchen at about the same time as Daniel's food was being prepared, which you were, Casey. While asleep, he suffers a cardiac arrest and dies."

"The pills he took were in the room with him!"

Tyrell smiled.

"No, they weren't. You made sure that Daniel Neville was in his room for almost an hour before you walked past, plenty of time for the drugs in his food to have killed him. You punched through the window to open the latch on the inside of his door, even though a few seconds more would have been enough time for the nurse to have arrived with the key. But you had to, Casey, because punching through that window was the only way to scatter that bottle of pills into the room, to make a homicide look like a suicide."

Casey blurted out a laugh.

"His mother's already been arrested and charged for the murder."

"Daniel's mother was released from custody the moment I got back to the station. I just had her arrested because that's what you were hoping for, ain't that right?" Casey swallowed thickly as Tyrell spoke. "You're on the same anxiety medication that Daniel was, aren't you? I'm guessin' that you figure there'll be no way for us to prove your guilt as you picked up the bottle of pills in the room, which nullifies the fact that your prints are on it."

"I sure did," Casey smirked. "Ain't got nothin' there."

"Sure I do. Daniel Neville was taking his medication at a daily twenty-five-milligram dose, but he died of an overdose of two-hundred-milligram pills," Tyrell said smoothly. "You had to use them of course, because it's surprisingly hard to kill someone using those kinds of medications. Thing is, Casey, you forgot that the different pills are different colors."

Casey stared at Tyrell for a moment and licked his lips.

"Ain't nothin' that I'd know about. I'm just a cleaner."

Tyrell hefted himself off the sofa and looked down at Casey.

"You were on the stand for a locked-room homicide twenty years ago, your own mother's suspicious overdose, but that time the prosecution didn't see through it. Who put you up to it, Casey? Kelvin Patterson? Your brother?"

Casey bolted upright to his feet, towering over Tyrell.

"They got nothin' to do with this!"

"They used you, Casey," Tyrell said, standing his ground. "They've always used you."

"You're settin' me up!" Casey wailed. "They tol' me you would."

"They made you kill your own mother. Are they the kind of people you trust, Casey?"

"Shut up, they ain't usin' me!"

"I can help you, Casey," Tyrell offered, fingering the can of pepper spray in his pocket. "But I can't do anything unless you're straight with me."

Casey's eyes danced crazily as though looking for an escape. His huge hands gripped each other in desperation.

"They ain't been usin' me," Casey uttered, halfway between a threat and a plea. His blue eyes welled with trembling tears. "The pastor's my pa."

"No, Casey, Bradley Stone was your pa. Kelvin Patterson's a man who has arranged murders, and you're the man he's put in the dock for committing them."

Casey shook his head, his voice strained with grief. "He's all I've got."

Tyrell belatedly realized the depth of Casey's attachment to Kelvin Patterson.

"The police are searching for a murderer but I believe that you've been manipulated by Patterson. If you just tell me what—"

"The police ain't interested in me!" Casey snapped with sudden vigor.

"They sure are, and there's—"

"You've been suspended from duty, Mr. Tyrell."

Tyrell blinked, feeling suddenly dizzy. "How the hell would you know that?"

Casey's mouth twisted into an angry grimace. "Ain't none o' your business."

Shit. A dawning realization began creeping upon Tyrell like a dark and ominous wave as it rushed toward shore, and he knew it was going to swallow him whole. Someone on the force? Cain? Lopez?

"I think that you're hiding something and you should tell me what it is," he uttered. "You need to cooperate with us, Casey."

"There ain't no *us*!" Casey shouted, jabbing a thick finger in Tyrell's face. "I ain't goin' to jail. You're here on your own an' there ain't nobody left to help you now, you black motherfu—"

Tyrell whipped the can of pepper spray from his pocket and shoved it into Casey's face, squeezing the button hard. A thick hiss of vapor blasted the Texan and he staggered backward with a cry of panic, clawing at his face.

Tyrell stepped in, lifting one foot and smashing it sideways into Casey's knee joint. Blinded and off balance, the Texan crashed onto the thickly carpeted floor with a strained rush of expletives as Tyrell turned to get away.

Casey's thick hand latched onto Tyrell's arm like a vice, the Texan swearing and shouting as he swung a wild punch. Tyrell ducked the blow before dropping deftly and driving the point of one knee down hard into Casey's plexus. The Texan's swearing gave way to a sharp, strangled intake of breath as his nervous system convulsed under the blow, but his thick arms and chunky hands kept their maniacal grip. Tyrell jerked himself backward onto his heels.

Suddenly, he felt his balance waver, stars and points of light flashing in front of his eyes. *Shit, not now.* He dropped down onto one knee again as his balance failed him.

The blow came from nowhere. Casey's grip relented for an instant before the shape of a fist flashed in front of Tyrell's eyes and smashed into his face, crunching through the cartilage of his nose. The world tilted wildly as he reeled sideways, tripping over a thick rug and slamming hard onto the carpet.

The Texan crawled onto his knees, wiping his eyes with his sleeve as his chest surged with chronic wheezes. To Tyrell's dismay, despite the liberal dosage he'd unleashed into Casey's face, he appeared to be recovering swiftly. In contrast, Tyrell could barely breathe, sucking air down in desperate, rattling gasps past his ruined septum.

Casey lunged toward him and Tyrell emptied the can into his face from point-blank range. Casey managed to shield his eyes, but the stinging haze forced him away.

Tyrell turned and crawled on his hands and knees, stars flashing before his eyes in a nauseating whorl of colors. Behind him he heard Casey scramble in pursuit, and looked over his shoulder to see the once wide blue eyes now puffy and contracted into slits. Tyrell lurched on rubbery legs the final couple of steps to the front door, reached out, and grasped for the handle as he sank to his knees.

The door swung open, the handle yanked from Tyrell's grasp as a tall figure loomed in the doorway before him. Tyrell looked up through his bleary eyes and a flush of relief flooded through his body as Captain Louis Powell stared down at him.

He watched as Powell took in the scene and dropped onto one knee, his gloved hands grasping the dull metal of a service pistol that glinted in the light. Casey Jeffs stared through puffy eyes into the gaping maw of the weapon, and then two deafening gunshots crashed out. Casey quivered as two bloody red splatters smeared his chest, and then he toppled over and slumped against the wall as thick blood oozed from his fractured heart to drench his shirt.

Tyrell, slumped on his knees against the wall in the corridor, looked up at Powell.

"Jesus, am I glad to see you," he managed to rasp.

In one fluid motion that seemed to take an age, Tyrell watched as Powell stood and swung one heavy boot deep into his belly like a freight train through a balloon. Tyrell felt the remainder of the air in his lungs expelled in a great rush that surged through him, his vision melting into a milieu of swirling colors.

Tyrell collapsed onto his side with his back against the wall, his mouth wide open in a silent scream, eyes bulging and skin sheened with a cold, clammy sweat. He tried to speak but no sound came forth. The pulsing agony in his chest reached a new and excruciating plateau that forced a strangled cry of anguish from somewhere deep in his throat.

Captain Powell squatted down alongside him, his face taut with regret.

"You should've left this one alone, Lucas. I gave you every chance that I could," he said softly. "Another twenty-four hours and this would all have disappeared, but you just couldn't leave it alone."

Tyrell tried to speak, but no sound issued forth from his tortured lungs.

Powell shook his head slowly.

"You and Lopez have turned yourselves into liabilities and there's nothing more I can do for you. Believe me, if there was any other way I would take it, but I'm sure as hell not giving up my share of Patterson's fortune or going to jail for either of you."

Powell reached down and shoved his gloved hand across Tyrell's bloodied face, leaning his weight behind it.

Tyrell gagged for air and struggled ineffectually against Powell's grip until the last remaining strength seemed to vanish from his body. His lungs burned and tears filled his eyes, a melancholy as vast as the universe weighing him down as he felt Powell force the still-smoking pistol into his helpless hand. In dismay Tyrell recognized the weapon as his own, taken from him barely an hour before by the captain himself.

Tyrell, entrapped in a throbbing crucible of agony, felt a sudden release from the pain.

And then the blackness finally enveloped him as Powell stood and vanished into the night.

86

FIRST DISTRICT STATION
M STREET SW, WASHINGTON DC

Istill can't reach him."

Lopez put her cell phone back in her pocket and looked at Larry Pitt, who pointed at the screen of his computer terminal.

"Here you go, Casey Jeffs is listed at 1216 Juventus Place, on the corner of K Street and Potomac Avenue, near the docks."

Lopez turned abruptly away from the terminal and walked out of the office. She was surprised to see Kaczynski hurrying toward her, his features strained.

"I just tried to call you," she said, and then caught the look on his face. "What is it?"

"I was speaking to Emergency Services."

"Don't tell me they've been called down to K Street."

Kaczynski looked at Lopez as though she'd grown horns. "How the hell did you know that?"

"Is Tyrell okay?"

Kaczynski snapped out of it. "I don't know. I'm on my way down there."

She didn't wait for Kaczynski to offer her a ride, dashing past him toward the exit.

K STREET SE, WASHINGTON DC

The sight of the squad cars amid a blaze of hazard lights beside apartment blocks on the corner of K Street and Potomac Avenue sent a shiver down Lopez's spine. She sat in silence as Kaczynski pulled the car in alongside one of the beat cops guarding the scene. He flashed a badge through his open window at the cop.

Lopez was out of the car before it had stopped moving, hitting her stride fluidly as she crossed to where an ambulance sat idle, paramedics standing in silence around the vehicle. *Jesus, no. Please, no.*

"Where is he?" she asked one of the paramedics.

The man gestured to the open front door of the ground-floor apartment opposite them. Lopez felt a flush of hot tears scald her cheeks as she saw Lucas Tyrell lying slumped against a wall, his eyes staring vacantly out of the open door. One arm was pinned uselessly behind him, the other resting on the carpet as though caressing it, a pistol in his grasp. Farther down the hall Casey Jeffs lay in the corridor, his features a lifeless mask. The lights gently flickering against the Anacostia River nearby made the scene seem almost serene.

Bailey, Tyrell's dog, must have gotten out of the car. The little dachshund lay curled up against his master's lifeless body.

"Christ's sake," Lopez uttered, turning away.

Kaczynski spoke so softly that he was barely audible.

"Paramedics say he suffered a heart attack. His car's parked around the corner. Looks like he shot Casey in self-defense but was too far gone to call for help . . ."

Lopez saw Kaczynski hold up a sealed plastic bag in which lay Tyrell's cell phone, switched on but unused. She could see alerts to her missed calls on the screen. Lopez looked away, trying to blink back her tears but in the end swiping them angrily away with her sleeve.

"He was checked in to see a specialist tomorrow morning," she said. "Took me three years to get the fat asshole to book an appointment."

Lopez felt as though the world had weighed in upon her shoulders. Her legs quivered and she slumped down onto the dusty sidewalk.

Kaczynski squatted down beside her and placed a hand around her shoulder.

"There's nothing more you could have done, Lopez. It was his choice not to seek medical attention. We all knew that."

Lopez thumped her thigh with a clenched fist. "Stupid asshole."

Kaczynski managed a feeble smile. "An epitaph he would have agreed with entirely."

Kaczynski stood, calling out to the paramedics.

"Okay, let's get him out of here."

Lopez looked out at the twinkling sea of lights rippling on the surface of the Anacostia. A tiny, muted thought infiltrated the veil of her grief. She got up.

"Wait."

"What?" Kaczynski asked.

Lopez turned to the medics as they approached with the gurney.

"Any of you guys touched him?"

The senior medic shook his head. "He's been gone for a while, ma'am," he said respectfully. "CPR or defib wouldn't have saved him."

"I want him checked over," Lopez said to Kaczynski.

"His number was up, Lopez. There isn't anything to find here."

"Then there's no harm in having him checked out," she pointed out. "I want ballistics out here too. How soon can we get a forensic team?"

"Right away"—Kaczynski shrugged—"but why would you think he'd need that?"

"Lucas just wasn't the type to shoot," she said softly. "I don't think he drew his weapon in thirty years of service. He was proud of that."

"You don't think he got whacked?"

"I'd put my salary on it," Lopez said. "Only other witness that we had committed suicide five hours ago in a secure and guarded room. That's two deaths in one day connected to Lucas's work on this case."

"Why?" Kaczynski asked, looking at Casey Jeffs's body. "What the hell's this guy got to do with the case?"

Lopez's features hardened.

"Casey Jeffs was born as Casey Stone, the brother of Byron and the son of Bradley Stone, founder of a security company called MACE that's run out of Maryland."

"How the hell would you know that?" Kaczynksi asked.

"Blood," Lopez said quickly. "Casey had a history of mental disorders. His blood was taken regularly during his treatment, and matches that of his father, Bradley Stone."

"Why? How would this guy's history link him in with all of this?"

"Tyrell had found links between MACE and the American Evangelical Alliance's activities in Washington and Israel. That's what he was questioning Senator Black about when the Capitol police busted him. Casey Stone had a history of violence and psychosis and was employed by the Evangelical Alliance at the hospital."

Kaczynski stared at her silently for a long beat.

"That's a weak link, Lopez. You're starting to sound too much like Tyrell did."

"Maybe that's not such a bad thing," Lopez said tartly. "We need to find out if Tyrell fired the gun that's in his hand."

"Ballistics could take days or even weeks to confirm."

Lopez said nothing. Kaczynski stood for a moment longer and then glanced at Tyrell's corpse. He exhaled softly.

"Guess we owe him this much."

Lopez produced her notebook and tore off a page.

"This is the name of a guy who works for the DIA who I spoke to a half hour ago. He's linked several homicides in Israel to ours in Washington with medical evidence from the autopsies. Tyrell was right. You need to speak to this guy as soon as you can and he'll confirm what I'm telling you."

Kaczynski took the number. "What the hell am I supposed to do then?"

Lopez kept her tone neutral, controlling her grief and setting herself a course upon which she could rely, one based on evidence.

"According to the DIA, this whole thing has something to do with fossils being shipped from Israel to DC tonight."

"Fossils?" Kaczynski repeated in confusion.

"My first suggestion would be to go to the Interpol Bureau in the District and request a Red Notice for the extradition of one Damon Sheviz. The district attorney should back the move if it comes from the FBI, and it'll let us intercept the MACE jet that's on its way right now from Israel and find out what the hell's on it. If it does connect Kelvin Patterson to events in Israel, then we have a real reason to apprehend him."

"The Bureau can broadcast an international all points bulletin to law enforcement agencies in nearly two hundred countries and the Interpol general secretariat in Lyon, France," Kaczynski agreed, "but we'll need a national security letter as well, and only the agent in charge of the Bureau field office can issue one. Boarding that jet without it is a crime, and there's no way Axel Cain's going to go for it."

Lopez nodded, well aware that to search private premises, documents, and bank accounts would need the contentious letter, designed specifically to override the need for judicial overview and accountability.

"Homicide is a crime too, Terry. Offer whatever you can to Axel Cain to get it."

"What about Powell? He'll have to clear this."

Lopez, gambling that Kaczynski was just too damned straight to have climbed up Powell's ass, took a chance.

"The only link between the events here in DC and what's happened in Israel is Powell himself."

Kaczynski thought for a moment, looked at Tyrell's corpse, and then began shaking his head.

"No way, Lopez. Don't even go there. It's so insane even Tyrell would have walked away from it."

"Would he?"

"Don't be an ass, Lopez," Kaczynski pleaded. "Let's talk about it in the morning. You're not thinking straight after what's happened, and—"

Lopez turned and strode to the car, retrieving the file that Larry Pitt had handed her at the office. She stormed back across to Kaczynski, opening the file to the second page.

"Homicide trial, San Antonio, Texas, back in 1984. Perp's name was Casey Jeffs, who we now know as Casey Stone."

"So he's a convicted felon too?" Kaczynski asked.

"No. Casey Jeffs was on the stand for the suspected homicide of a prostitute who'd apparently overdosed and who, it turned out, was Casey's mother. Prosecution reckoned he'd planned her murder to look like a suicide, while the defense held that he wasn't smart enough to premeditate the crime. But the defense was gettin' screwed because on the witness stand Casey just couldn't handle the stress and kept slipping up during questioning. He was looking at twenty to life when next thing you know, he's off after a late witness testimony gives him a cast-iron alibi. Now, look at the investigating officers listed here, and the officer who supposedly found the witness."

Kaczynski looked at the list of officers at the bottom of the page, and stopped at one.

"Sergeant Louis Powell," he whispered as he read the name.

"Ring any bells?" Lopez asked. "A body found by Casey Jeffs, a locked-room homicide, an overdose? Tyrell must have worked this all out after he was suspended. Casey Jeffs is the bastard son of Bradley Stone. Bradley must have been paying Casey's hooker mom off for years to keep her silent and avoid a scandal, and MACE has paid for Casey's hospitalization and treatment both then and ever since. Somewhere along the line the hooker gets too greedy, someone decides that enough is enough and has her iced. What if Tyrell worked it all out, but it's not Casey who's planned this and he's just the fall guy?"

"Patterson," Kaczynski guessed, "or Byron Stone. And you linked Casey to his dead mother through the blood taken at the scene of the homicide?"

"Exactly, and to his father, through genetic profiling that wasn't available when this homicide case went to trial. Powell must have been in Byron Stone's pocket for decades, ever since this case put a black mark on his career. It's no wonder nobody's picked up on these suspicious overdoses in the District before now if Powell's been sweeping them under the carpet. He's covering for either MACE or the Evangelical Alliance, maybe even both. You know he's retiring soon, got himself that nice condo down in Florida? Think it's worth finding out how he paid for it?"

Kaczynski stared at her with an expression of bewilderment.

"Christ," he finally muttered. "If I get the national security letter we could tap some bank accounts, see what they've been up to, but what about jurisdiction? This case was signed off by the commissioner herself. I go strolling down to Dulles without any paperwork I'll get my cojones chewed off."

Lopez nodded.

"I'm officially off duty, Powell's orders. Just get the letters. I'll head down to the airport and see if I can find the jet we're looking for before Axel Cain hears about what's happened here and screws the whole goddamn thing up."

Kaczynski nodded and hurried away, leaving Lopez to stand over Lucas Tyrell's body.

"It ain't over till it's over," she said softly.

87

NEW COVENANT CHURCH
WASHINGTON DC

Kelvin Patterson walked around his desk as Senator Isaiah Black swept into his office with two staff on either side of him, extending his hand and smiling brightly.

"Senator, thank you for coming by at such short notice."

Black's jaw creased into a smile.

"My pleasure, Pastor, but we must be swift. The rally begins in an hour and I can't afford to be late."

Patterson nodded.

"I understand. Please," he said, gesturing to one of the chairs behind the desk, "take a seat."

The senator sat down, his two guards flanking him. Patterson took his place behind his desk, folding his hands together for a moment, looking at his own two security guards as they appeared in the office doorway before speaking.

"The polls are with you, Isaiah. The people are following you, with or without the support of the alliance. I realize that now."

"Faith is no match for good policy when the people need a leader," Black said simply. "That is the true power of our Constitution."

Patterson gritted his teeth as he smiled.

"Indeed, and we must make every effort to sustain our campaign to ensure that the wishes of the moral majority are carried through by Congress and the Senate."

Black took a deep breath.

"What's your point, Kelvin?"

"That perhaps we can find a compromise between the practicality of leadership and the enlightenment of spiritual guidance that I can bring to your administration."

"It's not my administration, Pastor."

"Not yet, but soon it will be."

Black shook his head.

"You still don't understand, do you, Kelvin? You expect your influence to penetrate the halls of Congress and the Senate, in direct opposition to the very voters who have considered your support for my campaign and rejected it. Democracy is the will of the people, and they do not want your theocratic agenda influencing our administration."

Patterson struggled to control his frustration. "The people know not what they do," he insisted. "What would you say if I told you that I could make you more powerful than you can imagine."

"There's no role more powerful than the president of the United States."

"There is one," Patterson said. "You could join the Lord's sons, if you wanted."

Senator Black sighed, and slowly stood.

"This may surprise you, Pastor, but even if what you're saying was true or even possible, I'd still say no. You want to know why?" Patterson raised an eyebrow.

"Someone like you should never be allowed to wield power because no matter how well meaning your motives, you'd still be a dictator."

Senator Black turned away and strode for the door. Patterson nodded once to the guards. Instantly, they shuffled closer together, barring the senator's path. Black paused in front of them with his two security guards, and then laughed out loud and turned back to the pastor.

"What are you going to do, Kelvin? Keep us here? Half of the country is expecting to see me on television within the hour. Don't you think they might come searching for me?"

Patterson stood from behind his desk, walking slowly around it and approaching the senator until they stood barely a meter apart, their respective security teams glowering at each other.

"Yes, Isaiah, I do. In fact, I'm counting on it."

Black's eyes narrowed. "What the hell are you talking about?"

Patterson nodded to his men. Instantly, they produced pistols, standing clear of the door and aiming at the senator's guards. Black's jaw dropped open, and he turned to look at Patterson.

"Tell your men to stand down. Let's keep this simple and without bloodshed," said Patterson.

"You're insane," Black uttered in disbelief.

"The weapons," Patterson insisted quietly.

Black looked at his men, and nodded once. Reluctantly, the two guards slowly lay down their pistols on the carpet. Patterson gestured to his men, and they grabbed the senator's arms, pinning him between them. Even before he could shout out, one of them held a hand over his mouth as the other drove his knee into the back of the senator's legs, forcing him to his knees.

Patterson watched as the senator was bound and gagged, and then smiled as he looked down into his eyes.

"Believe me, Isaiah, you will thank me for this before the night is over."

For the first time since entering the room, Senator Black's eyes betrayed the presence of fear, and Patterson felt an inexplicable rush of adrenaline surge through his veins.

"Bind and gag his men," he said briskly to the guards. "And take the senator to the chamber."

DULLES INTERNATIONAL AIRPORT
WASHINGTON DC

Lopez drove into the airport's industrial park, her path smoothed by calls from Larry Pitt at the First District Office to the airport's administration facility. She could see the blinking lights of an aircraft taking off into the night sky, the airstrip marked by a seemingly endless line of glowing orange lights. The sound of jet engines on the hot night air reverberated through the chassis of her car as she cruised between valleys of steel shipping containers and pulled in near the edge of a large servicing pan, extinguishing her lights.

The servicing area was separate from the main terminals fielding domestic and international flights. Industrial units and hangars surrounding her were mostly darkened, long since closed for business. Lopez climbed out of the car, looking at a curved row of blue lights in the tarmac marking the boundaries of a taxiway. The jet would come in from there, and she would be in place to intercept it.

She placed a hand on her service pistol beneath her jacket.

"That's far enough." Lopez froze as the voice spoke to her from the darkness. "Show me the piece, slowly."

Lopez obeyed, slowly drawing her weapon and holding it between thumb and forefinger as she turned around. Captain Louis Powell loomed from between two shipping containers, his pistol pointed at her. Lopez felt a sickening apprehension compress her stomach. The captain stared at her for a moment and then lowered his weapon.

"Lopez? What the hell are you doing here?"

Lopez swallowed. "Following some leads."

Powell holstered his weapon and moved across to her. Lopez realized that she'd never before noticed how powerfully built he was.

"What part of being off duty are you failing to understand?" Powell asked.

"If the case is closed, then what the hell are you doing here?"

Lopez saw the captain's larynx rise and fall as he swallowed, and above his voice the sound of two turbofan jet engines whined as a jet taxied toward them.

"You did the right thing telling me about Tyrell and the senator, but now's not the time to get all smart-ass. Are the FBI on their way?"

Lopez knew that it wouldn't take Axel Cain long to find out from Larry Pitt where she was, and when he did he'd bring half of the Bureau's manpower down here with him.

"Axel Cain's leading a boarding team," she lied. "Just waiting on the paperwork. He's been in contact with you about this?"

Powell nodded slowly, still not looking at her. Alarm bells rang like claxons in Lopez's head, and she edged slightly farther away from Powell. Powell turned, jabbing a leather-gloved finger at her.

"If you two are so sure that there's something in all of this, then where's Tyrell now?"

For a moment, Lopez thought that she'd gotten it all terribly wrong, and that Powell really was trying to get to the bottom of the case. She opened her mouth to speak, and then her heart stopped beating in her chest. Beneath the soft black leather of Powell's glove, the cuffs of his shirt were thickly stained with blood.

Powell's expression wavered with concern as he caught the direction of her gaze. Lopez jerked her pistol up to point at the captain, but Powell's arm smashed her weapon aside. A chunky fist slammed into her stomach and she gagged and folded over the blow, the strength leaving her legs as Powell hurled her against the steel wall of a shipping container.

A crack reverberated through her head as it struck the hard metal, her vision blurring as Powell tore her pistol from her grip. She felt the barrel jammed against her face, saw Powell's features loom before her as the sound of the approaching jet reached deafening proportions.

"Move!" Powell shouted.

Lopez was shoved toward the Gulfstream V550 that had parked within twenty meters of them.

"You'll never get away with this shit," Lopez shouted above the engine noise.

Powell didn't respond as he manhandled her alongside the Gulfstream. As the engines wound down, she saw the fuselage entrance door open and a set of steps unfold with a mechanical buzz. As soon as it touched the tarmac Powell propelled her up the steps, the pistol still wedged against her head.

As she reached the doorway, a tall man blocked her way. A pair of clear, cold eyes locked onto hers, narrow irises floating in gray discs. They took in the pistol at her neck and Powell holding her before the man stepped back and out of the way.

"We've been compromised," Powell snapped as he shoved Lopez into the aircraft. "Get the consignment off but leave the crate on."

"That wasn't part of the plan," the man said, Lopez detecting a hint of a Chicago accent.

"The plan's over!" Powell boomed, and shoved Lopez toward the man. "Empty the crate and get those remains out of here. When you're done, put her inside the crate."

Lopez was caught in the man's iron grip as he looked at Powell.

"What are you going to do to her?"

Captain Powell looked down at Lopez. "You're the last remaining link, Nicola. Once you're out of the picture everything goes back to normal. I'll make it quick, but I'm afraid you're going out to sea."

Lopez felt acid seething through her veins as an image of Lucas Tyrell lying dead in the apartment filled her mind.

"Just as gutless as I thought you were."

Powell's eyes flared and he struck out at her with the back of his hand.

Lopez flinched, but was surprised to see the hand of the man holding her flick out and block Powell's blow easily. Even before she had registered what was happening, she felt herself being spun away as the man with the cold gray eyes rushed forward, gripping Powell's gun hand in his own while driving the points of his fingers into Powell's eyes. Powell growled and stumbled back, trying to swipe the hand away. In an instant, Lopez's savior stomped on the inside of Powell's left leg while twisting his gun arm up and away from his torso.

Powell's gag became a brief scream as his shoulder

dislocated, and Lopez heard a popping sound as the tendons snapped in his wrist, the pistol dropping onto the Gulfstream's carpeted floor.

Lopez scrambled to her feet as the man grabbed the pistol and stood back from Powell's crumpled form.

"Who the hell are you?" she asked.

"Ethan Warner," the man replied, keeping the weapon trained on Powell. "You?"

"Nicola Lopez, MPD. What the hell's going on?"

"You need to call Doug Jarvis at the DIA and tell him that—"

"I spoke to him an hour ago; he's the one that got me into this," Lopez said briskly. "You came here from Israel?"

"Direct," Ethan confirmed. "Who's this?" he asked, gesturing to Powell.

"Your worst nightmare," Powell snarled, struggling to his feet. "You've no jurisdiction and have entered the country illegally. I'll have the both of you in a cell within—"

Lopez stepped forward and swung a roundhouse punch that connected to Powell's jaw with a crack that seemed to echo through the aircraft. Powell's two-hundred-pound frame spun 180 degrees and plunged facefirst onto one of the couches.

Ethan Warner looked at her in surprise as he lowered the pistol.

"Bad day at the office?"

"You have no idea," Lopez said bitterly, massaging her knuckles. "Now, I need you to tell me everything that's happened in Israel."

89

Your fiancée?"

Nicola Lopez seemed genuinely appalled at Ethan's loss.

"No worse than you losing your partner," Ethan replied. "At least my fiancée may still be alive. If I'd put everything together out there sooner, none of this would have happened."

"Wasn't your fault," Aaron Luckov said from beside Safiya. "We all did what we could."

Lopez shook her head, swiping a strand of black hair from her face.

"Wouldn't have changed much anyway, not with this asshole protecting everything that MACE has been doing," she said, pointing to where Powell now sat gagged and bound against the couch. "Those remains, they're the ones that Patterson's been after?"

Ethan glanced briefly at the crate lashed to the rear bulkhead.

"He's been after the DNA in the bones, some crackpot campaign to bring angels back to life. He either has no idea or doesn't want to entertain the fact that the remains aren't of an angel, they're of some kind of alien humanoid."

Lopez stared at him blankly.

"Alien? You're shitting me."

"Afraid not," Ethan said. "Look in the box if you don't believe me."

"Then what's with all the experiments, the dead drug addicts over here?"

"This guy Patterson is the brains behind everything," Ethan explained. "They wanted to conduct blood transfusions using the bone marrow of the supposed angels to genetically alter the human population, something to do with fulfilling a biblical covenant between man and God. Sheviz was taking it one step further and trying to impregnate women with Nephilim eggs created from embryonic stem cells extracted from the remains."

Lopez winced.

"Gruesome. He get anywhere?"

"No," Ethan said.

"You want Patterson," Lopez guessed.

Ethan nodded once, and she shook her head.

"Powell's a worthless piece of shit, but he's right, you're in the country illegally, and if the FBI finds you, it's game over. There's enough evidence here to convict Patterson without you running around playing the Lone Ranger."

"He's not done yet," Ethan insisted. "Whatever he's planned, it's likely to go down soon. He'll know by now that MACE is dead in the water and that his precious DNA is beyond his grasp. Whatever he's got left, he'll know that he's got to use it now before it's too late."

"The Bureau won't let you out of this aircraft, let alone loose in the city."

"Then you can help me get to him," Ethan said.

"The hell d'you think I am, the mayor?"

Ethan looked at her strangely as a thought occurred to him.

"No, as it happens. And where's your backup? Where's the FBI?"

Lopez sighed.

"It's a long story, but we're both screwed. The FBI's been trying to shut this investigation down since yesterday. Boarding this jet was illegal and is likely to cost me my badge."

Ethan nodded.

"Then you've got no more to lose than me. We can be utterly worthless together."

Lopez chuckled bitterly. "No use getting cute with me."

Ethan leveled her with what he hoped was an honest look.

"If we're going to lose what little we've got left, why not bring that sanctimonious bastard Patterson down with us and make it worthwhile?"

Lopez glanced at Powell lying nearby, and an image of Lucas Tyrell drifted in front of her mind's eye.

"Come with me."

The sudden screech of car tires and a blizzard of flashing lights reflected off the Gulftstream's fuselage as the sound of a loudspeaker blasted Special Agent Axel Cain's ears almost clean off.

"Police, nobody move!"

Cain sprinted from his vehicle and followed four heavily armed FBI agents as they plunged into the fuselage of the Gulfstream, weapons sweeping the interior and finding Powell.

Cain strode to Powell's side, squatting down and tearing the gag from his face.

"About time," Powell spat.

"What the hell's going on here?" Cain asked, looking at the crate nearby, the bearded man, and the Palestinian woman standing near the cockpit of the jet with their hands in the air.

"Detective Lopez has gone off the range," Powell said. "We need to arrest her and the man she's with, some guy called Ethan Warner. He's here illegally from Israel and could be a suspect in one of our investigations."

"Where the hell are they?"

"They took off, not more than ten minutes ago," Powell said. "Most likely they'll head for the District, probably the New Covenant Church."

Cain looked at the crate again. "What's in that?"

"I've no idea," Powell snapped. "Cut me loose."

"I wouldn't do that if I were you," said the bearded, barrel-chested man near the cockpit.

"Who the hell are you?" Cain muttered.

"My name's Aaron Luckov, and there's something on that crate you should see."

Cain ignored him and reached for a Swiss Army knife he carried. He was about to cut Powell's bonds when one of the FBI agents called over.

"Sir, this guy's right. I think you should see this right now."

Cain got up, and the agent gestured to a piece of paper that had been hastily scribbled upon and tacked to the big crate.

Powell killed Tyrell. Treat the blood on his sleeves as evidence of homicide and use ballistics to match it to the crime scene in Anacostia. Doug Jarvis at the DIA will confirm the origin of the remains in the crate in the aircraft, as will the commander-

in-chief of the Israeli Defense Force, General Benja-
min Aydan. Hurry, there isn't much time.
   NL

Cain moved back to Powell and looked at the captain's sleeves. The whites of his cuffs were speckled with dark bloodstains, and a thin rim of black spots lined the edges of the fabric. Cain slowly put his knife away before producing a set of steel handcuffs.

"What the hell are you doing?" Powell stammered.

Cain smiled coldly. "Hedging my bets."

Cain cuffed Powell, and then looked at the FBI agents standing around him.

"Send everything we've got to the New Covenant Church in DC. I want Detective Nicola Lopez in custody within the hour, understood?"

90

NEW COVENANT CHURCH
WASHINGTON DC

The church glowed in the light from powerful lamps set into the lawns that cast their beams across the facade as Lopez drove Ethan into the parking lot.

"It's huge," Ethan said as they pulled up and Lopez killed the engine.

"Biggest in the District," Lopez agreed, climbing out. "Patterson's property portfolio is worth millions of dollars alone."

Ethan fought down a surge of fury at the opulence of the church as he envisioned Joanna, a genuine messenger of truth, either dead or abducted and held beneath ground in a hot, dusty chamber in some obscure derelict building in Gaza City.

"Looks like there's a few people inside," he said.

"Which bothers me," Lopez said. "Patterson was endorsing Senator Black's presidential campaign. Thought he'd be at the rally by now."

Ethan peered into the foyer and saw a pair of heavily built men in suits standing with their hands clasped before them, talking to another smaller man.

"That's him," Lopez said urgently, pointing at the small man, who turned and walked out of sight down a corridor away from the foyer.

"You ever heard of a church needing door security?" Ethan asked.

"No," Lopez said. "Maybe we should find another way in. Patterson may know we're coming."

"They'll have locked every other entrance if they're expecting visitors," Ethan said, the fury still coursing through his veins. "You look to see where Patterson's gone. Leave the guards to me."

Lopez threw Ethan a mock salute as she followed him.

Ethan made his way to the two huge glass double doors and eased his way inside. One of the two guards lumbered over to intercept him in the foyer.

"Have I come at a bad time?" Ethan muttered.

"The church is closed," the guard said, reaching out and grabbing Ethan's arm.

As the guard yanked him back toward the doors, Ethan turned and pushed him off balance before slamming the palm of his right hand under the guard's jaw. The heavily built man staggered backward and crashed down across a table that snapped in half beneath his weight with a crackle of splintered wood.

Ethan turned as the second security guard rushed him and a meaty shoulder ploughed into his belly. Ethan felt himself hurled onto his back on the thick carpet, the security guard pinning him down before reaching out to grab his wrists. Ethan waited until the guard got hold of them and pushed them toward the ground, before he arched his back and butted his head forward. His skull impacted the guard's nose, shattering the nasal bridge with a crunch. Ethan thumped his knee into the man's groin, and the guard rolled off him with a strangled groan.

Ethan leaped to his feet to see the other guard draw a pistol and aim it at him.

"Stay where you are, hands on your head."

Ethan obeyed as the guard edged closer, the gun never wavering from Ethan's face.

"On your knees."

"Go to hell."

The second guard staggered to his feet before slamming a fist deep into Ethan's flank. Ethan gasped as pain erupted across his side and he sank to his knees. The guard was about to speak when Lopez pushed through the glass doors with her pistol in one hand and her badge in the other.

"Metro PD, drop your weapon now!"

The guards turned in surprise and Ethan jerked upright and backward onto his feet, slamming into the man behind him. The guard staggered backward into the wall as Ethan turned and grabbed his pistol wrist before the guard could bring his weapon to bear. Ethan yanked the arm toward him, turning and throwing the man over his shoulder before twisting his wrist away from the direction of the fall and stomping down on his armpit.

The tendons in the guard's shoulder rippled as they parted under the sudden unbearable pressure, a gargled scream issuing from his mouth as the pistol was ripped from his grasp. Ethan lifted his boot and delivered a sharp blow to the guard's temple, abruptly cutting the scream off.

Lopez looked at the remaining guard, who had turned to point his gun at Ethan.

"Don't even think about it," she said. "Drop it."

The guard obeyed, and Ethan strode across to him and smashed the butt of his pistol across his temple, the man collapsing instantly onto his side.

Lopez picked up the guard's pistol. "Didn't fancy talking it over with them then."

"Where'd Patterson go?" Ethan asked.

"Leave the guards to me," Lopez echoed. "You think you're Russell Crowe or something?"

"Patterson," Ethan said sternly. Lopez watched him silently for a moment. "I'm not going to kill him," Ethan promised.

"Sure," Lopez murmured.

"Unless he tries to kill us."

Lopez said nothing, leading him in the direction Patterson had vanished. Ethan followed her down a long corridor until they reached a large door at the end bearing Patterson's name.

Lopez tried the door handle.

"Locked."

Ethan stood back. This would be the moment to heroically kick the door down, but in truth doors couldn't be opened easily in that way.

"If we use guns and he's here, he'll hear us," Lopez said.

Ethan looked around and saw a seat with velvet cushions back down the corridor. He strolled across and picked the cushions up before returning to the door. Lopez understood immediately, aiming at the door as Ethan pressed the cushions against the lock. Lopez buried the muzzle of her pistol into the cushions and fired three times.

Ethan heard the metallic crunch as the door lock was mangled under the blasts amid splintering wood. Lopez pulled back as Ethan dropped the cushions and pushed on the door handle. The heavy door opened partially, enough for Ethan to see the shattered locking mechanism.

Ethan leaned out, and then barged his shoulder into the door.

The door flew open, Lopez rushing past him into the office with her pistol held before her. Ethan looked at the broad windows and the huge chrome crucifix on the wall.

"He's not here."

"You didn't tell me you were a genius," Lopez muttered, looking around her. "He's got to be around somewhere."

"You sure he came in here?"

"I look like a moron?"

"No, but he could have sneaked off somewhere else."

"He didn't," Lopez said. "He came in here, I saw him, and there's no other exit from the corridor."

A flash of light caught Ethan's eyes as it traveled across the wall in front of him, and he turned to look back out into the corridor. Through a window on the opposite wall, he saw pulsing strobes and car headlights flash past as they entered the parking lot outside.

"Wherever he is, we'd better find him fast," Lopez said. "The FBI's here."

91

Ethan looked around the huge office in desperation as Lopez grabbed one of the chairs from Patterson's desk, using it to wedge the office door closed.

"You said that Patterson had this place built to his own specifications," Ethan said.

"Yeah, about fifteen years ago."

"So he wouldn't have used his charitable institutions like the hospitals for his experiments for fear of whistle-blowers among his employees."

Lopez glanced over her shoulder at him as she pushed the chair into place.

"You think he's got a secret chamber here or something?"

"Either that or he just spontaneously combusted into thin air. Maybe God really is looking out for him."

Lopez snorted as she began experimentally tapping the walls of the office with the butt of her pistol.

"The only reason God would be looking out for a slimeball like Patterson is to send him to roast in hell."

Ethan walked to the middle of the office and slowly turned 360 degrees, observing his surroundings and stopping as he looked directly at the vast crucifix dominating the wall above the altar.

He strode across to it, looking closely at the chromed surface.

The crucifix was made of three tightly fitting pieces: the central vertical pillar, the upper tip, and the horizontal crossbeam. The vertical pillar was just over six feet tall and a foot wide, and as Ethan looked at the surface he could just make out a translucency to the metal. He looked down at the carpet beneath his feet and saw a mild thinning of the fibers, as though someone had walked or stood on the same spot many times.

"Here," he motioned for Lopez to join him.

Lopez examined the surface of the crucifix for a moment, then the carpet.

"He went through here somehow. There must be a release mechanism," she said.

"It's got to be something mechanical," Ethan agreed, turning.

His eye caught instantly on the large bronze eagle on Patterson's desk, beside a small monitor. Lopez followed his gaze even as they both heard muffled voices approaching down the corridor outside. Ethan grabbed the eagle's head and twisted it sideways.

Silently, the vertical pillar of the crucifix revolved into the wall, revealing a narrow passage that opened into a wider descending tunnel beyond. Lopez slipped through the opening, Ethan following a moment later before the crucifix silently closed behind him. He realized that he could faintly see through the crucifix back into the office, the chrome surface some sort of two-way mirror that Patterson must have used to enter and exit the office unobserved. Figures burst into the office, torch beams sweeping this way and that.

"The FBI's here," he whispered. "It won't take them long to figure out where we've gone."

"We won't need much time," Lopez said.

The passage opened out ahead, Ethan guessing it to be about twelve meters long and descending two meters in total, enough to put it below the auditorium of the megachurch. As they descended, Ethan could make out a door with a heavy handle, and before it a gap of some six inches. Lopez stopped in front of the door, and as Ethan came alongside her he could see that the gap extended to either side of them, above and below, the door the entrance to a large boxlike structure suspended in midair within an underground chamber.

"An anechoic chamber," Lopez said loudly. "Don't worry, they can't hear us and we can't hear them until we open this door."

Ethan shook his head in wonder, having heard only rumors about such chambers. An anechoic chamber was a form of room that was isolated from exterior sound or electromagnetic radiation sources, preventing the reflection of wave phenomena. The chamber was supported slightly above the actual floor using tensile springs, and surrounded on all sides by soundproofing layers of anechoic tiles, a concrete shield and a full six inches of near vacuum-pressure air.

"Shall we?" Ethan suggested, grabbing the door handle.

Nicola raised her pistol, and on a count of three Ethan yanked the door open and they burst into the chamber together to hear the voice of a man shouting.

"You're insane!"

The voice sounded dead, monotone, its vocal resonance lost within the room as though Ethan were listening to it underwater. He blinked in surprise as he saw that the steel-walled room was an operating theater, replete with a heart-bypass machine, refrigerator banks, computer monitors, and a single, large light suspended over a gurney in the center of the theater. Upon the gurney, lying restrained on his back, was Senator Isaiah Black. The senator stared in terror at Ethan and Lopez.

"Get this bastard off me!"

Pastor Kelvin Patterson stood on one side of the theater. In one hand he held a syringe filled with a deep-scarlet fluid, the other hand on the door of a refrigerator filled with mysterious-looking vials. Before Ethan or Lopez could speak, Patterson lurched sideways, reaching out for the senator with the syringe.

"Freeze!" Lopez shouted, aiming at the pastor. "Don't you dare move!"

Patterson hesitated, the needle twelve inches from the senator's neck.

Senator Black's face was contorted with a volatile mixture of outrage and fear.

"What the hell is in that?" he shouted, staring fanatically at the syringe.

Ethan spoke quietly, his gaze leveled at Patterson and radiating hatred.

"It's the blood of an unknown alien species."

Senator Black's skin paled visibly, but Patterson snarled back at Ethan.

"This is the blood of an angel, a Nephilim." He looked down at the senator. "Fear not, Isaiah, for you are about to be invigorated. Imagine, the blood of angels running through your veins. You will become invincible."

Senator Black balked, his skin sheened with sweat.

"I don't want to be invincible!"

Ethan spoke up as he took a pace closer to Patterson.

"If you're so sure it's the blood of angels, then why not invigorate yourself and save Senator Black the trouble."

A cruel smile twisted Patterson's features.

"Better to be safe than sorry."

Senator Black gritted his teeth.

"Don't do it," he said to Patterson. "It's not worth it."

Lopez gestured with her pistol to the syringe in Patterson's hand.

"You put that shit in him he'll be dead within minutes. You might as well jack him full of diesel."

Patterson's gruesome smile crumbled into a look of pure disgust.

"How little faith you have," he spat. "This is the first chance in history for man to reach out and touch the hand of God, and you filthy liberalist secularists would snatch it away from humanity. You would deny even the blood of God in your fear of the truth. Do you even know what 'covenant' means? It is a bond in blood, sovereignly administered by God."

Ethan glanced around the theater at the transfusion lines and oxygen bottles, searching for a way to hinder the pastor for just long enough to get hold of him. Patterson was standing only ten feet away, but he was closer to the senator than Ethan was.

"Go ahead," Patterson dared him, as though reading his thoughts. "One step and I'll put this through his heart and finish him for good."

"The FBI is here," Lopez said. "It's only a matter of time before they find this chamber."

"Yes, it is," Patterson agreed, "by which time this will all be over."

"You'll kill him," Lopez said, her pistol fixed on the pastor. "What the hell makes you think you'll achieve anything else?"

"This is the purest human blood in existence," Patterson said, his eyes ablaze with the furor of the righteous, "an unbroken line that goes back to Adam's presence in the Garden of Eden, six thousand years ago. The rest of our blood has long since been contaminated, soiled by the filth and depravity of mankind's soulless existence, but our true bloodline came from the Levant, from Israel, from the time of the patriarchs. This blood will bring God's children back to this Earth and with them the dawning of a new age."

"No, it won't," Lopez uttered. "You're nothing more than a murderer."

"I am the savior!" Patterson cried out. "We have waited two thousand years for this moment, but why should we have waited at all? If we cannot find God here on Earth, then I shall bring God to us!"

Ethan glanced at Lopez before he spoke to Patterson, putting his gun on the floor and moving toward him.

"You think that by doing this you'll find some kind of illumination. I think that you'll plunge us all into darkness."

"You're already in darkness," Patterson sneered.

Ethan judged the distance. Six feet, maybe seven.

"Are we? You know, it's always bugged me how people like you claim to be the light, the truth, the saviors of mankind, yet you threaten to kill anyone who doesn't believe the same things. To me, you're the one who's in darkness."

Patterson edged closer to the senator as Ethan took another pace. Five feet.

"When God's will comes to pass you and all other heathen will see the light, but it will be forever beyond your reach."

Ethan nodded.

"Then let's bring God's will to pass, right now."

In that instant Lopez fired her pistol at the light above the gurney, the shot deafeningly loud in the confines of the theater, and the entire chamber was plunged into darkness as Ethan hurled himself at the pastor.

92

Ethan rushed forward, intercepting Kelvin Patterson as he lunged for the gurney and smashing him aside with his body weight. He heard a crash as Patterson spun away into the refrigerator door, and faintly saw the syringe needle glinting in the light.

Behind him, he heard rather than saw Lopez scramble across to the gurney and begin unstrapping the senator.

Patterson screamed in outrage and rushed toward Ethan, who swung a wild left hook that connected with the pastor's cheek. Ethan heard Patterson slam sideways into a bank of steel cupboards at the back of the chamber and he plunged into him, desperately searching for the syringe that Patterson still held.

"Get the senator out of here!" Ethan shouted at Lopez.

Ethan leaned away desperately as Patterson tried to sink his teeth into Ethan's neck. The world tilted crazily in the darkness as Ethan toppled over backward and smashed onto his back on the unforgiving tiles. In the scarce light from the open doorway to the chamber he saw the syringe plunge down toward him.

Ethan grabbed the pastor's wrists and stopped the

tip of the needle two inches from his own chest as Patterson tumbled down on top of him, teeth gritted with effort as he pushed his entire body weight down on the syringe.

Ethan gasped beneath the pastor's furious attack, sucking in air as he struggled to hold Patterson's body inches above his own, the pastor grimacing and starting to laugh maniacally as he drove the syringe another inch toward Ethan's chest.

Ethan felt the tip of the needle pierce his shirt and skin, a tiny prick of pain. He felt his muscles bursting with effort, his eyes bulging as he heard his own labored pulse rushing through his ears. Spots sparkled before his eyes as he felt the last of his strength deserting him.

He heard the pastor's voice above the rushing in his ears.

"Prepare to meet thy Maker."

Patterson shoved his body higher up on Ethan's, bringing his full weight to bear on the syringe. Ethan sucked in a lungful of air and twisted the pastor's wrists downward, turning the needle away from his own chest.

Patterson grunted as he fought this new and unexpected counterattack. Ethan let the pastor's body weight help him, placing all of the strain on Patterson's wrists. The pastor gagged as he struggled to control his balance.

The syringe turned between them, facing down toward their feet, and Ethan changed his grip on the pastor's hands, ready to push the syringe upward. Patterson panicked, scrambling up and away from the needle. Ethan hooked one leg over the pastor's and kicked it out from beneath him, twisting him by his hands and wrists as his body flipped sideways and over onto his back. Ethan scrambled on top of Patterson, the needle now pointing down at the pastor's chest.

In the faint light, he saw Patterson's eyes swimming with panic.

"Joanna Defoe," Ethan hissed, glowering down at the pastor.

A tremor of recognition flickered across Patterson's features.

"Let me go," he gasped, "or I'll tell you nothing."

"I know she's alive." Ethan grinned coldly. "I know MACE took her."

"I had nothing to do with it," the pastor croaked, straining to hold the syringe away from his skin. "I don't know what happened to her, I swear."

"Then what use are you?" Ethan growled.

"No, please, don't—"

Ethan slammed his entire body weight down on the syringe. Patterson screamed as the needle plunged deep into his chest and the fluid flooded into his body.

Ethan hauled himself off the pastor, yanking the syringe free and tossing it to one side. Behind him, he heard a clatter of footsteps as flashlight beams sliced into the darkness and a handful of FBI agents burst into the chamber, Axel Cain at their head.

"Hands up, don't move!"

Ethan complied, not resisting the FBI agents as they cuffed him. He saw Lopez being cuffed alongside him.

"*Illuminated?*" she said. "*Darkness?* You're a riot, Warner, you really are."

"You got it, didn't you?"

He watched as they lifted Patterson to his feet, the pastor holding his chest where the needle had pierced him. Slowly he straightened, and began to chuckle as he looked at Ethan. For a terrible instant, Ethan wondered if the insane old man had been right as he stood four-square and looked Ethan in the eye.

"The Word has been spoken, and this is God's judgment upon us all for . . ."

Patterson's voice trailed off, and the fevered delight vanished as his face folded in upon itself in agony. Ethan took a step back as, bowing over at the waist, Patterson looked up and wailed a scream that sounded as though his innards were being doused in flames.

Patterson lurched to one side, the FBI agents leaping out of his way as the pastor slammed into the side of the gurney and sprawled onto his back, his eyes bulging and his mouth wide open as a foamy mess of bloodied mucus bubbled out to spill onto the tiles beneath him. Ethan winced as the pastor gargled and thrashed, dark blood spilling from his cavities as his internal organs turned to mush inside him.

Patterson gave a last anguished cry of despair, his limbs contorting at impossible angles as his spine arched over to the sound of cracking bones, his head twisted back to almost touch the back of his legs before he froze in position, his eyes staring wide and empty toward the exit of the chamber.

Ethan stared at his body for a moment, and then looked at the FBI agents.

"You might want to seal this room off. It could be contaminated."

"You think?" Axel Cain shot him a look of mock surprise. "Get out of here."

Ethan gave the dead pastor one last glance, and then let himself be led out of the chamber and into the light once more.

93

J. EDGAR HOOVER BUILDING
WASHINGTON DC
AUGUST 28, 1 P.M.

I've told you everything."

Ethan sat in a hard metal chair with his wrists cuffed to the legs. A camera in one corner of the cell recorded the conversation, an FBI agent guarding the door as Ethan sat staring at the pockmarked face of Special Agent Axel Cain.

"Everything," Cain repeated cynically, smiling with his lips only. "Mr. Warner, you've been embroiled in an international conspiracy that has resulted in several deaths, one of which was at your own hands and witnessed by a half-dozen FBI agents, myself included."

"It was self-defense." Ethan shrugged, beyond caring by now.

"You injected him with something that caused his innards to melt and pour out of his eyes, ears, and ass!" Cain shouted. "Overkill, don't you think?"

"Not for a man who committed the crimes he has."

Cain looked down at his notes, shaking his head.

"The district attorney won't see it like that. You left

Israel without passport or papers, entered the United States as an illegal immigrant, and then proceeded to injure several men, acquire a firearm for which you were not licensed, and commit the homicide of a respected local pastor." Cain grinned coldly. "And that's the way I'll be presenting it."

"Bullshit baffles brains," Ethan muttered.

Cain's grin didn't slip as he stood.

"Sticks and stones, Mr. Warner. You're going away for a very long time, make no mistake about that."

The cell door opened as Cain made his way out, only to be pushed back in by two men in smart suits. Before Cain was even able to protest, the two men flashed badges at him.

"We'll be taking Ethan Warner into our custody," the taller of the two said in a voice that brooked no argument.

"He's our suspect," Cain blustered. "We've got evidence, witnesses, and—"

"Presidential pardon," said the shorter of the two men.

Ethan experienced a brief sensation of disbelief.

"Presidential pardon?" he echoed, as though he were as appalled as Agent Cain.

"If you'll come with us," said the taller man, who then turned to Cain. "Release him, now. This case is closed."

Cain, his blotchy face flushed red with restrained fury, nodded to the guard, who quickly released Ethan from the chair.

"This is insane," Cain protested. "Who the hell has the authority for this? The president doesn't even know about what's—"

"That's classified, Defense Intelligence Agency information and well above your pay grade," the tall man said. "Any more questions and we'll take you into our custody as well."

Cain blanched and stepped back as Ethan walked out of the cell, following the two men down the corridor.

"Seriously?" he asked them. "Presidential pardon?"

"Not quite," said the shorter of the two, "but close enough."

Ethan saw two more suited men appear ahead, Nicola Lopez wedged between them and looking equally bemused.

"How do we keep meeting like this?" he asked her.

"Bad luck and timing?"

Ethan said nothing as they were led to the underground parking lot of the FBI headquarters. Three black SUVs were waiting, an ad in themselves for government-agency business. Once inside, they were driven out of the parking lot and turned for the District.

"You tell them anything?" Ethan asked Lopez.

"I'd barely sat down when Secret Service turned up," Lopez explained. "Cain's got sand up his ass about the case being shut down."

"So I noticed. He a friend of yours?"

"You think?"

The SUVs drifted down Pennsylvania Avenue, and for one moment Ethan thought that they were really heading to meet the president. He felt slightly deflated as the vehicles rolled past and on toward the Capitol.

"We're not that important," Lopez said with a wry smile.

"That's what worries me," Ethan said. "Where are we going?"

"For debrief," said one of the agents in the front of the vehicle. "Then to the Hart Senate Office Building."

"How's Senator Black?" Lopez asked.

This time the agent looked over his shoulder and winked.

"He's fine; you did good."

Ethan and Lopez shared a glance, and Ethan wondered what the hell was going on as the vehicle turned away from the District and headed through nondescript industrial areas near the Anacostia River. They finally pulled up outside what once was part of the old navy dockyards, the towering old storage warehouses. Nearby, extensive building work was under way converting the unused buildings into flashy new apartments.

The SUVs rolled toward a particularly battered-looking warehouse that faced away from the city, and as they approached a loading door raised automatically, allowing the three vehicles to roll inside. Ethan looked over his shoulder and saw the rollers close up again as though swallowing them whole.

"Why the cloak-and-dagger routine?" Ethan asked the agents.

"Keeps you out of the media eye," one of them explained. "FBI would have broadcast your arrests to the world, and we don't want that to happen."

Ethan felt a slight tension return to his body.

"Are we going for a swim wearing concrete flippers?"

The two agents laughed, but said nothing as the SUVs rolled to a halt. The doors were opened by agents from the outside, all of them competent-looking men with earpieces and carefully concealed weapons.

Ethan stepped out, and was quickly hurried away by two agents in the opposite direction of Lopez.

94

You understand the importance of the situation?"

Ethan nodded.

"I can understand why you're doing this, yes."

Ethan was sitting in a comfortable room buried deep in the center of the old warehouse, his voice sounding oddly muted and monotone in the anechoic chamber built into the solid concrete of the dock. The differences between this room and Patterson's macabre operating theater were the soft couch, the coffee and doughnuts, and the straight-talking man who sat opposite. In his forties and with a long, serious face, he was the epitome of the discreet but capable government agent, and called himself Mr. Wilson.

"The DIA can't afford this kind of security leak right now," Wilson explained. "People think that to maintain security around delicate matters people like us use violence or intimidation, even murder. We don't, if at all possible. We prefer to keep people on our side and explain to them why we are doing what we're doing."

Ethan nodded.

"That's very reasonable and convenient, as I quite like being alive."

Wilson smiled.

"The simple fact is that we don't know what these aliens were, what they were doing here seven thousand years ago, or whether they visit us now. The remains found in Israel by Dr. Lucy Morgan will remain under lock and key for further study, and will not reach the public domain for some decades yet."

Ethan frowned.

"Surely people are ready for this kind of thing?"

Wilson nodded in agreement.

"Absolutely correct, Ethan, if you're referring to the educated, prepared countries of our Western world: barely one sixth of Earth's population. We in the West might be mentally prepared for the presence of extraterrestrial species and their visitation of Earth, but what about the rest? What chaos might be caused in the Middle East, the former Soviet States, South America, and elsewhere?"

Ethan raised an eyebrow.

"Surely they're prepared enough not to commit mass suicide."

"Perhaps," Wilson conceded. "But combined with that uncertainty is the fact that we ourselves don't know why these . . . beings visit us. We don't know what they want. We don't know where they come from. We don't know if they'll arrive in greater numbers in the future. All the talk about conspiracy by government to conceal the truth, like Roswell, is utter crap. We don't know the goddamn truth ourselves and are just trying to keep a lid on things until the rest of the world stops blowing itself to hell. Then, maybe, we'll start seeing how we might deal with all of this."

"If they're hostile, we need to work together," Ethan said.

"Exactly," Wilson said. "And even if they're not, we don't want one country welcoming them with open arms as another opens fire or tries to steal technology to get the upper hand. It's just the kind of shortsighted thing that some dictatorships might try, and God knows what would happen if we pissed these beings off. As it is, they can infiltrate our airspace with impunity and make a mockery of our defenses even when we do detect them."

Ethan finished his coffee and set his mug down.

"So, silence all around then?" he guessed. "It never happened."

Wilson nodded frankly.

"Dr. Sheviz is in the care of Bedouin nomads, which I think we can both assume will not be a pleasant experience for him. Most of the other key players are dead. Lopez and you will sign an official secrets declaration, as will your friends Safiya and Aaron Luckov before their return to Israel. All trace of events will be removed from the records of all agencies involved, and Kelvin Patterson died tragically from natural causes."

"What about Lucas Tyrell?" Ethan asked. "Lopez said he was killed during his investigation."

"He died a hero," Wilson said with genuine intensity, "and that will be on the record."

"What about Joanna Defoe, my fiancée?"

"That will be for Senator Black to explain."

"And the bloodline?" Ethan asked. "The message in a bottle that those remains represent? Surely we all deserve to know what the message is?"

Wilson's features hardened, and he stood from his chair.

"They'll be studied. Let's just say that if you leave someone a calling card, you'll make sure there's a way of calling back on it."

"And what if any one of the others goes public with what happened?" Ethan asked out of curiosity as he stood.

Wilson smiled as he shook Ethan's hand, but his eyes were cold.

"Three things. First, nobody will believe them except the cranks and weirdos. Second, they'll find themselves experiencing a long and continuous run of bad luck. If that doesn't silence them, then the third thing will happen, and nobody wants that. Enjoy a long life, Mr. Warner."

95

HART SENATE OFFICE BUILDING
WASHINGTON DC

Why wasn't I told?"

Ethan sat on the edge of a finely furnished couch opposite Senator Isaiah Black. The senator sighed, picking his words with care.

"It was a difficult time," he began, "and the administration didn't know how to handle—"

"The truth?" Ethan cut in. "It was a difficult time for me, in case they hadn't noticed. They knew what had happened to Joanna Defoe and they refused to tell me."

Black nodded, raising a placatory hand. "Please, I'm just the messenger here."

"So what happened?" Ethan pressed.

Senator Black spoke quietly, holding Ethan's pensive gaze.

"According to the Defense Intelligence Agency, Joanna Defoe traveled into Gaza before Operation Cast Lead, Israel's retaliation for rocket attacks by Hamas. She was talking to high-level militants and filming them as they attempted to launch Qassam rocket attacks into Sderot. At some point MACE operatives decided to abduct or detain Miss Defoe against her will near Jabaliya."

Black hesitated for a moment. Ethan waited, keeping his gaze fixed on the senator until he was compelled to continue.

"Jabaliya was hit by aerial attacks at several points during the conflict, each of which caused numerous casualties among the Hamas leadership. Israel believed that Joanna Defoe was inadvertently killed during one such attack, but it would seem likely that she may not have been there at all, held captive by MACE forces elsewhere."

Pain pinched the corners of Ethan's eyes and his top lip quivered.

"Why wasn't I told?" he asked again.

"Most of the details were kept from the public because, essentially, the apparent passing of your fiancée was considered a direct result of Israeli military action. However, that action was against legitimate targets."

"And Joanna likely wasn't even there."

Senator Black nodded.

"Pastor Kelvin Patterson was behind the entire operation, having gained a controlling share of MACE in order to provide security and mobility, as well as plausible deniability in the form of advanced cryogenic battlefield surgery for his experiments. This was nobody's fault except his, and at least now you have the truth."

"All lies lead to the truth," Ethan said. "Do they know what happened to Joanna afterward?"

"I'm afraid the trail runs cold at that point," the senator said. "If Byron Stone or Spencer Malik knew anything about it, they took their secret to the grave."

Black looked down at a legal file in his lap.

"It has been decided that in recognition of your efforts both to liberate Lucy Morgan and, not least, to prevent Kelvin Patterson from killing me, the administration should compensate you for your loss. They understand that you have suffered a great deal, and that any court hearing would find in your favor. I do not think that the terms of your compensation will be disappointing."

"They would be disappointing to Joanna."

"I know," Black said, the line of his jaw hardening. "But I think that you're by now aware of the delicacy of what's come to pass and of the need for security. All other parties have been compensated to their satisfaction, including Lucas Tyrell's family. I owe you my life, Mr. Warner, and if it's of any consolation, I'm willing to offer my support to you in any way from this day on. I never forget a debt."

Ethan stood up, and finally managed a faint smile.

"I may call you up on that one day, especially if you make it into the White House."

Senator Isaiah Black grinned as they shook hands.

"I hope that you do."

96

CHICAGO, ILLINOIS
SEPTEMBER 12

Ethan sat on a bar stool at a tall table outside a restaurant, watching nearby choppy, white-crested waves whipped up by a cool breeze sweeping in off Lake Michigan to take the edge off the late-summer sunshine. His first beer in over a week tasted better than he ever remembered, not least since he no longer had to worry about money.

"Mind if I join you?"

Ethan turned, looking straight into the eyes of Nicola Lopez.

"Sure," he said, gesturing to the stool next to him. "Your call sounded urgent."

Lopez sat down, looking entirely different in a summer dress and with her hair long and flowing like black velvet.

"I quit the force," she said simply.

Ethan's jaw dropped. "You did what? You were up for promotion after what happened."

Lopez shrugged, ordering a drink from a passing waitress before replying.

"Never was one for rank. Besides, after what happened to Lucas Tyrell and all the interagency bullshit, I thought I could do better on my own."

Ethan found himself smiling.

"You're going freelance, like a gumshoe? You going to wear a trilby and a trench coat?"

"Maybe not," Lopez said tartly, "but right now I need the money, both for myself and for my family down over the border. I'm pretty damned sure I can do better financially this way."

Ethan took a sip of beer, looking out over the lake.

"So where'd you think of setting up this grand new empire?"

Lopez shrugged.

"Anywhere there's business, but somewhere I can live without having to worry about going out late at night."

Ethan took a chance, gesturing out over the water. "Maybe the lakes?" he suggested. "Indiana's good in the summer."

Lopez smiled. "Maybe. What about you?"

Ethan shrugged.

"I've bought an apartment. Chicago's my home, and I've still got some money left."

Lopez raised an eyebrow as she studied her drink.

"So you're at a loose end then," she suggested.

"Kind of."

"Feel like killing some time until you've decided what you want to do?"

"Doing what?"

"Whatever comes up," Lopez said, smiling at him over the rim of her glass.

"Didn't think innuendo was your thing."

"It's not."

Ethan looked at her for a moment, then chuckled and glanced out over the lakes as Lopez leaned forward on the table.

"We're both at a crossroads in our lives," she said. "We both know what we're good at, so why not join forces and see what comes up. People don't always want the police on their doorstep; they want things done discreetly. Besides, I've had enough of uncovering corpses in Prince George's and Anacostia. I want to look for cases that are a bit more interesting." She sat back. "We could make a good team."

"I'm not sure how I fit into this great design of yours."

Lopez smiled brightly.

"You can be the brains, I'll be the hard ass."

Ethan laughed out loud for the first time in what felt like years.

"Why not?" he said finally. "Trouble is, we need a case first."

Lopez's dark eyes sparkled as she gave a little shrug and looked away from him to study the opposite shore of the lake.

"Hello, Ethan."

The voice came from behind, and Ethan turned to see Doug Jarvis standing behind him. Ethan stood impulsively from his seat as a stab of anger lanced through him.

"You knew," he said. "You knew about MACE and Joanna."

"We suspected," Jarvis said, raising a placatory hand. "The DIA couldn't investigate without Congress finding out about it, and that would have put pressure on the administration to prevent the media from sniffing the story out. The incumbent president authorized

MACE's contracts when he took office—it doesn't matter that he didn't know what they were up to, if word had gotten out, his reelection campaign would have been over."

"Two birds, one stone," Ethan said bitterly. "They ever really have any interest in finding Joanna?"

"No," Jarvis said flatly. "They wanted the remains Lucy found, and they wanted MACE investigated. Both needed a discreet operation, one that wouldn't be traced back to the DIA."

Ethan sat down, shaking his head.

"You did a great job," he said, and looked at Lopez. "You sure you want to work for these guys?"

"They've got work for us, Ethan," she said seriously.

Doug Jarvis gestured to a man waiting nearby. Adrian Selby walked over and extended his hand to Ethan, who took it cautiously.

"You did a fantastic job, Mr. Warner, no doubt about it," Selby said enthusiastically. "So good, in fact, that I brought you and Ms. Lopez this."

Selby handed Ethan a thick blue file.

"What is it?" Ethan asked.

Doug Jarvis spoke for his colleague.

"All of our investigations with the agency have to be justified, if not to Congress then to our own superiors. We have a budget and it has its limits. Nobody at the DIA would back the operation in the Negev; that's why I came to you. But your success has generated new interest. The agency has given us a limited budget to investigate cases where we'd find it hard to justify committing resources, where the subject matter in hand is considered . . . unusual."

Ethan frowned.

"Unusual? As in weird?"

"As in unique," Selby said promptly. "There's a situation developing, in New Mexico. It's a bit of a tricky one and we're not sure how to deal with it as we don't have enough information on the ground. The agency would appreciate it if you could take a look at things for us . . ."

ACKNOWLEDGMENTS

It's surprising how many people come together to publish a novel. For fifteen years it was just me, a computer monitor, and an ever-growing pile of rejection letters. Now there's an army of hardworking, enthusiastic people turning what was once a dream into a reality. I owe an immense debt of gratitude to my brilliant agent Luigi Bonomi, who saw potential in my work and nurtured it so expertly; to my wonderful editors Maxine Hitchcock and Emma Lowth, and the fantastic team at Simon & Schuster, who have made me feel so welcome in what has become a very different world to live in; to authors James Becker, Matt Hilton, and Rebecca Royle for their advice and guidance on my journey to publication; to my friends who read countless manuscripts; and to my parents Terry and Carolyn, who along with all of my family have unfailingly supported me throughout these long years. Every day has been worth it.

Turn the page for a peek at
the next heart-pounding thriller from

DEAN CRAWFORD

IMMORTAL

Coming soon from Touchstone

They're out near the Santa Fe Trail. Shots fired."

Patrol Officer Enrico Zamora pressed down hard on the gas pedal, the Dodge Charger's V-6 engine growling as the patrol cruiser accelerated along the scorched tarmac of Interstate 25 winding into the shimmering desert heat ahead. Broad plains of desiccated thorn scrub swept toward the Pecos Wilderness on either side of the highway, while ahead the jagged peaks of the mountains loomed against the vast blue dome of the sky. The late season was turning the thick ranks of aspens that coated the mountain's flanks a vivid yellow, the forests glowing in the afternoon sunlight as the cruiser plunged between the steep hillsides of the pass.

"Any fatalities?" Zamora asked as he glanced at his partner, his eyes veiled by mirror-lensed sunglasses.

"Not yet." Sergeant Barker shook his head, one hand resting on the Smith & Wesson .357 pistol in its holster at his side. "One man is down and another's injured. Park ranger says that they came under attack."

"Chrissakes," Zamora muttered, wondering what the hell had happened out there in the lonely mountains.

The call had gone out ten minutes previously for emergency response teams to converge on Glorieta Pass. Eight tourists, tenderfoots down from the Big Apple on what Zamora suspected was some kind of bullshit team-building exercise, had been caught in the crossfire of a gunfight. One of the park rangers had led them out on a horse riding expedition, in itself a liability, Zamora thought. Most city types didn't know what a horse looked like, let alone how to ride one. He had seen every injury under the sun suffered by twentysomething investment bankers who earned more in a day than he earned in a year, yet couldn't lift a saddle onto a horse's back without pulling a muscle

But this was different. He had heard it in the dispatcher's voice, her tones edgy. Shots were being fired. People were being hit.

"Just up here," Barker said as they turned off the interstate and roared up a narrow, dusty track that plunged between the walls of a deep gully. Zamora saw his partner still fiddling with his pistol as he ran the other hand over the bald dome of his head.

"Will you quit it with the weapon?" Zamora said as he followed the track. "I don't want to see another wild bullet let loose, okay?"

Barker put his hands in his lap, but his face remained taut like canvas stretched across a frame. Zamora slowed as, ahead among the trees, he saw a group of horses tethered to tree trunks. Crouching among them were several men, each staring wide-eyed at the approaching cruiser.

Zamora killed the engine and got out, drawing his pistol and hurrying across with Barker in a low run to where a park ranger was waving urgently at him. The ranger looked at Zamora. He was young, and his skin was flushed with a volatile mixture of excitement and fear.

"You guys bring backup?" he asked.

"Four more cars and an ambulance are on their way," Zamora replied calmly, glancing at the ranger's pistol. A faint wisp of blue smoke drifting from the barrel told him to expect the worst. "What's the situation?"

The ranger shook his head in disbelief.

"I ain't got a clue, man," he said. "We were makin' our way back down here when all hell broke loose.

Some old guy's having himself a shouting match with a tenderfoot up on the pass, then he pulls out some kind of old musket and shoots the tenderfoot at point-blank range." The ranger gestured over his shoulder to the city slickers behind him. "Damned if he didn't take a shot at us too. One of the guys here panicked and tried to ride past, an' then everything went to hell and the horses bolted. The greenhorn's still lyin' up there, bleedin' out." The ranger looked apologetic. "I didn't want to go back up without support."

Zamora took a deep breath and gestured to the ranger's pistol. "Did you shoot the old guy?"

The young man glanced at his weapon as though he'd forgotten he even had it.

"Yeah," he whispered.

"You did the right thing. How far away is he?"

"A hundred yards, give or take."

"Stay here," Zamora cautioned him, "and keep an eye on the tourists. Don't let them move."

The ranger nodded as Zamora checked his weapon again and moved forward, hugging the rocky side of the trail that climbed up between the tree-studded hills on either side of the gully. The sun flared off the rocky terrain. Zamora could hear no birdsong as he climbed, no crickets chirping in the scorched undergrowth. Gunshots could do that, scatter or silence wildlife.

"You smell that?"

Barker's voice was a husky whisper, and a moment later Zamora caught the scent of woodsmoke drifting invisibly through the trees. He wiped beads of sweat from his forehead as he edged around a bend in the narrow track, hemmed in by thick ranks of trees glowing in the sunlight.

He froze.

There, lying facedown in the center of the track, was a black man dressed in a checked shirt and gray slacks, not the kind of attire one would wear when hiking in the hills. Zamora could see a thick pool of blood congealing in the dust around the man's body. A pair of spectacles lay alongside the body where they had fallen.

"He a dead'un?" Barker asked in a whisper.

Zamora squinted, lowering the rim of his hat to shield his eyes, and detected the man's back gently rising and falling.

"He's breathing," he said, "but he's also leakin'. We need to get him out of there fast."

Barker nodded, holding his Smith & Wesson with both hands.

"You want me to do it?"

Zamora looked up at the steep cliff to their side. The faint smell of woodsmoke was stronger now, closer.

"Looks like whoever did the shooting spent the night here," he whispered. "Maybe the tourists spooked them or something."

A soft whinnying caught their attention. Zamora turned to see a horse tethered to a nearby tree, its head hung low. Across its back lay a blanket, and Zamora felt a twinge of concern as he saw the blanket was thick with dried blood.

"The horse?" Barker said.

Zamora shook his head, swallowing thickly.

"That's not the horse's blood," he said, realizing what he was looking at. "The ranger got 'im all right. Go up that gully there," Zamora said, pointing up to his right. "Get to the high ground in case this lunatic comes back."

Barker nodded, and they broke cover. Zamora hurried forward, reaching the body and squatting down alongside it. The nearby burgundy spectacles were those of a rich kid, a tenderfoot. He paused for a moment, looking around for any sign of an impending attack, before reaching down and touching the man's neck. A pulse threaded its way weakly beneath his fingertips. He was about to holster his pistol when the man groaned and rolled over. Zamora judged him as being no more than thirty years old, clean-shaven and definitely not a native.

"Don't move," Zamora cautioned, looking at the bloodstain soaking the man's left shoulder. "What's your name, son?"

"Tyler Willis," came the dry-throated response. "Don't shoot him."

"Don't shoot who?"

"Conley. Hiram Conley. He's . . . he's unwell."

Zamora squinted up at the heavily forested hills surrounding them.

"You're goddamned right there, son," he said quietly. "We need to get you out of here. You know anything about this Conley?"

Tyler Willis swallowed thickly, grimacing with the pain.

"Don't shoot him," he insisted again. "He's extremely old."

Zamora was about to respond when a voice broke the silence of the pass around them.

"Stay still. Identify yourself!"

Zamora flinched and peered up into the woods. The voice bounced and echoed off the walls of the pass, concealing its location. He could see nothing.

"Officer Enrico Zamora, New Mexico State Police," he called back. "This man needs a hospital."

"There ain't no such thing as a state police, and that man ain't no part of the Union!"

Zamora frowned in confusion. "This man is injured and he needs treatment. I need to take him back down the pass."

"He ain't goin' nowhere!" the voice yelled. "I got no beef with you, boy. You turn your back to me an' I'll let you leave, but I got forty dead men up here if'n you try to cross me!"

Forty dead men? Dispatch had only mentioned one man down. Zamora's gaze edged upward as he searched for corpses among the trees, and he saw a flicker of movement.

It took him a moment to register what he was looking at through the dappled sunlight shimmering in pools of light beneath the trees. The man was old, perhaps in his sixties, a thick gray beard draped down across his bare chest. A navy-blue jacket clung to his emaciated frame, the sleeves marked with narrow yellow lines running from shoulder to .cuffs. Across his chest was a thick band of dressing stained crimson with blood. The old man was aiming what looked like an antique rifle over the top of a boulder at him. Zamora looked down at Tyler Willis.

"He's killed forty men?"

"No." Willis shook his head. "He's got forty cartridges for his musket. 'Dead men' is what they used to call their ammunition, back in the Civil War."

Zamora frowned at the wounded man beside him.

"Why's he using a musket? And how do you know him?"

"It's a long story," Willis rasped. "A real long story."

Zamora looked up to the woods and called back. "I can't leave this man here."

"We had an accord, he and I!" the old man cackled. "But he did betray me! No secessionist is worth a dime o' dollar, goddamned southerners been aggervatin' us for years! What regiment are you with, boy?"

Zamora blinked sweat from his eyes, and saw Barker's silhouette creeping through the trees toward the old man.

"I'm not a soldier. You?"

"New Mexico Militia!" the old man shouted. "Born and bred to the Union!"

Zamora realized the old man was either insane

or delusional. Maybe from alcohol or exposure to the elements, or blood loss from the bullet wound.

"He's ill," Tyler Willis rasped from beside him. "He's already been injured, lost a lot of blood. He could have shot me in the head, but he didn't. He just needs help; he needs a hospital."

"You're injured!" Zamora shouted up at the old man. "Come down here—we can treat the wound."

"Only thing I'm gonna be treatin's your balderdash, boy. Now hike out!"

Zamora saw Barker stand up and take aim, and in that instant the old man sensed the threat and whirled the old musket around. Zamora saw Barker rush forward.

"Barker, hold your fire!"

Two gunshots crashed out simultaneously through the canyon, and both men vanished in a cloud of oily blue smoke. Barker's ghostly shape shuddered and dropped into the undergrowth. Zamora leapt to his feet, pistol at the ready as he squinted into the swirling cloud of cordite.

An anguished cry burst out as the old man charged out of the forest, the veil of smoke curling around him. A long-barreled musket cradled in his grip was tipped with a wicked bayonet that glinted at Zamora in the sunlight as it rushed toward him. But in that terrible moment, it wasn't the lethal weapon that sent a spasm of terror bolting through Zamora's stomach.

The left sleeve of the old man's jacket had been torn off, and as he burst into the bright sunlight Zamora could see the flesh of the old man's arm, a tangled, sinewy web of exposed muscles and ragged chunks of decaying gray flesh spilling away as he rushed forward. His hands were gnarled and twisted like those of some ancient crone, his knuckles exposed like white bone beneath almost transparent skin. For one terrible instant, Zamora had the impression of being rushed by a man suffering from the terminal stages of leprosy.

"Get back!" Zamora shouted in surprise, raising his pistol.

"You're gonna be singing on the end of my pigsticker!" the old man screamed, charging the last few paces. The ragged navy-blue uniform, kepi hat, and torn pants seemed to have leapt from some hellish Civil War battlefield, filling Zamora's vision with a nightmarish image of decay and rage.

On the ground beside him, Tyler Willis raised a hand.

"Don't kill him! He's too old to die!"

The bayonet flashed in the sunlight before Zamora's eyes as he staggered backward, taking aim and firing a single shot at the emaciated face charging toward him.

MEDICAL INVESTIGATOR FACILITY
ALBUQUERQUE
NEW MEXICO
MAY 13

Okay, who's tonight's lucky contestant?"

Medical Investigator Lillian Cruz strode down a corridor toward the morgue with a practiced stride. Tall and proud-looking, Lillian had worked in the morgue for as long as anyone could remember. She was leading the night shift, as she did twice a week. If working the small hours virtually alone in a morgue had ever bothered her, she couldn't recall. In contrast her assistant, Alexis, was new to the facility and looked nervous, her squeaky student voice mildly irritating Lillian as she filled in her boss on the details of the night's first autopsy.

"White male, approximately sixty years of age, died from a single gunshot wound to the head fired in self-defense by Officer Enrico Zamora, state PD. The trooper reported that the victim seemed to be suffering from some kind of wasting disease."

Lillian frowned. Probably a drunk who had got himself injured, or some loser strung out on peyote buttons or crack who fancied himself attacking Injuns and heading them off at the pass out Glorieta way. In her many years as a medical investigator, Lillian had seen just about everything.

"When did he die?" Lillian asked as they turned the corner and approached the morgue.

"Yesterday afternoon, time of death called in by the response team as three forty-five p.m. Victim's been on ice since four twenty that afternoon."

Ten hours then. Lillian led the way into the morgue, where a steel gurney awaited them, the contents concealed by a blue plastic ziplock bag speckled with smears of fluid. Lillian checked that the door was closed behind them before donning gloves and a plastic face shield and tying her surgical gown.

"Okay, let's get started, shall we?" Lillian spoke loudly enough to be heard by the recorder sitting on the worktop nearby. She picked up a clipboard, ready to make notes as Alexis grabbed a digital camera to document their findings. On cue, Alexis reached forward over the gurney and with a single smooth movement unzipped the plastic bag.

"Jesus!"

Lillian stared at the gurney as Alexis stifled a tight scream, one gloved hand flying to her mouth. Overcoming a momentary revulsion, Lillian took a cautious pace forward and peered into the depths of the plastic bag as Alexis began taking photographs.

The body that lay within seemed as though it had been stripped of its skin: the internal organs were exposed and decayed, the slack jaw only held in place by frayed tendons and muscles that had either contracted into tight bands or fallen off the body altogether to coil like snakes beneath the corpse. The eyeballs had shriveled and sunk deep into their sockets, and what skin remained drooped in leathery tatters from the bones. Tentatively, Lillian reached out and touched a piece of skin. It felt brittle, like a leather rag left too long in the desert sun. Specks of material crumbled beneath her touch to lightly dust the steel surface of the gurney.

"He's mummified," she murmured.

Alexis shook her head as if to rouse herself from a daze.

"That's not possible. He died yesterday," she insisted. "The rangers and the police independently verified his age, and there are photos taken at the scene by state troopers. He's been on ice ever since. He had papers on him too."

Alexis handed Lillian an evidence form that listed the deceased's name and Social Security number: Hiram Conley, born Las Cruces, New Mexico, 1940. She then handed her the photographs taken by the troopers. Lillian looked at the images of the elderly man killed at the scene of the crime, and then at the decomposed and desiccated remains before her.

"There's got to be a reason for this. Let's see you make the case."

Lillian started making notes and drawings of the observations as Alexis led the autopsy.

"Weight at time of death, approximately one hundred forty pounds. Some evidence of malnutrition and exposure prior to desiccation. Victim had applied field dressings to numerous wounds around the area of the chest, right shoulder and left arm consistent with . . . er . . . some kind of gunshot injuries." Alexis hesitated before continuing. "Victim is clothed in what appears to be some kind of fancy dress or memorial attire, consistent with Civil War era. Note: attire may provide evidence of cause or location of death."

Lillian set her clipboard down and took another long, hard look at the body as Alexis carefully undressed the corpse. With the broad-shouldered jacket and baggy pants gone the body looked entirely skeletal, a bone cage from which hung shriveled tissue and muscle, but this was not what shocked Lillian the most. The remaining tatters of skin on the man's chest bore multiple lesions, deep pits of scar tissue peppering the surface.

"You thinking what I'm thinking?" Alexis asked.

"Smallpox." Lillian nodded, noting the position of the lesions before examining the remains more closely. The body was a silent witness to more scars and lesions than Lillian had seen in her many years working in New Mexico. Barely an inch of his body seemed clear of damage, and even the bones bore testimony to breaks, cut marks, and disease.

"This guy looks like he'd lived a hundred lives," Alexis remarked in wonderment.

"And all of them violent," Lillian agreed.

"Most of his teeth are missing," Alexis said, "and his gums are heavily receded. Could be the mummification, but it could also be scurvy."

Lillian stood back from the body and shook her head.

"Doesn't explain the mummification," she answered. "Smallpox was eradicated in the late seventies and scurvy disappeared over a century ago."

Alexis peered into Hiram Conley's sightless eyes and examined the strange blue-gray irises.

"Odd," she said. "Looks like extensive cataracts, but the cataract cortex hasn't liquefied. This guy should have been blind as a bat by now."

Lillian leaned over for a closer look as Alexis shot more photos.

"Long-term ultraviolet radiation exposure," she said, identifying the cause of the cataracts, "denaturation of lens protein. But you're right; they should have blinded him by now."

"And they're an odd color," Alexis continued, "blue-gray. It's like the proteins were constantly being repaired, fending off the liquefaction." Alexis gestured to Hiram Conley's recently removed clothes, now lying nearby in an evidence tray. "And he was wearing clothes that look a hundred years old."

Lillian stared blankly at her assistant.

"Where are you going with this? You think this guy walked out of a wormhole to the past or something? This isn't *Star Trek,* Alexis. We need to keep our brains engaged here."

"I'm not saying anything like that," Alexis said quickly, reddening. "You ever heard of that Japanese guy, Hiroo Onoda? He was a soldier during World War Two who was on operations in the Philippine jungle when the war ended. He didn't believe the leaflets dropped to inform soldiers of the end of the war, thinking it was propaganda. He only surrendered when his former commanding officer came to get him after he was spotted by a traveler in the region."

"When was that?"

"1974," Alexis said. "He held out for thirty years. My point is, what if this guy's part of some family out in the Pecos who've just kept on going as they were? The Amish have been doing it for long enough. It explains the injuries, the disease, the old-style uniform. Bad water and improper sanitation can cause dysentery, and exposure to the elements frequently leads to pneumonia. Typhoid fever, chicken pox, whooping cough, tuberculosis—I bet if you screen for them half will turn up."

Lillian shook her head.

"It still doesn't explain the mummification, especially not when it occurred overnight. This isn't somebody who's walked out of an Amish town. The only explanation is that this is absolute desiccation—the body has dried out in a matter of hours."

Lillian was about to continue when a metallic sound echoed through the morgue, as though someone had dropped a coin into one of the steel sinks and it was rolling round and round toward the plughole. She looked at Alexis, who stared back before glancing down at Hiram Conley's remains. The metallic sound stopped, and then something fell with a sharp crack onto the tiles of the floor. From beneath the gurney rolled a small, dark sphere no bigger than an acorn. Lillian squatted down and picked the object up in her gloved hands.

"That's a musket ball," Alexis said in surprise. "It must have dropped out of him and rolled down the blood-drainage chute."

Lillian turned to Conley's remains, moving slowly across to where the crumpled, emaciated flesh was dropping in clumps from the very bones themselves.

"He's still decaying," Alexis gasped.

Lillian shook her head slowly. "He's not decaying," she said. "He's aging."